THE HIDDEN GERMAN

and not about the yet-to-be latex water-based paint. I finished and laid it down on brown wrapping paper.

I walked around the living room, touching this and lifting that, and came across the ration book. It was thick and lumpy. Were the rations pasted in? I don't know. Maybe someday I'll do some research on that. My memory is not too bound by factual empirical details. I do remember that I decided to hide it under the rug.

It was such an important book. More important, it seemed, than all the books in the house, and there were many. My father was a professor. That meant something in Europe, but very little in America. It meant something in our family. His presence could make us cry with fear. Little girls and big authoritarian Daddy. I still fight and sneer at my fear of authority and give respect, even when it is not their due, to suited men.

My mother usually held the ration book whenever she went out to the store. She hid it in her purse, and she covered her purse with her coat, slinging it over her arm unless she wore the brown wool coat in winter. My older sister said she hid her pregnancy of me with her coat too.

It wasn't until the next morning, Saturday, that my mother discovered the book was missing. She paced up and down the room and walked over the treasure about three times at least.

"I know I left it there on the desk," she lamented.

"Look, you've looked a tousand times und it's not here," my father said. "Go file for another von." He had an accent at times and I could hear it when he was frustrated and couldn't hear it when he was calm. I couldn't ever hear hers until it was on a tape we recorded years later in Malibu.

It pleased me to see this drama mostly because I realized I was in control of it. If I wished, all the consternation would be removed instantly and they would be so grateful to find the ration book was safe. I think I slipped it into some papers on the desk. I was never found out, and if I was, the punishment was nothing compared to the power of the scene I created.

My parents had always known about rationing. They rationed love and money and fun and food and TV time. Not openly, with rules, but inwardly with sacrifice and austerity. My father would rebel and always put huge gobs of butter and jelly on his bread and say "piss" or "hell," and later we would giggle. He looked to me to understand him but not because I was to have been his boy. He was strangely wary of his little three little girls but seemed to have no desire for a boy. I would listen and that was what he wanted.

Both of my parents grew up in Germany. All my life, I would carefully explain that they came to the United States in the 1920s, "before Hitler."

My mother would give us snippets of history when we would play canasta while my father was teaching graduate education night classes in statistics.

"We would run out and watch the bombs and later collect shrapnel." "For my confirmation in the Lutheran church, I wore shoes four sizes too big and stuffed paper in them." "The very best birthday I had was my sixteenth when my father got a huge bunch of bananas on a stalk for my party and all my girl friends and I ate them."

There were always interesting people at the house. The Hauns: he a naval officer who later died of pneumonia and she pregnant and sitting with a cup on her belly, spitting saliva into it calmly. The Finleys: he a red-headed doctor and she studying to be a lawyer and wore high heels because she said she could stand flat-footed anymore. Leckler, who spoke about education with a grand accent and married a blond woman to take care of him. Michael Bistrisky, a Russian and a high school music teacher and conductor of a symphony. The Winklers, who never seemed to do anything and always had time to visit.

The Fact Finders Club and the Faculty Club came over and talked and talked, and we served drinks and food while mother stayed in the kitchen and father told jokes and lifted a chair once with his teeth.

He couldn't tell jokes about the Americans or the Jews because he had to watch what he said. He had to be careful about extolling German virtues too, and so Beethoven and Brahms and Richard Strauss were played only occasionally on those big breakable records. To counter any suspicions, both my parent were air-raid wardens and had helmets and flashlights to patrol the neighborhood. But at school, a teacher questioned me once, and I was caught not knowing if my father's name was William or Wilhelm.

Had it not been for such things as the sinking of the Lusitania, I know now how close we came to joining Germany against England in World War I and how much secret respect certain people expect because of their German names. When I was young, the press and I were allowed to feel pride in Einstein who was as German as he was Jewish, and Marlene Dietrich, the heroine who had beauty and the brains and stood for freedom outside the barracks. She was powerful and never an ingénue, always a woman of principle and sly talent. A queen who was not seen as wicked even though she was old and German and made political stances. These were the few that were not secret Germans. Later, I guess, Werner Von Braun had a brief bit of glory, which was not entirely tainted by his German rocketry experience. Who else? Of course, years beyond, there was Günter Grass and *The Tin Drum* and then the painters like Kiefer depicting war and ruin and corruption. Now Schwarzkopf and Schwarzenegger are American names, hidden Germans.

Going to Germany in the fall, the ivy leaves drip crimson down brick institutions and the chilled air catches me aware of the need for shelter and warmth. The flat-faced houses are still neat and stiff-shouldered against each other. When I went with my father after the war in the early fifties, those houses were still there, beyond the central city rubble that buried the past of before the war.

The war is still the milestone now, even greater than the fall of the Berlin wall, and there is the constant reminder via comments and photos of the restitution and rebuilding of the old palaces, state houses, and churches that had been bombed during the war. In Nuremberg or Nürnberg, how to spell all those names always taunted me, and Würzburg, they let bits of bitterness taint their reemergence as though there had been no reason for the destruction. Berlin is involved with redoing the eastern section and recovering its stature. The above-ground gas pipes are brightly painted pink, serpentine guides to more shops and hotels, and yellow and green cranes pecking over the western section, swinging beams for more and more buildings.

The taxi drivers say it is a "secret," but all point out this mound of dirt that covers Hitler's sealed bunker near the remnants of the Wall.

Munich, München, is long into its songs and sales along the pedestrian retail passages. Freiburg and Stuttgart have their cuckoo clocks. Köln thrives again with museums and as the travelers' crossroad via the river and the trains. Hamburg still has its ships of industry, while most taxis are Mercedes Benz.

FRITZ WOLF

The shopkeepers and hoteliers are eager to speak English and won't let you stumble through words of German, proud of their multilingual capabilities. This causes me to feel less than them, despite my being American and my success and wealth. There is the faint arrogance of the sharp-nosed blond reception clerk at the Dom Hotel in Köln in her spoken English phrases, while she tried to get us to take a $300 room with a stain on the chair and in the train porter with a cigarette clamped in his scowling lips mumbling and disgusted that I won't let him take my rolling suitcase. The old couples are quiet when they see us, and there is a neutrality among the civil servants, but the young train conductors and waiters are sweet and undiscriminating in their willingness to help.

Everywhere, there are yellowing and reddish leaves clustered around the glass and tiled fifties buildings as well as the granite edifice survivors with intricate iron works of lions and vines. The woods of maple, elm, poplar, birch, and pine blur colors, shades, and tones of yellow, red, and green. Linden trees, lime yellow in the cold, have patient grace.

Trees and wood dominated the museums with chests, chiffoniers, and commodes of inlaid tulipwood, satinwood, purple wood, sycamore, oak, burr walnut, filled in with touches of tortoise shell, silver, mother of pearl, brass, and ivory.

"These doors were taken down and preserved," said the English-speaking guide, and he told the story of Bossi with his dragons of rebellion on the bishop residence walls.

How come Germany attempts to rectify horrific deeds even while restoring itself, while the French and the Swiss and the Catholics and we are just now slipping in admissions of all our culpability, our hidden complacency and compliancy, and collaboration and complicity in Hitler's ruthlessness?

CHAPTER 2

Hunter Thompson meets Mary Poppins.

Father, forgive me, I have sinned. Father, I have sinned because I cannot suck up to you. You, sterile in white miter and shaft, never gave forth, bled, never pushed out life in its slithery cover.

Mother, forgive me, I have sinned. Mother, I have sinned because I cannot take care of you, you, haus frau, who never thought or fought out there among the phallic warriors.

Goodbye to both of you, meat for my mind's conception, carrion of my grief, polluter, retroactive contaminant of my future life, ghost in men I've lost and dreams I've drowned.

You have died so human.

And left me midcentury amid life of floundering and flowering, slapping tales of suffocation and bursting colors of creation. Your story begins so simply.

WILHELM AND HELENE, were both born in 1903, the year the first Wright brothers' airplane took flight here in America. My father was born on May 23 in Cologne, Germany, and my mother on July 6 in Stuttgart, Germany.

Three months older than my mother and the eldest of three siblings, my father was born from a mother that looked like a mule and a father that looked like a cock. Pictures of his parents' fiftieth anniversary show them together like animal characters from the fairy tale "Town Musicians of Bremen," who saved themselves with the music of their own voices.

In the Middle Ages, Köln was one of the city-states that concentrated on the Three Wise Men for its religious ideals and inspirations. Some say that because of this multiplicity of worshipping, Germany never integrated religion and government successfully, like France or England did. The disparate kingdoms and principalities united only in 1871 after the other European states had centuries of being nations. For those who spoke the Germanic tongue, borders were never clear.

Then there are the Italians, we'll talk about later. Suffice it to say, most of the Germans longed for the Italian emotional landscape, the cypress and mists of Tuscany or the burnt sienna and cobalt blue of Sorrento. Religion was not the point, and neither was government. Life was. Warmth was. But north of the boot, it was a cold and isolated woodland when Köln was the meeting place for all travelers coming from the exotic East and the warring West with goods and trade agendas. The city grew despite its life being disjointed.

Willi, as he was called by his parents, never seemed to bother with propriety of living his parents carefully guarded life and, along with his love of a good time, seemed to have a touch of the Italian in him. Although he claimed he had traced his family lineage back to the Visigoths who sacked Rome. Anyway, he made his way in the world by paving paths rather than walking on tried and tired ones. That modus operandi got him into trouble and also endeared him to many.

Right from the moment my father was born in that upstairs bedroom of their first house, his parents thought him strange. He did little crying after being wiped off, and opened his eyes immediately, looking around the room, as though he could already see clearly, hindered only because he couldn't tell them in words.

This small, wizened newborn had reddish brown hair and grew tall and curious. Like his younger brother, he played with the hoop, but he was more interested in emptying bottles out in the sink or watching sugar dissolve in boiling water and turn into burnt caramel. When he was five, his parents had given my father, their first boy, a chemistry set because he had been fascinated with the bottles in the pharmacy

trillion marks was equivalent to one American dollar in 1923; and to get by, his father planted a garden five blocks away in a neighborhood plot, growing tomatoes to trade for flour, and promising to deliver large post office packages in exchange for sugar.

He sat there listening to his father complain about Woodrow Wilson, about his worthless declaration that the Germans would be allowed to negotiate a settlement, and how, instead, everything was taken away from Germany and the Allies were still occupying Köln to that very day. How were the Germans supposed to pay the trillion of reparations if all their industrial areas were given to the French? And why wouldn't they let Austria join Germany to stop trade barriers? On and on he went, blaming and praising Erhard and hoping that Stresemann could do what he promised. Willi didn't want to enter in to his father's distress, so he sat quietly with his head resting on the wing-back chair, his eyes closed, thinking about the periodic table.

"Are you listening? Did you only give up on Catholicism or Germany as well? What do you make of article 231 of the treaty? Never has a nation been responsible for other nations' damages. War crimes, that is what they call it now. We Germans must pay for it all. How did this come to be?"

His parents had never forgiven him for abandoning the church and for continuing to call their priest crazy. His distain and avoidance of politics were the final evidence of his strangeness.

Soon Joseph and his mother came in, and they had cherry cake and coffee while talking about soccer. Joseph had scored two goals at school, and they knew that was good. That Willi had helped him pass his math exam was not mentioned.

Willi finally stood up and, almost bowing to his mother, said, "My train is leaving in an hour. Hans Burger is going to meet me. It's time for me to go." His father and his brother stood up and shook his hand, and his mother looked down and fussed with the tablecloth and said, "Go then and write if you can, to tell us where you'll be."

He closed the door softly and listened to his father ask for more coffee and complain that soon they would not be able to afford it. With a sigh, he looked around the hall, every door was shut to "conserve heat" they used to tell him even in summer. The parlor, the dining room, his parents' bedroom, the kitchen, the bathroom, all doors shut and partitioned off from the hall. He knew years ago that shutting the doors also gave Mr. Baum little opportunity to see their goings-on. Mr. Baum worked at a bookstore by the main market and always nodded to Willi on his way up the stairs into the house's attic. He lived there for nine years before Willi ever said anything more than "good day" to him. Before departing, he went upstairs to the third floor to knock on his door and say goodbye too, but there was no answer.

After that, it took him six years and a new life before he came back for a day's visit. Hamburg absorbed him easily. It was full of factory chimneys sending forth the smoke signals of private enterprise and docks that held huge crates unloaded from formidable ships owned by rich families. The Hamburg-America line had a ship leaving every day, and he began, it seemed, to say goodbye to as many people as he tried to meet. All on their way to America. The university was crowded with students heralding the colors of their fraternities and overflowing with the time-honored rite of passage, beer drinking. Housing was scarce. He talked his way into a room with three others by offering to teach one of them chemistry so the downtrodden student could finally pass his exams and go back to teach in Bonn, a little town near Köln.

Within three weeks, he had his room and his courses set and had his picture taken near his classroom blackboard jauntily sitting on the edge of his big desk with his little students, all dressed in stiff shirts and dark jackets, sitting seriously and attentively at their wooden desks. What it is about pictures from that time that always show big sad baggy eyes and pursed lips? It's as if no one was sure what would happen to them when the flash exploded and they watched in a limbo of concern and conformity, never consciously admitting fear and yet hoping to survive the whole process.

He was the revered teacher already, and yet there is another picture of him standing with other smooth-faced young men around a table where the sitting professors held a profound court. He is bowing slightly, looking at his mentors, not at the camera that the others stared at audaciously. He clutched a few slim volumes in his left hand tucked close to his chest. Respect and solemnity reverberated in the two tiers of academicians. Maybe this was his real family.

Years later he told the story of how he survived. "One Saturday in October, I valked into a small smoky restaurant near the ports und vas seated at one of the dark pine booths along the long wall at the back of da room. Red cabbage und roast pork were the meal of the day, and as I nodded to the waiter a confirmation, den I saw a young boy duck behind a pillar und den try to dart to the kitchen. I recognized him as one of my students und, frowning slightly, signaled him to come over immediately.

"'Aren't you in my class? Why are you running in here?'

"'Yes, sir, I am. But you see, I, I mean, I . . . my father, he owns this place,' the boy said, taking his cap in his hands and twisting it unmercifully.

"'Yes, yes. Master Brummell, right?' I said, contemplating his words.

"'Yes, sir.'

"'And what have you done about your math?'

"'My math, sir?' the boy whined and dropped his hat and picked it up to strangle it again.

"'Yes, yes, your math. Your performance suggests you'll never pass your examinations,' I said while I pierced a piece of meat on my fork and pointed it all at the boy. I vaited for a reply and then continued, 'Bring your father here und I will talk with him about helping you.'

"The boy ran again through the smoky crowded dining room and into the kitchen. I ate quickly and rehearsed vat to say. I felt my pocket where my last pfennigs, which were valueless, lay with the wad of marks I received for that month's teaching. The father was a tall man with only a few stands of black hair crossing over a head dat was full of sweat. He wiped his forehead repeatedly mit a stained white apron and greeted Herr Professor Wilhelm with multiple bows.

"The deal was easy, and Mr. Brummell very grateful that his son would receive full tutoring in exchange for the professor taking one meal a day at his restaurant. I now had regular food as well as my rooms, und I ordered another dark beer free of charge. Dat is how I fed myself during all those years of inflation until about 1925 when the mark stabilized."

These teaching arrangements made him immune to the '20s inflation in Germany and would protect him during the Great Depression in the United States as well.

While one of his roommates who knew Rosa Luxembourg was cut on the face during a communist riot in 1923, Willi worked on his chemistry and made friends with the roommate's brother, who had a chemist shop and was named Otto Menz. Neither Otto nor Willi wanted to hear about the reparations and inflation when they could talk about creams, perfumes, and possible ways to tint Willi's hair so it wasn't so full of red. It darkened all by itself by the time he was twenty-two.

Otto's shop was a narrow two rooms with one long counter full of drawers and wall shelves everywhere. There were ceramic jars with filigreed fronts and dark corked bottles placed in careful rows on the shelves; the drawers had delicately painted scripts for labels, and the brass scale stood on the counter with special felt boxes for the weights. The shelves held all that Willi cared about, liquid and crystal compounds. When Otto was busy with a customer, Willi climbed the rolling wooden ladder and lift a bottle from the top shelf to bring down to the counter. He would remove the etched glass stopper and tilt the bottle, examining its contents, smelling its vapors, gingerly tasting a drop of liquid, or a smidgen of crystal. He nodded knowingly and then wiped the bottle clean of dust and returned it to the shelf.

When they were alone, they distilled ethyl alcohol in the back of the shop, letting it drip into 1000 mL beakers, which they banged together, toasted and drank from, while they talked of plans to open a perfume factory. After all Cologne, the American way of spelling Köln, was Willi's birthplace, Otto would say, and therefore, it would be fitting to have him make perfume in the USA too. Willi said he'd send his mother free samples always. They also conspired to find a wife for each other. This they felt was necessary to further their careers. One particular night in following summer, Otto brought a singles magazine with ads from young ladies inside, and they each decided to write to the ad writer who interested each. That was how Willi met Helene.

"She was very accomplished, played the piano, und came from a good family. She liked to write," he said as he narrated his side of the story.

CHAPTER 3

There is the need to understand time and sequence, history and chronology, but there is a timeless time as well. Those daguerreotypes, snapshots, photos, slides, Polaroids, videos taken by each of us with his and her emotional cameras. We sort through the piles of film scored on the sweet silver of emotion and find that pixilated image, which conjures timelessly a certain time, and it becomes a hologram in the mind.

Throughout her life, she brought forth the negatives of her father not listening to her business sense and the brutal etching of her mother dying of breast cancer at age fifty-two when she was only twenty-three. Shame and sorrow sowed in her soul, not being recognized because she had a brother, watching being a woman causes death.

I can see her now sitting in front of her typewriter in the living room, writing letters to her brother in Stuttgart, and I can see her now sitting in the chair at the retirement home lobby, going through her purse the tenth time to check for her keys and, most of all, to have something to do, to have something to do.

MY MOTHER WAS Helene, not Helen, but with the *e* that drew out the name to an elegance and slight strangeness, which belonged to different people. Hel-leene.

I remember she used to call us "little eagles," and I knew from her use, it meant a messy little animal, like how we call people pigs. "Little ichsl" were hedgehog-like, I found out years later. Still in English, it sounded like our soaring national bird. I took that meaning and flew with it. It was one of the discrepancies that I understood somewhere in my mind and never examined until I was looking for answers to "living life." It bobbed up along with someone calling my father "Willi," which was a word in Detroit that belong to the black boys who were beginning to play football for white audiences. She was raised speaking High German, he Low German.

She called him Bill in front of others and Lutzi when they were at home. I never asked anyone if that meant anything like *sweetie* or *honey*. It was my mother's name for my father, that was all.

"I liked your father. He had energy and plans. He talked about all these dreams he had for a perfume factory and being a chemistry professor. He came to visit me in Stuttgart."

She was the second child and only daughter of these austere-looking middle-class people. Her mother had upswept hair and a bodice of propriety, and her father was mustached with authority. A photograph shows them stiff with hard-earned respectability. They owned a bakery and small grocery store.

"In the basement, there were large wooden barrels, and we would go down and chop cabbage and then add water and let it ferment. I pushed and pushed the cabbage to soak it, and that was our sauerkraut. We stored apples and hard pears when possible along with potatoes and onions. Upstairs, we hung all the beer sausage, salami, and tongue. I loved to smell it all. I came home from school and took a big serving out of the stew pot, and that would be dinner. That pot held meals for the whole week, and my mother would add potatoes and little scraps of meat as the week wore on. We never sat down for dinner together."

The store was on what I heard was "the Lenzhalter," a long winding street up one of the hills in Stuttgart. She always recited a poem about its beautiful hills. Her parents' store was on the first floor, and above it were the apartments where they lived. Her room had thick lace curtains and a view of the city. There were pictures of her with plump cheeks standing with her rabbit in hand. I never knew his name, but I knew about Jacob, her raven, and Roland, her harlequin Great Dane.

"I never forgave my father. One night a man had climbed over Roland and into the kitchen from the window facing the yard. My father said, 'What kind of a dog is this that I feed?' and got rid of him the next day. Roland had been such a friendly dog, and my father saw no use for him. He would not listen to me."

Every morning, Konrad, who was the tall, broad-shouldered baker her father had hired when she was only six, made rolls and cakes to be distributed up and down the neighborhood. Little bags would be hung on the doors of all these regular customers, and Helene would wait for surplus if someone had gone out of town or left a note saying none today. She went into the bakery area sometimes even before school and looked at the trays of little cakes and cookies with fruit centers and great lengths of strudel. Konrad gently put new creations in the cases and gave her halves of special designs or leftover apple tarts.

The smells of coffee, stew, and cinnamon-apple combination stayed with her all her life, and she remembered at about ten years of age that she decided to have her own business. The customers always asked for her mother, saying, "Mrs. Wolf, please. She understands my needs." They didn't want to talk to her father who would say, "This is what I have, and that's all. I can't bake special for every one," and mumble under his breath, "Damn Jews." Many of the customers were wealthy Jewish families, and her father resented having to serve non-Christians.

Helene didn't care much about religion; she liked her confirmation dress for the Lutheran ceremony, but as she repeated in years to come, her shoes were two or three sizes too big and that was about all she invested her memory in when it came to religion. However, there was always the belief about "going to heaven." It was an automatic thought, not a born-again Christian entitlement with gold reward, just heaven as haven. All people went to heaven, and animals were not a problem either if someone remembered to include them.

She had that elegant and simple combination of spiritual vagueness with a practical sense. When she was sixteen, she went to Lindau on Lake Constance in the southwest of Germany. She was a student at the exclusive girls' school Maria and Martha. Of course, the names reflected the curriculum, and the girls were to emulate the essence of holiness for woman, like, of course, not getting pregnant and the core of servitude and learning household skills.

"I never had my period the whole year I was there. None of us girls in the top room did. That is where I met Maria, the real Maria, and she and I became friends. She crocheted for me, and I wrote her poems for literature class. We laughed over that, and Helene Post, my friend who lives in Düsseldorf, kept our secret." Maria became the wife of Helene's brother for thirty-four years until her brother met Olga who owned a hotel in the heart of Stuttgart and took him over.

Richard Strauss and Richard Dehmel were the composer and poet Helene recalled with an intimacy that appeared as erudition to me, but was really a familiarity with the artists of her time. My discovery of Dehmel in a poetry book was like a myth becoming real after finding evidence in an archeological dig. My realization that those men were her contemporaries, made her young with bobbed hair and full of petulance, determination, romanticism, and a 1920s woman.

"I met your father through my brother," she said, and only when we were older did she admit that she and Maria wrote her ad for the magazine late one night while it was raining. They were up in the corner room with its rounded window overlooking the street and the rails of the streetcar glistened while they looked out and giggled over possible responses. "We wanted someone with some ambition and not one of the boys nearby."

So Helene and Willi wrote to each other and met some awkward Sunday when he took the train down and called at the house, and her father looked him over and couldn't understand why he wasn't in business and her mother gave him a big piece of cherry cake with white icing and whole cherries ringed around the top. They took a walk because it was already 1924 and they were modern sorts. He discussed his ambition to be a professor, and she told him she could play the piano and paint. She liked his dreams, and he liked her accomplishments. Yet she didn't wait for him and went to the United States.

CHAPTER 4

Somewhere just below the scrub that crawled up the mountain, they built fires and chip stone to make the pointed weapons they latched onto the wooden sticks. They walked in soft leather and made sayings white people say, like "Don't judge a man until you've walked in his moccasins for a day." They disappeared into reservations and alcohol and finally oil and casinos while the immigrants kept coming with hard-soled shoes. Nine million from Germany and five million more from Austria, and the next biggest group from England with seven million and then Ireland and Italy with five million.

ALL HIS LIFE Willi wore the wingtip shoes with carefully puncture dots designed around the top. He wore them running to the ship of the Hamburg-American line and leaving Otto's Mercedes on the dock. He wore the same pair when he found Helene in Chicago at her Uncle Christian's and when he stood at his graduation, clutching books in his hands. When he traveled back to Europe, he bought some brown as well as black shoes, but they all were wingtips. He married in the black pair and promised Helene he would take care of things and realize his dreams, and she played the piano at her uncle's when he went to class at night after she had worked as a housekeeper during the day.

He came to visit in Los Angeles, and I found him sitting in the Biltmore with his dark suit, legs crossed shaking that long thin foot in his size 12 wingtip shoes. He was a professor and wondered why I missed the freeway entrance on 5th when I had lived so long in LA.

The last time I saw him, he was almost eighty-three and slightly shuffled those shoes through the Detroit Northland Mall as we looked at all the men's clothes and then went out to dinner before I went back to LA.

Helene had had the black confirmation shoes of fine leather; and in two photos, one of her wedding in 1926 out in a garden, the other of their fifth anniversary, she wears very pointed toe pumps like elves have with high fronts that complemented her long lightweight print dresses. I never saw the actual shoes; by the 1940s, she was wearing plain flats or blunt-nosed pumps and had her hair combed back where it curled especially in the humid summer nights in Detroit. After one visit as a married woman in 1927, she never went back to Europe until 1977, and that was all. Everyone looked so "worn out," she didn't recognize them.

Grasshoppers, cloth with leather soles, were all she would wear for the last twenty years of her life. We went and bought leather loafers and sandals. She'd say she liked them, and then put them in her closet to mold. She always wondered why I wore high heels.

My sister fought with my mother because she could never find size 10 shoes and my mother always gave her gifts and money to make up for what she felt was her mistake. My mother wore a size 7. They would spend a whole day looking for school shoes and come back with my big sister slamming her door and not coming out for dinner and my mother saying, "Shhh, your sister is upset."

My big sister gave my little sister and me instructions about her ballet lessons and said I was clumsy and I had size 9 shoes, which were the biggest size carried at most stores in the 1950s. To this day, I have trouble relaxing and letting my legs and feet dance.

My husband had big black loafers when I saw him do the Twist before we were married. He'd been drinking and was telling jokes and I was embarrassed for him, but he didn't seem to care if people laughed at how ungraceful he was. He was a Fair Oaks Jewish boy who had a wonderful chest and twenty-eight-inch waist when he was twenty-two. I couldn't remember his shoes because I focused on his Levi's; I called them penis pants, which was what I looked at the most below his waist. He never wore sneakers or tennis shoes but had some leather boots as well as the ubiquitous loafers.

"God damn, fucking cat sucked a hole in my last pair of socks. I'm wearing these boots to the interview, and I don't care what they say. No wonder I'm having troubles getting a new job. I'll kill the cat," he'd say, and he'd bite his lip and stump around the house till he caught the cat and we'd all yell, "No, no, don't hurt Arnie! Please, Dad." The kids would beg, and I'd say, "Roger, Roger, stop it, stop it. I'll go get you some socks out of the drier right now."

Later, he'd tell me how he really liked cats, even Siamese who suck socks. "Cats are dispensable though. I remember on my grandfather's farm, the cows rolled over in the barn and if a cat was trying to keep warm—*squash*, and my grandfather would come and take his foot in a big rubber boot and nudge the body off the cement with the hay sticking to it. Sometimes, the pigs would eat it, but mostly it stayed in the garbage heap, and ants and flies and stuff would help it rot away."

"Thanks a lot for the story. Couldn't you tell the kids something less gruesome? You're always talking about awful cruelty."

"That's not cruel. That's life. Cruel is when they used to call me kike and laugh at me. You'll never know what that's like. But the kids will. You've got more sympathy for the 'hairback' Arab your sister sucks than you do for me."

"Oh, damn it, now we're into that. I was called buckteeth and skinny. You even called me buckteeth and imitated me when I first met you and you were already twenty. Besides, none of us have really had it bad compared to the rest of the world."

"Ah, the great martyr. I'm going to sleep. Let's drop it."

The day closed with bathing the kids and tucking them in bed and reassuring them it was okay, and the cat was not going to get hurt and everything would be better in the morning. I could hear him snoring, even able to growl in his sleep.

All those years hearing patients tell me of the abuse, physical and sexual, burns, beatings, batterings, being hung by the hair, hands held over gas flames, penises hammered, labia stretched and sewn, babies being starved, little girls being abused by father, grandfather, and brothers for years and years, being thrown from windows, being chained in closets. What was this yelling he did? My kids called him Sasquatch, but to the world, this was tiny tyranny not worthy of the tabloids. No matter, it would echo on for years and years, fossilized footprints of his presence, which all my rain of tears could not erode.

CHAPTER 5

I look for the attic of my mind. In all those Midwestern houses, there, on the second floor, open the solid wooden door, of oak most likely, and see the narrow dark steps with solid risers going up to the heaven of the past where all valuable records were stored along with things from which we could not be parted. Those things had to stay quietly docile while we worked at separation by forgetting them. Find me my attic with gabled windows and heat so intense the wood seemed a shelter. Find me that high hidden solace where secrets unfolded in photos and camphor quilts.

I HAVE TAKEN TO photographing old clothes, scribbles on paper, an unfired clay statue, stuffed animals and wine bottles covered with aluminum foil and burnished with black paint. It's like some secret mandate. Things my children made years ago or my mother wore before she died or my father sent when I was young, all of these still have to be preserved.

It is a compromise that let me have the attic in a small drawer and hide that neurological need for the memory-prompting stimulus. The actual stuff is going to go to the garbage dump in my brown pails of the past, which sit out in front of the house each Tuesday and Friday.

Garbage was what my sister and mother called the stuff I picked up as a kid in the alleys or that I still keep today. I liked rose buds that were dried a blackish red. I cannot get rid of the long flower box on which my mother taped the ribbon a sailor on the Bremen Line gave her when he flirted with her in 1926 as they steamed across the Atlantic. It is a gold foil box, and it showed off the beautiful woven ribbon like a road to romance. I cannot get rid of the plastic camera case my father gave me to carry the Ikoflex when I went from Detroit to New Haven to photograph my baby nephew. It is faux leather but it holds evidence of his attention to me.

My sisters can keep their drawers empty, have a few items as necessary, and clean things routinely. My older sister collects antique lacquer boxes, and they are empty. My younger sister collects silver dinner flatware and keeps it in the bank safe deposit box. They are in control and competent, masters over things. They are able to use discretion, separate out foreground value from background waste.

I am an accumulator, not a collector. It is quite a paradox since I live in a house without an attic or a basement, struggling with the ubiquitous California two-car garage that seldom holds cars.

"How can you keep all this junk? I'll order a dumpster and you can throw it all away. I want you to have a nice house," my younger son says periodically. "You're like a gypsy, Mom," my older daughter tells me routinely.

How can I tell them that I had too much to do? Help them grow up and work and buy groceries. I didn't drive myself to clean the garage; I tried to make it through the day and year. Now I have time to clean the house and it only dusts off my memories when I find old skateboards and wetsuit jackets, a Barbie doll coat and a Snoopy doll tuxedo, oil paintings of dolphins and green plastic arrows. My house is like a memory dump, and I rifle through it like some memory scavenger, not a recycler. Show me the Chinese checker marble and I will conjure the games. Show me the old bedspread and I will have daydreams.

I liked to run as though I were a horse, galloping and feeling my throat raw from the breath that streamed in and out through it. I liked to exhaust myself and could tolerate him lying to me and lifting him in a unison passion until I couldn't breathe anymore.

I remember I played this song before. I remember the telephone number of our house, Townsend 83430, or was it 82250, before area codes and only numbers, Pennsylvania 6-500 is now history.

I wish so little. I wish I could call either of my parents now and hear anything they had to say. I would know there was still the real link, not only the memory chain.

When my father died, I had to fly back to the Midwest. Detroit was dead too. Grass grew in the sidewalk cracks and paper trash drifted to curbs and crevices like the men out of work to the liquor store corners.

He had been at the peak of his career when the smoke stacks had been four and five in a row streaming gray clouds of strength and General Motors, Ford, and Chrysler were avatars.

"Let's sit out on the back steps and watch the cars," Mother had said after dinner was over. We sat still on the four steps and yelled, "That's a Ford . . . Studebaker . . . Here comes the Buick . . . and look, see three DeSotos in a row."

And my father brought home papers of profundity for his big wooden desk.

CHAPTER 6

"I dream of Jeanie with the light brown hair / Floating like a zephyr on the soft summer air." The song goes something like that even though it's supposed to be 'vapor' I like it better with zephyr, longing and sweetness. Why does hair turn gray and longing end and sweetness sour? To be blond to please your parents, to be blond on a gray-haired man's arm, to be blond to indicate worth. I want the comfort of a kiss, and I have brown hair.

CURLY HAIR HAS it advantages, which my mother used by combing her hair back and letting it join in tumbles at her neck. She always looked like the nineteen twenties girl who let her bob grow out a little for sway. Waves framed her forehead, and they foamed into gray as she got older, but I doubt she tried to get wiser.

My older sister's hair was a strawberry blond, and my younger sister's a burnished brunette. Now they hide the gray, and I should start to streak my hair with the new brown as the new gray takes over from the old brown. So am I to hide me again from the top?

If I want, I can lie on the bed with my eyes shut and see the three of us in a circle, sitting on the floor with gradations of hair and our legs bent in z's. We are dividing up things in groups of threes. We are sorting all the odds and ends of my father three months after he died. In a closet by a big dresser, we found a silver cigarette box, one of the first-hand calculators that wound around at the top, a few Omega watches, and all sorts of assorted coins and clips that I have no idea about but surely missed when I didn't get them. I had picked the other hand behind someone's back or they'd picked my hand that held the good thing in it. Chance, like the genetics of our hair and minds, got me that trivet "Ve get too soon oldt und too late schmart."

CHAPTER 7

When they begin the beguine . . . Love makes the world go round, love makes the world go round . . . Love me and the world is mine . . . A song of love is a sad song, Hi-lili hi-lili hi-lo, for I have loved and I know . . . What is this thing called love?. . . Love me tender . . . All you need is love . . . I can't get no satisfaction . . . Every move you make.

Not sonnets or couplets, but popular songs in airwaves. They ask me how I knew my true love was true . . . Mind floaters, like the cell chains that drift in your eye fluids, across your vision sometimes, when looking into the microscope, trying to see something else. Inescapable. Illusive.

ACCORDING TO SIGMUND Freud, the Victorian, who first offered his psyche to the world as twentieth-century scientific theory, love is libido, sex with some rationalization attached and sublimation suggested.

Melanie Klein, not related to Anne or Calvin, of the United States schools of analytic thought, still referred to as *Mrs.* Klein in psychoanalytic schools today, went further back in human developmental *his*-story and postulated positions via love related to the breast and how the savage beast could be soothed if the breast produced the milk of human kindness and not the toxic poetic fluidity of depression and paranoia.

Winnicott decoded emotional components of love and thriving and said the mental health of the loved baby was in the mind of the mother-lover.

Who really knows what Bion claimed with his alphabet?

Franz Alexander had a great name and said inter-psychic oral conflict produced peptic ulcers, even though it was doctors who gave milk and Mylanta before Zantac, Pepcid, or treating *H. pylori*. His conflicts mentioned resultant asthma, arthritis, ulcerative colitis, neurodermatitis, and high blood pressure, not sad songs and funny feelings in the chest and gut pining over lost love.

Florence Dunbar wrote about "types" of personalities and sickness, compulsives and constipation types.

Otto Kernberg and Heinz Kohut looked in mirrors and split prisms.

New York still debates these philosophers of psychoanalysis but in LA, all that was put mainly in the past. Dopamine and serotonin reuptake inhibitors along with Naloxone, Crisis and Cognitive Therapies were the prevalent approaches to understanding the mind.

Poor Camille, poor Werther, poor me. Never able to figure out love, only able to live it. Under this adulthood is the motor of narcissism, a grandiose 5 liter, 8 valve, 60 in less than 6, if I love hard enough and well enough I can get the rotten son-of-a-shithead father (not bitch, you chauvinists) to be nice to me and acknowledge my type of motor. It ran me in hopes of earning my father's love, my mother's love, my sisters' loves, all my lovers' loves. Not my children's loves, for theirs' was nothing but love in return without any earning.

Hidden in there among the piston heart and tubes, the carburetor alveoli, the gastrointestinal tank is the German manufacturing seal and this auto . . . mobile who is in a female form.

It was smart in a nonlinear way, in an intuitive way, a way that sensed and felt and, what shall I say, "divined." A way that read emotion, as well as logical thoughts.

The lasting love I have is for ideas. Beyond math or physics or engineering, the joy and angst of time and space and matter.

In the living room of the dark house with the porches on the first and second floor, the little girl I was read comics and *Life* magazine. The house was wood inside and out, except for the cement pillars and posts that held the steps to the porch like an accordion. You walked under the second floor porch to get to the front door, and woody darkness took over. Oak framed the 960 Atkinson entrance, and the floor and the paneled dining room was also made of oak. The front room traversed the whole front of the house like a front room should, and individually framed windows accompanied it. On one end was the fireplace between two built-in bookcases, and on the other end was the big chair my mother or father would sit in while the floor lamp cast its yellow light.

Erp, erp was the sound my father would make, with his hand in his armpit pumping his arm. "Hear that little monkey?" he'd say, and we'd all laugh and pretend we were too wise for that kind of foolishness. Then he'd take his two hands and squeeze them together and make all sorts of farting sounds, which of course was neither a word nor a sound we were supposed to acknowledge.

At dinner, in his double-breasted suit after teaching graduate students, when he said "piss" or "hell," the three little girls giggled at what a devil he was, and dinner would continue in silence for a while, the 'bad' words ringing in our minds.

My mother didn't really have a sense of humor or the ability to be on stage. She had what we call the serious gene or the sensitive gene directed to seriousness. She made gingerbread houses before all the schools did and collected silver brooches she never wore. In the late afternoon, she would be at the piano playing chords and no piece in particular, her own improvisation of gentle lyrical sounds.

I can't figure out how they grew so far apart from that German couple who wrote letters to each other and admired each other's attributes.

Today, my male type shows all his feathers in an immediate display. There's the talk about how many woman are after him and how this one wanted to marry him and all the ones he's fucked. He'll tell you about the money he made and the cars he owns and the plans he has and the people he dines with. He'll dress well and try not to fart for a while.

I, as the woman, am Miss Docile and Sweetness and Light. She'll listen and keep her feathers tucked hovering in a brown posture and wait. I didn't learn to preen and demand, but I'm learning now.

"Be happy you attracted those flighty birdmen" was the underlying motto, but after a while, it became necessary to reveal plumage of opinion and ideas and wants and experience and risk losing love that was based on giving in and cooperating to have the comfort and sex.

Anyway, there in the late 1940s, this little kid sat reading the newspaper that had eight columns, not the paltry six of today. There is no recollection of anyone else being in that long room. Her mother was probably in the kitchen and her sisters upstairs. Her father was gone as usual. The sun led her across the floor as she looked at the photographs and read what intrigued her until she turned to the comics. Then all became still and warm. She usually didn't read what she remembers as *Gasoline Alley*, but that day, the last frame caught her eye.

It said something about a baby growing up and the years passing, "1949, 1950, 1951." Future was born for her, and it stunned her.

I remember the concept standing unadorned in my consciousness, and I realized that another decade could exist. Now time and future stand brazenly in front of every day and century 2000 shouts, but then the idea of future was a pure thought of time, clean and unencumbered by needs to plan and prepare. I didn't know if I was to tell any one of my great discovery since even the comics seem to know it before me, and yet it was one of the original anchors to place me. I kept it hidden, and the 1950s came anyway.

Time to go forward then, and time to go back now and conjure riding in the time machine of the mind. Grasping airy memories while feeling their punch like wind, those are real ghosts I know. Leading a middle-aged life I can ride the time machine both ways.

How does each of us come across time and its arms of past and future? Do we bump into it as it stands serenely in our way, or does it pick us up like some Father Christmas and carry us into the snow flurry of doing? Maybe it rocks us in its arms like a mother, bringing our cat so we can have it up in bed with us, and we fall asleep covered up by its arms.

The next great idea for me was one my father gave to me in a narcissistic display. The thirteen-year-old girl was sitting on the floor at the Irwin's apartment. She had never been in an apartment for adults before. Her friends had been in houses down the block, and she met high school classmates that lived all over the city in apartments and houses and duplexes.

The apartment was on Six Mile Road, way out from downtown Detroit. It had built-in shelves and oriental carpets and china displayed on shelves and tables. There were a collection of Irish mugs—damn the name for them escapes now—made by Dalton, which was annoying in its open celebration of being Irish. Who could do such a thing as be proud of where they were from?

The discussion had to do with philosophy and the issues of teaching creativity and thought.

All three of them had PhDs and were university teachers. I sat on the rug by the coffee table a little farther away from the adults, listening and moving glass ashtrays into straight lines.

The Irwins were letting her father hold court, and they were courting him. He was the tenured university professor, and she assumed they called him professor in the European style out of respect.

The male Irwin was round-faced and balding. He did the serving. The female Irwin was slightly jowly and chose a reddish clay hair color before it was on every TV sitcom star possible, unless of course the TV woman was blond. She acknowledged the men's ideas in a way that had to do with being a woman speaking to the Y chromosome, and her bracelets jangled and they responded, the humiliated one and the selected one.

Being so young and inexperienced, it was strange to see this interaction with her father at the center. This was the wizardry of sex working, and it left her isolated, a mere observer, spaces away, daughter of the desired, princess to the king, and rival to his sycophants.

She knew that ideas were not really the issue, vaguely feeling scents not sense were what drove the interaction, and what she learned had to do with narcissism, not philosophy. That was so until her father said, "I am God," in this definitive manner, which would have seemed audacious from anyone else. She was initially shocked at his daring. He continued to expound and contradict their provincial concepts, which of course allowed them to worship the professor even more.

The idea precipitated out slowly in layers, jutting out into all areas of her consciousness like a forming crystal. This was not conceit, not narcissism, not self-centered idolatry; this was an ultimate acknowledgement of creativity. God, the big unifying field theory idea, overseeing all the space of the universe, and all the organized religions was made of man's projections.

Years later, I look at this and see the recent struggles to make it man's and woman's projections and to neuter the projection as though that would make it all-encompassing. What is it: the Father, the Mother, and the Holy Spirit JC? Or is it God, you, rather than God, he? This

Jews' head of household, ultimate of Plato's ideal, all-powerful, all-knowing, all-forgiving, everywhere and nowhere on earth.

My father continued to put globs of butter and jelly on his toast and read. And I went on to look for gods, not even finding heroes forever, nor loves that lasted, or standards that stood untouched. I was fooled by the idea. Somehow encompass the whole of space with the idea of an ideal. It haunts me still, this unified field theory born in humans.

Finally to complete insights, organic tissue came to her. She felt. It was insidious in its coming to be. Gently brushing the tangles of her thoughts with touches, tastes, and other senses into sensuality. Time and space would not be complete without it. She might have called it matter.

She felt juice of the crisp apple in fall and burnt leaves smoking flavors and smells into memories. She felt her fingers burn for playing too long in the snow. She felt small clots pass her cervix and, years later, whole babies came from her. The tolerance for another being easily accomplished by her body, similar yet different from those bodies that rejected parts like kidneys, livers, lungs, or heart. How were those possible? What and where was the hidden placenta of life without rejection?

Dirt smells, especially when wet, and had a cunning seduction about it. She would poke holes and place seeds and plants inside. Sight did not tantalize her like touch. Sight was a cold, albeit colorful, sense that colluded with intellect. Men she met used sight to erect themselves, but she would close her eyes to create herself. Hearing was warmer because of music and the sound of wind and human breath. Taste was like certain touches, sweet or sour, salty, bitter, and peppery.

The gentle tapered fingers of her mother politely moved about the ribbon and made bows. She'd touch the bowl of applesauce and cleared the sides with the spoon. All night long, she could hear her mother go to the back door and wait for the cat to come in. She remembered her mother telling her about having her arms and legs put in boots to hold her still while she was in labor and she never slept with her husband after the girls were born. Her mother kept beautiful sets of manicure scissors and delicately trimmed her cuticles. She didn't like company and had little to do with the outside world. She was the "haus frau" without caring for the house or without caring for her "mann," Herr Professor. Yet she had the gentle touch for items she cared about, papers and pens, scissors and silk scarves for her sensitive neck, which she tied and retied as she listened to her favorite tenor aria after aria. She and her mother could share those kinds of moments and even appreciate the feel of a good potato.

Love convoluted into memories and loyalty and stubborn resistance to discovery of illusions.

How displaced then, to grow into a young woman who wanted sex instead of solace, to leave coveted things to her mother and move on to tissue and flesh. To see the little curious penis peeking out of Peter's or Ricky's pants in the school playground or hold hands with Thomas Callero in seventh grade or feel the full lips of a boy of fifteen on her own mouth, to hug and be stroked. Being touched was when she writhed alive. She hid that until that secret would be discovered and she would no longer be able to resist. Penetrated by a felt idea of another. Time, space, and matter.

CHAPTER 8

Why is it so easy for some to cross lines? To dare, to run across borders that weren't always open, to risk exposure for their own good? Others can lie and cheat and further themselves no matter what, no matter what ethical or moral borders they cross. Still, others extend borders and enlarge perimeters of decency, compassion, creativity. But the spectator, the conservative, the girl with propriety salted in her brain, stews in torment before she acts and then must hide herself to make sure she is unobtrusive and good like a middle child, watching glory for the older and TLC for the younger, glory and TLC for the male, glory for the other and TLC for the vulnerable.

S HE HAS THIS desire to give him a bath. He claims he only took showers. He said her face is pretty, and she caught him looking at her breasts. He says she needed a "manly" influence and then makes little suggestive remarks about a stiff window like he is or she should find ways to keep warm besides hoping the remodeled doors get put in quickly.

He splayed his whole life before her, all thirty-five years, and talked so openly and guilelessly like the way he builds, perpendicular lines and open spaces. He said he wanted her, but he wants her to be his Jocasta, jocose without knowing it, or the Mrs. Robinson she knew and he might have heard of. Now the "process" has ended, and he is away entertaining himself with other fantasies.

She was touched. How sweet that he should be intrigued and say she doesn't look much over forty to justify his lust. It amused her even while she was courted by executives and engineers who push for their way with her. They were her match in wariness, but he only wanted to "do it."

She would add her bubble bath pour bain and let the water run very warm. The bubbles would begin at the end of the long stream of the water falling and would mound and spread as floats of white on the water. He would be lying on the bed, and she would lead him by the hand to the bath after all the candles were lit. The water would churn and foam like whipped egg whites.

Why would he be so easy and yet absolutely foolish to make love to? She was in her fifties and had repeatedly vowed never to return the attentions of the younger men who had noticed her. She wasn't bringing up any more children. Liz Taylor had had them all and could easily run across borders where no dogs patrolled and could rip others to shreds. The stars were above gossip and made their own rules. But she, on the other hand, had her neighbor to think about. He was the neighbor's prized son.

He would sit in the foam like Neptune and spear her, and she would have him. That was the point. She would make love to him, bring forth all her powers of sensuality for him, not only to be shown his. She would remember that if she ever married again, it would have to be alternating seduction, taking turns being the lover and the loved.

Why would she care about him, such a different being than her? A self-made man, but never traveled, never graduated, never had parents that cared much for him as a child but only wanted him to be a man quickly.

Better yet, she would start on the couch and sit him down in a dark room with only the hall light in the background. She would position herself on him, her legs apart. They would be fully clothed. She would begin by lightly kissing his eyes and then licking them from the corners out to his temples. Like a great tiger, she would overcome the bars of her skin and let passion free. Purring, she would lick his cheeks and rub her nose on his, and brush his lips while holding his hands still by her thighs.

She would touch his lips half-open, calling for the depth of sensual pleasure inside the mouth. And they would kiss. Only a kiss and roll in that, smear in passion, and be happy with that meeting of minds and tongues. Their secret, hidden and pleasurable.

Could she do it and not miss him or feel embarrassed at her taken pleasure from a son of her friend? No, she was chicken shit and would always attach her heart to her sexual self. She would be caught in love and sex again. Penetrate the hidden vagina and find hidden love was the sad rule.

CHAPTER 9

December holds the season to hide.

S HE HAD RED berries and silver bells around the table.
For three years now, she had done "nothing" on New Year's Eve and had stayed at home to be alone. There was something strange about being with people now. She could tolerate parties for only a half hour or so, and interactions other than at work strained some sense of herself.

She walked into the house where the party was held. She had driven alone and followed a long curving road holding houses on stilts overlooking lush hills. Her girlfriend had been sick with a cold and had not wanted to bother going to another singles party. To reveal there was no one, as you walked in all poised and groomed and dressed very well, took all her effort. Her ex had made sure she felt alone when he married another willing woman to show the world he was not the one alone. Those willing women who'll let a man insult her and give her gifts and run her money and act superior for the privilege of a ring and safety, is she better off? She never knew the right answer. Why did one have to subjugate to get and give love? Her generation's bargains were painful for the man or the woman.

It was a warm house hidden in the Hollywood Hills and was full of paintings of women's faces. The paintings were hung in a random manner and sometimes were even slightly askew as though an earthquake might have occurred but was not noticeable enough for its owners to bother checking the house for damages. The wood was dark, and the furniture had the look of worn wealth. The great underbelly of LA was not crime or sordid souls, but the middle class, the warm, flea-infested, milk-giving beast of mundane life. The host was one of the same. He and an ocher blond were the receptionists in the den.

Dr. Bond, the host, was in his early sixties and had a goatee, which suited him well because he liked to eat almost everything and had provided a nice assortment of nibbles. For the thirty dollars, one had company and dinner.

He told her he was a psychologist and had been a member of this group for close to ten years.

"It is a very select group, and we're happy to have you here. How did you find out about us?"

"My friend told me, but she couldn't come tonight. Bad cold."

"Go right on in down the hall," the blond said with a smile. She must evaluate all the desirable men as they come in and send all the women to the "back room."

No one introduces you, and no one notices you directly. Like all cocktail parties, there is a feeling of acute aloneness unless you have friends somewhere in the groups. You hide your shyness. It is not a very adult thing to have when others are laughing and talking and being the social animal you are not.

She went immediately to the bar to get some sallow white wine that was being served by a very young woman in a white blouse and black bow tie. She smiled as she poured the drink and asked if she wanted some ice in the wine to chill it a little more.

"No, that's all right. I'll take it at room temperature," she replied and took the thin plastic cup in her hand. She looked around the room. Most of the people were outside on the patio because there were gas heaters planted like guards every ten feet or so and any December chill Southern California had could be vanquished by this ingenuity. That was not so for the people.

Everyone was very well dressed and was very old it seemed. The ubiquitous gray-haired men and dyed fuzzy blond or red-haired but equally grayed women stood in groups, talking and occasionally laughing. She looked outside for one face to greet her and of course knew that was unlikely. The thing was she no longer had the patience or gumption to stand for a while or to walk over to someone. She had been alone too long now, and it didn't really matter. That human need to be with one's own kind couldn't drive her anymore, and if she were not accepted, she couldn't wait or try to help herself anymore. She turned and went back to the bar and its room of quiet.

She went to the table where the nibbles, just crackers and nuts, were and tried a couple leftover pretzels but knew she was too queasy and frustrated to eat.

"Well, he certainly is eclectic in his collection of records," she finally said to a tall man standing and looking at the woman's faces above the CDs. She should have said CDs, but he knew she was old anyway so what the hell? Why not use anachronisms?

They talked about the host's paintings and musical tastes, and he said the host was very creative and interested in a variety of things and she said he was unsure of his interests and had rather tacky taste in paintings, pointing out this paper mural of the moon's surface.

She knew this was another of the species she was very ambivalent about. He had some virility, but what went with it, which annoyed her, was the openly indiscriminate acceptance of what was. Not really smarmy, just gormless. She had some hidden pleasure in calling him such.

He was an engineer. "What type?" she asked.

He seemed surprised and pleased. "So you know there are differences."

Actually, he turned out to be a rocket scientist for Rockwell. She wanted to ask him all sorts of questions about the Challenger and space, but he capped his introduction with crusty resignation.

"Can't wait to retire. I'm tired of working at this job." He sighed.

She tried anyway. "But it must be fascinating to be part of the greatest engineering developments of our time." It sounded stupid, so inarticulate, but maybe he wouldn't notice.

He looked across the room at Dr. Bond as though he were waiting for permission to speak.

"Well, it's had its moments, which I really did enjoy." He smiled and put his hand on her back to move her away from someone stumbling in with a drink in his hand. She knew she was one of the more attractive women there from her fast survey of the patio and hoped he knew it too and the two of them could talk about these real things.

"What exactly did you do?"

Instead of answering her question, he said, "Oh, there's Dr. Bond signaling. He wants us to go out on the patio for the mixer, you know, for the dance to get to know each other."

She didn't know, but when he suggested they go out by extending his hand to indicate the way, she declined and went back to the bar for some peanuts. It was getting to be too much. The need to be patient was a demand too great to obey. No one was going to come after her. She was too old and too sick of the court in courtship, judging her, judging them, to earn some male company.

She put her drink down, and even as she asked herself why she wouldn't wait a little longer, she went through the hall to the living room, past the ochre blond and Dr. Bond, who was scolding his little dachshund for trying to get a cookie, and into the dark where she could cease to exist.

It was best during these attacks to get in the car and drive back down to the freeway and then decide whether to go home or to a movie.

She began to cry a little. Why couldn't she give herself a chance to find someone? He could be shy too. She would be lonely again tonight. So what?

She went past a couple of the theaters in Santa Monica and parked. She bought her ticket for seven-fifty and thought about Roy Roger matinees when all the kids on the block walked down to the Alhambra Theater Saturdays.

The cashier asked, "One?" as though she too had hoped that an invisible partner would come up behind her to make it two.

"One."

It wasn't as though she couldn't get attention from men. It was that none of them melted her butter enough, as she liked to say, to make it all worth the effort. The feature had already started, and it was dark and cozy in the theater. She could make out a few heads when the screen got bright with sky and was startled for a moment when she thought she recognized one of the men sitting with two women. He didn't have the right shape for the head though, and she finally relaxed in her anonymity in the dark. She could hide here like the escapees in old movies who sneaked by ticket booths into theaters as refuge from the police pursuing them. No one would notice for very long that she was alone. In a while, Christmas would be over, and New Year's have come and gone.

Paradoxically, being alone was a family trait. On Christmas Day in 1892, Helene's mother, Sophia, was at home after her parents and two brothers and her had eaten a goose. She was doing dishes after dinner while the others had gone to the small village church for day services. Their farm had provided a good harvest that year, and she thought about her mother's promise they would go into town at the New Year and buy material for two new dresses. It was time for her to think about marriage. After all, she was getting old at seventeen, and although they would miss her helping her mother in the kitchen, it was time for her now. She had received a small silver-encased pink glass flower vase, which she kept all her life on the window sills of all three bedrooms she had in her life: the one on the farm, the one in her first house with her husband, Helene's father, and the last one in the big house where she stayed with him and her daughter until she died. She preferred to help balance the farm accounts and to order the seed by running her hands through the barrels of grain, but the gift had come from her grandparents so she hid her disappointment in not getting a ledger book.

Helene's father, Karl, was already in the city and had set himself up with a boyhood friend in a small confectionery shop; the friend did the baking, and Karl delivered to customers in the morning and sold at the counter late into the evening. He was asleep in the back of the store hiding on Christmas Day after working until midnight and going to the minister's house with the last of the cakes after night services. Stuttgart was growing over its hills, and the people loved to eat sweets, like Black Forest cakes with cherries strewn over white frosting and apple strudel with flaked sugary baked flour that broke in the mouth like shards of satisfaction.

Willi's mother, Francesca, was alone in her room sewing again as the day waned because she had linens to finish embroidering for her older sister's marriage. They were hidden in a great chest by her bed, but she could open the lid easily with one hand whose thumb seemed to jut out, signaling great flexibility. She was a big-boned woman who, when she finished with milking cows, turned to beautiful embroidery. Her mother, sister, and she had stewed rabbit, dumplings, and red cabbage with apples they had fetched from the cellar before the fruits had become too wizened. She used to cry when the rabbits were killed, but that had stopped after her father had been hurt in a plowing accident and bled to death in the barn. She only whined a little thereafter and hid her tears.

Willi's father, Jacob, dressed in a black braided uniform, was riding a train from Hamburg to Köln taking tickets from the few travelers of that day, men in warm long wool coats who sat beside women in feathers and furs gently tapping children on their gloved hands if they moved around too much. He had hidden his lunch in the back of the baggage car and sat on a barrel eating quietly after the train had pulled into the station. He had nowhere to go and didn't need much to eat, being a rather slight narrow-nosed man. Later, he sold post office stamps.

She, too, the granddaughter, one hundred years later, was alone. Her children were grown and busy with responsibilities, her husband long gone in divorce, for her and the children's sake, not in spite of it. Noisy memories of eager screams and questions and running around the house with toy cars, planes, Snoopy and paints and begging for telephones and records before CDs sang through her loneliness. Their riffs of red, green, and blue paper with trails of ribbons, game setups and sweater or sock piles, candy canes, and felt Christmas stocking hanging on the fireplace played in her mind, while she saw only furniture and stillness. Christmas Eve dinners, German style, with fire in the fireplace and dinner at the table, modified gift opening, waiting until the children were old enough not to have to delay until Christmas morning, and Santa Claus's appearing in person.

She could hear her father on Christmas Eve bellowing, "Ho, Ho, Ho," and not letting her and her sisters down the stairs. She had married a man who had eight candles to light and dreidels to spin with guilt and mockery. How easy it was for them to find each other.

Better to be alone and look forward.

CHAPTER 10

molest /me'lest/ vt

I KNOW OF A woman whose grandfather, uncle, father, three brothers, and a cousin molested her throughout the years she was at home from age seven until eighteen, and then she ran away and got married. It was during the '40s and '50s in Texas where they're known for doing things in a big way. They each cornered her in the barn when the others were out farming. "Exceptin', of course, Daddy," she said, "who came at night and dragged me out from under the bed." She went to Indiana and was only raped once there by her husband's brother. She had three children by C-section; one of the kids was born without a brain and died three days later. The woman's jaw was wired shut after her husband broke it because she wouldn't stop crying over the baby. When I saw her, she'd come to the hospital for cancer of the cervix. It had already spread, and she had to have radiation and chemotherapy. She shot and killed her husband when he tried to have anal sex with her right after her surgery and her first treatments.

Someone else said they knew one of the fifty or so men who reported the priest had molested them when he was in their parish. They had been little kids but had the ability to remember. He also told me about the girl whom the priest got pregnant and sent to have an abortion in the Bronx.

Those things remained hidden for almost fifty years. What about all of the others, she wondered, like herself who only had one episode and it was a "minor violation" by the Texas woman's standard. What little dirty secrets were still hidden?

Irangate, Watergate, S&L bailouts, adultery by England's heir apparent and whomever are poor news compared to taking gold from teeth, lying, stealing lands, rape, killing and burning humans. Dead babies in nunnery walls, children beaten and strangled. There is no comparison, no parity with everyday molestations after seeing the photographs of the children coming out of the concentration camps.

What do the everyday people with their everyday wrongs against them do but hide them? Who cares today if one was molested once, or someone cheated you out of some monies, or fucked you, or fucked you over, or fucked you up. Monstrous violations are what get exposed with acknowledgement and supposed cathartic results through justice or even by the mere exposure itself. So it is as if the floodlights of knowing created goodness and withered gross evil. But no amount of time smoothes over those photos of the concentration camp victims. What do we do with the little transgressions? Is there a flashlight, a candlelight for the little molestations? Will that help the healing?

What do you do with your everyday lies and self-deceptions, with the little molestations of life, and the violet violations, that can't bring purple prose?

There was this little girl who sat on the friend of her dad. Sitting close to a dark oak table, the two men talked and worked on a proposal.

"The budget allows for the full-time item, if you think you can justify it," the friend said and added, "I've spent the last few weeks every night adding up the numbers, and it will work. You can have the contract and produce the coffee machine with the one salesman."

That day, her mother had gone to the store with her other sisters, and she had stayed home to listen to the men talk because she liked to hear them and watch all their important papers be moved about.

The friend lifted her up on his lap and let her mark a blank piece of paper with his ink pen.

"I'll get us some coffee. Vat do you need? Cream? Sugar?" her father asked solicitously.

Her father was always kind to others even when they weren't German and he was superior.

Herr Professor. He was always trying "to make a go" of some business deal, to make a fortune in America, which he never did; his hidden desire was the fortune. He had respect for American physicians and lawyers, not teachers, just like Americans in general, except they really liked businessmen best. He liked this lawyer from Toledo, Ohio.

"Both, please, Bill. Thanks," the friend said as he lifted one of her curls and twirled it gently. Now she thinks of that phrase, lifted from

Thomas Wolf's "You Can't Go Home Again," "kinder and gentler." He could not have been kinder or gentler as he pulled her pants down.

"Sit still, little sweetheart. Don't move," he whispered while he held her arm with one hand.

"Vat was that, Jack? I thought lawyers didn't talk quietly," her father called from the kitchen.

"Nothing, Bill. Only thinking out loud. How about a little toast and cheese too? I haven't eaten all day."

They bantered back and forth from the different rooms for over half an hour, and during that time, she could feel something in his lap harden and his fingers explore her and stick her and he held her tightly and told her, "Don't move." He leaned over and looked down at her while he watched his hand. The afternoon light from the yard flickered through all the leaves of rose bushes nearby and then entered through the beveled glass dining room doors and on to the table where she had her important paper.

He put her down before her father came in with the coffee, and when she grew up, she never ever drank coffee. Later that day, when her mother came home, she scolded her for being such a mess and having her dress caught in her underpants. "You're a little gypsy, wandering around and not caring about how you look." She remained quiet for she did not have the words to describe what had happened, nor could she understand it then.

When they were all adults, her older sister had told her once how, when she was fifteen, she had been grabbed and kissed "with an open mouth" by some Bible salesman. Her younger one said that her mother had cautioned her not to sit on men's laps when she went to college.

Her daughters had been grabbed and pinched at school or on the subway, but they could tell her at least. Did knowing or telling help?

How many secrets are out there that aren't "that big a deal"?

"Gentler" and "kinder" and supposedly less brutal secrets that are still molestations?

What about pooping in your pants from fear? Or losing your lunch money to a bully? Or being touched by another boy when you are a boy? Or being hit by your father? Or being abandoned by your mother? Or being mocked if you can't get an erection? Or losing all your money in a robbery? Or just being afraid of that group? Or failing a class run by a sarcastic shithead? Or not knowing the right answer and being laughed at?

Who cares? Why bother? When, as they say, do you give a shit?

CHAPTER 11

Once upon a time, the princess kissed the frog, and he turned into a handsome prince and they lived happily ever after.

I THINK OF ALL the Grimm fairy tales where the ugly male turns into a handsome prince with the love of a pretty girl. Frogs and beasts are transformed into heroic kind handsome rich men. Stepmothers abuse little girls who are rescued by princes. There are neither cruel stepfathers who sexually abuse little girls nor husbands that beat wives. That's real life.

Fairly tale women get to be physically turned into sleeping objects waiting to be kissed so they can "wake up." They can be turned ugly into cruel witches and stepmothers so they can be aggressive. The only other transformations they make are as poor girls into girls wearing designer clothes. The heroine's inner beauty manifested in fancy dresses.

Padded bras went the way of science into silicone implants and girdles into liposuction. If you have wrinkles, you must anguish over whether or not to have a face lift to fit the fairy tale princess and never get old and be a horrible, wicked witch.

She took her ideas of time, space, and matter, along with the sphinx of shame at being too smart from her father and the cat of "too interested" from her mother, and went out into the world.

I have launched my children now, and I am left to find new ways to service. The house, full of years of things collected to serve, now needs to be served. Also, there's the job catering to all the working egos. Of course, there could be a man to soothe and transform from beast to banal being. Taught well, I gave myself up for selflessness to avoid selfishness.

There are moments of such morbidity when I smile and turn them into trite contempt. I could take some sedative like Seconal or Phenobarbital for no more second chances and put some warm sweater on with my Levi's. I could go out into the fields beyond the back of my house and lie down in a garbage bag, seal myself up, and fall asleep. Of course, the bushes would be sticking their branches out to protest the intrusion and the ground would be moist and full of dead debris that preferred to ferment without me, but I would overpower the wild with my death, and the wilderness would be quietly accepting soon enough.

The idea comforts me. Women seem to think that they must kill themselves while men allow themselves to kill others.

I tell patients who raise the idea of suicide that suicide is always an alternative. Most people think of it like I do, as an idea, an alternative to the shit of the day.

There are even doctors who want it over for good, like one of our internal medicine doctors who chained himself to a rock at low tide and overdosed as well. Or the intern bride groom who thought he'd picked the wrong honeymoon spot for his bride and could hear the freeway traffic while he said his eyes were falling out of his head and couldn't his new wife see that? He blew his head off with an old .45 he'd been given from his dad's collection of guns. The radiologist hooked himself up to two IVs, one with potassium chloride and one with barbs way before the Michigan doctor's euthanasia contraptions. They didn't find him for three days. He was in a motel outside of Bakersfield. The two women physicians from our hospital who killed themselves did it with drugs. Another let her psychotic husband cut her up in little pieces for the garbage.

My father was like the serrated grapefruit knives that cut into the pulp and separate out the fruit of thought clearly and swiftly. He would have said, "Oh, you're just crazy," to think about suicide since there's so much in the world to enjoy. Didn't I tell you he put gobs of butter and jelly on the toast he made for us and himself? He was reading about arrhythmias at his bedside when he died of atrial fib at eighty-two.

My father's father, Jacob, took other people's tickets in life and never crowed too loudly as the trains he traveled on went always on the tracks and he came home to Francesca with her royal name and her plain handmade perfumed linens.

My mother Helene's father, Karl, I never knew, but he was more like a Luger pistol, firing sharp verbal bullets at anyone he found annoying.

Helene was always allowed in the family bakery and loved to watch "Konrad, my baker," she told everyone. He told her of the great bakeries in Hanover and all the modern machines that were used to mix the dough for bread, cut chocolate squares, and pour out molded cookies to bake in huge ovens. While he talked, he shifted trays full of round rising dough from tables to ovens, which would soon produce glowing brown glazed rolls. He would always give her the one on the right side end, until she was about sixteen and left for boarding school, plump and petulant. Ovens and Germany no longer conjure sweet fragrant bread, but during her time, rich woven breads and glazed buns were what ovens were for.

She remembered crying the day she was to leave. Sitting quietly in her upstairs room, in her south corner, centered in the half turret ringed with windows, she was reluctant to part from the warmth of those ovens. It was raining, and business had been slow. Her mother had been able to go upstairs from the grocery on the first floor of their big gray house on the Lenzhalter overlooking the whole valley of that gradual sloping Stuttgart hill. She had come up to help her pack and smooth out her new lace collared blouses before they were wrapped in tissue and packed. In the store, she and her mother wrapped rolls and cakes in handmade boxes and sausage or bread in shiny waxed paper and tied it with thin white string, which was easy to get again now that the war was over.

Helene's father, Karl, had grown up during the time of Bismarck, openly celebrating alliance with the Austro-Hungarian Empire who had made secret treaties with Russia. Anything to guard against France taking back Alsace-Lorraine was the rule of the time. Karl felt that to gain money to survive was the tenet of his time. He made secret treaties with the mills for flour and took a generous dowry from the family Sophia had so wanted to account *for*, not *to*. He hid the money in a small chest of wood behind their huge mahogany armoire. The 1890s passed, and he prospered with the new wife he had by 1898.

As his children grew and the 1910s heralded a new openness of skies and seas, he did not understand the overt declarations of war and all the commotion over Bosnia, which clanged death that knelled again eighty years later but to the more deaf ears of the Austrians,

Hungarians, and Germans, as well as the British and French. Then it meant something to the balance of power with little Balkan states near Turkey. The round robin of declarations in the glaring newspaper headlines of his day and the flat print of today's encyclopedia swarmed over him: "Austria-Hungarian declares war against Serbia," "Germany against Russia," "France mobilizing against Germany," "Germany against France," "Austria-Hungary against Russia," "Serbia against Germany," "Montenegro against Austria-Hungary," "France and Great Britain against Austria-Hungary," and "Austria-Hungary against Japan and Belgium." It appalled him to have all these open fightings, and he swore under his breath and kept selling food.

Life splayed itself even more openly and continued so even after the war had closed. Fertilized by dead young men, young women were forced to bloom by melding their ways with the lost men they would never have. Helene bobbed her hair and even wore slacks at home. When it was time for their Helene to go to school, Sophia hid but did not give up her hope that her daughter would be free to add numbers or account as she wished.

For Helene herself, it was a strange time to go away while the very fear of France overpowering Germany came true with the treaty talks, held in that palace of the French Sun King, Louis XIV. World War I, named the "last" ever war in 1918. The French soldiers who were prisoners of war and worked on her grandparent's farm as well as other farms near the Freiburg village had stayed and didn't want to go back to France. That seemed so strange to her since she had wanted to leave Stuttgart ever since her father had sent Roland away for not barking. If she barked, he could not forgive her. She told herself she stayed only for her mother, now that her brother was at the university, and also for the bakery.

"I hate the way he orders you around. What will you do?" Helene sobbed. "I shouldn't go. What will you do?"

"It is fine. He'll be fine. He is a good man. Only not good with people. His yelling, that's our secret. He is disappointed in Germany."

They finished packing, and she went away for that year. Resisting the Maria and Martha doctrines of purity and cooking. Her knitting stitches were too tight and couldn't be forced off the needle or back on. Her readings of English and French were good, but she hated to stand and quote the passages from Shakespeare they were required to recite.

She and her friends giggled about the clean-shaven math teacher and wrote poetry about him.

When she came back home, she worked in the grocery store with her mother while her father and Konrad baked. She told the story many times of how her mother ran up the few stairs to the bakery when she heard her father yelling at a customer.

"Ah, Mrs. Wolf, I am sure I would not come back here if it weren't for your kindness," almost all of them said as she gave them extra rolls with clear candied fruit and raisins inside.

Karl would not listen to Sophia begging him to be nicer or to Helene's prescience about the economy.

"Don't you see, Father, it is time to get rid of your cash and buy some things. The money is worth less and less," Helene pleaded as they stood at the big pot of stew. Her mother cut dark brown chunks off huge bread loaves and then sliced yellow cheese to top the soft brown pumpernickel. Sometimes, they would have the bread and cheese with a little sausage, especially if there had been no time to make more stew the night before.

"Don't tell me what to do. I have worked all my life for the money. Do your lessons and stop listening to your mother and her strange ideas." In a few years, people would come to him with real wheel barrels spilling money for that bread and he would ask for silver or gold instead. He would take the tea sets or little lockets and get more flour. He never acknowledged Helene or his wife being right and only cursed his customers more.

Karl could not listen to his daughter, and she was the one that loved the business. His son wanted what his mother wanted, and he became an accountant who collected money and wrote in the ledgers his mother had always loved.

Days of selling and making more to sell were the everyday days. Years of pleading for recognition were the every year years. Helene continued to try to earn the right to be interested. If she could only find the right words, the right kisses to change the stubborn beast, her father would finally understand.

It took the slow rotting to death of her mother to stop her hope. She watched her father carry her mother back and forth to the bathroom and help her get into the bath. Those huge seven-foot bathtubs had outsized chrome cross faucets of hot and cold and long writhing metal cord and spray attachment for elegant avant-garde showering and bathing. They had been installed before the war at the beginning of the modern age of the automobile and the flying machine, but they always reminded me of sterile operating room paraphernalia, not opulence; they were so German in their big-boned serviceability and lack of delicacy.

My grandmother died, and my mother wandered the streets with her brother asking "Why her?" all that cold spring. "She was such a good woman" was the phrase I heard when my mother was dying sixty-five years later. It was as if that grief of losing her own mother at the beginning of my mother's adult life never let her step fully into adulthood.

She made only one great effort at independence and then settled into the gray of belonging to someone else's agenda, but I thank her for that one-time grand gumption. In the fall after her mother died, Helene left Europe and Willi and kissed her father goodbye, no longer waiting for the beast to turn. She went on the North American line from Bremen to Chicago, Illinois, and her Uncle Christian's house. She left the grief for her mother, and she left the hopelessness of her father. Hers was a repeat of the great migrations to America: the Puritans, the Huguenots, the potato famine families, the defeated, all those who left for freedom from big or little oppression to come to an unstructured potential.

Most of all, the Germans had come and the Austrians. More than any other migrating group, they had come to America, and she rode one of the last great waves in the 1920s before it was too late. More millions than any other European nationality moved into the hinterland of the United States, seeking familiar terrain, inland, rolling foothills, woods of evergreen and elm, encompassed seas and waterways, until they found the Midwest and the central plains and were safe to raise wheat and bake. While many Italians, the Irish, and, of course, the English stayed near the great waters, the Swedes and the Czech went with Germans, who had stories told about them in years to come. After WWI, Germans remained hidden. That heritage seldom claimed with celebration. Helene also agreed to cover her beginnings, to become American.

"I remember getting on the train in New York. I didn't have to go to Ellis Island because I had a sponsor in my uncle, really a distant relative, and so I went from the ship to Grand Central Station and on to the train. There was this woman next to me, by the window, with her little daughter, and she talked to me.

"'In America, we have many roads, and in American, you can go where you want, and in America, all types of people have cars,' she explained after finding out about my origins. It was the 1920s and her hair was bobbed and she was wrapped in a coat with fur on the collar and big cloth buttons down the front and she wore pointed shoes. The American woman didn't know about Stuttgart and the Black Forest, only about the poison gas and her uncle who died from dysentery somewhere in France."

My mother continued, leaving somewhere for somewhere else, but they were all little leaving-takings compared to her one great journey.

CHAPTER 12

*Everything in Nature contains all the powers of Nature.
Everything is made of one hidden stuff.*

—Ralph Waldo Emerson

S HE HID AS a mother. She left her girlhood and womanhood
and became a mother. The cape of a mother image encompassed
her, and later she would realize it was a way of escape. I understand her.
To be a mother is a formidable presence, and one that is unassailable to
most demands of the id.

One takes the car's suicide seat, not the driver's or backseat, and travels
along protecting and assisting others. She could avoid almost everything
as a mother except those things that showed her to herself as good and
kind and loving as well as altruistic and, occasionally, self-sacrificing.

"Are you sure she's never been kissed?" Alex asked Roger. She,
Alex, and Roger were in medical school in the 1960s when less than 10
percent of the class were women.

"Well, pretty sure, the way she talks. Never had it in her, and I'm
willing to change that." Roger told Alex. She liked Roger's big blue eyes
and the darkened area where his beard was shaven. She wanted to rub her
hand up against him and then mark him with her cheek against his. He
didn't know that. He thought she was "innocent," and he of course had had
already "seventeen women," which to him meant he was an experienced
lover. Her innocence amounted to her allowing herself to open her legs for
the first time like the horns of a dilemma and to "come," to come to an

amazing orgiastic popcorn of life below him and on top of him. She was careful to hide that even from herself thereafter and localize the sensation.

She had babies and became a mother, and in the middle of the night, they would sneak up upon each other and redo pleasure and redo it again. The children didn't know their secret until much later when they kept their own secrets about touching themselves and others.

He had to keep her a secret when he first met her for whatever reason—others, religion, shame, guilt, fun. I even understand him.

It became apparent to her late in life that the stuff of infatuation, romance, and sex materialized at different rates for the man and the woman. Male highs were fast and stiff. Men infused with infatuation and readied to couple early on, but she never took advantage of anything to keep them. She ascended more slowly and intensity built for her into a trust that it was all right to release one's self. That came with sex, sex but not with soul.

She wished she could have learned to enjoy it all by herself or with vibrators or just suppressed her drive.

She bought light green pajamas for her first time with him, and he touched her. He was interested and jealous and impatient. He wanted her for himself, and that was all that mattered. If Alex came over to see her, Roger became mad and threw books rather than tell her how much he loved her. He never said that.

For some reason, there was a despair about her. The ones she loved had never told her they loved her and the ones that were interested in her were unrequited and she avoided. It was the German angst, Sturm und Drang. A writhing romantic nature that never let it work out, never could see that she could be loved, and never could accept the one who did tell her he was right and trustworthy.

It was not so easy anymore to fall into propriety and have to be together. They'd been married two decades before she couldn't stand it anymore. He made the kids cry and yelled at them for thinking for themselves and forgetting to put candy wrappers away. He couldn't ejaculate joy and only spewed forth anger and restrictions on the basis of preserving money. When they parted, the omniscient gray fog shrouding her evaporated into a sparkling vast night sky of infinite aloneness. Absence of pain is sometimes the most one glimpses of joy.

Now there is the descent into the circles of individuality that had been rimmed with the patina of mothering and crusted over with service and precipitated on by whatever man had needs she could try to fulfill.

She was alone, and in some ways, it was better. She was alone, and it was curious that after all this time of longing to be with someone, maybe she would like to be alone instead. Men came and went, and she didn't want any of them since those days of green pajamas and eager sex turned to red nightgowns and black nights.

Her daughters were with young men, and they too suffered the role of lover. Confined by his jealousy or devoted to helping him rather than themselves or criticized for being of a woman's mind not male minded, they tried to make some reasonable compromise, holding him in the horns of their dilemma just like she had.

I, of course, of inevitable course, had a similar story. I was the shy child or rather the quiet child. Ashamed I had needs, sorry I had bodily functions that could demand gratification or release, that could make funny sounds of hunger or repellant smells of which somehow my sisters never seemed to feel guilty of and boys lauded as distinctly part of their own sex. I hid in big sweaters and bulky skirts, books to stay home and exchange ideas; stereo in my room for Chopin nocturnes at age fourteen; in class "brainy" boys wanted to play chess with me rather than have their chests and crotches rubbed; girlfriends said I was lucky to be with them to look at them with admiration or to give advice.

Still I could not escape my brain and its gift of thought. I heard that ignorance was bliss, so what is knowledge? Is the Garden of Eden really meant to let human minds be fallow?

A place to supply all our needs with no effort? What was the purpose of my having any brains, Eve? Tell me. Thank you for being blamed for eating the apple. The problem when I grew up was I was ashamed of that ability to know. I traced the kind of algebraic X of desire and the shame of wanting to my mother and then my grandmother; the other X marks the spot to be able to love and project and procreate to my father and his father, who needed to have some means to carry on the race. Women carried the burden of life while men possessed the Y chromosome along with an X and therefore whys of the world for themselves.

There is no stopping the menstrual flow unless you get pregnant with a baby, are overworked, run over, let the surgeon gut you or let age pleasantly surprise you and tell you, you have bled enough.

CHAPTER 13

I am a part of all that I have met.

—Lord Alfred Tennyson

T HAT PHRASE ENCAPSULATES a good result I hope in what I try to do in psychiatry. To have some *influence*, which is a pretty word to me. It is melodic, gentle, and quickly over, considering the possibilities attached to its meaning. *Influence*. It turns things outward rather than in toward the one who is aware. Children are the best example, I think, both literally and figuratively, of one's self being a part of them.

My father was a traveler like Ulysses. He went to Hamburg and made himself a teacher to students who were really only a few years younger than him and he took the train to Stuttgart and saw Helene. He could not believe she would leave him and Germany, but he saw her do it and he followed in his usual dramatic fashion.

"Dat day, I saw the best ship about to leave from Hamburg. Your mother had gone on about one mont already and had written me about the buildings, skyscrapers dat really scraped the sky, and about Dewey at the University of Chicago. She was staying with Aunt Mema and her Uncle Christopher. I ran to the dock und met a man who said he would sponsor me, right dere on the dock. He wore a striped suit and wingtip shoes. I told him I was a teacher and they could use me in America. I left the car, a Mercedes, und got on the ship."

He had that con and cunning in him that is called gumption and leads to some sort of success. He went back and forth after the war and visited all over Europe as the American professor who brought an American study group and was welcomed. The buildings were mounds of rubble piled up away from the streets, which were cleared.

Though when I think of him now, he belongs in the same category as my mother. A type of person who makes one great move, book, invention, thought, musical composition, and settles into understanding it or living within it and not going on. He caught the ship to here. I had always seen him as someone who would continue to do and create, but he really only learned more and dreamed differently than she did. He never did more.

His were the trays to sell and the coffeemaker to market and statistical computations to evaluate others' performances and an article or lecture and some bookshelves he built to store the ideas. Hers were to win contests and publish a book and die in a plane crash after taking out insurance. Mine were to understand and keep moving.

Today, the clouds puffed up as the sun sank, and they were like plump little memories. I remember making fried potatoes with onions by slicing boiled potatoes into round disks and frying them to sizzling satisfaction. There were canasta games and checkers and watching the Red Wings skate and score at two in the morning. Prophet Jones would say, "Let's give a little hand for the Lord," and his congregation would sing, "Hallelujah." Further back before TV, I remember the paper drives and binding the piles of newspaper in tough narrow string that could sear the skin and stepping on cans, which sometimes stuck to our shoes and made us hoofed like horses.

Now, every Wednesday, the recycling truck comes and picks up aluminum cans, glass bottles, and newspapers. Did I tell you that?

I have worn long skirts and short skirts and miniskirts and long shirts again and flowered dresses and straight dresses and flowered dressed again. I have traveled almost everywhere except the Galapagos and have made my great move to California. Now, it seems everyone is moving back to where they came from.

I kept going west, but went once to China, as east as there is, yet west of me here. I remember seeing pictures of World War II women working machines and standing on the outside of an airplane either touching its belly and gunning the rivets, or smiling under caps with straps that dangled the authority of being a pilot.

Today, women in the United States are in suits and give speeches and are accused of nefarious attempts at power. Yet in hidden places like fish canneries, sewing shops, and in China, they are lined up chopping and scaling, pushing machine pedals for designer jeans and in front of huge steaming water bins soaking cocoons to spin silk threads. Women don't have to die here or there now because they are good worker bees and can find the end of the cocoon thread to hook it to the spindles, and they can sew fine threads to make white kitten pictures or weave red threads into flowered rugs until, of course, they become literally blind. The Good Earth is a market economy now. Our Golden Streets country is too. East and West dream in terms of eating and money. What is the better life now? Here it seems only prostitutes and cocaine and deals.

I do not want to recycle my parents' lives by dreaming. I do not want to start a stripped down cycle of eating and money only.

One day, this woman sat down to eat her dinner, and she put a newspaper in front of her plate to the left of her water glass filled with elliptical ice. She read the "View" section where there were articles on bungee jumping, street taggers who wanted their names everywhere they could pee, a child who was carried by a surrogate who was really the mother who was married to the brother of the donor who was the lover of the mother in coma who had been shot by the surrogate's sister. Below all that was a picture of a movie star who was getting married to a rock star. Inside, the next page had a full spread on skinheads.

The woman wore her jockey tee shirt and some Levi's. She hooked her thumb between her skin and the denim and pulled the snap open as she ate.

Her ex-husband was divorcing his second wife and had called to see how the kids were doing. Of course, the kids were no longer kids and were off on exotic weekends away from their apartments and houses. She felt a slight nausea as she tried to eat. He always worried her. He would be suicidal periodically, and since he was in another state, she was relieved and yet burdened with helplessness as though she might still owe him something.

The skinhead had supposedly planned a killing to cause a race riot. They believed in purity of race and were neo-Nazis. They were all good-looking even if their faces were rounded from being shaved of all hair and eating a little too much steak and potatoes. Next to them was the picture of the latest murder victim; she was a dark-haired Caucasian, age twenty, and a student. There were no clues as to who had killed her and dumped her in the ravine over the pass on the San Diego Freeway.

The woman ate her dinner as she read. It was a somewhat strange fare for dinner because it consisted of breakfast food, sunny-side up eggs, and leftover bacon with some fried potatoes. It was a secret dinner since she usually ate the recommended pastas or a big salad. She wasn't sure if the grease or her ex-husband's mood was making her sick.

She was alone that weekend and had tried to clean up the house, but it bored her and she went to the table to eat at 5:30 instead of a more customary time. As she finished streaking the egg yolk across the plate with her toast, it occurred to her she was alone. That she had to think about what she was going to do on this Saturday night of the weekend to play and rest.

She could read some more about the events of the day, or she could finish a detective novel or rent a movie or watch TV.

She thought of Richard. He was her last "relationship" as she had learned to say. He had wrecked her car and now wouldn't call her. It was still amazing to her that after all those years, he could abruptly stop calling her. She thought of two other men who had done that and a woman friend she's had for twenty years who didn't like depression. She always had to go through prolonged grieving and parting scenes to satisfy her internal goodbyes.

Suicide floated to her mind like it always did when she suffered. A while ago, she had asked herself, "How much longer?" and that had frightened her. She really didn't care about life anymore.

"Really though," she thought, "I hate Richard. He could dismiss me at will. How lucky he is to have that discipline."

She continued to read the newspaper and saw an article of another killer getting five years for his crime. It was then that she recalled the statistics that you can kill and get off in an average of seven years. She wondered why women didn't take advantage of the system and do some killing too. When they did, they got all publicity and the men went about the business of making a killing with killing.

She told me that day that she had been thinking of killing herself and changed her mind with those thoughts about prison terms. She finished her dinner and read some simple detective novel where she only turned the pages to the end to confirm what she already knew and who the killer was.

That night, she dreamt she was being followed by a man who looked like a buffalo, but not the friendly Beauty and Beast variety. The big head with a long gnarled nose in a graveled face was set in his huge shoulders, and the tuffs of his beard sprang out like rusted wires. He moved toward her in the street, which she recognized as her own, and into her house as she ran from the downstairs entrance up into her bedroom to shut the door. There had seemed to be no lock on the front door, and she waited only a second or two before she gave up looking for it and turned to scale the stairs two at a time. He meant harm. She knew that. Somehow, as in dreams, his face appeared at the window of her bedroom on the second floor, and she took the gun her sons had given her and unwrapped it to fire it. She had to pull the barrel back to put the bullet in the chamber and then release the safety. She did it calmly and with the knowledge that she would die if she didn't do it right. He was coming for her, and his eyes would not see her as anything but his prey. Close up, he had huge ears like satellite disks coming from the top of his head and horns like a bull; he was charging, and the window glass was shattering and he was on her, crushing her with his weight. She felt him strangle her with stubby hairy fingers and felt him ejaculate as she pulled the trigger and shot him.

The shot startled her awake, and she felt the proverbial distress of her heart pounding to get free of terror. She did not try to go back to sleep again but sat up against her soft pillows while the light stayed on, and she stared or closed her eyes to redo the scene again and again. In the morning, she went to work quite tired but with a pleasant kind of resignation that killing was okay for her too. Killing was the way it was now. Skinheads were the news, not goodness.

She continued her life with little variance except when she was too lonely, and then she would go with a friend to find a man. He would never have rusted hair but would be bald or with the gray hair of the wolf. For her, it was all right now. She could kill for herself, not only for her children or a man.

What part of me was her and how could I get her to trust not because of innocence but because of wisdom? There wasn't time, and she worried about insurance payments and told me about her eating breakfast at dinner frequently. She was happy going to the movies alone and didn't feel the feeling of failure for not having a companion to sit in the dark with her. She'd tell me that talking men were as big a bore as the ones that didn't talk. It seemed to amuse her that no matter what they were, they no longer fascinated her or determined what she did each day in the hopes of winning their favor. When I saw her last, she said she was in love with Beethoven. He was perfect. Tormented, needing love and kindness, creative, deaf to all but his heart and music, but also dead enough not to take her away from herself. She said she even wrote him love letters and hid her secret fan club from her kids and friends who would think she was crazy. She was quite happy.

I think she picked a pretty good Ludwig to love, like the mad King of Bavaria in his beautiful castle Neuschwanstein built for love and sorrow without regard for money and copied by Walt Disney, but maybe this Ludwig was even more beautiful. A Ludwig with a lion's mane, furrowed eyebrows, determined jaw, and that inner ear of joy. I love him too but know he can't be mine.

CHAPTER 14

"The horror, the horror." Is the free will we supposedly have just a little randomness that nature allows us as long as we conform to the preservation of self for reproduction and nurturing or as fodder for others?

I FELL IN LOVE with black men. I loved them like they were my vindicated self—so misunderstood, so maligned, so imbued with the qualities of anarchy and sexuality, that every success they had seemed closer to me than all the white-haired white men, with their eyeglasses of erudition and striped ties, hearing and telling tales of power and money. Black men could be my champions because they overcame the odds against themselves each time one of them made the newspapers and newsreels and television of black and white. They were not born with the white mantle of gratuitous endowment, but their penises were shrouded in that dark skin of inferiority. They were the visible smudges on society's conscience, which women were never allowed to be, until I was already a quiet doer in the fray of the 1960s.

I can still see Joe Louis in those grayish chiaroscuro photos in the *Detroit News*. His swollen, cut eyes, and full, protruding lips. His torso, not defined like a weightlifter, but huge and smooth, stemming from his shimmering satin shorts. The biceps ballooning and the forearms ending in the bulbous gloves that hid his own fists. The tight high-laced shoes for stepping forward and forward again, to hit and hit and hit.

I never saw one of his fights. The "Brown Bomber" was a legend already when I cared about him. He overcame the odds with a physical prowess. Of course, there was Marian Anderson singing for the

Washington DC crowds and Jesse Owens running over the Nazis, but I didn't really know about them except in history books until way later.

There was the gentleman Jackie Robinson. Somewhere in that vague territory of peripheral memories, he made it to first base and on to home plate as a hero when I was trying to throw a ball. He overcame the odds like Louis, and the white male press allowed him to be honored only later after the slings and arrows.

The most cerebral of my loves was Nat King Cole. I listened to him tell me of the ballerina who had to dance, not marry, and the woman in the painting had only been the painting Mona Lisa before he sang her story, and then I would look at those gentle eyes in the blackest of black faces with what others would mock as "liver lips" and I would hide how I cared and work at reconciling how I could love him and not betray the boys I was supposed to love.

Frank, the baritone, and Gene Kelly, the muscular dancer, and Elvis, the sensual, were of course wonderful loves to allow me to give my sexual urgings free rein. But the black men, they were my hope at redemption for my hidden sins. They were my avatars. The Mills Brothers, my big brothers. Soon it was Cassius Clay, Marcellus Clay, with his Latin name, Muhammad Ali his Muslim name, who overcame all that Rome stood for with "its might makes right" for white men. He fought for me. Mike Tyson was sacrificed. Today is there anyone more beautifully carved than Michael Jordan? He has a streak of the first black man heroes, but in some way, he has been lost in the familiarity of his face.

Nat King Cole and Oscar Peterson, Louis Armstrong, and Stevie Wonder played to me. *I have a dream.*

I tried to find the white man hero. Schweitzer, Sabin, Mantle, Gordie Howe, but they didn't represent the striving me. I remember calling Stalin a great man when he died because I seemed to know early on "great" had nothing to do with "good," many times as far as history goes, it only meant powerful and influential. I remember Joseph McCarthy, evil incarnate, screaming, "Point of order! Point of order!" on television as he hunted humans through labels, creating a greater scare than communism would ever be and getting other white men to hide their beliefs and their pasts.

Still the black men in the news back then were real heroes, *overcoming* their imposed supposed destinies before it was a cause. I was secretly hoping to be one of them.

Where were the women to hold up? Then I didn't know of the 1930s Mae West or Irene Dunne playing with Cary Grant. I didn't know about Amelia Earhart other than she died and Marlene Dietrich sang outside the barracks. Eleanor Roosevelt was only laughed at for her buckteeth like mine as she traveled the world after her husband died. I had to see Marilyn Monroe worshipped for having a baby doll voice and buxom body and Audrey Hepburn being beautiful dressed and innocent eyed. The 1950s put women in their least-threatening intellectual place and didn't ask men to really have sex with sex goddesses, just imagine.

Black men were my fighters, Sugar Rays of hope, and you could, if you dared, celebrate them even if you weren't black or male. The *Second Sex* and *The Feminine Mystique* were only book titles then, and now they are part of history, demeaned as "feminist," supposedly interpreted as "anti-men."

Now of course I know that the Japanese or Chinese men defined their standard by their own image, and the Arab men by theirs, and so the European man was the white image of perfection and all else was "other" and "less" and black or woman.

What can you do if the dictionary of divinity was male in concept and definition? I guess you pick the lowest of the males.

The night she moved to her first college apartment, he drove up in a cab. It was strange to see him park the familiar yellow car as his own. He took some bags of groceries into the apartment down below her.

Later, he smiled, a smile of glistening eyes and white teeth against mottled dark gums, and he touched her hair. She touched his too, and it was soft as down, and they kissed this tentative kiss that broke apart like a soap bubble. They laughed at their daring and ate hamburger they fried on a little charcoal grill and drank jug wine like big people.

Of course, they hid all this from their families.

"You think I like you talking to those white guys?" he'd say and then throw the pillow he's been squeezing back on the couch.

"Do you think they're interested in me? I'm the brain in the class, and they like the blonds. Stop worrying," she'd console. Secretly, she liked him to complain because it revealed he valued her. There was this open declaration between the two of them, not to their families, that each felt dangerous and special with the other's company.

The muscles on his brown back mimed the work he did for her in painting the walls of her bedroom and a finesse that spoke of newly practice roles of love and partnership. Her long fingers folded the Levi's he threw on the floor after returning from the Laundromat. They lived together, alternating nights in his or her apartment, and although he had some friends over occasionally, they were alone that whole year. He had shown her the French kiss by gently but insistently pressing, and she discovered the wetness of passion for all of her, and she had learned his urgent spasms through her own lips and tongue.

Her father asked if she had a boyfriend, and her mother wondered why she didn't want to come home more often. How could she tell them she wanted to be with him and not them if they made her choose? She rode the bus with him from Ann Arbor to Detroit and defied the world with kisses to his cheek and he would smile and look out the window, knowing that the other passengers were surprised and annoyed at their openness to such a social taboo. Rosa Parks had already said she wouldn't give up her seat on another bus a few years ago and hundreds of miles away.

Once she brought him home with her, and she saw the disparity between her open adoration and the polite demeanors of her parents as they tolerated the meeting and would not even think of what was really going on.

"He's nice enough, but you go round with this young negro man and you won't have any friends but bohemians," her father said. Her mother only looked at her with brown questioning eyes. They didn't know about the white sophomore poet she'd met in English class who had taken her to his attic apartment where the beanbags, floor mattresses, and pillows were dumped between canvases and books and the drapes were black and always drawn. The second time there, he had put it to her and in her, and she was wide-eyed and too tense to know anything except this was sex. Sucking and touching and probing her body while not knowing her favorite color or her middle name. He was her first boy, and after he finished, he got up and went into the john to wash himself. She walked down the stairs and met a long black-haired girl, with fringes on her jacket, who was carrying a bag of apples up the stairs. She never saw either of them again. She never even considered that he would call. He had serviced her and served as her initiation into the fleetingness of fucking the unknown.

Her downstairs neighbor, her real lover, her molasses man, was not the bohemian. He was aspiring to the middle class, while Beats were aspiring to the classless and modeling for younger sibs who were to be the hippies. How little her father really knew amused her, and she smiled her wise smile.

Later though, when she had asked her father why he shaved his legs and why her mother slept in a separate room, her father showed her the bugs he picked up at some hotel he stayed at for one of his business trips and how they looked like little crabs crawling on a white sheet of paper. The wise smile of hers became pained at thoughts she could not repress.

Her lover's father, her boy friend's father as she said then, died of a heart attack at age forty-three, and his mother was a tall and very thin woman, who carried on. She'd had six children, four boys and two girls. He was the third oldest. The boys were lean like his mother, but the girls were busty and somewhat overweight. They had all been at the house when he had come home with her. They lived on Chicago Boulevard near Hamilton in a huge house. They had the top floor and the attic, and his aunt and her husband and three sons lived on the bottom floor. The younger children were playing outside and stood still as they got out of the Ford. His older brother had picked them up from the bus station.

The house had been a mansion of some importance, and reportedly a judge had lived there in the 1930s. It had the flat face of architectural prestige, with only protrusion on the left side of the house for the carriages and cars of better days. The wooden floors were covered with carpet when she visited, and the wood paneling had been painted blue. There was laundry all over and an ironing board in the dining room.

"I understand you went to Cass High School. I work in the office there now," his mother said with the slightest accent of Southern upbringing. "My youngest son is to have schooling there, I hope, better than Northern High now."

They ate dinner with the family, and everyone was quiet except the smallest girl who asked to touch her white skin because it looked funny without color and she wondered if it was like paper. Everyone joined in to say, "Shut your mouth, Florence." They were as ashamed of her and their sister as her parents had been of him.

Neither of them went to the other's house for the rest of the year, and when June came, he said he wouldn't have time to see her in Detroit, it was goodbye, and he was taking a scholarship to go to Howard University Law School. He wrote her once when she came back to school in the fall, and that was it. He said he was very busy, had met a girl from North Carolina but would always remember her shinning eyes and sweet tongue for words and other things.

She wrote him once after that and said she hoped he did really well and she would look forward to reading about him in the news when he handled a big case. As an afterthought, she said she would probably go back to school too. But she never heard about him again, but sometimes when she returned to Detroit, she would go by that big house, bigger than any house her parents ever had, and look for his mother. She was never outside though, and after a while, she stopped thinking about him or his mother. She hid what had happened. Only when someone would make some remark about "niggers" would she think she knew better and defend those colored people, those blacks, those men who marched for their "dream" and while she watched on TV, she cried for those little brave, colored children who went to school.

About the time of the secret black and white lovers, Sylvia Plath was writing her pains and lamenting her father, her feelings, her femaleness, her fortunes. She would become a symbol of how women were supposedly caught in the maze of their roles while I went quietly on to school to become a medical doctor, a physician. I inadvertently made it out of that labyrinth, twisting with Chubby Checker and singing the "Yellow Submarine," examining dirty old men who coughed and vomited with chronic obstructive pulmonary disease and cirrhosis of the liver and then going to the next examining room to help thirteen-year-old girls have babies.

There were eleven girls in the class of 125 students, and the rest were boy-men. The black and white stories were from one of my classmates who smoked and laughed and went shopping with me when we weren't cramming facts I can't even remember now. We endured the slides of women's breasts used to break up dull lectures before there were actions against sexual harassments, and we suffered remarks about our own supposed puny pudenda. We took the flags out of our male cadavers' penises and ate sandwiches over dissected brains. Somehow, as the years went by, a metamorphosis occurred, and we became acclimated to thinking medically and pursuing the body gently and thoroughly to find its health and its pains and its diseases. I didn't understand that my own march forward for my daughters and my sons was important; I stayed hidden in work. My CV is without any fame but framed in devotion.

CHAPTER 15

I am restless. I ache. I cannot find something, some lost legacy trails my days and hangs back in my nights. Move. Move. Move forward, move back. Stay in this city, get transferred to this office, find a new house in a better part of town. Find the hospital. Move, move. Find new homes, go back home.

I am restless. I feel this wail across my breasts and chest and arms. Winds rustle in me, and no mind can calm them, no kiss can tell them, "Wait."

The rollicking rolling grasses, the soft moaning sand mounds, the ocean white caps are in me—they fill me and restlessness undulates within my heart.

Yet all that is caged in ribs of conformity. Help me.

YOU REMEMBER 1903 when my parents were born. Of course, that was the year of the Wright brothers taking off in the United States.

Köln was where Willi was born.

Frederick Barbarossa gave the bones of the Three Wise Men to the bishop of Köln in 1164. Those white splintered collections of calcium had steadied the flesh, which held the gold, frankincense, and myrrh, to offer to the Babe in the manager. Then the muscles decayed away and the bones were recreated and consecrated to lie for a while in Constantinople and then Milan. Finally, they were sent to Köln as a gift for the thriving crossroads city's huge cathedral. Those constructs were appropriate relics for the city where early on, the northern world converged to exchange its wares.

The cathedral took over six hundred years to build, finished I think in the 1800s and has tall statueless spires and gaunt folds of stone to hold up its entrances like crevices in rock. It rises as a majestic visual representation of awe. Deep underground, where the vaults form, lie those royal traveling men's bones in a golden cage.

Going up the stone stairs from the visit to the vaults and walking across the hard floors, I can look up in the honed stone space and almost believe I might reach goodness.

I once went to Köln by train from Frankfurt. We walked out of the station of gray cement and glass from the 1950s bleak age of utilitarianism and saw all the colored cars and the busy people who seemed almost all dressed in red. The cathedral stood very close by like a huge homeless hag, grayed and wrinkled by the modernity that ignored her. Her grounds were also an all-cement plaza, and milling around them were protesting students, with painted white skeleton faces mimicking radioactive deaths and not the bones of the Three Wise Men. There was no grass, and only a few flower boxes surrounding a hotel nearby.

I think the Three Wise Men hidden deep in the great Gothic womb would like to have been born again and traveled under the night sky looking for innocent hope. They too must be restless.

Stuttgart was where Helene was born.

Stuttgart, with its green hills and Black Forest longings and Swabian tales, was where Herr Benz named his new car after his daughter Mercedes. Eight hundred years after Frederick settled the Wise Men, Ferdinand Porsche joined the Benz Company in 1923 and worked hard for his bosses Mr. Benz and then Mr. Daimler. Professor Porsche offered electrical cars and air-cooled engines. Later, aside from the Volkswagen rear air-cooled engine and airtight body, which could float, he made his own cars. Those cars revved up the dream of going fast that dominated fantasies about prowess and seduction in the United States while I was growing up and learning to drive.

Winding roads in mountain passes and engines that rumbled and roared and rushed sensuality and power were the images that carried the emblem of Stuttgart to the world's view. It was all right to own those famous cars from Germany, and many a big boy drove his Mercedes or his Porsche regardless of his politics or killed relatives.

In my garage, a genuine 1957 red Porsche Series A 1600 Speedster nestles under the obligatory car cover. It is the model the kits copied when the originals were hidden away. It is gently rounded from its hood, which is for the storage, up through the windshield and convertible roof to the grated rear motor compartment. The sides slope to soften each fender, and it is my little Victorian bathtub. People tell me to keep it hidden, to be careful about driving it, or it might get stolen or bumped and it is worth a lot of money. I wonder though if it wouldn't like to try Topanga again, top down, unaware of its value and aware only of wind its own speed makes.

I was born in Detroit, the motor city, Motown, the home of Ford Motor Company, General Motors, and Chrysler Corporation, known as "the big three." Huge plants dominated suburban Dearborn where Henry Ford allowed the blacks to work but not live. Outside Detroit, Ford is credited today with the assembly line and Greenfield Village where he preserved Edison and himself. The big halfway landmarks going to downtown Detroit, which was an interminable six miles, were the General Motors Building right next to the Fisher Building named after the Fisher Body Division that made GM car designs. Chrysler put its factories out farther and always had the Chrysler Building in Manhattan, which in some way made it more prestigious.

I was allowed to drive the first little boxy unrounded trunk Ford my parents got. It was hell to turn around in tight spaces, which I'd get in visiting high school friends in narrow streets hedged in by frame houses, but soon we had one of the really new finned and chromed cars of opulence, which was even bigger and had a poorer turning radius.

Detroit was not too ugly then, and it had not become forlorn like someone trying to capture a fleeting good dream on awakening.

When I grew up, the big three were in power. Mercury is disappearing, and De Soto is gone now. Swift explorers lost to the Asian adventure. Those big three were not wise and did not retool for the journey. I still like them. Their power is male and muscle and bigness. Their factories are empty wombs.

The new convertibles, the Mazda Miata, copy of the Porsche 1957 Speedster, the Mercedes 500, and the Porsche 914 are powerless and polite. My Mustang GT, a rugged ride, is waiting to inseminate.

CHAPTER 16

*Once upon a time, this story came to be, and with it,
old and classic daughters and sons of kings and queens who
plant seeds and eat flowers. They hear the birds and lambs
talking, and all who are killed by shame rise up again, and
with special lotions on their eyes, see themselves; it is good.
In the heather and at the hearth, they kiss, and passion is
for them alone.*

S HE HAD BEEN sentenced to being a mother who could not
provide a father for her children. Fuck the nuclear family. It had
explosion written in its atoms. How adeptly her children accused her of
not looking out for them, with their stories at the dinner table of what
happened when their father was around and what happened when he
wasn't. They knew fear when he was present. They never dealt with the
dilemma of how to survive when he was gone. She wanted to scream at
them: what would you have done? I was like a tigress choosing to leave
her cubs to hunt for food, risking their safety while I was gone to get
them food, or they would die. What would you have done? I went to
work to make sure we did not have to rely on him when he was out of
our lives. What would you have done? Tell me, what would you have
done?

CHAPTER 17

Open your mouth. Don't bite down. Open wider.

I GOT OFF THE bus and crossed Woodward Avenue to get to the dentist, who as on the eight floor of the David Something Scott Building. In those days, all types of professionals were in downtown buildings. Now it seems only lawyers and accountants have remained in high-priced, multi-floored structures. The dentist's name was Dr. Rice, and it seemed that he was the prototype for all Dr. Rices. White, thin, and slightly balding and gray. I wondered if he had been put in hot water for torturing me so, if he would have swollen and expanded to something soft and mealy. I could have bitten him in half now.

I had fourteen cavities one year, before Crest and better dental care. He drilled on me without Novocain because he said "it wouldn't hurt that much" and "it would take too long to take effect." The smell of the burning enamel of my teeth mixed with sprays of water still signal outpourings of saliva. The piercing, high-pitched pain that came when he worked on a molar traced nerve distributions better than any dissections I did on the jaw of my cadaver in medical school. That pain is what I still expect when I am told to "open my mouth."

My mother had her three upper front teeth knocked out in an automobile accident, which was why she never drove ever again. Sometimes, she said it happened after we were born, and sometimes, she said it was before we were born. I liked to see the bridgework of the delicate scaffolds that held her porcelain teeth is their place. Her teeth were multicolored like opals without the gleam, and her lips were thin and tentative. She set them tightly against themselves to show her determination and came across the Atlantic. After that, her lips framed a different mouth, and her teeth were pulled out one after the other as the years' offerings. She was left with only three front bottom incisors, one medial and two laterals. Her false teeth shown white with homogeneity and lined up in ridged conformity, while the real teeth stood like icons of age even as the gums shunned them.

My father had the "good" teeth, and the myth was he never had a cavity in his life and therefore never needed any fillings. I saw though, when he laughed and when he died, the gold in the back of his mouth. For all his bite, he lived three years less than she did. Yet he was always able to bite. At the dinner table, we could all laughed as he said "hell" or "piss" and would clamp down on his sliced beef.

The last time I saw Dr. Rice was during a Christmas break from college; I was nineteen. I had to have all my wisdom teeth pulled because my mouth was too crowded. My front teeth were a little prominent, but I only started wearing braces when I was thirty-one. I had nitrous oxide for the extraction and rode some pixie dust ride in the sky while I dreamt. Then I got up and spit some oozing blood, had my mouth packed with cotton, and walked down to the bus stop by Hudson's and rode home.

I much prefer oral sex to the dentist. In oral sex, you open wide after some licking, if you like, and then you slide the saluting penis in; or if it is somewhat shy, you slurp in the reasonable potential. If the man has a respectable one, sometimes my jaw feels stretched in my effort not to hurt him with my teeth. You can withdraw and relax and try again. In the dentist's chair, he is in control. Of course, you can gag, and usually the technicians, hygienist, or dentist will at least ask if you're all right.

All the times I've had cavities, crowns, root canals, gum surgeries, molds made with progressively gagging cold plastics, I close my eyes and pray for oral sex instead. And the dentists are asking, "Are you all right?"

My children's teeth are lined in fine order, and their gums are pink and homey with the teeth's enamel. They never put up with drilling without Novocain and in their teens hated their braces.

Some people at work have dark teeth slimed with tartar and swollen gums, but they don't want to see the dentist.

I was a good German. I did not show my teeth and covered them with my hand when I could not easily cover them with my lips. I respected authority, I kept my place, I suffered for my own good, I wore

FRITZ WOLF

the uniform of gratitude that girls should wear and saluted the uniform of power. I did not know yet what would be brought out about the "good Germans" over in Europe. The good Germans, who went about their business and ignored hell in hopes of staying out of it and denied the vengeance that spewed ashes in the sunny days of denial. Then, gold was pulled out of teeth. Everybody disowned the defeated Nazis, but the really good Germans, what do you do with them and their children? Where did I fit in, both villain and victim, born of German parents?

Now there are little Christmas tree brushes for gums and patriotic toothpastes and orthodontists to apply hidden braces and tooth implants and endodontists and really good Germans.

Dentists quietly carve away our bites and give us longer-lasting teeth and hours in chairs meant for putting metal and porcelain in our mouths.

There is this theory now that those that get abused are really temperamentally predisposed to the abuse. They do not protect themselves and are in a sense victims waiting to happen. Could you have been a good girl and said no to Dr. Rice? Do you understand "repetition compulsion"?

CHAPTER 18

All the news that's fit to print.

—The New York Times

"ALL THE NEWS that's fit to print" is the motto of our great American newspaper. I am of the generation that loves the newspaper and doesn't want to hear the news and see the images over and over from four o'clock through five o'clock and on and on until seven o'clock. To spend Sunday morning in bed with the *LA Times* and the *New York Times* in Los Angeles makes for a transcontinental paradise.

I made a report once in eighth grade on Abraham Lincoln and the press. I liked going through the books about history and finding photos of clippings and descriptions of his run for congress and then the civil war opinions. The press hated Lincoln until he died. The press doesn't remember that now. Most people know about the zealot that killed him; in fact, most high school students probably do better at remembering John Wilkes Booth or Lee Harvey Oswald or James Earl Ray and their middle names than knowing the first or middle names of the people they killed. I remember John Lennon; at least I don't remember who killed Lennon.

I guess people were killed to gratify supposed beliefs, just like they are killed now for the right to do abortions. Take away the right of someone who you think is taking the right away from someone else. Hide until you can hit. Spring from the bushes and slash, shoot, smash.

During our lifetime, the hidden revealed had been commonplace. In the 1940s, what Hitler and Stalin were doing was hidden, denied, disbelieved; in the 1950s, you hid what you believed in so the press wouldn't get your name and McCarthy wouldn't ruin you while the government hid the atomic explosions and nefarious syphilis experiments; in the 1960s, Nixon tried to hide his five o'clock shadow and Kennedy his Addison's disease, love of golf, and his multiple affairs. The press helped him. Then it wasn't fit to print. In the 1970s, when Nixon couldn't hide a different shadow and Deep Throat talked, blatant denial still took place, and by the 1980s, you could do what you wanted if you didn't admit it. Closet doors were opened, and more than innocent gays came out. In the 1990s, you hide confusion and disequilibrium and fear because the only course you have is not common sense, hard work, or the rights of others, but machinations from lawyers that ask their clients to hide the truth and stall the proceedings until they are found not guilty. The finger is pointed at the inadequacies of the "good side" as a defense against culpability. You hide qualms and O. J. Simpson sits quietly and obediently by their sides until he is freed, only to pay with money for lives he took.

The newspapers have fewer columns and more pictures, and all the news that's fit to print is whatever is left over from TV. Millennium fever doesn't hide all the reflections of the past.

How ambivalent I feel about the exposure fifty years later of the Swiss and their bloodied gold extracted from the mouths of the suffering, and the French and their moral flexibility, and the Italians forgiven for incompetence, and the United States controlling who they took into the country while refugees floated in limbo and onto death refusing Ann Frank and her family. They all were collaborators with the Nazi poison and stood in self-righteous excrement, admiring the paintings they confiscated.

It was so easy to name the Germans, the Nazis, they stood up in their fearsome uniforms and their arrogant openness and it was easy to point a deserved judging finger at them. I am unsatisfied because I want those others exposed; their culpabilities heaved the Holocaust forward. An exposure means that we all share guilt and exploitation, and it cannot only be focused on the part of my soul that is German. Who claims ugliness? I want the sanctimonious Klan and the chilling

Catholic priests and the Red Guard and the gang bangers to all plead guilty with me.

Yet I also want the ugliness to persist in being hidden, and the neighborhood news of what is happening to John Travolta and how Elizabeth Taylor's brain is doing and whether Jennifer Lopez is really acting to continue since I know them better than the people across the street. I want the pictures of Tiger Woods walking and Kobe Bryant jumping even more than the next killings in Bosnia or the deaths in Zaire, now the Congo, or human rights incarcerations in China. I try to draw the limit with the stained blue dress and perjury and Bush making light of being dumb and I look at the Victory Garden program and the Simpsons cartoons. They are for the next century, to grow vegetables and learn how to behave.

CHAPTER 19

"A hidden cancer" can cause anemia and fatigue and depression. It can manifest itself only after it has metastasized.

HARRY HAD ALWAYS been an alert impish-looking child. He played with an intensity similar to his father who was a radiologist who chomped beef jerky and unlit cigars. Harry held pencils in his mouth and blew puffs of air like his father. His mother, who was a nurse and liked the story of Florence Nightingale, had named him Henry because of her British grandfather who visited from Vermont every year in January and brought maple syrup. The grandfather wanted to swim in the ocean even with the January temperatures, but Harry didn't like water. He said he felt sick if his grandfather asked him to go with him in the winter; and in the summer, Harry hid his dislike from his brothers by explaining that he had to construct some Hot Wheel road and could not go into the pool. Although his brothers were younger than he was, they swam "like fish," his parents tell his grandfather. By four, Harry insisted on showers rather than baths and gave rubber duckies away to his brothers while he played with soap on a rope.

One spring day, he was washing his hands under the fine shower spray, being careful not to get his head wet too soon, when he felt the lump around his ring finger. He held the soap between his hands and slid it back and forth while capturing it in his interlocking fingers.

He thought maybe he was turning into a fish because he had seen the webbed feet of lizards and the educational programs on evolution. He decided there was hope that he would someday be able to join his brothers in the pool and not be afraid of water. He sat down in the

biology and having to travel. I remember early on his gumption to live by the beach and have the waves near us all.

My younger daughter knows how to draw the blood of the Orca and care for the skin of the dolphins and help them to live and thrive as she doctors them and dives with them in their ocean. She heals injured paws of tigers so they can walk on the hot earth and teaches gibbons to come to her for insulin shots. She has the greatest perspective on who humans are.

My youngest son is a surfer and sprayed water all over the deck when he was a toddler playing. He is the calm and profound one and waters down fires that break out within the family when he is not a physician treating emergency room patients.

I am indebted to their wills and their being water babies. At the kissed edge of the land and the ocean, that is where we are. They are still diving into new areas and riding new waves. So lucky.

I remember going to camp and looking down into lake water from a dock, not seeing the hidden bottom and then jumping. I still remember almost drowning and the whirl of thoughts in the whirl of water, knowing not to suck in water and yet desperate for the air. If water gets into the lungs while I am asleep, I will be grateful. I do not want to gasp. It seems the worst of all deaths and yet I have had pneumonia twice and knew the weakness of air. Water will win. It will be soothing and I will rock to sleep and oblivion.

CHAPTER 20

Play hide-and-seek.

HE COMES IN the dream. His hair is like crashing waves around his rock face and I was floating like some rendering by Arthur Rackham with my hair flowing and twirling with my body. We are mixing, tides pulling and pushing, moons watching.

I have come across my children's readings, and when they were teenagers, sometimes seen *Playboys* and *Playgirls* strewn about in their rooms. I feel sad and old-fashioned. I could not look at those centerfolds, even though I have seen it all as a physician. There, where the women held their labia open and men aimed with their penises or both part their buttocks for the eyes, there was such a loss in the revelation.

It was really true that their names were Dickie and Peter. At the time, I did not understand what their names meant. Dickie was dark-haired with blanched skin and a pumpkin smile with a top and bottom front tooth missing, and Peter had the pale peppered skin of the freckled blond. We were there on the playground, that dusty and graveled plain where so much was pioneered after school.

We stood by the chain-link fence near home plate and dared them to show us their things. They did, and we laughed but did not reciprocate and ran away to our house.

They still played with us, and it reminds me of the young man who tried to show me how worthy he was by telling me what he knew, smelling nice with aftershave, and shivering near me. Still, I would not reveal me. His was not love but infatuation. I guess I was afraid of pure passion and no inner connection.

The mouth's tongue and the legs' tunnel, I don't know how to exhibit them. I wanted that blind kiss of the glans with the cervix, those dimpled lovers who kiss in the dark.

They hide their activities and she hides hers.

CHAPTER 21

I hate you.

THE GERMAN SHEPHERD had been trained by the police and was retired at five years. He was 150 pounds, and when he pushed up against you for attention, you had to brace yourself or be set off balance. His eyes were sorrowful and the same beer bottle brown color as that of deer and seals. He knew all his commands, and you had to be careful not to say one by mistake in some causal conversation.

The German shepherd is the wolf dog that Europeans fear. Of course, there were the Rottweilers and Dobermans as well. The other German dog is the Dachshund, brown sausage of devotion and eagerness.

In England in 1913, many of these little dogs were kicked because they were considered German like any human with a German last name. The British king himself had to renounce his relations with all his German and Russian cousins and change his name from something weird like Saxe-Coburg-Gotha to Windsor to avoid hate from his own subjects. The Kaiser had been the King's cousin and was wearing a pointed hat of imperialism although the sun never set on the British nation.

In Germany, my mother skipped up and down the gravel and picked up shrapnel for souvenirs along the railroad tracks in Stuttgart after bombings in 1918 and didn't know how much she was hated.

In Tennessee in 1921, the father of a man I know named Schumann said he tried to tell people he was American too, but they called him "Kraut" and told him he was lucky they didn't deport him as a spy.

My parents refused to speak German while they were in Madison, Wisconsin, and Chicago, Illinois, during the '20s and '30s. Even the German Jew was considered German first. My father couldn't delight at being a Visigoth descendant and admitted he was afraid for his job at the university. My mother made sure no one heard him say anything that suggested the Germans were angry at the Treaty of Versailles and were justified in fighting back. When their children were born in Detroit, they were Americans, although they stayed by themselves except for a few other German and foreign friends. They were discriminated against out of fear and respect and hate and, of course, patriotism.

Discrimination had no problems metastasizing in the United States even though the point was to come here to get away from prejudice. In Indiana, the Ku Klux Klan first got together and hanged "niggers" and "the wet backs" get renamed and still kicked out of California when times were too tough; there's got to be someone to hate for this time. Maybe now Clinton is the centralized Internet's focus and everyone can band together in a rainbow coalition of hate, the legacy of the twentieth century if Hitler gets to be *Time*'s man of the century, not Einstein.

Each of my children flirted with the phrase "I hate you." Once or twice, they each said it to me and waited to see what I would do. They hoped, of course, I might reconsider whatever it was they wanted, but I refused and wanted them to do what had been asked. They had those big round eyes of varying shades of brown that watched me for the reaction to that painful dart. Would I fall? Would I believe them? That was never their issue. They had hoped for a useful weapon in the parent-child negotiations, that's all.

They hated homework and certain teachers, kids who ate boogers, the Dallas Cowboys, crap in the sack, driving to the orthodontist, having to get up early, onions, their father's temper, but I knew they didn't hate me. I knew that. It was one of the only things I was really sure of.

CHAPTER 22

And I took the road less traveled . . .

—Robert Frost

OVER THE BLIND thrust faults and the San Andreas Fault and little tremors of 3 or so on the Richter scale stretches the 10 Freeway.

There was the Mayflower and the Bremerton Hamburg-American lines crossing the Atlantic, and the covered wagons and the railroads of the Union Pacific, Santa Fe, and Amtrak, and there was Route 66. From the great migrations in the 1600s of both the red man and the white man to the crossing of the Mississippi for good, to the 1800s when the millions of humans, many who prayed in German, came again from Europe and the freed slaves moved north and Chinamen sailed east and through to the early 1900s when more Europeans migrated than ever before to the 1920s and 1930s when the so-called paranoid European Jews came following their accurate intuition, to the 1930s when the Dust Bowl Okies were blown west to California while the Japanese were moved away and the Hispanics were retaking North America, there came another move and it was mine.

In our Ford, we drove by the Midwest forest, lakes, blast furnaces, and smoking chimneys through the golden wheat and farmhouse and barn dotted plains to the West Coast in the '60s. Then after the post-World War II era, during the Vietnam schism the Americans of the Northeast liked to say the United States was lifted up on the eastern seaboard and all the scum slid and settled in Los Angeles, and I came too.

My freeway is the 10 from the Coachella Valley and San Bernardino, inland, where Azusa came into being as "from A to Z in the USA," to Santa Monica and its palisades of palms and views, where in the year 1923 the city council refused to pay the back taxes of $23 for the beach to the state. I drive about 25 miles every day to work and 25 miles back. I used to think that was a major trip when I went away to college 30 miles away in Ann Arbor, now it is nothing in the 1990s.

There are other freeways going to big places in California from the first freeway built, the Pasadena, which only has these short little on-roads you can't even call ramps to the Golden State, the Hollywood, the San Diego, the Long Beach, the Ventura to the newer Foothill and Century freeways, but the Santa Monica, USA 10, is mine. It transverses the whole Los Angeles basin from ocean to mountains.

In February, the rains and cool days allow the air to pass over the mountains so no smog collects and the view is extraordinary for its clarity. Grated office building fronts and river like road lines in the mountains are so clear you can map them from your car window.

These years of the 1990s while I have been tired and searching, the Los Angeles basin had been burning. With the riots over the trials of the man who drove through the city and wouldn't stop until the police force stopped him with furor and the policemen who were culpable, there were the plumes of fire and black smoke to the right and left of the freeway. I drove cautiously but as fast as I could. The plumes were like the Indian signals in movies sending messages of all kinds. Back and forth, I went as the days past and the media displayed the charred evidence and the smoke blew away to history and disdain from the Midwest.

Burning your own neighborhood like Detroit and LA did in the '60s extended to burning any neighborhood, and instead of enclaves of security, there were enclaves of fear. In the '90s the ashes were found every morning settled on cars driven to secluded neighborhoods as well on the burning places.

Still driving, I saw the fires from the mountains in the autumn drought. Turner would have been stirred to paint again at the colors that fulminated out of the dark. In the mornings that followed, I drove across the basin with a car covered in gray ash that had floated about the air for hundreds of miles and landed on trees, pools, and cars. This was the Southern California snow. In the 1940s, there were the ashes from Poland that landed too but were mainly ignored.

This fire advanced for days, and it curled over each of the Santa Monica Mountains toward our house and then it came over the last edge. The color outlines the tops of our mountain. The heat hits the face suddenly and you know that hell had come in its horrific beauty and power.

Yet back and forth I still go, across the rich alluvial plain of this basin ringed by the mountains. The sky is smudged from flames as the freeway leads me here and there and here again. I have all my precious things like photographs and children's drawings in suitcases ready to leave again with the next biblical happening.

In 1994, the earth shook on Martin Luther King Day. The San Fernando Valley and Santa Monica fell. You sit up in bed immediately. You know what it is. This time it goes on forever, and you move away from books and shelves. The ground rolls like hard waves, your house sways, and there is nowhere to go, only to wait. If you use the telephone and called immediately, almost while it was going on, you can reach loved ones but in seconds no electricity and no phone service. Then people go out to the streets, crying and clutching and laughing and mobilizing. The supermarket gives free water and batteries and people, being greedy, take food in the dark that seals the store from the sun and survival.

You have to go in and assess the hospital to help patient loads. You drive again on the broken freeway, jag off onto the plain avenues and old streets with houses and stores and secret detours, and then on again to the rest of the intact freeway, across the basin.

CHAPTER 23

Legacy is the mind's filigree.

H ER MORNING RITUAL consisted of repeating what her parents had valued. She took the precision clippers and nipped off the hangnail. Then she put the clippers back in the drawer with their cupped cutting edges, like praying hands, and picked the scissors, which were light and had two finely hewn blades that overlapped each other perfectly. The handle's holes were oval and accepted the thumb and forefinger with graciousness, not constraint, making it easy to enter and leave. Cutting was definitive. She seldom cut her cuticles but remembered her mother performing a ritual with the instruments and filing her nails thereafter into closely aligned covers of her tapered smooth fingertips. They had to be short for the piano and the typewriter, her mother explained. Her mother could sit at the piano and improvise soft cords and you could hear within the music the soft clicking of those perfectly curved nails.

She liked the hemostats and their curved necks, which brought their noses into tissues and allowed the clamp of their two prongs to hold on for dear life. They let go only when you popped the sliding wedges on the handle loose.

"I'm German, so of course I like precision," she heard someone say. Was that stereotyping from movies or a true legacy that makes one trust Lufthansa and BMW? We Americans made it to the moon in wings of stretched aluminum and created the bombs of all bombs with that precision, and yet we stuff old boards in our metro tunnel casings when no one is looking.

She put the scissors back in the drawer, pushing the clippers, emery boards, bobby pins, and clips around to make room for them. She never could be neat enough.

Then she took the camera to take a photo of the cat sleeping with her belly up, which she could send to her child in college. She pressed the square button, which caused the whizzing sound. Her father had known all about cameras and lenses. Ikoflex and Zeiss, and then Canon and Nikon, focal points and light meters had pleased him as challenges to get the results right. In the magic "dark room" in their basement, he would conjure and she would watch with respect. He told her to push the paper with large tongs gently back and forth in the white enamel pans and soon the image would emerge like some rising ghost sunk below a visible surface as his magic summoned it to appear.

It was Sunday so there was no need to dress for work. Dressing was important to make a good impression. Everyone had a uniform of sorts, maintenance men and surgeons, lawyers and Hells Angels, rappers, and new nuns. Her parents had often talked of uniforms. The movies had immortalized spiked helmets and long black boots, those leather gloves, held in one hand and used to slap someone across the face, signaling authority and impatience. There was the imperial eagle stamped everywhere, forever sibling to our own bald eagle, one black and regal, the other white and clear eyed over all domains. Impeccably groomed uniforms still marched in bands. They were the remains of the Garde-Grenadier her mother first remembered seeing when she was seven. There were the headdress tassels, chinstraps, stiff collars, and golden buttons down to belts with buckles that clasped all authority together. The stiff stance and guns held to the side, red, blue, white accented and the resultant pride.

She secretly liked the young Brando in his leather jacket or Cary Grant in a beautiful tuxedo, and she kept her ex-husband's Navy uniform with its gold stripes and a gold emblem on the brim of his hat like a golden beacon of authority, or tuff of Buddha's wisdom to put on and take off. Her sons didn't like anything that had an emblem on it, except for Levi's. Polo shirts were not for them. They gave away the medals they had collected, and the gas masks were stuffed in boxes at the back of closets. She herself never bothered with uniforms of the Brownies or the white coats she was to wear as a doctor. She was, however, always trying to wear the right things to each occasion and

CHAPTER 24

I need room to remember.

THIS MORNING, I thought of the little dots of candy on strips of paper we bought from a candy store and how we ate them, pressing the paper to our lips and closing our teeth around the tiny mound. Those candies belong with the era of banks that had marble pillars and mounting wide steps, and Saturday afternoon movies walked to by stepping over sidewalks avoiding cracks that could "break your back" and skates that widened to clamp on to your regular shoes.

My memory finds are similar to what it must have been like coming across that ancient beef jerky–looking iceman in the mountain snow, which was on an episode of the *Nova*.

I am surprised at what appeared when time melted away. Today, I also came across a journal my father kept when he was first here in the United States and unsure of what direction to take in his career. He wrote about money worries and not having enough intellect to accomplish something meaningful. In a time warp every day, I think the same things.

He also clipped articles out of newspapers listing admirable goals and underlined inspirational lines. It was something my mother did too. I have folders of articles on everything from mountains to meals taken from old newspapers and *Parade* magazine. It seems somewhat mundane to me in my semi-sophisticated world, but then people read *The Bridges of Madison County* and I am unrealistic in my expectations for myself and others.

In his journal, my father writes about being a cultural orphan, not willing to continue being German as hate began to ferment here. He even wrote in English after only one year here, and yet he felt unable to assimilate inconspicuously, he said in 1929, the worst economic time ever with the plunge of the stock market.

It was the same somehow moving from the Midwest to Los Angeles. I still don't know how to work hard enough in a land where appearance was everything. I cannot wear shorts shopping as my father could not go hatless all his life. We remain strange.

To quote them now that they were dead is eerie, a violation and yet a comfort. I touched base with their being there for me, a first-generation American. I had a tape of each of their voices and some photographs, but it was their writing to themselves that covered my heart in comfort. I knew those torments and those minds.

To distract myself, I go out to dinner with one of my few friends since I have become manless and unwilling to attach. After drinking a little wine and while zooming home in my convertible, following white lines and red taillights, I pass through downtown Los Angeles and it is night. It is night, and the funny-shaped buildings are like stalactites dripping from the dark sky and their crystallized windows were outlined in light. I love the feel, looking up to cool light and dark shapes. I am in a different universe than Helene and Willi. To transform myself back and forth, strange woman in the West, girl of the Midwest, child of the heart of Europe—those feats are beyond light years.

I go into my house with all its empty rooms. It is quiet and yet echoes of busy, pressured, living days were in the chips on the wall corners and the chairs circling the table and the child creations of clay statues and framed drawings. The stairs lead to my bedroom, and like a Steppenwolf, I go up.

My dreams are of houses and rooms that I could never have lived in. In those dreams, I am forever trying to fit everything in: man, children, furniture, friends. There may be some problem. I can't get a cupboard door to open, or I am surprised by the extent of a room and how it led to other rooms. There were passageways that lead to whole new complexes of rooms and apartments within houses. I don't know how to arrange the rooms and the furniture so it feels right, so it is like a home.

There were different dream houses. Some were full of mahogany cabinets and shelves and brass knobs and handles rising above warm burgundy rugs and inner doors to closets with transient musty smells to trigger reminiscences. There were finished basements and bricked spaces. They enclosed ghosts. Some of the dream houses were beautiful, made of glass and stone. They were endless and open. I could see out over huge city territory and others could see in. The house overlooked busy streets or cliffs. Although there might be flowers in the yard, and I feel I have mastered the layout, then I have to watch for cars or rocks and most of all for intruders.

Someone dark and real was coming to the door. Do I lie still and hide? Do I try to run out the back door? Do I take knife or gun? I never get the answer. I sit up in bed. Startled. Ready to hit him off. He is not there, and there was no one beside me to help me. I thought of my husband of old. I calmed down, alone, and returned to sleep.

CHAPTER 25

Consultation-Liaison Psychiatry is the specialty of interviewing medical and surgical patients, reviewing their charts, and then presenting the medical problem in the context of each patient's whole life and recommending/ advising treatment of the patient to the primary physicians.

A PSYCHIATRIC CONSULTATION BEGINS with a request from the primary physician. In the private sector, many times, the consult request comes late in the hospitalization of the patient, late in the week and late in the day. Multiple procedures have already been done for whatever the problem is—gastrointestinal, neurological, and cardiovascular being the most common. The consultation is called when the problem's answer is not readily apparent or the patient isn't getting better after medical interventions. Many departments employ their own psychologists to do hours of testing and give gentle equivocal conclusions about what is going on beyond the Minnesota Multiphasic Personality Inventory or MMPI, which really doesn't explain the crisis.

Physicians from other specialties are prone to think they can do most anything a psychiatrist can do during these managed care days. They believe that it is only prescribing medications that differentiate psychiatrists from the non-medically oriented psychologist, and the primary physician can do that easily. The PhD degree had been stretched beyond its respectful meaning in such areas as biochemistry, neurobiology, molecular science, physics, and even clinical psychology. Now clinical psychologists were turned out in awful numbers with no university affiliations and no real training. Even though psychiatrists are medical doctors, many believe they indulge in a "soft science," and the other types of medical doctors wonder why psychiatrists pursue such a career, not knowing the difference in knowledge and experience demanded for a meaningful consultation.

In our Weltanschauung as consulting psychiatrists, we hear thoughts of a patient's self while tubes go in and out of orifices and fluids flow, while procedures using minute cameras examine cells and stir sterile surgical magic, while medication gets swallowed and pushed into bodies to relate to specific receptors and science itself becomes the great monstrance of today. It is the current TV program *ER* that fascinates people even though the 80 percent of them apparently believe in God. Who does cure? God and/or science? Although there is great emphasis on people keeping themselves healthy with diet and exercise, the Weltschmerz we discover demands an understanding in the hospital and medical clinic of the patient's mind set and past experiences to make sense of why a patient's hospital medical course may proceed or derail from the way it should go.

There is hate glimpsed in an anorexic patient who went down to Mexico to get diuretics and secretly swallow them to defy her doctor father, celebrating her course in and out of the hospital for low potassium, thin as a skeleton covered in vellum skin. There is the convulsing, terrified patient who preferred blanking out to remembering his father's beatings and sexual assaults as a child; the manic-depressive patient who could not settle for even moods and even took decongestants to get high; the patient who had multiple surgeries because of migrating pelvic pain rather than face her husband's impotence; the patient who stuck stones in his penis to get into the hospital, the nurse who took her own femoral blood taps and swallowed the blood to appear as though she had a GI bleed to gain attention; the destitute young male prostitute who had a dildo stuck in his trachea; and the patient who rang for the nurse and when she didn't come, hanged himself on the vent above the toilet.

Consultations appear different if you are in a private hospital rather than the public hospitals, but the patients are mainly the same, except for the openly mainlining drug-abusing ones at the county hospitals. There are the usual deliriums caused by infection, toxic doses of drugs, electrolyte imbalance, medication side effects, stroke, brain abscesses, drug or alcohol withdrawal, whatever can affect the brain. I never used the acronym I WATCH DEATH, which stood for "Infection,

Withdrawal, Acute metabolic disorders, Trauma, CNS pathology, Hypoxia, Deficiencies, Endocrinopathies, Acute vascular shock, Toxins, Heavy metals," which was taught as the headings of causes. I think about the patient to find the cause.

There are the psychoses caused by the hospitalization due to suicide attempts like bridge jumping to get rid of hallucinations, or those precipitated in the intensive care unit after a month of constant lights, procedures with no reprieve and no love. There are the mood disorders of anxiety, mania, depression frequently glamorized but living hell, and associated very often with physical illness, early signs of lung or pancreatic cancer, or side effects of ace inhibitors. There are the tormented adjustments and subsequent infantilism of independent minds to some unfair illnesses: multiple sclerosis, myocardial infarct, CVA with a residual paralysis, necrotizing fasciitis, cancer chemotherapy, or the cutting out of cancers of hand, arm, and shoulder, throats and necks, breasts, bladder, rectum. There are the everyday anguishes over the results of the HIV antibodies tests or the early onset of dementias and the diagnosis dumped in the family's laps.

Freud was a medical doctor who specialized initially as a neurologist. Apart from the fact that he was discriminated against because he was Jewish and German and smart, I think he was a great writer of patients' stories. In typical cases, neurology is headaches and backaches that are transient worries and headaches and backaches that alter life forever suddenly or insidiously. What pills that are available are given to both types of patients. Psychiatry wanders in all the areas between black and white; all the colors are there, I tell my patients. When Freud and Breuer looked at hysterical patients, ones we now call somatoform disorders like conversion, they saw what later was called the unconscious, working its wonders, and they were hooked. So am I, hooked to discovering patterns and unrealized connections and ripples of childhood conclusion carried into the adult's conduct.

Psychiatrists kill themselves at a higher rate than most other doctors, except maybe pediatricians, head and neck surgeons, and anesthesiologists. Most theories based on research as to why psychiatrists do this are they suffer the hazards of a depressing profession or they are inherently mentally ill and so attracted to it all. Who knows? It depends on the studies cited. It is hard though to be alone and to love the mind only as the science of the brain. If you are supposed to be a medicine man, an empirical observer and pills giver, appreciator of neurons and dendrites and the synapses, you keep secret the poetry of the mind, its rhyme and reason. As Blaise Pascal wrote, "The heart has reasons the mind knows nothing of."

Still I know things. I know all patients have signs and smiles and tears even when hidden; that there are ways to give solace and solution. I know the hidden hate formed long ago and gnawing at security, the mind left amputated of a good self, struggling to find redemption through exploitation; there's the wish to ignore and mock any relevance to my work and yet the techniques expose so often the insult that was thought to be sealed away in past days. I know the resonance of past pains with today's hurts and the freedom that follows release from supposed destiny and finally with absolutism. I know the need of humans to feel superior to animals and children and yet crawl with them and seek nurture from them.

The trip through space and time of each human being secretly elates me in this day of hopelessness and destruction; it is like the stars compared to their physics.

CHAPTER 26

Pop Theory and Loose Associations evolving

S HE WAS MAD at the TV lectures: It is up to the parents to act like parents and let the children be children. The mature relationship wherein each gender accepts its limitations and seeks the other for completion and sharing. The child has to move beyond the dyad of mother and child to resolve the Oedipal complex and accept each parent, share each parent, and go on to form his or her own alliance with his or her mate. A boy needed to give up the fear of castration and a girl needed to give up the loss of the penis. The good Jewish boy paradigm.

Sometimes there was the acceptance of giving birth and the breast as having importance.

There was the intimate intrusion of the man wanting the triad and his place in the family and yet never really accepting the equality of the parents, resenting it seems the original dyad of which he played the child, and asserting the adult as the inseminator and finally guardian. Why, if Freud was right, doesn't society give women the same authority as men? If the parents, each offering their own gender qualities, are really to be equal components of the family team, why are mothers so denigrated so many times and feel their power only when they have a child sucking at their breasts?

Countless times, men have waved their penises in the streets in between cars or even walking behind her; men have brushed up against her and tried to touch her in the crotch; men have pressed her breasts with nonchalant forearms while she sat in the dentist chair; men have looked her up and down like appraisers and men have fucked and fallen asleep after sex, leaving her alone.

Why is the old mother woman a mockery, her wisdom disdained? Is there a day for Susan B. Anthony or Eleanor Roosevelt? For the little old lady from Pasadena to rise up and be heard? Grandmothers, all old ladies unite! The old man forgiven or admired, looks to inseminating his younger lover or being courted by his peer cooking and cleaning for him.

This is old hat and said better in all the feminist literature her friend, a financial counselor, retorted, and besides it's up to women to assert themselves. Do they have to be alone then? Is that the only way, or take some docile boy-man to have in bed and keep warm? "You are rambling," her friend said. "What are you reading in the magazines? And besides, what are you lamenting? You have a career that can be defined in a few words and have kids. What are you complaining about? Your husband is with you, when he's not gone?"

It is said the ultimate human father is what the Nazis were about in a perverse way, using tyranny for authority. You could be their girl friend or they can come and get you for not conforming, for being Jewish, or for caring about the rights of others or painting pictures differently. They will knock at the door or grab you in the street and you are at their mercy. Fear of being found out. Being made to disappear. The ultimate S&M fantasies. Whatever you need to digest your helplessness and sins. To eat or be eaten, that is the formula of life.

To nurse your baby at your breast comes before you allow yourself to eat. She knew the ultimate surprise and pleasure when her babies started sucking with such enormous force while their helpless bodies were held close.

Mary is the Virgin Mary, and yet she is considered one of the ultimate mothers. In the "Pieta" by Michelangelo, she is calm and white and cold marble as the grown Christ is splayed in her lap after having given birth to him, nursed him, and stood there at the cross. She was helpless in the affairs of her life, God, the story goes, decided she would be pregnant and that she would have no sexual claims with Joseph and she would have no say on the death of her child. Yet she felt him.

"You must be a Kleinian instead of a Freudian," her friend observed. "Believing in the breast and all the good and bad and paranoid positions."

"What's that?"

"It's theory about the dyad, but it applies today. So many lost, incomplete little egos and trust steps of Erik Erikson disturbed."

"How do you make the jump to adulthood after being left beaten and penetrated in orifices, small and delicate, only capable of being open to hope?"

"First one must feel lovable, then be able to love, and finally be able to share love. Shakespeare's Sonnet 10, 'Make thee another self for love of me, That beauty still may live in thine and thee,' is lovely to read, but impossible to obey."

She was confused, her friend told her. "People recover from these assaults and go on, reveal the scars, and in revelation find release and go on."

"But what do they do? Are they afraid of their hatred and helplessness?"

"They need to express anger."

"Anger again. Is there no other answer? What if they have no sense of self to fight for? Do they choose not to have children or stay away from them by hiding in their jobs? How do they recover?"

"Lighten up and try to look at the Internet chat rooms and watch *Seinfeld*. They have fun even if they're losers. Look at John Bradshaw and Martha Stewart. They do all right."

"You mean divorced or single and telling us how to be happy."

"Talk about it and make a pretty table."

"Good parents for all of us, right?"

"You're confused," her friend said again.

"Help me understand then. Help me."

"You'll grow out of it and learn more soon."

"Help me, please. Now."

CHAPTER 27

Stat

THE LOS ANGELES County Medical Center, called the General Hospital in reality as well as in the TV soap opera, is a 1930s marble building. It is tiered gracefully as it rises nineteen stories high, and its layout is like a great cathedral's floor plan: the baptistery and choir are the intensive care units, surgeries, and administration; the transepts are for the four-patient wards on all the floors above the first three; and the naves are for procedures. I never saw the parallel until now, during my mature years of irreligious reflection but visits to cathedrals. I admit I love it dearly.

In 1971 and in 1994, the hospital withstood the large threatening earthquakes to its well being, and even though the stairwells' plaster cracks are gouged out farther for justification and demonstration of the need for a new hospital and minimal hope for repair, it stands now in 1999 supreme, usable, and active among the 1950s smaller hospitals that are abandoned as unsafe. They were all connected to it with tunnels like umbilical cords to the "mother."

Approaching the hospital's front were the iron gates perpetually open and then the plaza with blooming trees and milling people. Going up to the building at the end of the tiers of broad stairs, molded stone Angeles topped the entrances and then through the arches, in the foyer she saw the engraving, wrote it down once, something about providing, regardless of finances, good health care for the poor, and all. 1932. It was very touching. The multiple-domed ceilings of the foyer had dazzling gold and blue homage paintings of famous physicians: Galen,

Vesalius, Pasteur, Hunter, Harvey, and Hippocrates and led to the art deco lobby with backlightening of Aztec like tiles.

At the time it was built, the hospital was some sort of political disaster for the sponsoring mayor. Too costly, too big, too far out of town. There was the outpatient building, the Psych hospital, the Ob-Gyn hospital, the Peds hospital, the intern-residents quarters and the medical school complex. Impressive, clean little colonies of the mother, Unit I, with over two thousand beds.

The actual lobby has art deco tiles and ceiling, with an ugly glassed-in information booth added at the back along with "blue coats," as we call the attendants with no protection of their own except an occasional walky-talky, checking for guns.

You can still get in past the lobby with its marble-squared columns if you have your badge or a sticker labeled "Visitor." The hallways are at least twenty feet wide, and the main hall is like a busy city street. There are the casually clothed patients with family searching for the ER or the 1050 ambulatory emergency area, the maintenance crews on breaks talking basketball, the nurses and clerks holding lunches wrapped in clear plastics from the cafeteria and waiting for elevators, and doctors talking and coming and going from the DDR, the doctor's dining room, attendants pushing gurneys with and without patients on them, volunteers in jackets of candy-stripe patterns giggling, and even admitted patients in knee length gowns pushing their IV poles like shepherds' staffs through the flocks of other people to get back to their wards or go out to smoke.

There are the psychiatric patients who wander around and sing songs, lecture about undecipherable ideas, dress in flamboyant colors, put costume jewelry all over their bodies, or use audio tape for ponytails. They get herded away sooner now and wind up on involuntary holds.

On the first floor, right next to the huge post office, where there are hundreds of mailboxes, are the emergency rooms that see thousands and thousands of patients a month in the walk-in, trauma, and ambulance areas. Down the hall are the bank of elevators, the pharmacy, and cafeterias. Stabbings have occurred in all these places. I knew the doctor who got shot right in the emergency room one afternoon by the man who brought the duffel bag of guns to protest. It is usually quieter by the security offices and the financial areas as well as the huge auditorium and conference room.

The second floor has the library, the morgue, and the labs. The third floor is all radiology and special procedures. The fourth, more special procedures rooms for cardiology, neurology, urology, and other surgical specialties. The fifth is for neurology and neurosurgery. Sixth through eighth floors are dedicated to internal medicine with the AIDS ward, and ninth and on up for surgical operating suites, burns, rheumatology, pulmonology, gastroenterology. The thirteenth floor is completely used for the medical jail and has long slit-like windows, which the twin tower county jail have duplicated. Eighteen floors up is for research and you can walk around the outside on the roof and see the sky.

In its best days, the hospital had a unit or clinic for everything from burn to lupus to leprosy to diabetes to pellagra and trichinosis. There is a medical intensive care unit, MIC-U, and a pediatric intensive care unit, PIC-U, too.

If you couldn't go anywhere else, you could go to the county hospital; its doors were always open to anyone. That was its claim to fame. The other hospitals punted undesirable patients and took only patients who were able to pay or were worth it for some other reason.

The staff felt they belonged with the outcasts, helping the downtrodden, teaching new generations of doctors. How guileless, unsophisticated, and sincere that sounds now when patients are counted by their cost per heads and money is more important than life.

When she first started working there, it was as a moonlighter, and there was no TV *ER,* just the old medical doctors, *Welby and Kildare.* It was the limbo time when everyone fucked around without causes and the "me" generation was alive and sick.

Between one wave rumbling on the beach and the next rearing, ready to fall, sometimes there is a lull, a suspended silence, and the past bobs up. In redolent moods like this evening, she filled it with W. T. Leon's emergency room.

It began during the time The Beatles broke up, but Elvis was still alive. There were two hundred million people in the Unites States, Nixon had gone to China, Roe vs. Wade proposed to make it safe for women to choose, and the microprocessors were announced. There were of course the assassinations, oil embargoes, the covert bombings, the flying out of Viet Nam and the tarnishing of the Presidency of the United States.

Here in LA, the hospital, the "Mother" to all that worked in her, stood proudly. She was big and cream colored and would be there forever. In February, the cauldron of putrid yellow gases was gone and there was a clear and distinct view of her.

The sun seldom ceased and Californians could afford to be blasé about that, but a view was special. Marcie was a view worshipper. She could see the streaks and paths of the mountain skins and the sharp grates of the glass office buildings, the pastel painted houses and wired streets, and straight ahead, the huge tiered building, erect, like a nipple in the slopes of the browning hills. The General Hospital to the patients and the "Mother" to the staff.

Down a long, wide hall in the guts of the mother was W. T. Leon's Emergency Room. "The pits, the armpit of the world, the place God would give an enema to the earth." At that time there was no specialty of Emergency Medicine and there was no designated Emergency Department at the Los Angeles County General Hospital – University of Southern California Medical Center, merely the emergency room.

The only place Marcie ever saw Mr. Leon was in the pits and she wanted to remember him. It was important to remember him for some reason. She was not sure why. When she came near him, he was thick in a breath of rotten teeth, alcohol, and tobacco, all rancid. His loud voice started vying for attention, trying to embarrass her, the doctor, into placating him. His face was not Ray Milland but a forty-three-year-old's, viscous stained, tall, black frame with ropes of muscle still showing in well and eddies under scared skin. His thin mustache sat like a gash under soaked eyes. Judging from the size of his medical chart, W. T. did all his business at the General. He was born there around the time it first opened.

Things are constantly changed, remodeled, rebuilt, moved. Brown curtains replaced by vinyl doors and then blue curtains. The pre 1930s nurses building torn down for parking, the tan doorways painted pumpkin and lime, and diabetes moved up a floor.

Anyway, W. T. Leon's emergency was in the main unit, first floor. He came day or night to talk with the staff, his doctors.

There were three sections at the ER, really already an emergency department, which is what the profession liked to call it now. Usually W. T. came to the walk-in area. The criteria for being seen there are just anyone over the age of fourteen who can walk. That's all. No one is refused. Of course, chronic wheel chair patients are seen there and a thalidomide teen transporting himself on a skateboard.

Sometimes walk-in lucked out and Mr. Leon went to the ambulance area. The stretcher cases and overt stuff are handled there and possible admission to the wards. The third place to which he might get channeled was minor trauma. He might have a fight or need his cast checked, sutures put in and removed, something of the sort. Knowing Mr. Leon, he might visit a couple places all in the same night and get away with it because of his multiple problems.

Approximately ten thousand patients were seen in the walk-in area every month. It was Mr. Leon's favorite place. He'd tell you that many times. It was the nebulous area. Doctors were constantly trying to define its purpose. Emergencies? General Medicine? What kind of patient should be seen here? It was the password into the specialty clinics and the source of the little blue appointment card. Someone could come there first to find a doctor who'd listen, or go to all the clinics and come back again to find a doctor who'd listen. The beauty and the curse is, there are no appointments for the rooms of emergency.

After curving around the twenty-foot-wide halls, walking on beige tiles divided in the center by colored stripes leading to the ER area, the pharmacy, all over the building and out, W. T. would make it to the waiting room. There was talk that a colored TV was going to be installed there, above the sign in desk.

W. T. would wait his turn, first filling out and turning in the simple form the computers handle now. Name, address, date and place of birth, mother's name, marital status, employer. The signature went on the consent sheet. No financial information now. Than he'd sit for three or four hours in the afternoon as it turned to night, waiting to see a doctor.

And he waited. Behind the doors, A and B, where people entered to be taken care of, existed a milieu of shiny counters and milling people, doctors leaning on brown Formica tops, writing on charts, nurses straightening papers and giving shots, patient and attendants coming in and out of doors with medicines and charts, people lost or looking for friends, sporadic coughing, gagging, yelling.

The room was enormous. Lines of booths were separated by long tables or counters wedged between square pillars. It was busy tonight. There were still seventy-five charts from the afternoon shift. Two wire baskets hold the papers with their card board supports and paper clips. Probably four hundred patients seen so far.

The booths for examining the patients were like narrow dressing rooms. They had vinyl sliding door entrances, equipment tables on the narrow walls of the rectangle, and the examining tables opposite two kitchen-like chairs on the long walls.

Temperatures and sometimes blood pressure and pulse were taken by an attendant in booth 1 and 19, on opposite sides of the room. The procedure then was the patients were brought to the booths by the attendants and asked to sit down on the chairs. Attempts were made to get the attendants to ask patients to undress and put gowns on but it never lasted very long and usually the patients sat and waited for the doctor to tell them anything.

Marcie was moonlighting until her husband finished his law school and then it would be her turn. He'd come home in the afternoon and she would start her freeway drive. Until he was done this year, she worked four to midnight shifts to help pay for the house they rented away from the smog.

Marcie or any doctor, who finished writing up a previous chart, picked up the papers from the little wooden slot in front of the booths. She usually looked at the name at the bottom of the form and stepped into the booth, leaned against the black-topped examining table and looked down into the patient's face. After a history of the chief complaints and anything related, the patient slipped on the disposable gown and sat on the table to wait for her to come in again.

She'd check the brown paper bags where the pills and liquid were carried. The pharmacy puts all the prescriptions in these bags and the patients bring them back and forth from home to the clinic. The thick paper is made soft at the neck and wrinkled and occasionally torn. It is wrung from pain over and over. It holds clear or brownish plastic vials with white tops and colored capsules or tablets, big liter bottles of red potassium chloride, light aqua plastic Mylanta bottles. Standard equipment.

Over and over again she'd half sit and half lean against the table and then hear the voices, see the people. Listen.

Hi Mr. Bobo, what's the problem?

I hurts.

Where do you hurt?

All over.

Well, where does it begin, where does it hurt the most?

Huh?

Where does it hurt most?

Oh, the head, the head hurts the most.

How long has it been hurting?

A long time.

What's a long time? A week, a month, a year?

Yeah, quite a while.

Could you tell me when it started?

I dunno, I guess about the time that my auntie passed away and I got the flu.

When?

About Christmastime, I'm a thinking.

How did it start? Has it been hurting all the time since last December?

What?

The pain.

Oh yeah. It begin real slow. Right here. That pain, it come and go and then it won't go.   The doctor back home, he telling me I have high blood.

Anything else wrong? Ever had heart pains? Trouble with your stomach or bowels; pain when you pass your water?

Well, I tells you, you understand, sometimes, sometimes I . . .

Blood Pressure 230/133, admit before he strokes.

Are you Mrs. Washington? Fifty-five and old charts.

Yes, Doctor. Hello, Doctor, I needs my medicines.

All right, did you bring your medicine bottles? I'll take care of it.

Oh, I forgot.

Do you know what medicines you're taking, then I won't have to get the old chart and make you wait.

Yes, three or four kinds. Some white ones, real little and . . .

Well, I need their names. Do you know what they're for?

No, never did.

What's been the problem with you? Do you know why you need the pills?

My doctor, he did never tell me.

Well, how do you feel? What did you use the medicines for?

I feels okay. But no one done told me what them medicines are for.

It's always best if you asked what the medicines are for, okay? Now why did you go to the doctor the first time?

I just got tired all day. I gots to be able to work. You understand, kids and grand kids and all.

Are you anemic? How are your periods?

My regular? It don't come down no more.

For how long? You're thirty-six years old, right?

Well, it been about eight month now. I had surgery that time, bleeding and all. They done said they hitched my rectum. Low blood and all.

Did they take your womb out, your female organs, a hysterectomy?

I dunno for sure, but ever since then it never did come down no more. I got seven at home. The grand babies is three years and the other is six months. I did some day work and told me that I wouldn't get tired no more and to swallow these pills for my nerves and blood.

Let's check you over. Any pain? Shortness of breath? Are you eating well?

But doctor, I needs my pills, you'll give them to me, right? I still tired and I been vomiking blood.

Throwing up blood?

Uh huh, every night after dinner.

Well, Mrs. Washington, we've got to find out what's causing the bleeding. Let me check you over while we talk. Any black stools? You may have to be in the hospital.

My furniture is all brown. I just wants my medicines, okay?

Heme positive. Hemoglobin 6.1. Admit.

The shift is eight hours and the voices continue.

It's the ear, doctor, it's been paining. It bothers me terrible and than I gets this gum ball behind it. That there tooth is bad and my neck it swelled up.

My problem? Everything's my problem, Doctor. I have this constant pain and lots of gas all the time. And doctor, see this area of my skin, it itches all the time and before I go to sleep a headache always comes right here and oh before I forget, I have bad nerves. My daughter she ran away and well . . .

I got the crabs.

There's a lump in my, you know, titty.

I dunno I just feels badly all over.

It's my stomach, Doctor, I ain't had a poop in ten days.

I strained myself and something is coming out of my privates.

I've had a tension headache for a month and it's killing me.

Dwelle mucho, pain, Doctora. Habla Espanol, yes, Doctora?

When you mash here it hurts.

My doctor he's been doctoring for a couple months but I ain't no better so I came to the county to find out what's wrong, man.

There're these white things on my legs, they come out of my skin. They gave me poison at the board and care place. I brought some these white pieces in this paper, can you see them? They're going to take over.

What's wrong? You're supposed to tell me, Doc.

I'm getting a cold, I can feel it.

I'm new in town and didn't have any place else to go.

My doctor told me to come here if I get that pain in my chest again. It's here.

I have this recurrent back pain and need a refill of my codeine. It's the only medicine that works for me. I've tried the Darvon and it makes me dizzy.

See like, I don't have a place to sleep.

This here estrogen is causing terrible spots on my face. I'm a female impersonator and this is terrible.

My legs, they got swollen. I can't bends them and hardly can walk.

It hurts when I tee tee.

What brought me to the hospital? The ambulance, I done called the ambulance.

Hour after hour she saw and treated. More and more coming to the emergency rooms, can't wait for appointments, don't believe in specialists, want to see a doctor when they want to, when they need to. Each patient another question and answer trial. Impression and disposition. Then the next one. People who explain themselves in clear middle-class terms and who question her conclusions struck annoyance as well as pleasure. It took time, it meant complications. Do they want to be indulged? Explanations, causes, she liked talking, explaining, and being understood, but more are waiting. For hours.

So many ways to classify; she'd been seeing patients straight since four that afternoon. A dinner break and it was nine o'clock and rows and rows of people were still sitting in pastel-colored chairs. The basket full of charts, like random drawings. File and sort each time there's a new person—age, sex, words, behavior, dress. Trying to find them, answer them, help them. There are the dazzling stories, horror and aberrations at the emergency room, but she wanted to understand, name the disguised, covert stuff. She hoped for insight into the patients separate from labels she placed on them: older, younger, male, female, gay, black, white, Chicano, Tibetan, quite a few people from Tibet, mother, child, student, husband, neurotic, psychotic, on and on, with all the titles for grasping another person. Nervous, drunk, stoned, filthy, scared, obese, loud, manipulating, weird, wired, short of breath, tremulous. Diseases, head trauma, ear aches, tonsillitis, tumors, congestive heart failure, cirrhosis, hepatitis, thrombophlebitis, TB, rheumatoid arthritis, syphilis, low back pain, lupus, warts, hemorrhoids, stasis ulcers, ingrown toenail. Head to foot.

Recently, there were physicians assistants who triaged special problems: pregnant woman to Ob-Gyn, the sick baby to Peds, etc. But there was still the schizophrenic woman found in the back booth wailing her liver was too big and too painful while holding her belly during contractions. And the guy, who came in a month after breaking his shoulder with his child's face blown out with an abscess dripping down the baby's neck, asking for pain meds so they could both sleep.

There was the old man, they wanted to send to psych, who came in saying something was moving under his skin and he was right. A genuine case of trichinosis, buried worms wiggling in his muscles.

The doctors were from all fields of medicine, full time during the day and moonlighting residents working the nights. All the staff had kids so we were trying for a few extra dollars. Marcie could get a curb stone consultation all the time. Surgery, neuro, eye, ortho, urology. Anybody she wanted was working somewhere on the floor and the radiology and minor trauma department were separate setups right next store just to handle emergency films.

"Hey, take a look, I think this is early papilledema."

"Look at this, Jean. The woman in booth 14 has these things hanging down from her legs, huge fat dehiscence flopping out medially from her thigh, hanging down to her ankles. They're like melted candles but no pain."

"Want to see this? Third case of secondary syphilis I've seen in two weeks, beautiful palmer lesions."

"Marcie, look at this, you're the expert on the heart, do you think that's a significant q wave?"

"Jesus Christ, I just saw a guy who had urine coming out of his back from a stab wound."

"Here's an active TB, not on the films eight months ago."

All night, exchanges of information go one if there were any doubts or interesting cases. The patient got the benefit even if he couldn't remember the doctors' names.

The idea was always to find out what was wrong if possible, treat if possible, and get the person assigned to a clinic for follow up or see them in walk-in again or admit them. Always those decisions.

When the patient doesn't speak English, she had to rely on filtered information. Clinics kept a list of translators for most languages. They come down from the jobs gratis. Spanish speaking translators are around all the time. Even with some Spanish words, it was better to get translators. Cubans, one day in California come to the hospital after years of back pain; teenage girls from Mexico with stomach pains like their mothers are common.

> *Mrs. Ramirez, Ra-mir-ez, what's the problem?*
> *Habla Español?*
> *Yo habla un pocito Español. Que es su problema?*
> *Ah mucho dolor, el pecho.*
> *And she begins to talk very quickly gesturing just a quickly. Despacio, por favor.*
> *Chest pain. Dizziness. Too many possibilities. Nebulous descriptions.*

With a translator the exchange begins again. She listens to her questions being asked in Spanish. The difference between the translators was sometimes the difference between solving the patient's riddle and not. The physical exam was only half the answer. Some translators approximate what she said because of their limited vocabulary or opinions about what they think is a self-indulgent patient. Others try to be machines only. A few work with her to get the keys to unlock the patient's words.

"Hi, Mrs. Alvarez, Ms. Lopez here had chest pain for apparently two months. Been here four times and keeps coming back. I see on her chart she had a negative chest x-ray. Would you tell her Dr. Walker left for the day and the x-ray is normal." Marcie pauses and listens to the Spanish, watching the patient. This one is shy, twenty-four, dark mascara lined eyes in a smooth face, who doesn't look at Marcie or the translator. A twenty-four-year-old with chest pain. Rare. Now to decipher the puzzle.

"Ask her, please, if the chest pain is with her all the time? Is it sharp, dull, cramping, what kind is it?" Both languages are inadequate in describing pain.

"Does she cough when she gets the pain, breathe fast, spit blood? Any stomach pains or nausea along with it, does the pain go anywhere, is it worse with certain food or if she's lying down? Are her nerves bad, does the pain come when she's nervous or upset? Is it related to exercise, is she taking birth control pills? Any wasting or weakness in her muscles, any loss of sensations? Any history of diseases like rheumatic fever or anemia."

Marcie wanders everywhere through the review of systems and got no solid replies, nothing she might relate to an organ or a disease. She reconnoitered. She explored and got too many inconsistencies, too much vagueness.

The old chart came and the story was as confusing in the notes as it was now.

"Ask her if she's worried about something. Tell her every time she comes here, none of the doctors can find anything wrong with her. I want you to talk with her please, and have her get on a gown so I can examine her."

In the interim, she sees another patient with ulcers and refills his meds.

Now the patient is sitting in a paper gown, looking at her knees and saying nothing.

Time and patience creep on. Full physical exam negative. She'll have to write it up. Head, ears, eyes, nose, mouth, pharynx—negative. Neck, heart, lungs—negative; no masses, no murmurs, no nothing. Breasts, abdomen no masses, no tenderness, bowel sounds normal, neuro grossly normal including fundiscopic and reflexes. Vital signs all within normal limits.

"Tell her I find nothing wrong, her EKG and chest x-rays are normal each time and many doctors think she's fine." She would get labels crock, hysteric, somatization disorder by women as well as men doctors. She was wearing the system down.

"All right we're going to have to get this out of her." There was a long exchange, talking, questions, waiting for the key to open her up and she had it with the questions about her family and her husband.

Her husband left her and she doesn't know where he is. She doesn't know anybody in LA, three of her kids are with her and two are with her mother in Mexico. She doesn't know what to do, she hasn't got money and can't get back to Mexico or stay where she is.

Finally the problem. "Let's see what we can do. Tell her we'll call the social worker to see her now. She was apparently married to a United States citizen, maybe that's something. Tell her she's to follow up here if she continues to have chest pains but we're hoping the social worker will be able to help her and those pains will go away. Thanks for translating."

Marcie leaves a note in the chart. This was the eighth time the patient had been in the walk-in area in these last months, waiting for someone to decipher her simple code, give her a better answer than nothing is wrong, and come back for test results.

Going to pick up another blank chart, Marcie wonders if this young woman will find a way out and her kids will be all right. Searching for hidden keys, how many locks do I miss and send the patient home so they come back to someone else, still hoping for recognition. Waiting for the translated frustration into bodily complaints to be interpreted into the original sources of distress.

She enters the next booth and sees a man about thirty, alert, relaxed, clean shaven, Adam's apple prominent. His leather jacket hangs on his shoulder, his arm bent so his index finger is providing a causal hook for the jacket. He wants a refill of his Neosporin. She looks at him and asks what it's for.

It's a sore.
Is it better?
Eh, a little.
May I see it? You may need something else.
Oh it's just a sore.
Let's take a look.
No need. Just the medicine. Okay?
No, it's better if I see what's going on.

Slowly he lets the jacket slip down, shy and reluctant, but resigned to the instruction. Under a clean shirt, a boulder rising above his scapular is revealed. She asks him to take off his shirt and there oozing pus is the tumor as big as the man's head. She says that must hurt and he needs to come in the hospital. He looks at her and his eyes brim with tears; he's relieved and readily accepts admission. I think of him still, wondering how he died.

Another chart.
I done been told I have the fireballs of the Eucharist and I does bleed and bleed till my doctor say I have low blood.
You're bleeding from where, Mrs. Jefferson?
From the hole there. I gots that hole dripping. My friend it's coming.
Your friend? You mean your period?
Yessum.
Mrs. Jefferson, women have three holes, one for pee, one for periods and babies, and one for bowel movements. Where's the blood coming from? Did the doctors say you had fibroids in the uterus, your womb?
That there's it. Fireballs. I done thought I was going to church enough. Lord knows, I is tired of praying. It's my womb, not my sins. So you mean I pees from another hole. Do you too?
Work up, hemoglobin 5.3, (normal above 12) admission to Ob-Gyn.

"Excuse me, Doctor, is this your signature? Marcie?" The intricately made up woman points to the signature on a chart.

"Yes, what's the problem?"

"Well, I never saw that name before. Marcie, is that right?"

"Yes, my parents liked it. What's the problem?"

The social workers, recently hired and old timers, took any opportunity to stroll over to walk-in to question doctors about the possible cost of the visits and medicines that would have to be paid on the outside. That frustrated the hell out of Marcie, since she had no idea of the outside cost other than in round figures. She also realized it all depended on what was going to happen to the patient. Whether there was a gall stone blockage and gangrene, whether the barium enema showed an invasive polyp, whether the EKG showed an MI, and so on. Within reason, the simple cases were sent out if the patient could afford to pay. The county charged as much or more than anywhere else because of all the facilities it maintained. All tests, drugs, therapy were included in its fee. The social workers interview all patients who were to get clinic appointments.

"Doctor, you've written here that you want placement for this patient because he had no place to live."

"Right."

"Well, you have to fill out Board and Care papers." Bored herself, the woman waits for an answer and scouts the room evaluating the men doctors. Social workers usually fall into three categories, young females who willingly have coffee with the doctors down in the public cafeteria, males with full bellies under tight corduroy pants and aborted ties, and older, any types, merely doing the job.

"Look he's not disabled to the point where he needs board and care." Marcie imagined the B&Cs full to the brim and really replied from a feeling that the patient would be lost if sent down that paper road.

"But I can't do anything without the forms."

"This man is a chronic alcoholic who can easily go out for his meals. In fact, he should have the most freedom we can give him. The county can't support everyone. I want him to have a place to live and meal cards. He'd never stay in a board and care anyway."

Marcie felt she was more aware of all the possibilities. Getting streetwise. A lot of senior residents hated the drain of funds by the indigents, but she couldn't be that wise and send them out on the street with bus tokens. Someday, she would get tired of them too.

"You don't want him to go to a board and care?" the case worker asked, while she scratched her back and looked at the neurosurgery resident in his scrubs.

"No, but I want him to have a place to stay."

"Well, I'll see if I can get him in one of the hotels, maybe some aid," and she meandered out.

Shadowing the country were the myriad of rooms for those without rooms. Missions, board and cares, closed and open nursing homes, institutions, rehab programs, state and private hospitals. She used to be dumb and admit some for an overnight stay if they were homeless, so they wouldn't sleep on Third Street cement sidewalks. With the inpatient bed and the meal, the cost would be one hundred-eighty. Now she wrangles a call from the attendants and unfailingly they find a mission bed.

A man could stay at a mission for about five days. A few refused to go back to them and opted for a hotel downtown. Afraid of TB or being jumped. It wasn't clear which places were worse. All the buildings used for refuge had been initially for other purposes and echoed in their structures past times and different interests. The people now wandered in and out like wounded birds using old abandoned nests.

Suddenly, after hours of sitting in the waiting room, Mr. Leon stood, swaying slowly like an elephant and then made up mind to start trouble. He came to one of the doors to the examining booths and the hunched-over doctors writing in charts.

"Doc, I've got to see ya now."

"Mr. Leon, please sit down. We've got lots of people ahead of you. We'll see as fast as we can."

"How come that guy got in, he was here after me."

"It's an asthmatic attack."

"Look I'm hurting too, gotta see the doctor now. I've been coughing all night, can't get no sleep. See this here, he addressed the attendant at the door, opened a brown paper bag with books, papers, pills. That's my class. I'm studying and can't get no sleep and study too."

"Mr. Leon sit down, there are people who've waited longer than you."

He retreated.

After a Tuesday full of stomach complaints, Marcie would finish writing up a case and close her eyes trying to censor the thought that she could not stand to hear another woman tell her she had gas or smell another fetid breath of a shaking drunk with gut pains. She felt them, the patients, like they were a continuous seeping jelly of grievances. The agenda was to survive one more evaluation, gather reserve at coffee breaks, fight boredom, fatigue, restlessness.

"Fuck, saw another bovine disease," Phil Goodman, an ophthalmology resident, hung over the desk and grumbled as he scribbled.

"Bovine?"

"Yup, you know, fat cow complaining of knees hurting. Jesus couldn't give out nutritional advice here, no way."

Marcie smiled and sighed. "I knew there was an epidemic but I thought it was mad cow, not fat cow disease. I stand corrected."

"Gotta keep up with the latest medical advances, Marcie. Really, get with it."

"What's the problem, sir?" As she talked she walked into the booth, leaned against the table, turned the chart over to his age, fifty-one. He was stocky, cleanly dressed in a flannel shirt and belted loose paints. There were those that could diagnose the problem by looking at the address of the patient, who was looking at his folded hands. She looked at him. His hair was dark and his face was tawny. Ethnicity helped but most likely this was an alcoholic. Blood sugar 220.

"I came for my pills."

"What are the pills for?"

"I'd been drinking and stopped my diabetes pills." He looked up at her and said, "Tell me, do I have to take them? I mean I'll be dead soon anyway."

Alcoholics tend to be melodramatic, asking for sympathy with their meds but this man had stated his thoughts rather blandly. "How come you think that, Mr. Perez?"

"Look, I'm an old grandfather, I haven't much time. Why should I live?"

"Have you been hurting? Leg cramps? Dizzy?"

"I take Diabenese, one a day. I'm not hurting. I feel okay I guess."

"There's got to be more to your idea about not living." She waited.

"I think I want to kill myself. It scares me a little."

If she would have only checked his urine, refill his meds, what would have happened to him? The age was pretty much in the ballpark for suicide among men.

What was she going to do with him? "Would you be interested in talking to someone about how you feel?"

"I dunno. Maybe."

"Not drinking is good but it takes more time to figure these things out. You could go down to the Psychiatry Hospital and get help there. You want to try to live, don't you? For your grandchildren. Do they care about you?"

"I guess so, but I got no job now and my daughter she not like me living in her house and all."

"Did she say that?"

"No."

"Don't kill yourself, you talk to your daughter one more time. You may feel better getting your diabetes under control. Want to try?"

"I guess so."

"Tell me about your grandkids."

He lights up and gives a rundown of the four grandchildren and how he teaches them everything from Spanish to math to how to plant tomatoes. He is invested in them. There is a chance. He hands her a vial of Seconal and smiles.

What to do? You can hold suicidal persons but eventually they have to be let go. Get the social worker and refer to psych clinic. Punt the pain. "I think we will have you talk to the social worker about your family situation and make an appointment at the diabetes and psych clinic. I'll refill your medication. Please sit over here to wait."

The next chart has to do with an older woman and another one accompanying her. The chief complaint is not eating.

Mrs. Hewitt, what's the problem?

I'm her sister. Viola won't eat nothin' and jus sits and stares.

When did that start? How long has it been going on?

She done stopped when her daughter died. She had the smiling mighty Jesus and slipped away.

I don't understand.

When Florence, she died.

What did she die of?

The smiling mighty Jesus, just like that. The doctor he told us. Florence was in San Francisco at school. She gots this headache and went into the hospital and died. Her and three other students.

It was spinal meningitis, but it was still a stretch to smiling mighty Jesus. Nevertheless the sister shook her head in agreement. The patient was markedly dehydrated, electrolytes way off the mark, urine dark brown, blood pressure 68/50, HR 128. She had to be admitted to medicine.

Again the voice of Mr. Leon.

"Just ordering people around. I's sick, I tell you. Sit out there for hours and nobody gives a rat's ass. Let me talk to the head doctor."

"Okay, you go sit down now, Mr. Leon, or go talk to the head doctor in his office down the hall, but no trouble here. We'll see you in a while," Marcie offered. "You don't want us to call security, right?"

Security was composed of large, brown-uniformed men with guns on their sides and short sideburns on their faces. They'd an impressive job, whether it was controlling the drunk or subduing the psychotic or taking pulled knives away from druggies. There was very little variation in their methods with swift, unhesitating force, subdue and restrain. Mr. Leon didn't want to deal with them.

"Goddamn doctors. What the hell are ya fo'? Shoving me out like that. I walked from seventh to the hospital, a damn long distance." He came in a black raincoat and it was easy to imagine him waking up on a stained striped mattress under a butchered blanket in a scuffed square room, knowing the shifty dread in his gut would disappear with a tepid drink. He did have a mother somewhere in LA but he only talked about her high blood pressure.

He sat down again, yelling his cathartic. He'd get up and he'd go temporarily. Black attendants nodded heads together, putting him down and worthlessness. Third time today he's been in today, wasting everybody's time and money. He should go someplace else if he don't like it here.

Let's see what else. Besides an aura of booze, he also wore a brown hat with Indian beads for a band. He carried those hard cover books but the ones she saw were of dubious distinction; *Nursing in the Mountains, Better English Quick, The Word of Buddha for Baptists.* When, where did he read them? In that square room, a window enclosed hotel lobby, maybe the tables in the public cafeteria at the hospital or Pershing Square?

Sometimes he would be gone for a week or more, not coming into the walk-in, minor trauma, or ambulance area. There was this paradox of comments like, All we need tonight is Mr. Leon. Yeah, it's eerie quiet.

He and the other drunks were a passé evil in these days of tampering with choice sociological categories. Their numbers did not diminish because of everyone's boredom with the subject. What's the estimate in the 1990s, nine to fourteen million alcoholics in the US? There were some programs for neat business men who over indulged and their depressed drinking companion wives, but the regulars she saw must have had psyches shaped like bottles. They knew all about programs, AA, and the rehab centers. It didn't mean much to them, they came to the General when they got in big trouble.

She'd pick up a chart, step into the booth, see a man. A fortyish man with an eroded face, channels of wrinkles meeting at thin lips, and crumbling teeth. His eyes, small, watery, red, look down at the dirty suit. She'd look too and see the torn shoes, white socks, trousers too short and stained at the crotch, suit jacket gray and underneath a couple plaid flannel shirts, white shirt rolled at the cuff and finally a gray T-shirt. The diagnosis had to include booze.

The body was stringy except at the belly where the liver swelled and then shriveled in old age.

The women drinkers were older and had purple lipstick overlapping taunt lips, and the blacks were springer and younger. "Oh, I've been drinking a long time, since maybe nine or ten, with my daddy at first but then he went away."

It was just a matter of seeing them when they began to run into trouble, wear out, break down, bleed, hurt. Not that they would be phased out by drugs. Alcohol was big among the young too. They were better dressed the first ten years, that's all. Druggies got all the press, maybe a couple million of them, but alcohol reigned in reality.

or angel dust with or without cocaine any better or worse than barbs, passé old dangerous Meprobamate, Librium, and the darling Valium and alcohol? All as fashionable as skirts go up and down and Levi's get straight legged or flared.

It had been fun to watch a few flower children and daring blacks wearing Afros and braids. Thin, tall girls with checkered suits and men loping in with net wife beater shirts and purple underwear. Now there is little inexpensive daring, all conforming to the street fashions.

People kept coming. Again she was strangely grateful. She still didn't know why. She still didn't understand. Everyone talked about the pain in the ass the hours and the patients were. She agreed but her secret was she was awed by the endless parade. A social maelstrom. At this time there was still the overt expression of need, amazing trust, and the humble willingness to be submissive to the doctor, the good old 1970s.

There was no question, regardless of woman's lib, that women still conformed to the unwritten rituals of decorum. The Spanish and Chicano did too.

Always polite and cooperative. The Blacks on the average faced her with warmth and respect. Even at the age of rebellion, teenagers invariably sat with their mothers who did the talking. Fifteen, six foot two and he'd defer, looking to his mother. If Marcie maneuvered it so he was alone, he'd talk readily but insists he only came because of his mother. There was the smile when he heard she didn't give a shot of penicillin for a viral cold.

If the patients weren't alone, after initial complaints, everyone seemed to prefer to have others talk for them, mothers for daughters and sons, husbands for wives, wives for husbands, doctors for patients.

My wife, she have barnacle pneumonia and is still coughing.

My son here, have the chicken pops and they left him this scar festering.

My son, he had a fallen out and needs his Dilantin.

This here bag is leaking after the construction of my pa's bowel.

See this here, Lettecia got pain in her neighbor and she is shying about it.

FRITZ WOLF

Low blood, high blood, sweet blood, bad blood, dirty blood were shortcuts to anemia, hypertension, diabetes, syphilis, hepatitis.

Don't mash here, mah nature's gone.

I done got the merseries.

Mah throat is sore, like when you start to cry and try not ta, said by a wrestler with crisscross scars on both cheeks. Face to face with a powerful man who had sensitivity.

CHAPTER 28

Learning

IT HAD BEEN a black man who had trusted her first and made her a doctor in someone else's eyes. Black men and middle-aged women. Those types must have given birth to more baby doctors than all the other patients put together. They were the teaching hospital resources.

Talking with patients was just like her first time, surgery rounds. Four or five second year students rounding with Dr. Cory, hollow cheeked and silver haired.

The ward was full and the sun made shadows of the patients. The staff surgeon led them past rows of iron framed beds with white open weave blankets to a place by one of the barred windows.

When they saw the white coats, men, mainly black men, who'd been milling around, excused themselves out of the room if they could walk. The cluster of white students in white coats came up to the patient who was to be examined. He was a black man, sixty-six. His arms, like gnarled chicken legs, were pushing against the window sill to keep him standing. He had burly black hair. He had a full face with multiple moles dotting his cheeks and he turned easily to face the doctors. The attending began talking about the body and liver. When they looked down at his swollen belly, everyone has this polite, intellectual look, including the patient.

Marcie was assigned the case. His name was John Washington Willard. She returned to ward after rounds and felt like she was two years old, little and stupid to the ways of the world as she walked to his bed. She went past sick men with tubes hanging out their arms and penises and cigarettes hanging from their mouths.

"My, my just look at the fine lady, my, my. What's under that there white coat?"

"Don't pay them no mind. You got business with me, Doc?"

He had acknowledged her, rescued her in that simple acceptance and it was easy from then on, pulled the curtain, get her stethoscope out of her bag and start examining him.

Eyes had only minimal retinal vessel narrowing. There were the black splotches of pigment against the pink mucosa of his mouth when he said *ahh*. His hair was soft, neck normal, chest like a barrel of ribs.

He let her palpate his liver floating in its juices and then she had him lie in a semi-fowlers position and she did her first abdominal tap, two quarts. He had cirrhosis and ascites. It was like sticking a needle in a water balloon.

"Damn, it that don't make a difference, Doc. I can get a breath fo' sure."

He did what she told him to do and took his pills, happy with the relief, knowing it wouldn't last and he'd fill up again as the scarred liver squeezed itself.

She came to see him twice a day, with staff and without. He'd tell her about his medical history, real river boat loading cotton bales like the song and his brew being the only stuff he ever drank for the forty-two years that he made it "hisself."

"I used to doctor myself a little too. Now this here is a cyst, a ball of water, it done grown on the ropes of the wrist. Yo' understands? Well, now, we jus took a board and hit it real hard and the ball, it break and never come again."

"We call that a ganglion cyst surgeons take out. You hit it with a board and got the same results?"

"Yup. You go on and feel right here. And that there is the place where my rib got broke when I was on the Queen steamer. A hurricane. Three men overboard and big cargo too. I gots slammed up against a packing crate. That done hurt a hell've lot worse like swallowing pills. Lord, doc, I do hate those vitamin pills but I takes 'em."

"You were a sailor all your life."

"Yeah, Great Lakes and South Atlantic but I done some train work here and construction when they was building downtown more. As I says all of it easier than those vitamin pills."

They would laugh.

He always shared his stories with her and never asked a thing about her or her qualifications. He was her patient and yet it was he who made her feel better.

They never said much but both knew about the illusion she wore with her white coat. They both knew reciting facts never substituted for truth and experience. She got better and he got better, a mutual agreement between doctor and patient.

Months turned to graduation and the agreements grew as others saw her as a doctor too. In the walk-in area, she saw people, letting themselves be called patients, over and over again. All the shirts are unbuttoned bottom to neck, and the pants pulled off by hooking the thumbs inside the elastic and pulling down. The eyes hoping to be understood.

There are two types of patients still. The highly neurotic, frustrated with multiple psychosomatic complaints centered on their bulging stomachs, or the stoic, unassuming figures who walk-in with heart attack, congestive failure, stab wounds, cancer that charred breasts away, rotting teeth with bleeding gums, skin ulcers eating up whole legs.

Mr. Travis, what's the problem?

Well, it's my hand, it's still numb.

How long has it been that way?

About three weeks now. It makes it difficult for me to do my work. I am a mechanic.

Did the numbness occur suddenly, did something happen to your arm?

Did you get hit or have accident?

No. No.

Tell me when you first noticed it.

After I woke up I noticed it. I didn't think much about it 'cause I thought it would go away.

Did you sleep awkwardly?

Well, I guess I slumped over the bathtub. I got dizzy. I cut my pecker off. It was always bothering me, always a bothering me. I was in the bathroom and I got kinda dizzy. I was bleeding pretty much . . . I tried to set down and I guess I passed out. My hand's been weak ever since.

A rich, large, well-equipped hospital, a beauty of a county hospital, but the prevailing expectation was medical help as a last resort, don't come to the county unless you're really sick. Routine physical couldn't be squeezed in unless, of course, the patient had a sickness or had a symptom or sign of one. However, with a little encouragement almost everybody could develop a symptom of something. Can't assume anything and had to examine everyone.

Is it only middle class women with neurotic hangups that willingly go to a doctor? Others feel ambivalent. To go or not to go.

Looking for hope here. Able to talk to a doctor. A medical confessional.

Monday chest pain, Tuesday high blood pressure, peptic ulcer disease, Wednesday back pain gall bladders and refills, Thursday Stelazine and Valium refills for the neurotic-psychotic, Friday admixed held together with depression. Weekends. Always talk and pain and a need to make contact.

Making contact inexorably and inextricable connected to pain. Tell us where it hurts. Like a mother, promising to make it better, come. Follow the ritual and be treated for pain as the patient. The communication, the dialogue has its bargains, its protocols. So intricate and so base as well.

Marcie liked the talking at night best. Along with the urgency to discover the problem, paramount in an emergency room, nighttime made facing patients more intimate. Less formality. The day staff hid in bureaucracy, doctor's aura, business procedures of the nursing personnel, peering social workers, physician assistant students.

At night everyone took it as it came. No buffers. The hospital was down to necessity, sparse, quiet in the halls, relaxed tired doctors, appraisal less loaded with jargon, less punting to other services open during the day.

Mr. Leon's best time is at night too.

It is 10:30 and someone is finally getting rid of Mrs. Ford.

"I tell you what you are, goddamn horse doctors, that's what. Nazi bastards. Where is that bottle my pills was in? Where is it? You can't keep it. Lousy doctors." She mumbled as she sorts through a big trash basket. "I'll never come back here, they're trying to lock me up. Give me electrical wiring. Torture me. Put me in a camp to gas me. They try to do that to everyone, I hear them on TV." She sees an attendant smiling with awkwardness and screams again, "You go ahead and laugh, I'll get you all. I'll come and tell them in the morning but they're bastards too."

"All right now, Mrs. Ford, take it easy. You go get your pills at the psychiatric unit. You're getting too many pills from too many places. It's best if you got them one place."

"They think they can laugh at me. I'm not a fool." Her thick glasses slide down her nose as she bends her bleached blond head, picks up her Bullock's shopping bag, and goes into the hall. "They won't keep me there. You wait and see. I want them more pills."

It was quiet for a few minutes as the insults sank and her pathos rose. The demand had slowed down until the next bus anyway. The lull was broken by the confirmation from the waiting room. Mr. Leon was seen in the halls. Bill and Marcie smiled and prepared the others.

He'd talk with Mrs. Taylor, the door attendant, about the cold weather and she'd repeat three times for him to go in booth 14 and put the thermometer in his mouth.

He tipped his Indian beaded hat to the doctors and leaned against the booth's sliding door, eyes glazed, mouth smiling, wearing his black ribbon tie.

It was Marcie's turn. She picked up the chart and he began. "Well, how are you, Doc? It's the green cough syrup I needs, Doctor, you understand, you know what I means. Have me this chronic sinus condition." He coughed, He spoke as clearly as possible and seemed in his nicer moments to desperately try for a polite interchange and not to degrade the whole encounter to a mundane county service. He had alcohol on his breath but his speech was not slurred tonight.

"Mr. Leon, what did you do with the bottle you got last night?"

"It was stolen right in front of me, see here's what happened . . . Three bums, I fought 'em hard."

"Okay." He had been in three times in the last twenty-four hours. Marcie's eyes were burning. She'd been up with the baby and her bad cough most of the night before. "How bad are you sinuses today? Last chest x-ray and exams have been negative."

"No, no, I's jus fine. My arm cast gone, feels real good. You know I am going to class, can't be coughing all the time in school. Can't hardly talk then. Jus the refill today." He unzipped his shiny gray Members Only jacket and waited.

"All right, sit back, let me check your throat and chest, then I'll fill this out and they will call you for your medicine."

"Thank you, Doctor, thank you. You know I can hardly talk without it and I used to be able to sing real good."

Shirt frayed but clean gray. Throat and lungs clear. She bent over the form writing for a refill, a simple expectorant, no narcotics in it. Mr. Leon was not after junk, just the visit. He'd been to the ear, nose, and throat clinic, medicine, neuro, everywhere but clinic appointments didn't contain him.

"This here green solution helps my singing voice."

How many drunks had come in singing? Not that many. Usually it was, "Take me out to the ball game" and a few repeats and then sitting down quietly again or whistling, "When the Saints Come Marching In" on the way to the pharmacy. Once she saw a tottering man do a soft shuffle in front of a seat in the waiting room, past a crying baby and an impatient housewife. But mainly there was no singing, just the yelling, crying, moaning, and staring.

Marcie finished writing up her findings and turned to Mr. Leon. "So you used to be able to sing really well, is that right? Okay. They'll call you over there, please."

"Sure did, better than on those TV programs."

"Better than TV, oh come on."

His small eyes looked around, alerted by the attendants' and doctors' smiles. "It's true too, and loud," he said. "You believe me?" He stretched his hands out as if ending a song.

The day had been long and she wondered if her daughter was feeling better and glad the dad was home with her and she wanted to be home with them too and a cup of tea and music. "Sure, let's hear some. Yes, come on and sing, Mr. Leon," Marcie coaxed, calling his bluff.

He stood himself in the center of the brown tile floor between all the examining booths and the long Formica tables held by thick, white plaster columns. He put his legs far apart to steady himself, pulled his jacket straight, and sang.

> O Danny boy, the pipes, the pipes are calling
> From glen to glen and down the mountainside
> The summer's gone and all the roses falling
> 'Tis you, 'tis you must go and I must bide.

But come ye back when summer's in the meadow
Or when the valley's hushed and white with snow
'Tis I'll be here in sunshine or in shadow
O Danny boy, O Danny boy, I love you so.

He cleared his throat, stepped forward a little off balance, and continued.

But if ye come and all the flowers are dying
If I am dead, as dead I well may be,
You'll come and find the place where I am lying
And kneel and say an Ave there for me.

And I shall hear, though soft, your tread above me
And all my grave shall warmer, sweeter be
For you will bend and tell me that you love me
And I will sleep in peace until you come to me.

She didn't recall having heard the whole song before. She always considered it maudlin. How long since she even thought of it. He sang it loudly and on tune. It took her by surprise, like finding a dandelion in cement walk ways. What she thought was an Irish song was sung by this West Coast wanderer. He was his own being for the moment. There was a silence, a respectable quiet at first as he finished.

And as he finished, clearly proud at knowing all the words, he extended his arms, his hands opened, and his fingers waved like sea anemones inviting morsels of recognition. Then there was clapping and she joined in.

Bowing to the applause, he said, "Good night, Doctor, and thank you. The green medicine, right?" He held up the papers and smiled.

"That's right, Mr. Leon. Good night."

Mr. Leon went around the corner, said good night to the attendant at the disposition desk, calling her by name, asking the time, discussing how that song makes him choke up most times. She told him he better get going to the pharmacy.

He went. Usually the alcoholics came back multiple times to talk, to fuss, to bother. Mr. Leon seemed well satisfied tonight and left thereafter quietly. The attendants saw him every night and didn't have much patience with his free loading county meds and time, but his singing still touched their moods and decorated their smiles. He wasn't the same person tonight, one of them offered.

The moonlighting neurosurgeon Ed Baxter said he'd never seen Mr. Leon in such a good mood. "He should sing more often. Marcie, you had the magic."

"Yeah, he's usually pestering and yelling, loves to argue with everyone."

"Jesus, he can be a trouble maker. Administration wouldn't let him sign in for a while. He'd been coming in so many times for nothing."

"It's enough to see people for their colds."

Mrs. Farmington, what's the problem? Fifty-five and full chart.

I need the disability. I am going through the change.

You're menopausal, is that right? What problems do you have?

Just can't work. Not able to work for the last ten years or so.

How long has it been since your last period.

Oh, I haven't had a period for six and one half years, before my grandson was born, but he's too tiring for me. Before when I was coming up I had lots of energy. I do housework for my daughter. She and her husband are running their own business and they pays me to sit their kids when they're home from school.

Those kids run around and exhaust me. I need disability payments. I got gas and can't eat peppers. No one cares about me.

Let me check you over.

I am tired, tired, tired.

Everything seems normal. We'll send you for a blood test to see if you're anemic but you don't appear to be.

I'm not getting the disabilities?

No. Maybe you could talk to your family about getting someone to help you out.

Oh lord, I better get something to eat before I take the bus again. I got today and tomorrow off to rest up.

It's okay. Good idea, Mrs. Farmington.

Disability insurance was a favorite pursuit by all sorts of patients. The Russian immigrants see it as their right and the poor see it as social security and entitlements for surviving. There is no issue of physical or mental impairment, just need.

The women, depressed, middle aged, expressing distress through physical symptoms that are demonstrable many times. "I tell you if I see another neurotic woman today, I'll freak out. Headaches and stomach gases give me the runs."

"Listen, Phil," Jean interceded, "these woman can't do anything. They justified their lives raising children and doing housework for their family. That's great, but what do you do when it's over, their kids raised? Enter servitude again as a grandmother or housekeeper? Is that all they have for the rest of their lives, sometimes more than half of their lives. They don't get to go to school. They never learn anything more. They come here saying it's my back, where are the pills you give me to shut me up?"

"Hey, take it easy, you and Marcie get too worked up. Some of these people are really sick, but I can't accept that the emergency room is the place for society's problems. Sorry, but no way."

"And it isn't only women. I had the all time record with a guy who had back pain for thirty years and an ortho appointment Thursday but he came in here for Tylenol."

"It's true. They like it here, waiting three or four hours on Mondays and Tuesdays."

"Wednesdays too."

"But you try telling them to go home unless they have an emergency and I'll bet the sick ones go and the ones wasting our time stay," Marcie added.

"Okay, okay, don't play bleeding heart liberals."

"I know your answer, let them starve and disappear."

"Well, hell, at least the ones who survived would know how to take care of themselves. Nobody cares whether any of us survive. Anyway I'm going to get something to drink, want something too?"

"Yup, I need some ice water."

She sat down on a tall stool pulled up to the counter. It was nearly midnight, no buses for a while. Bill thumbed through the newspaper, discussing football, stocks, the insurance agent who kept following him around. Everybody's got problems he allowed.

The next Monday she talked with Ed, the neurosurgical resident, who also moonlighted in the walk-in area regularly. They were at dinner, Brunswick stew no less, and he remembered the Danny Boy concert but said Friday Mr. Leon peed all over his booth and hit one of the lab messengers. Security came and took him to the drunk tank. Eating in the doctor's dining room rather than the public cafeteria always made things worse.

A couple other stories got back to her, something about a fractured rib from a bar fight and five other visits to the walk-in area in one day. Then there was quiet as a runoff of warm days decreased the patient flow.

Wednesday, Mr. Leon was dead. Mrs. Taylor informed her as Marcie came in for her night shift.

No eulogy.

She could picture him still with his outstretched hands, had this queasy feeling about the news and some sadness about the inevitability of his story. Dead before they got him to the OR. Beaten up, skull fracture, massive brain bleed.

The void of the noisy, infantile man caused much conversation on the main floor. For a while. Everybody had known him better than most of the drunks. She continued to feel a vague annoyance at his disappearance. It was puzzling.

What was it? Nothing unique, no touching or strange story. Maybe the big generalities of death, determinism, self destruction versus the could-have-beens and might-have-beens. Had his song been all sung? Mr. Leon had died. What did it mean? Did it pose the question in *The Brothers Karamazov* of who's worthwhile? But that was stupid thinking.

Certainly she knew by now that the alcoholic will booze and battle and the red-toenailed blond will swallow her overdose as inevitably as the smoker's cancer will consume the lung. They die.

She and the others supplied the exams, the pills, the appointments to fill up their days and to fill her days too. Her contact with them wasn't going to change them. Maybe specialists and specialty clinics could do that. Specialists always say they can do marvelous things. Of course, the alcoholic has to go to the AA meeting. That's the rub.

Still people kept coming here. These patients intrude aspects of themselves besides bodily functions. Mr. Leon had done that. I didn't ask about where he went to school, I didn't know about where he used to sing, I only knew he liked his green cough medicine. Nevertheless I will remember him for my sake.

It would have been nice to spend a whole hour with a person but here were thirty more for her to see and evaluate and thirty more for everyone to see.

She knew the litany. These people are different. You can never understand them. That was the standard argument. See them quickly. You have nothing in common with them. They're sick and poor and ill educated. Not you. Besides you're here to diagnose medical problems. To make decisions about where to send them.

Years ago, the whole doctor thing was based on everybody complying to the rules. Right from the beginning. Medical students are programmed to know facts and cover up what they don't know and sympathize with their comrades in rounds who were slightly inept, glad to protect themselves, and get the diagnoses right. The majority of patients did their best to make the least noise and ooze humbled images, to get what they want. She knew she too was susceptible to that *Magic Mountain* total care and would even settle for a hell of a lot less. Maybe in years to come, the relationships would get better and doctors wouldn't wear out and patients could come down from high mountains of expectations and fight the war for health practically and reasonably.

"I'm taking a residency in psychiatry," Jean announced stunning the others.

"You want more of this craziness?"

"Hey, hold off, Jean," Jim pleaded. "You're tired, not that crazy yourself."

"I like it. It's like exploring a foreign world much like mine and easier than trying to learn the German my parents spoke."

"Good luck to you, Jean," Marcie offered.

Fifteen minutes until midnight and her shift's end. Her eyes burned, her back hurt, and she was fucking tired. It would be ever so nice to go into a booth and tell the white-coated doctor she hurt and hoped for some relief. Now she was going home instead. She thought of the woman who was raped by her father for ten years who can't get better from obesity surgery; the man whose brother had anal intercourse with him when the patient was six who now worries about being homosexual in the days of gay pride; the man who's complaining of losing his hair because of amphetamine abuse; the woman who won't hold her newborn baby; the wife who hated her husband for asking her to be kind to him; the woman who cried at everything; the man with the hand and head tremor that made him ashamed to go outside; the boy who heard voices telling him he was a shithead; the girl who knew she was being watched and writes in mirror writing; the woman who was afraid she'll be shot because she filed a sexual harassment suit on a policeman; the man who hated his father because he was weak from Parkinson's; the couples who were afraid to get married and the couples who were afraid to get divorced; the people who were lonely and yet don't trust anyone; the people who came from somewhere else and couldn't decide what customs to keep from before and what ways to adopt now; the people who couldn't decide anything, and those who could leave nothing to chance but feel they control all hideous things. On and on came the heart attack fears; three-hour seizures that weren't from brain damage but from fear; getting old and retiring fears; ways to keep people close and yet keep away.

Somehow her tolerance threshold had been reached that night.

Under the blackened sky, driving the long freeway home, she knew it was time to specialize, go beyond general medicine. She had to move on and not be one of the permanent staff of the walk-in clinic. She had to walk out and on.

This had been the place to get help. In daily shootings, in the riots and looting, in the cyclical burning of the hills, and finally, in the endless quakes of the earth, the heart of the city had held. South and a little right of the downtown, the brains, the huge white hospital, the heart, had been there to help and heal and care for the home of the soul. Yet in ploys and political machinations, it was threatened with closure by money-minded administrators who never needed refuge, never had pus or tuberculosis or gangrene or suicidal depression. There was a 6.7 heart attack earthquake in 1994 with the threat of closure and all the pride of doing good was replaced with the recriminations of spending money. Concentration was on survival, but now it was for the place itself, not its patients. Mr. Leon need not worry about it anymore, but creeping forward in metastatic numbers were the "for profit" hospitals, and delays in care, deals, and death were the ideal. "Purification" was an old dirge sounded many times in this century. Now it was the immigrants, the sick, and the poor who had to go away. She felt like an "other," old enough to remember caring in a modern era of medieval motives now called "rightsizing," "reengineering," "capitation," and "managed care." How do you move on?

What specialty would she choose?

CHAPTER 29

Skin Deep

THE IMAGE CAME to me today after I shaved my legs in the bath and studied all the spider veins, which were trying to spin webs on my calves. Sliding my hand over my body, I touched my fecund skin, always making some sort of experiment with acne to abscesses to moles and warts, now gave me dilated capillary veins, color variations, and wrinkles tracing lost frowns and smiles. My skin had always been busy since I was a teenager.

When I helped my mother bathe and dress, I saw her drawn breasts, pouting belly, and wasting shanks, but her back had been so smooth and clear of moles, scars, senile keratoses, and freckles. No red little hemangiomas or scars from cystic acne, only a long curved plane of back, hunched from age but with pure even skin. It had been sheltered from the sun and never exposed to field work like the Chicanos I'd treated in the migrant camps, and yet my mother's back had also gotten bent over from life and unrealized wants, or so she said. She was so unexposed to poverty or slavery, so lucky in that sense, and yet so timid and frail at eighty-five. I remember though she could still hunch over a piano and play made-up songs, her little hands moving gracefully, coming out furtively from under her frame.

The last time I saw my father, we sat on a wooden bench together and talked about education. I told you that it was in Detroit. His hands paced the brim of his hat, a proper Robert Mitchum hat, rotating it to each side of his crossed legs. My father's hands were full of interlocking distended veins and brown age spots that come overnight and stay in old age.

My cats have pale skin covered with soft, multicolored fur.

All my sweet babies had the skin of smooth lives. The plump cheeks, moist lips, feathery heads, arms attached with folds of fat at the shoulder and at the wrist, legs like rolls stuck to the doughy full thorax and rotund belly. Baby bodies are fat with potential and newness that is worshiped by most dreaming parents.

My girls sat in the bathwater and helped soap themselves thoroughly and pleasantly, enjoying the ease of the process and washing toy whales and fish accompanying them. My boys squirted the soap from their hands and let me wash them while they were busy sinking ships and watching them pop up again.

Then they disappeared into their rightful skin privacies and needs to monitor breasts and faint mustaches.

Tattoos are acceptable now, and they are also taboo. Little crying daggers, crosses, concentration camp numbers. All sorts of additions to the skin's own creations.

For me, all is cover up now, cover up the spoils of age and the sun's singeing, wear anti-aging alchemies and maybe succumb to being skinned alive by plastic surgeons.

I remember my mother saying, "I can't believe how I look in the mirror. I feel so young inside." I am called "ma'am" now but I still use that sliding scale of memory to child and young adult with great ease. That is not only skin deep.

Bombarding my consciousness is our little family's vulnerability. Dead grandparents of my children, divorced parents of my children, separation of days, interests, ills, and ideals of my children. Me, alone and not lonely enough to seek others.

My father died first. I heard about it from a clerk when I called the hospital to ask to talk to him—"he's dead"—there wasn't even a sorry.

That last six months of her life two years later, my mother had constipation, the bane of the old. Holding on to anything and not giving forth.

We were in the downstairs bathroom of the retirement home, which was surrounded by the pink wallpaper and beige artificial marble. She was sitting on the toilet, and I leaned against the sink. "Wipe again,"

I said, and repeating myself in a more patient tone, "Try again. It's almost clear."

"We'll be out of toilet paper soon," she commented with learned parsimony.

"I'll get some more if we need it," I rebuffed and looked down to open the cupboard under the sink. It had three rolls tightly sealed in crinkly paper.

She showed me her last wipe, and there was still brown on it. "A few more times and you'll have it."

She looked at me with hate. She tried again. The room smelled, and I reached over and flushed the toilet with her still sitting on it. She jumped and looked at me again startled and angry.

"I'm sorry. Did I scare you? I thought we should flush." I knew she and I were both angry. She didn't want me to control her and I didn't want to, but I had lost patience. I wanted to cry. My back hurt. What kind of a daughter would be so mean?

She showed me another fold of toilet paper. It had only a tiny bit of brown. I said, "Okay," and smiled, helped her tuck in her blouse, and watched her wash those small tapered hands with a dollop of soap. Then we went to lunch.

Weeks later, she went to the emergency room for the impaction. There is so much to remember and forget. My oldest daughter was there to help me and tell her brother to carry his grandmother to the car and my daughter along with her siblings will be there when it is my turn for compiled shit and death.

Whenever my hemorrhoidal tags give me a pain in the butt of an unclean wipe and I have to try again and again to get myself clean, I think of her, her stiletto stares and her hate and my hate. Shit. Both hates hiding the pain of losing her.

There is a gray-speckled dove in my wild lemon tree. She sits on her twig nest in the fork of the center branches within green leaves forming the sphere of the tree. I caught her eye, and she moved slightly, not hating, not quite fearing, but wary. I left her and went inside. She makes me think of my mother and hope.

FRITZ WOLF

CHAPTER 30

Gains and Losses

I AM BACK HOME in America. I've walked by the Carmel Hotel in Santa Monica where Thomas Mann stayed and I've sought out Billy Wilder's movies. A whole colony of Germans came to live in Los Angeles before I was born.

Now when I walk on the sloping streets and look into houses, there are heads sitting at tables watching television and eating or dim lights signaling emptiness or cars parked in driveways and people hidden. They are thinking of eating and money, not survival and art. The neighborhood gives off an aura of sunny safety at day and nocturnes at night.

I remember the crisp nights with white lights dazzling the dark, while Christmas trees filled windows otherwise closed by thick drapes; hot Santa Ana wind nights that carried voices laughing and yelling in the lit pool that splashed joy in the air; and the egg and shaving cream fights on Halloween between boys wearing black turtle necks and knitted caps sneaking around bushes. The little people carried cloth pumpkins and stood still at doorways quite unaware that they were elaborate dinosaurs, ballerinas, or cape crusaders. The football games in the street and the walks and talks and giggles. Curb sitting and dressing Snoopy dolls or Barbies and dogs way off barking greetings. Our walks with hands held and dreams sparkling like Fourth of July nights rimming Santa Monica Bay with fireworks above city lights.

Time settled these dusty thoughts but wind on balmy nights stirs them and lets them float around me again. Puffer bellies were what we called the tiny parachute seeds from dandelion plants, and I see them now each delivering to my mind old memories to plant anew in this present.

I see the long low valley of green, spotted with dandelions, and to the left side, the chunk of rock the fairy tale castle Neuschwanstein crowns. My father brought me there once, and I brought my children there, and then here. I have a watercolor of the castle on my wall. Dream castle and California suburbia, both places to live.

Over and over, the past is rewritten. This century we had Hitler, Stalin, and Mao. Who feels this horror? This capacity to slaughter without remorse? We carry on in our good German, good American, good somebody, good god, ways and try to forget we are them.

It is late and all over, descendants try to sleep and lay down confused heads and hearts, unable to resolve such capacities of love and hate, creation and destruction, aloneness and togetherness, self and state, pride and shame, God and you, life and death. The descendants toss and turn in pettiness and vengeance, pulling covers of penance over guilt and cruelty. They sleep and try anew tomorrow, if they have tomorrow.

Death steals around the sloping streets too and settles in cubbyholes and corners for forlorn leaves, as it settled down with crazy Ludwig II into the lake waters by the blue grotto he built near his castle.

I wonder how they rest, my people. I felt them flying, circling, when they first died but now they seem to precipitate on parts of real soil and come in little thoughts, not full-bodied ideas anymore.

Auf Wiedersehen, meine lieblichen. I speak English. Goodbye. Hello. We laud our consciousness, a superiority of awareness, but think clearly for the moment. Our consciousness is limited. I cannot get beyond the past and some of the present; I distort the past and cannot integrate the conscious with the unconscious as I write to you in the present. I am teased with a puny perspective of awakened, alert, conscious, but out there in the stars of thought, I am forbidden. I must pretend, make up or lose you. Now I become.

Listen to three of me. Voices I've taken in. These creations—Jean, Frank, and Tom—will speak their stories for the hidden German in America as the century ends.

BOOK II
Assimilation

CHAPTER 31

Stages of No

The children cry to let their wishes be known and then point and then begin to verbally express what they want and what they don't want by saying NO at about the age of two, the so-called terrible twos. That power determines the sense of self being honored. Then YES comes again.

S HE WATCHED AND listened. The patient looked around from her chosen chair and began by saying, "I just wanted to kill myself honestly. I'm so humiliated." She shimmied farther into the chair, put her multi-buckled purse and diaper bag down, and wiped some drool from the baby she had dressed in yellow. The baby looked up at her mother and smiled.

"Remember I told you on the phone, Dr. Volk? In their minds it was no problem. What a rotten thing to do! I should kill myself. That would show them."

As a therapist, she could intercede and counter that thought. But as a psychiatrist, having heard this story many times, she said nothing to the bait to reassure this patient.

The patient waited, looked at Jean expectantly, fussed with the baby's bib while she kissed her, and looked at Jean again.

"Why did they do this? I worked hard to have my career and still care for my baby this last year. I thought all this shit was over in this day and age. I mean it's the fucking 1990s, almost the twenty-first century, but I seem to have less credibility now than ever before."

Jean remained quiet.

Left to her own devises, the distressed woman bent over the baby, fussed in her purse for something, and asked, "What else can I do?"

"Good question. What else can you do?" Jean reflected back. Suicide was something she told patients was always an option, but what else was there?

The woman gently fingered the fine hair on top of the baby's head, repeatedly stroking a long lock, and the baby pushed up against her. "Well, I'm glad that my baby is all right. It would have been too much otherwise." She smiled. "My husband says I should sue and I could retire on the award. But how could I? I've worked there a long time. I mean how could they do this to me? The guy doesn't even know half of what I know."

She talked about the kind bosses and the arrogant bosses, the insecure yes-men, and the thwarted women. In Jean's own department, few women stayed long. Instead, they usually went into private practice and got away from the bull. It was easier than saying no to the men who determined roles and didn't promote women. It was easier for those who could get free, not to compromise and just leave.

At least, Jean had some autonomy in her own office, so she chose the compromise after her residency; it gave her security for the kids' college money. LA County and this university were tolerant of someone who didn't pester them and did the job. Quietly ignored, she enjoyed her practice and teaching; only periodically did she feel stymied as far as influence on policy.

What disparities! She knew at least one doctor who remains at the hospital even though he had been implicated in examining teenage boys "inappropriately." His family had promised a large donation to the university, and he insisted that he did nothing wrong.

The patient deliberated, "I can't go back there, but I need my job. Should I accept this?" It was as though Jean heard herself talking, and her ire rose. She could feel an urgency to persuade the patient to sue. She contained it. Her job was not to tell the patient what to do, but to let the patient find out what the patient really wanted. She began gathering more information and asked about the patient's childhood.

"Is it always necessary to talk about your past? I want to deal with the present." She put a pacifier in the baby's mouth.

"Well, the past is relevant to find out what patterns you formed and how you dealt with stresses early on. However, we can look at today as well, to find those patterns," Jean said calmly.

Immediately, the patient sat her baby on a pink blanket on the floor with some plastic colored rings, telling her to play, and started to talk about her parents and her younger brother, who was always getting attention from her mother while her father was always off on business trips.

The interview became therapeutic after the patient expressed more frustration and was able to see the obvious parallel with her brother. After the rest of her history was touched on, vegetative signs were pursued. Had she lost her appetite? Did she lose weight? How disturbed was her sleep? Did she have trouble concentrating? Headaches? Suicidal thoughts? How early in her life? How severe? How long?

"How often does this have to happen in my life? It isn't fair. I didn't cause this. I mean I didn't find these bastards, did I?"

This late-afternoon patient was the distressed Mrs. Lindsey Laurence. She didn't know how to say directly "No, I object to you, powers that be. I will not accept this."

She was a well-dressed woman in her thirties who attended to her child and rocked back and forth in agitation. She explained that she sought help only at her husband's insistence, and when asked if there were any particular stresses at the home that might also influence the sleep problems other than having a young baby, the woman started crying and explained her anger every night at being passed over for a promotion again. The man who got the promotion had been her assistant and now was taking over her project. Her husband didn't understand her disappointment with her bosses.

Mrs. Laurence was short and full-figured with big glasses encircling her red eyes. She wore an immaculately tailored suit and crossed her legs at the ankle. For some reason, which Jean filed away to look at later, the properness of the position reminded her of a school girl wearing lace-trimmed anklets.

"He tells me, 'Shirley, it's an outrage. You should sue'," she lamented while sobbing and then added, "That's Lindsey, my husband's always up for a fight. I can't do it." She looked at Jean for confirmation. It was as though uttering any words that had to do with fighting her bosses caused her greater pain than what they did to her. "I'm humiliated. How could they do this? I got nothing but positive performance reviews. My supervisor was always praising me. Then they say that it's better this way because I'm really too good at personal relations, not administrative work, but I've run the program for six years."

Before Jean would go further into doing and undoing and repetition compulsion, she knew it was best to understand the type and degree of blame the patient accepted. This patient had posed the question of her selecting certain types of people. Everyone accepted blame somewhere. They worked until the end of the hour, and the patient wanted to come back.

"I have to decide what to do, right, Dr. Volk? My priest, he tells me to accept the change and move on. He's known me since I was a kid. He knows how hard I work. He says concentrate on the baby. Is he right? Just accept this? I have to do something, and coming here will help me decide what to do, right, Doctor?" The patient stood up, hooked her baby to her hip, and nodded. "I have nine more sessions left and one month vacation. I'll see you next week and decide then."

Here was a woman who asked everyone's advice and was immobilized by their conflicting opinions. She was articulate, attentive, groomed, and involved appropriately with her nine-month-old baby. Struggling over the insult to herself, she sought resolution through many support systems. What were her own views and rights? Jean wrote up a history and detailed Shirley Laurence's mental status, summarized in the assessment. She concluded this person didn't fit into the borderline or hysterical personality that many women complainers got labeled. How could she even be thought of as an adjustment disorder with depressed mood? Was her presentation a disorder?

Her alternatives thoughts of killing herself or quitting her job and suing did not include the idea of facing the powers that be and negotiating the best deal for her. That would be the real goal. She would learn.

Driving home, Jean concluded it was "same old, same old": run or hide and suffer. The patient's history conjured up her own stepfather who told that stupid story about her. She would cringe, but he would proceed. "I sat her there in front of me and held her while she cried. I told her mother to go to bed and that once and for all she was going to stop protesting. No little kraut kid was going to get the best of me. She was amazing; it took the whole frigging night. I held her upright, straight in front of me. Oh sure, she would cry or nod off, but if the truth be told, it wasn't until the dawn the next morning that her mother came and got her and she went to sleep. After that, she modified her behavior and immediately went quiet when I held her or put her in her bed."

She was nine months old when that happened, and when she graduated from college with a major in chemistry and a minor in history and philosophy, she finally told her father, the only father she had known, stepfather in reality, to stop telling the story. "I didn't know that bothered you, Jean" was all he said and then started talking to her mother about getting the car to drive to dinner. He never let her use his last name, Perisano. It seemed she'd never been good enough.

Her biological father had died at the beginning of the war. That was the phrase used then and now. He had fought for the United States of America even though he had been born in Germany before the First World War and came over as a teenager all by himself and had sent for her mother later.

After she asked her stepfather to stop, she almost felt obligated to tell the story herself. Her adherence to what she remembered and what she thought were the facts of her life constrained her and muffled an already thwarted creativity. When she painted, it had to be gray clouds and gray water with only traces of the warm tanned sand. She could feel that granular massage as she lay in its heat, but she could not let anyone know that sensuality. The truth was in the gray reality of the day. She had trouble with piano lessons and gave up her exercises with Bach and could only play dark but simple three-key minor chords when she was alone. When she wrote, she wrote carefully and never showed the sloppy spillings of her urges.

She kept records for accuracy, the ones she could not let pride distort. There were photos of her distasteful serious face and scraps of her poor spelling tests, along with her citizenship marks, in her closet at her parent's home. She saved any letters she received, including a few Valentines from grade school when everyone gave everyone little silly cartoon figures with hearts sprinkled about, and one had said, "You're a funny-looking valentine." She kept the typed notes from her mother, which her mother justified for "clearer correspondence" than the large German script she brought with her from her first home. She had the Thompson Construction stationary her stepfather wrote for his "Happy

Birthday from your father" note every year. She kept her first saving account book and her yearbooks. She threw away anything that was too messy, and in all senses, she colored within the lines.

Ever since that first Memorial Day weekend when she had stayed home to clean her closet, she came across some of her writings in junior high and high school, and they nauseated her in their naiveté and prosaic prattle. She kept only school records in chronological order.

A picture of Mary O'Brien and her standing stiffly by the big 1930s porch of her parents' house, which they bought in the 1950s, always unfroze a different memory, a free girl. Down the block from her house, after school, she and Mary played wild mustangs. Her throat and chest ached with the cold air rushing in and out in puffs of joy as she galloped along the sidewalk and through the alleys. Sometimes, she attacked and killed Mary when she played a rattler; then, it was Mary's turn to kill.

Running, celebrating her legs, turned into covering them wearing a full skirt with a leashed poodle appliqué on the front and pockets for gum on the sides. She wore that every Thursday to school for her junior high girls' club.

She was tall and her legs grew long, and the last year she played real basketball was the year she played in the backyard and peed in her pants rather than leave a one-on-one game with Peter, a college student next door.

She always hated dodge ball with its big hard smooth brown balls trying to hit and hurt. Why was that a child's game? But the textured orange skin of the basketball, which she could push into the air, was her favorite. She did not notice how she could declare herself so openly when she dribbled down the court at twelve and slipped back to dodge any attention she might get, derogatory or not, at thirteen. That, of course, was the reason she would not kiss Walter then. He had wanted to target her, and so she must say no and not be hit.

Grade school and dodge ball, and junior high and dodge pimples, and high school and dodge being labeled a brain, and college and dodge getting fucked over instead of fucked.

Her stepfather made her set the table each night, and if she set it without the forks handles being at the same distance from the table's edge as the knife, he would fold his newspaper in half and sweep everything into a pile at the center of the table. If something fell and broke, she would have to replace it with her own money. Afterwards, she would have to eat all the dinner he served her on her plate, and if she would hesitate, he would make her eat all the leftovers from everyone else's plate. Her mother made spaghetti with Campbell's tomato soup for the sauce.

Both teenage brothers smirked in petrified pain and gratefulness it wasn't they who had to eat it all. They would only get beatings on Sundays with the brown leather belt he wore. If her mother objected, he would yell at her and say, "You Prussian bitch, shut the fuck up. I'm in charge, you hear?" Sometimes she would quietly say she's not Prussian, that she and her parents were from Bavaria, as if that would support her protest against the beatings. He would say, "A Kraut is a Kraut." She would stand and watch. He was Italian, but three generations away from Italy.

Later, he came into her bedroom and sat on the edge of her bed. He had that sweet sick smell of alcohol and cigarettes, which would coat her face as he reached to kiss her good night. "You know that you have to listen carefully to get anywhere in this world, right, honey?"

An hour or so later, her mother came in and made sure she didn't cough or cry too loud to wake up her father who by then had fallen asleep in the soft curves of the pillows of the long blue couch in the living room. Her mother believed in letting sleeping dragons sleep. Did he come in again later?

She heard kids say, "When I got A's they said nothing, but if I got a B, they asked what happened?" How different for her. She longed to keep her A's hidden as they were like Hester's mark for a brainy girl. "You are to get a degree in science and teach. That will make you secure. You know you're not beautiful. Who's going to marry you? I can't pay for you after you're eighteen," he would say and she would nod.

When he wasn't there, her brothers would scream out to her, "Be prepared. That's the Boy Scouts' marching song. Be prepared, as through life you go along. Don't solicit for your sister—that's not nice—unless you get a good percentage of the price." They'd throw some spit wads at her and run off when her mother would finally come up from the basement after washing their dirty laundry.

"Be cautious when sitting on a man's lap. All men can fit into you. Don't let them try." That was all her mother could say about men and about menses. "If it had been something good, I would have lost it a long time ago."

So she would sit in her room and talk on the phone and discover other girls liked the boys she liked after she liked them, and they would go out with them and she would sit in her room and talk on the phone. Two boys liked her while she was in high school. One was husky and black-haired and was kind to her. Still she reared away from him because no one thought he was cute. His name was Walter. They were lab partners. He and Mr. Brand, the inorganic chemistry teacher, told her she was smart enough to be a doctor. The other was a tall boy who was trapped in the ectomorphic body of the nerd but thought himself quite wonderful. His name was Warren.

She would study Warren carefully in all the classes they had together. He was the prototype of the unabashed male ego, the one that can stand in front of the mirror like some weird Opus the Penguin and think himself Hermes. He got a look of lip-licking satisfaction when he answered questions asked by the thin-haired, waistless math teacher, who afterwards would let him copy all the homework problems on her newly washed blackboard.

The white chalk was like a magic wand as he pressed it against the black slate and produced fine spheres and angles with the pleasant curves of 6s and 8s or the uprightness of the 1s and 7s. He not only knew what he was doing, but also knew he knew. She would get A's on the exams too, but he had the glory all to himself.

He was a phenomenon to her. So confident, he stood like the Colossus of Rhodes she found in a book her senior year, without of course the great thighs that held the harbor between them.

There was one thing that really bothered her, and that was when he saw her. He would tilt his head and scoop his forelock back with his thumb and index finger. It would stay for a moment while his head was askew, and he smiled and then the hair would slide down over his forehead again so he looked like some well-groomed little Dutch boy. She hated him and his artsy-fartsy appreciation of himself.

There was a lean but not very tall boy in college. His name was Philip. He wrote for the college newspaper and tried for a Hopwood Award while she distilled solutions and precipitated spiked crystals no one knew about. She watched him too, and when he wasn't fucking long-black-haired stubby girls, he took a moment and penetrated her for her initiation into a mutual disregard for her. He played Wagner over and over again and said his grandparents were from Tennessee. His sexual prowess was in getting in and out without really doing anything else before or after. She wondered if he dressed in military uniforms in secret like other men dressed in silk panties.

Her brothers had gone on about life a little like their mother and stepfather. One finished high school on beer and college on pot, got drafted for Korea, and, after he turned thirty or so, played the piano off and on at a steak house in Windsor, Ontario, across the river from where he grew up. During the day, he worked at the automobile club giving out maps, and he never told anyone about his DUI when he was seventeen or about the war. He had a sweet girlfriend who went to night classes in accounting.

The other brother got sentenced for vandalism. He was in his first year at college just twenty, in the ROTC, and registered for the draft. He and a friend from the dorm, drunk and defiant, decided to take over a restaurant in protest over his buddy getting drafted. His buddy didn't have connections to get a deferment. He wrote her sometimes about how all the guards were like little Hitlers. His letters filled up increasingly with his research on the Nazis and his hopes to take LSD when he got out to look for the meaning to life like an urban Carlos Castaneda. Later, both he and his buddy were sent to Vietnam. After a while, her younger brother got out of the service and looked around the world with a pale interest that faded further into going to school to teach and paint.

When they were both in their twenties and she was just twelve, each had written her letters while they had been in the service, and she had so treasured them that she had requested that they continue instead of calling on the telephone. They wrote of the color of bombs exploding and napalm flashing through green foliage. She only understood the horrific beauty of their description, and they never mentioned the bodies of birds and children.

She wrote asking questions about being in jail and what regimentation meant, and they got into long discussions about their German heritage, their Italian stepfather's way of the world, army life, and the comfort of music. They were being sentenced for thinking differently, protesting rules, being young men, and she, for being the daughter of a covert fascist.

Korea, the big news in the lab about the Israeli conflict and call up for further drafts, and then Vietnam were in her consciousness while

World War II was in her unconscious and World War I was in her legacies.

She understood her brothers' pacifism and their trotting along through life. That was their secret to survival. Yet there was no way she was going to marry into a set role. She had to take care of herself and not have rules laid down like the Gestapo or the SS Italian, which is what they called their stepfather. Her stepfather did what he thought was right for him. Her mother did what she was told. Those were facts. They both wound up in Detroit when it was the image of smoke stakes for war and might. They lived in the times of the automobile factories, bread lines, Rosie the Riveter, and Marilyn Monroe worship.

Although it was rare for girls, Jean chose differently. She fell into the grind of premed, precipitating crystals in organic chemistry with five-hour lab experiments three times a week, limping along through physics, looking at human embryology slides, counting fruit flies for genetics, generally preparing for medical school. She got through college and, without knowing again how rare it was in the '60s, got accepted to medical school, to find out more secrets. She did not have to go home because of all her work; she did not have to go home and have him tell her how to study or what to wear.

Instead, she sat years later on this faculty hot seat of disdain and disrespect among her outward peers, the Dr. Albrecht dwarf of medicine. Placed there in another conference, listening to the Siegfried masters; she watched as they flailed about slaying manmade dragons and lauding their CVs.

She was emancipated, out and free now, but still wary and could stay hidden without harm to herself, always conjuring that film of the child climbing out of muck who had hidden in the latrine when the Nazis were searching for Jews.

She remembered talking once in a jammed examining room to a tiny man made of one giant head and maybe two feet of body. He was wedged into one corner of a wheelchair seat, and his head seemed to wobble around on his legless torso with sprouts for little arms coming forth. His fingers moved like sea anemones' tendrils, fine and almost translucently pink. He had a beard and talked like a grown man. His Adam's apple moved up and down like a yoyo trained to work to words. He was a dwarf crippled and stunted, probably from thalidomide given to a distraught pregnant woman, his long-gone mother. Jean tried to put together his outward paradoxes while looking in his alert brown eyes.

He in turn looked at her and could not see her inward paradoxes. He was there only for his headache, the biggest part of him.

That was when she worked in Emergency Rooms. She saw giants too. Four-hundred-pound people who dressed like they were men or women but were more like huge clothed liberty bells created in the celebration of fat and food. She wrote her brothers these stories, and they wrote back to her.

As she got older, she wrote her brothers, and their correspondences reminded her of Jane Austen's characters writing letters to each other during the times when a brother meant something and a sister meant something. When not writing, the rest of the time she and her brothers worked at the daily tasks of living.

She wondered why her brothers could write her so lovingly and feel so little motivation to get power and authority, while she felt excluded from it by virtue of her being a good girl and sought some sort of redemption in the label of "good." She would write and ask, and they would write back. They couldn't stand to be like their stepfather, so they willingly and knowingly opted out. It didn't make a lot of sense, but they went on with their lives anyway. She, always trying to rein herself in but wanting to run, while they, moseying along, nibbled at what pleased them.

Years went by and they were middle-aged. One rainy morning, they all sat down to write each other. They still avoided e-mail and preferred paper and pen, even if it was just words written using a ballpoint pen. Loves, marriages, divorces, children, accidents, betrayals recorded, and little bank accounts of money and success, and life had a consistency of water running downstream, constant in direction, eroding but pleasant in sound and sight. The greatest loss was her oldest brother's grandson, dead in the Gulf War.

She married, took her residency in psychiatry, and discovered her mistakes. Her own children formed their own brooks and streams and soon became rivers of power and turmoil and fecundity, and she was left again to her correspondence. She and their father had divorced, and she saw him, the ex-husband everyone seem to have, periodically as his hair fell away replaced by pounds. She had kept the girls away from their grandfather and, inadvertently, from their grandmother who was usually not courageous enough to fly west. Her stepfather didn't come home one day in the '70s and no one seemed to care. Her mother was gone, gone too soon, eight years later.

There were other men, and one of them she thought of daily. When she was alone and he left for his own life, then she could flow and slide her mind over him and love him. She wanted to touch tongues. There was paradox and pain in not experiencing him in reality, but then he would trap her with the key of his penis, locking and closing her to anyone else, including herself. The trap door between her legs must be closed. Freedom and loneliness were the banners flying in her reality, no matter how it hurt. When starved longing urged her to come down the mountain and surrender, it was countered. She'd be damned first.

She worked on as her face began to carve out her story. Then there was the day at work when the chairman of the department asked her to meet with this researcher who was involved with a project on correlating brain chemistry with clinical syndromes. She had been offered up, she knew, as one of the clinicians who would do the scut work for the grant's execution. Late and great county hospitals crawled under the managed care of the universities and businessmen who wanted money, not human bodies, as the evidence of health.

The researcher drove a Lexus and had a son who was dyslexic. The minute she saw him, she popped up an engram that he was like Warren of high school notoriety. Medium height and somewhat good-looking with the mustache of intellect to fuss with while he talked. He would run his forefinger back and forth on the hairs, seemingly impressed with their appearance on his lip. Maybe he was getting some sort of enhancement to thought by stimulating them, or having a little masturbatory foreplay. Each time she saw him, she wondered about the motive but would use the behavior as a signal he was going to offer some idea for general discussion.

She disliked him. She despised him. She distrusted him. He would eat her ideas like a tapeworm that could smile. The proglottids, egg sacks that spill out the rectum with the animal feces, were white sheets of paper for the grants he wrote. He was published and known, and she figured he really hadn't done anything unique since his mentor retired twelve years previously. Her children were far more original in all their endeavors.

Why didn't she say no to the chairman who was younger than she was but groomed as the replacement for the old chairman, who nevertheless called his successor a wimp behind his back and screamed at everyone to their face? Cloaked in the aura of vertupitude, tall gray men passed power to little sharp-nosed men to defy today's political correctness. Glass ceilings for women in academic medicine were solid and constantly polished with the efforts and ideas of women working for men. Researchers and secretaries seemed pleased doing their jobs.

Why didn't she say no instead of bitching? Why couldn't she speak up for herself and take her own reins and spit the bit out and gallop? It would soon be too late, and private practice would turn her into a managed care employee before she even tried it full-time. She would have the bit in her mouth out in practice full-time or at the university.

Her ideas floated in a slop of indecision. She ran for others, like the racing horses and dogs, who didn't care about cheering but ran because of the whip or the meat or the praise. Yet the attention of winning the race was too uncomfortable; she could not take the acceptance and the praise. She was suspicious. She had enough trouble taking money for her work. To hide, unsung and busy at what she liked was the best compromise. Only alone with a patient could she use herself to full advantage. Now she had another unasked-for assignment.

"Well, we want you to run the screening examine interviews on the patients," he said as he sat before his computer screen and inserted the discs, like wafers for absolution, into the machine's mouth.

Her heart rammed up against her ribs, wanting to get out and run away. She was going to do for someone else again. Why couldn't she say no?

Five more patients that afternoon: a seventeen-year-old boy who couldn't move his right arm but had no discernible physical problem, a twenty-four-year-old lung transplant patient who was having trouble with her mother accepting that the patient could now go out on her own, a fifty-one-year-old computer programmer who had had his second surgery for a malignant melanoma brain metastasis and was depressed, a forty-five-year-old teacher who had lost 150 pounds with gastric bypass surgery and hated her husband because he said now she was too attractive for him, and a thirty-six-year-old engineer who had been beaten up as a child by his father and was afraid of hurting his own two girls.

It was dark when Jean wrote the last of her notes, made her calls, and drove home. She reviewed the dynamics, strengths and weaknesses of each of the patients, put pieces of their puzzles out before her and tried to reassemble them with the strengths each patient had. She thought about the different dilemmas and then about what was in the refrigerator to eat.

She was hungry. The house was empty of children or a man, and she could eat what and when she wanted. What she wanted was what could cook up the fastest. The bittersweet dinner again.

Afterwards, she went upstairs. Lately, she had taken to welcoming her cats to sleep right next to her in the king-size bed. It didn't worry her that she was becoming a cat lady.

CHAPTER 32

The Stage of "I"

At about two and a half or three years old, the child is able to conceptualize his or her self as an "I" and begins to say "I want this" rather than "Me want this" and thus to become a subject, not an object.

FRANZ JOSEPH HAD been named after his grandfather on his father's side, who, of course, was named after the emperor of the Austro-Hungarian Empire. Franz has been born in Wisconsin. He usually told people his name was Frank. His grandparents, his father, and his sister had come over from Germany in the 1920s. His grandfather worked a small farm, and his grandmother stayed home to take care of four more of her children and then her grandchildren. Franz's father died in 1942 in an army airplane accident over Georgia. His mother received some sort of medal anyway, but it was unsettling to Franz that his father hadn't at least died in battle. Even though he was seven when it happened, he couldn't remember his father.

His mother stayed at his grandfather's farm. She said there wasn't room in her parents' house for her and her two daughters and son. She then went to work as a typing teacher and, in the summer, as a secretary in the research division of a brewery. His grandmother took care of his sisters and him until they went to school and then afterwards while they waited for their mother to come home.

Every morning at five and every night at five, Franz's grandfather milked the cows, and Franz was supposed to help. If a cow rolled over on one of the barn cats at night, his grandfather kicked the stiff carcass out of the barn, and the pigs got it before Franz could get the courage to pick it up and take it to his grandmother. Only once was he able to rescue a little kitten so it could be buried. After that first summer, he couldn't remember the number of cats that died that way. He dreaded going to the barn in the morning. His grandfather thought he was a boy with an ill disposition.

Franz felt safest in the warm and worn kitchen of the wooden farmhouse. The table was covered with bang scars. In front of the stove and by the big bin of a sink, barren of the speckled linoleum, the floor's blackness was the designated place to stand to truss chicken or wash dishes. On hot days, Franz stuck his hands in the wooden ice box—now a valuable antique according to his ex-wife—and put his cold palms up to his forehead and cheeks. In the corners of the great "sideboard" whose plates displayed smiling faces to the room, he hid his favorite stones from an old quarry.

At night, when the cone of lampshade light from the kitchen ceiling came splaying down on the table, he and his grandmother went through some of the old writings she had from her days at school. She had saved them because oddly enough, she and his mother both liked poetry. His grandmother had been a broad-shouldered woman with hands that picked turnips and plucked chickens. His mother had been a woman whose hands held cigarette holders and fountain pens. Yet both their hands held these papers as they read aloud the likes of Hölderlin, Schiller, and Rilke and debated the translations. His grandmother would never allow him to learn the rough language her hands resembled. The hidden meaning in the original language was revealed only through what his grandmother wanted him to know. While he and his grandmother read, his sisters played with the big dog that his grandfather let in the house on cold nights, and were happy with the stories in English.

Franz was attracted to girls who knew poetry. He thought they were delicate, their hands fingered lace and turned onion thin papers. Shelley and Byron pleased them. His ex-wife was one of those poetic types, slight, black hair in a bun, and a "widow's peak" pointing to her frowning face.

It was she who found out that there had been another Franz before him, a brother who had died before he was born. She had asked his mother how she had decided on three children. His mother had said she had four.

Frank had been only listening in between reading the newspaper. This had been an obligatory visit according to his wife and she had been trying to make it interesting for herself. Facing his mother, she sat with her expectant belly dominating her life in the last few months of her pregnancy.

"What are you saying? I had a brother also named Franz? You weren't ever going to tell me?"

"Why would it matter to you? He was dead before you were born."

"He had the same name as me," Frank said slowly.

His mother answered as though it were a question. "I liked the name Franz. He was Franz Karl and you are Franz Joseph."

"So the great man had a double? Oh my, my." his wife exclaimed.

Lately, she seemed to resent everything about him, especially after his last series of papers were published. At first, it seemed she was jealous of his time away from her. But as he published more, he realized she was jealous of his success. She began to hate him and accused him of discriminating against nameless menopausal and depressed women. As their sons became teenagers, she ignored him, stayed up nights reading political science, and writing essays on the distortion of the human body because of pregnancy.

He never forgot his mother's cavalier explanation about his name. He was the son who came afterwards, the son who couldn't replace the first, the baby left to his own devises. Now he understood why he had been given over to his sisters and grandmother because of the death of the special son. She, his mother, was either in her bedroom with a headache or at the kitchen table tapping her empty cigarette holder on a coffee cup.

"What did he die of?" Frank asked.

"It was pneumonia. He got pneumonia. I couldn't help. There were no antibiotics, and sulfa didn't help. We tried mustard packs and steam. Quinine and cough medicine, and I would sit him up and tap his back up and down to loosen the phlegm like the doctor taught me, but he died anyway. He got hot, night after night, and cried and cried, and then he went to sleep and never woke up. I was pregnant with you when he died."

"How old was he?"

"Nineteen months and three days, and so smart. He had been saying 'Me wanna up' and smiling. It was hard for me to hold him on my lap because of you," his mother said and smoothed her belly and got up. "Anybody wants coffee?"

His mother had stayed on the farm until his grandparents had died, three weeks apart, grandfather first and then grandmother, after sixty-three years of marriage. Their children, her sisters-in-law and brothers-in-law, didn't want anything to do with the place. She sold everything quickly and moved to Chicago, to a downtown condominium complex, and lived there now on her pension and the money his sisters and he sent her monthly. She taught typing for computers at an adult education program at the high school near her until she was seventy-five, and then she quit.

About three years ago, Franz came to see her in Chicago during a meeting where he had presented a paper. She had seen an article in the newspaper with his name on it and tucked it under the pie plate she brought on the tray with the coffee.

"Thought you might like this for a scrapbook. Are you still keeping one?"

"It got thrown away when Amy and I split up," he said causally.

"I'm sorry," she said as she poured out the coffee from an old painted pot he'd seen on his grandparents' farm cupboard for years.

"No big deal, fifteen years have gone by," he said and rubbed his eyes.

"You know I was cleaning some storage boxes out and I found these suction cups. Would you like them?"

"What are they?"

"Your grandmother used them to remove the fevers," she said with an instructive tone. "She'd put them on the back and chest and try to suck away the illness."

The suction cups were half-moon-like glass attached to red rubber bulbs. She squeezed the bulb and then put the glass on her palm and it held like a kiss.

"I don't want them anymore. They're like a medical antique, you know. Your grandmother had them before she came to the United States, so they're probably over a hundred years old. That last night, we used them on Franz, but it didn't help," she trailed off, sipped from her cup, and then looked into the dark brown coffee as though it could evoke the past.

He looked at her and then at the little suction cups lined upright in the intact carrying case. That was all there was of his brother.

"You never did recover from his death, did you?" he stated rather than asked.

"I should have stopped after him."

He took the newspaper clipping when he left and crumpled it into his coat pocket. He knew he could never make up for her loss and didn't even try after that. He put the suction cups in their speckled black box up on a shelf in his office. Sometimes it was hard for him to remember he had a mother.

"I am a professor, a researcher, a noted writer, an authority on cognitive functioning and memory," he'd say in the shower, but in front of the mirror, he'd wonder who he could really be.

Although women at the office giggled about him the first few weeks after his divorce, he saw only a few socially and never ones from the office. Later, he was with his kids most of the time and took them permanently after Amy remarried and had another baby. They came to the lab and office with him, and he went to their basketball games. The boys, George who had finished law school and Matt who had finished college with a business major, moved north to Seattle and Portland at about the same time he began looking for a new place to live. No one needed the house. He felt they were both successful now, even Matt who'd had dyslexia but was computer literate and made for Internet life. How hard he'd tried to help them both, building desks in their rooms and playing catch with them like a good TV daddy. He was tired of the big house he'd maintained for the backyard and the half a basketball court he had paved. Both of his children called him on the phone about once a month now, and George's wife was expecting. They were doing well, but they wouldn't be staying in that house anymore for more than a few days to visit.

He met two real estate women who initially pursued him with a vengeance. Lucinda Leaven had copper hair and loved to go out to the "best restaurants." She skipped the entrée in favor of three desserts to sample. He let her have all three. She invited him everywhere, and he came for her laugh and her amazing ease at happiness. She introduced him as her doctor and took him to her place for coffee. She didn't

Of course, now, Franz was in California, and he appreciated the tan sand and dunes of the warmer landscape over the snowy one of his past. He ran his fingers over his mustache slowly, remembering when he'd grown a mustache to distract from his nose. It really didn't matter now. Bobby Johnson was in some iron lung of his past forever, having air sucked in and out of his lungs, lying on his back and looking into the mirror to see his vicious eyes tamed by a virus.

On his twelfth or thirteenth birthday, he'd been reading about the atomic bomb and Sheriff Whitehead came to the door. "Some cruel boy stoned the Hansen's red dog in the head." The sheriff pulled Franz outside by his right ear while his grandmother stood on the porch rubbing her hands in anguish. The sheriff looked down at him and interrogated him. "Why did you do that, stupid? Don't let me catch you using that confounded sling shot, Frankie, or you'll be locked up as soon as I get you." Every time Franz tried to deny it, the man's eyes would squint further and he'd say the same thing again. "Don't let me catch you, or I'll lock you up. Think you're such a smart boy? Just wait."

When he got into college, he never wanted to come back to the farm; and later when his grandparents knew he was already an assistant professor and published, they didn't really care, and he didn't see the point of going back. His grandfather had had to sell the cows and take nitroglycerine, and after he died, his grandmother forgot everything and looked around the farm for her husband of sixty-three years. Franz called her a few times and spoke to his mother. She complained.

Once Maria, as his mother called his grandmother, put a jacket on the scarecrow and told it to come inside. His mother locked the doors from the inside after that, and she wrote that his grandmother sat by the window in the kitchen looking out the window and singing "Du, Du, Du bist meine hertzen, Du, Du . . ." She called her a damn old woman with no mind of her own, screamed at her for singing day and night, and wondered when she would die because she couldn't stand taking care of anyone anymore. It took only three weeks and she was gone. He hadn't been able to get back in time because of the paper he was giving in San Francisco. His mother left a message with the department secretary on Friday. He got it on Monday.

His mother moved to Chicago then. His mother was still disease fearing, yet not superstitious enough to be considerate, very like Amy, his ex-wife. His mother was over eighty now. He should show more mercy. The wine quieted him and he got up from the black barrier the window had become to turn on a light or two. He wandered about the house and then went into the kitchen. He had a few messages but didn't want to call anyone back. He looked through his briefcase to prepare for work. Jean Volk's name was on his last series of notes. She was cold enough to be a psychiatrist; he wondered if she was smart. Probably was if she got through med school twenty, thirty years ago. She didn't go for a mail order clinical psychology degree whereby he'd seen bimbos interpret the world. Wonder why she chose psychiatry.

He fell asleep watching *Letterman* and, about four in the morning, woke up to an erection. He got out of bed and stood before the toilet until his penis relaxed, and he peed. He lay back on stiff pillows exhausted and awake.

CHAPTER 33

To Serve and Protect

TOM'S PARENTS, FREDRIC and Sarah Zeitman, were both blue-collar workers in Hamtramck, Michigan, for the first six and half years of Tom's life. After he heard one of their neighbors complaining about being stuck in demeaning blue-collar jobs, Tom always looked for their blue collars in the small closet of his parents' bedroom but never found them. By the time he realized the phrase had become figurative while he was growing up, his father had moved into a white-collar job as an inspector with the city and his mother had moved into a supervisor's job with the telephone company.

They looked to him for the answers on what to do with their savings and how they could help their only child get ahead with a college education so he could be independent.

His paternal grandparents, the Zeitmans—not a Polish name, but a German Jewish one—had come from Prussia, which bordered on Poland. When his father was three in 1913, he, his sister, and two older brothers had all made the journey to America, but both brothers died in the influenza epidemic of 1918 and 1919. Tom's father, raised by his older sister Mirabel because his parents worked, continued to speak Polish, German, and Yiddish and went to work at fourteen in the big tire factory outside of Detroit. Later, after marriage to Sarah and after Tom's birth, Fredric had read in the newspaper of the opening at the city for a clerk, and since he had been good at numbers, his father applied. He would always tell Tom that the smell of paper was better than that of rubber. It had a special meaning to him, which he compared with the great sayings of scholars like the wise men of Chelm. Tom couldn't remember those references of old but knew that paper smelled better than rubber.

Tom's mother had grown up on a farm, the eighth of ten children. The Greenbergs migrated to upstate New York from Hamburg when she was six and then on to Ohio. Although intent on growing things, they weren't used to farming. She had been diagnosed with rickets even though her parents said they had a cow for the kids' milk.

At ten, she was sent to live with an aunt in Ann Arbor, and after the aunt died, her uncle married again and Tom's mother was on her own at age sixteen. She took the bus to Detroit. Sarah's legs were always slightly curved to the outside, but no one ever called her bow-legged, at least not to her face. His father forbade that.

Sarah would tell Tom how she kept tract of all the calls she put through at the switchboard because of quota demands and would get certificates from the telephone company for her great efficiency. She always made her quota even when she wound up only giving out telephone numbers in "information" during the last years before she retired.

The year he started grade school, Tom remembered being the first one of the three of them to get home every day. He assured his mother that he would be a big boy and wait in his room for her to come home after work. The back door of their two-story frame house was always open for him. His parents explained to him they had wanted to save more money to pay for his college, and it was his job to be brave. They did not want him going to Hebrew school because it would cost money and, according to his farther, rabbis were as mean as nuns and what was it worth here in America where he must, and he was, to speak only English everywhere. There was whispering about the Holocaust, the discoveries of the camps, his parents' moaning interrupted when he entered the room. There were efforts to tie newspapers for the paper drives and evenings wrapping packages to send to cousins in Europe. Explanations only came later when he read about WWII but his parents dismissed his questions by saying it was the past, look to the future.

The walk from school was only four and a half blocks, and he would carry his books back and forth bound with a small strap made of leather his mother had made. The house would be quiet and cold when he first entered it that first September. He would take the clinkers out from the furnace and put new coal in to make it cozy and warm for his parents when they came home from their long bus rides down Hamilton. He greeted them with his homework done and dishes set for dinner.

He still had that faint scar on his eyelid from the cut a clinker made one day when he had fallen on the basement stairs carrying the clinker, a scarred shell of coal up to the garbage bin. He held an old rag to his eye and waited for his mother to come home two and a half hours later. His mother insisted that they go down to Receiving Hospital to have his vision checked even though he said he could clearly see she was crying.

The smell and the clamor of that first floor in the hospital with its octagonal black-and-white-tile-checked floor and brown wooden shelves full of bottles and packages wrapped in green cloth were amazing to him. There were old men with blood on their matted hair, wearing dirty shirts and lying on carts with shelves down below for their shoes. There were babies screaming while mothers paced up and down with them in their arms, and white-coated doctors and nurses in white dresses and white shoes, even in winter he marveled, moving everywhere it seemed. Later, he wouldn't watch the new 1990s TV program *ER* because he knew it was full of running people trying to help screaming people but it didn't have the vivid colors in blatant relief against the black and white and the smells of alcohol, acetone, vomit, and pee of that day.

His doctor was a carrot red-haired man who smiled at him and wiped Tom's eye and the laceration itself gently. It took five stitches, and the little black threads of silk were each tied in knots and ends that stood out against his pale skin and brown eyebrow like a Hebrew word in stitching. Later he came back with his mother to have them pulled out and could hardly see the scar. He decided then he was going to be a doctor. He didn't know about the medical school quotas for Jews.

When they moved to their own duplex on Dexter so the Zeitman grandparents could live above them, he could only think about being nearer to that chaotic healing place downtown.

He got fitted for "seeing far away" glasses, and although he could hit a baseball regularly at the school playground where the boys would go after their snacks and changed clothes, he usually stayed home even though the house had a new gas furnace so nothing had to be prepared. He read most of the time: comics in the newspaper, *Modern Library* books his parents gave him for his birthday, and the *World Book Encyclopedia*. A black-haired doctor told him that if he read with his glasses on, he wouldn't need reading glasses as early as other adults would. He didn't know what difference it made since he still had to wear glasses, but he did what he was told and told his mother and father to do the same when they read.

When they had been at the Dexter house for three years, a new family moved in next door. There seemed to be some uproar about it all, and he heard his mother talking to Mrs. Goldman across the fence, whose only son had been killed in the war, and she was saying they were moving because of the property values going down. That was 1954.

He met WP who was a year older than Tom. He was a "schwartza" as Tom's grandparents named him, and he had brown-black eyes set in clear white sclera and a big grin with teeth Tom thought were perfect. He was sitting on the cement-pillared porch of the same kind of brick house as Tom's, chipping off paint drops of the steps with a chisel.

Tom stood at the sidewalk and grass boundary right in front of the Negro family's house and looked at him.

"See, they paints and drips and I have to clean up behind them," WP called.

"Who did it?" Tom asked.

"My older uncle, Washington."

"I'm Tom. What's your name?"

"They call me WP."

"Those are letters. Your name is just letters?"

"Nope, stands for Wassermann Positive Jones, after my father. He was Wassermann Negative Jones, but my mama, she didn't want no bad attitudes and named me Positive, so I'd get along fine in the world." Tom would smile about that name years later when he knew the Wassermann test was for syphilis. WP was a positive man without the disease.

"My father's named Fredric. I'm Jerome Thomas Zeitman, after my dead grandfather Jerome Baum. My other grandfather didn't like Jerome so I'm called JT or Tom."

"JT and WP. You like the Tigers?"

"They're okay, but I like the Redwings better. I stay up doing my homework and watch the games on TV."

"Is there chess on TV? You play chess?"

"Chess?"

"Yeah, chess. My mama say that we got to be educated and her daddy, my grandpappy, taught me chess before he stroked from high blood. He learned it in New York at some park and brought his pieces and board with him here during the war. He worked at General Motors till the day he died at age fifty-eight and a half. I thought all white boys played chess, not hockey."

"Not all, but after I finished high school in a year, I'm going to college, and maybe then I'll learn or you gonna teach me?"

"Teach you? Sure, but I gotta finish this first?"

"You want my help?"

"I don't know. Mostly Jewish people, they don't do this kind of thing. Do they? I heard they was all burned up in the war. Not you though, huh?"

"We're Americans just like you. My parents have been blue-collar workers. Doesn't that count?"

"My daddy was blue-collar at Chrysler small parts division," WP carefully elaborated as though these words were special, "but he died of drink, liver got him doctors said, but my mama she got insurance savings and bought this house and she work as a house keeper for a lawyer on eight mile and nights she sews dresses she sells."

All summer and through the next fall, WP and JT sat in the backyard of one or the other and played chess. In WP's yard, they played on crates and an old metal table with a hole in the center for the long missing shade umbrella, and in JT's yard, they sat on a wooden picnic table Mr. Zeitman had made from planks he got at the lumberyard. In the winter, they played at the kitchen table of WP's house, which always had some exotic smells of cornbread, pork knuckles, and turnips or collard greens cooking in a big iron pot. After Tom's mother stopped crying over having a Negro in the house, they went in Tom's room lying on the floor, elbows dug in the rug, hands on their chins, arms propping up heads, and played out games in books borrowed from the library.

Sometimes, after they were done and JT wanted hot chocolate and WP wanted a coke, WP would stand at the hall arch and peek in at the great Detroit Red Wings coming out of the TV console and shake his head back and forth while smiling as Gordie Howe scored. He would always refuse to sit down.

No one ever used the living room in WP's house because it had dresses hanging everywhere, and the sewing machine was right in the center of the room.

By the time graduation came about, both of them had been on three dates with proper girls and had gotten some playing cards with different sexual positions from the Kama Sutra. WP got a job offer from his uncle to do house painting, and JT had applied to Wayne State University to go to college and had seen two dermatologists about his persistent acne. Tom washed his face, combed his hair, and showered at least twice a day while WP got kidded for liking to take a bath daily and had beautiful smooth skin with no effort.

They lost touch with each other when Tom's parents moved to Southfield and Tom got an apartment with a fellow student down on Warren in the Forest Arms.

Ten years later, as Tom was finishing his residency in internal medicine, Tom's parents died one after the other, first his father from colon cancer, then his mother from pancreatic cancer.

There had been no one to talk to about it all. They had gone to Mount Sinai when they were beyond anything but palliative treatment, and each had told the other and then Tom they didn't want to spend the money on hopeless radiation or chemotherapy and they didn't want to get sicker doing it. Tom always thought about how little the side effects were now when instituting such treatment and all the good medications available. Then the doctors kept the narcotics restricted so his parents wouldn't get addicted to them, and he watched his father turn yellow from liver mets and get confused and his mother help wash and change his bed when he was incontinent of a bright yellow stool and dark brown urine.

One morning, coughing up bright red blood while Tom was sitting with him on the weekend before his final boards, his father smiled, looked at the white Kleenex full of his blood, and said, "Good thing this is paper, not rubber. Blood won't scare you. Don't let this stop you, son. You're almost thirty, twelve years of training, don't stop. Keep going like I did and made it out of rubber into paper and you made it out of paper into respect and human service. Mazel tov."

They smiled at each other and ate real chicken soup Tom's mother had made from big green ceramic bowl Tom held in his lap. He fed one spoonful to his father and then one spoonful to himself. When he came back after two days of exams and a night on call, his father lay on the bed in a coma.

His mother refused to have him taken to the hospital. The room smelled of ammonia from the urine that had leaked out around the catheter and dried blood was caked on his teeth. His mother was washing his father's lips with a blue washcloth and talking to him in a soothing voice.

Two days later, after his mother and Tom had sat on the bed counting respirations, when they came to take his father's body away, his mother covered him with a crochet blanket she had made long ago. She said, "Goodbye, Fredric," and, wrapping her hands around her own shoulders, sat down on the big brown upholstered chair by the bed.

Hers had been the silent tumor, and by the time she admitted to pain, it was all over her belly. She died one night unexpectedly of a heart attack while up in the attic looking for some photographs she had mentioned to Tom. He had moved back with her and gotten a Plymouth to drive to and from the hospital for his fellowship, his thirteenth year at zilch pay, and was in the living room watching the Lions game that Monday. By the beginning of the second half, he looked around for her and then wondered what she was doing for such a long time.

He found her lying over a big box of photos and books as though she were taking a little nap before starting her search again. He knew she was dead before he ever touched her or felt her pulse; the silence had been breathless. There were fading pictures of the family left in Europe. Nobody was there anymore.

She was heavy as he held her and rocked her back and forth, saying, "It's okay, it's okay."

When he called for an ambulance, WP was driving and they looked at each other and smiled.

"Hey, bro, what's going down?" WP said.

"It's my mother. She died today, up in the attic."

"Mine, she's still makin' dresses. We'll share her, okay?"

Tom sat all those days on a worn chair in the smelly funeral home, and WP came with a cake, and except for three telephone operators and Mrs. Goldman who still lived on Dexter, they sat alone. WP came every sundown for the whole time.

His parents left Tom the house and the car and life insurance of $10,000. He gave WP the car and sold the house. He became staff at Harper's and then moved to LA in 1971, alone and pretty much broke after the last of his training. His hair was getting thinner and his face still had pockmarks and an occasional persistent pimple.

CHAPTER 34

The task of the boy is to give up competing with the father for the mother and identify with the father. The task of the girl is to also give up competing with the father for the mother, identify with the mother and then give up competing with the mother, or something to that fashion, according to the old-time religion of psychoanalysts.

J EAN GOT A request for a consultation the first thing Monday morning. She would have to read the research proposal afterwards. The "PI" line, which she always read as private investigator rather than principal investigator, was of course the great Frank K. Schlager, MD, PhD. What did he know of the muck she would find in each consultation?

What would be the problem? Grief over an amputation, suicide attempt, conversion, pseudo-seizures, depression, delusions? She only knew from the message the primary physician, a neurologist, had left that the patient was having difficulty talking and had lost twenty-five pounds in a few months and yet there was no neurological reason, no multiple sclerosis, no tumor, no AIDS. The patient was cleared medically but was starving.

She reviewed the chart and then went to the bedside. There was this woman in her thirties with bleached blond hair watching TV. Her cheekbones were taut and her shoulders stood out like small matching globes juggling her head.

Jean introduced herself and began the interview. She noticed how the patient responded, what kind of smile there was, how long the eyes made contact, where the patient's hands were and where they went pulling and arranging the hair in the back of her head, when her leg would begin shaking, and what she was talking about at the time.

She could talk. Initially, there were a few nods rather than one-word answers to the questions Jean carefully phrased to be answered yes or no, but then orchestrating a more open-ended question produced tears and words.

She'd been raped three months ago by two men her husband had brought home for dinner. As a child, she'd been molested from age seven through twelve by her father's best friend, every Saturday when her parents went to bowling. She couldn't talk. Now she wanted to scream at her husband but couldn't tell him. He had been on a business trip when it happened and still saw the men. She gagged when she thought of them, and she gagged when she thought of what they had done. She had never told anyone before. Her husband questioned her when she refused to let her daughter stay alone in the house with those men but shrugged his shoulders and went out with his buddies. The patient and Jean talked for over an hour, and then Jean told her she'd be back the next day.

There were a few days to work with the patient while she was being hydrated and monitored for anorexia and bulimia as a possible diagnosis before she went back up to Bakersfield.

Apart from her insight-oriented patients, her day went from that patient's history to worse with a patient who had terminal liver disease who attempted to hang himself with IV tubing, a patient who refused his cyclosporine knowing he would reject the transplanted lung if he didn't, and finally a visitor of a patient who was depressed because his wife was in a car accident and was paraplegic and couldn't have orgasms.

The last one was the most difficult because the husband flirted with her while complaining about his wife. She remained professional, wanting to scream too, and went to the patient as soon as she could. What do you tell medical students about these types of encounters?

As the day died, she walked slowly to her car. Her back was burning from fatigue, and her feet wished her to have a place to sit. She'd just talked with a teenage girl who had been abused by her older cousin. There were too many stories now about abuse. It was tiring, and nobody really cared anymore. Fifteen-month-olds with gonorrhea or two-month-olds with subdural hematomas from being thrown against walls, and all these women's endless stories that bring symptoms to medical doctors for the hope of exorcising their pain.

She was to have dinner with Richard Stone tonight, Richard who hung the tennis ball from the garage rafters so it would knock at the windshield to prevent him from driving his car too far into the garage's back wall. Richard who was sixty-one years old and still wanted to know whether she liked him in boxers or jockey shorts. She couldn't have cared less if he wore diapers. Richard who wanted her to spend her whole Saturday of sun watching war movies like *Platoon*. She was to meet him at a steak house where old people sang old songs. She liked that best about him. He liked that steak house, probably because he flirted with the waitress who had teased red hair. That was okay though because Jean could hear the music of the '30s and '40s played by a fat Hoagy Carmichael type with a toothpick, not a cigarette jerking around in between his lips.

Richard was an engineer, and in the 1980s and '90s, engineers were everywhere in Los Angeles except at work. She met him at a play when he sat next to her and began talking. They had the proverbial coffee date during which she drank tea and then, approving, started going out. He thought she was married at first because she wouldn't let him come to her house to pick her up. She said it was caution, but she also wanted to be able to drive away and not be stranded in his company.

It was pleasant that he was amorous and could get it up easily. But it was disgusting when he made vulgar talk like some stupid Prince Phillip about sucking and poking. Stroking turned her on, not babbling. She wondered if she was getting old or bored or too wary of the simplicity of men.

They had their dinner and house wine, listened to the piano until the eleven o'clock break, went to his condo (sorry, townhouse), and had sex; and afterwards, she found herself with her eyes open and the room too hot. He snored gently, evenly, contently, constantly. She got up and left.

It was cold out, and the air gave her a sense of herself again. It defined her in her skin, and she drove home listening to late-night classical music and the soft male voice of the announcer. She wondered what he looked like.

It would be eleven years since she had lived with a man, her ex-husband, and Richard on and off thereafter. She couldn't really think about moving in with someone or him moving in with her. Eleven years. Sex and then home alone. Freedom and loneliness were getting to be a permanent state.

Richard was impressed she was a physician. How funny. At work, she watched grand rounds audiences, and for years, the women all sat by themselves, what few there were. It was the alone generation for woman, especially if they were at all attractive as well as professional. She took the snide remarks, the defiance, the kidding, and couldn't be denied some advancement if only because she stuck it out. Sexual harassment was rampant news, but sexual containment was the hidden agenda.

She pulled into her driveway and got out of the car. Was she a bitter bitch? So be it. She liked the alliteration. She wasn't afraid of the labels anymore: bitch, nag, frigid, castrating, ambitious, the sin of sins. Go to sleep. "Tomorrow and tomorrow creeps in this petty pace."

Monday came, and she had to meet with Schlager after lunch. His office was a mess of stacked books and twin computers protruding from bookshelves of properly arranged journals.

He asked about the usual: schooling, interests, time constraints, married or divorced, and then got looser. "So who influenced you to become a physician?"

"I personally can't identify with either of my parents comfortably. My mother was a German house Frau and my stepfather an Italian tyrant. What a combination! You probably want to know why my name isn't Italian. He wouldn't adopt me, and Volk was my mother's married name from my biological father, rather common in parts of Germany." She smiled as she threw back his question during the interview. "I wonder, also, if this is relevant to whether you and I could work together."

He looked at her to reassess her. "Well, I meant to see if your parents were in science or your brothers or sisters were. You know, it took a lot for a woman to go to medical school then," he justified.

"No one but me in my family, and your influences?" she replied. It pleased her to see that she didn't really give a damn about this and could not be fired for not accepting this extra bullshit. She had really come a long way even if her CV showed only children for her honor society and raising them as papers published. She felt like she was finally able to speak up to the elitist sneering Jack Nicholson type who would have successfully demeaned her in the past for being old and unglamorous and smart.

He answered sincerely. No one had ever asked him about himself in a long time. It was unsettling but not unpleasant. "No, my mother worked in other things, and my father died when I was young."

"Since you suggest it had to be someone who influenced our careers, who was it then? For you, that is," she continued brazenly. Maybe he would let her off the hook and take some young grad student or a psychology clerk. Why should she have to do this?

He looked up to the ceiling while pondering her question. He didn't seem to be annoyed and responded, "I'm not sure how it happened. I guess I wanted to find out about things, and I was good at it. Making electric circuits and growing molds for science projects, stuff like that. Teachers loved it. Maybe they were the ones who influenced me the most, especially seventh grade Mrs. Haas."

"What did she do?" Jean prompted, pleased she was now the interviewer.

"It was about osmosis. She said if I couldn't explain it to the class, the class might as well be dismissed since I was her only hope." He smiled and then looked at her as though she had caught him in a forbidden reverie.

She stared at him, thinking multiple things at once. His brown eyes were warm, his hair was thinning, and he didn't seem so arrogant. She knew she would turn their interaction into a take-care-of-him relationship because she was grateful he was as benign as he was.

"I was a good kid, good citizenship marks all the time, attendance, never yelling or throwing spit balls, all that stuff, and so I read," he offered, smiling.

She wanted to protect herself, and she shot back, "I was the unnoticed kid. I had to wipe snot on my dress and rub it in because I didn't have a tissue or I had to hide in the john while I washed my dress because of period leaks and had to wait for it to dry next to the window. Still, Mr. Brand in tenth-grade chemistry helped when he had me breathe some alcohol to clear up my nose and told me I was a good scientist because I found all the unknowns in my test sample. It's too bad citizenship isn't rated in the workplace like it is in school. His kindness helped me more than all his lectures on valences."

CHAPTER 35

Cluster A are the personality types who are lost in the self and distrust interactions: schizoid, schizotypal, and paranoid. Cluster B are the personality disorders of a particular type intent on gratifying self with certain styles: hysterical, borderline, narcissistic, and antisocial. Cluster C are personality types who try to find ways to allay anxiety and please others: obsessive-compulsive, dependent.

SHE SAT AT the kitchen table writing a paper that would never be published. She'd never had a mentor and no one to tag her name with at the beginning to get published. She didn't even know how to do it all, and she really never forced herself to find out. She would go home and take care of the children, not sit and schmooze ideas. Hiding was better than showing yourself anyway. She'd tried a couple times in the past to get good ideas and some research proposals off the ground. They'd get approval, but she never had time to lobby for them and seek grants. Some of the clinical stuff she'd worked on got read, and sometimes she'd find her ideas lifted.

Now she wrote her ideas in a journal and left them there. She was too old to care about publishing and not confident enough to think the big white men would care about her observations.

She began: There is a capacity especially in woman, and particularly in mothers, to project as a component of nurture. Projection is the process by which the mother, in this case, takes her thoughts and puts them into the baby and in such a way explains such things as "why three-week-old baby is crying," for example. "The little sweetie wants me to hold her." "He has a little stomach gas." "She had a bad dream." "He was upset because of all the noise." "The kid is trying to irritate me." Later, she can read the baby's thoughts, but in the beginning, she projects and interprets, and she and the baby are further bonded. There is the smile and the eyes following as proof of the baby's attachment. The mother knows she is right. That capacity to understand and project into others continues the bonding and ensures survival.

Sometimes, the projection becomes a style of interacting and explaining others. It is carried out into other relationships that are very different, and the projection blinds the woman from a real appraisal of others.

Her mind drifts.

Mother was always explaining him: "He's only tired and doesn't mean it really." "He's got so much on his mind." "He yells out of frustration." "He feels like a prisoner in his life, and that's why he yells."

Mother, it is you and I who were prisoners. He is a tyrant. Is there really a core of something else there? Some misunderstood child who now tortures us? We project kindness on to him and hope he will direct it toward us. How long must I wait to see evidence of anything but selfishness? Mother help me.

"He's the only father you have. Try to be respectful."

She practiced her skill on her husband. "I know he loves me even though he can't tell me." "He is hurting." "He was jealous of his younger sisters." "He was all alone and no one cared." "If I love him and be patient, he'll come around."

When she lost patience, she remembered falling for the reprimand, called a nag and bitch, and saying nothing rather than being called those hateful names. It took her fifteen years to begin to call him the bitch. He didn't know what to do with that.

She looked back at her paper. Projection. The phone rang. It was her older brother.

"I heard from our brother today," he said in between crunching on some crackling food. "Wanted me to see some new car he got, a Japanese job. Did he call you too?"

"Wouldn't you know it, a car got you to call me. How are you?"

"I'm doing all right. Grandkids getting ready for Halloween. Fun stuff. The mothers like it too."

"What about you?"

"I'm doing all right, like I said. I miss having thirty kids in the classroom, but I'm happy. I wanted you to know I've been smitten by another teacher." He paused and then went on, "She's a junior high teacher and retired."

Jean paused for a moment and realized her brother was almost seventy and he kept up with the grade-school statistics. His wife had left him twenty years ago for no one else, only to be by herself.

"She's lied about her age and is really seventy-two, but you couldn't tell. How about dinner with her sometime? I'll get us all together."

She smiled and agreed.

"When are you going to retire?" he asked cavalierly.

As she had passed from *Miss* to *Ms.* to *Ma'am* now she had to hear that question. "You know, that question irritates the hell out of me, and I don't know why. How can I really think of relaxing? I've got to take care of me."

"Well, I don't know, but maybe you should before we're all down the drain." He laughed and snorted at the thought.

Her beeper went off there on the desk hidden in her pile of bills and books.

"Oh, call me later, please. I'm on call this weekend. Beeper went off. Please call me later, okay?"

She had watched how all the younger generations carried beepers for the fast-food contacts of their friends. Cell phones were debuting everywhere. She was of the profession and generation where calls meant trouble, interruption, emergency, not immediate gratification for bullshitting. On call this weekend for Larry meant fielding trouble.

She dialed the hospital operator. The patient had overdosed. She was no one's patient and had broken up with her boyfriend. She was on the line, and the operator put her through.

"Hello, Doctor," a small voice started to talk, "I'm tired of fighting. I finally took all my Klonopin and Tylenol. I want to go to sleep, but I got scared. They wouldn't let me come in the hospital 'cause, you know, I wasn't suicidal, so I took my meds. Doctor, help me."

"What is your name?" Jean said clearly and calmly. Tylenol could kill.

"My name," the voice paused as though not sure what to say. "My name, my name is Julie. What's yours?"

"Julie, I'm Dr. Volk. What's your full name Julie?"

"Like the Volkswagen, Doctor?"

"Yes, that's my last name. What is yours, Julie?" She had to be careful and get the name and address and not lose her to the morass of calls the operator got and could not trace. She had to be kind and careful.

"Doctor, I cut my wrist too, and it hurts. What shall I do?"

"What's your name and telephone number, Julie, so in case I get cut off from you, I can call you back, okay? And I'll tell you what we'll do?" She used the *we* deliberately.

"Julie, Julie Ward. One, two, three four, no, I mean"—she laughed a short sad laugh—"oh, here it is." She read it off and repeated it three times.

"Now, Julie, I need to get your address and we can help you to get to the hospital."

"Nah, I have to call my case manager person before or I'll have to pay and stuff like that. Nah, just talk to me, Doctor. They don't like me. I've cut my wrists, lots."

"Julie, do you . . . do you have someone with you? Let us help you."

There used to be the county patients and the private patients, and she could get help for both right away. Now with managed care, the patients are scared of the public hospitals, yet afraid they'll lose their insurance with the private. They just ignore all of it, to leave the losses to the hospitals and the doctors. Lifetime benefits of a few thousand mental health dollars and that's it.

Managed care places could be on the East Coast for the West Coast insured, and special telephone numbers for inpatient vs. outpatient and screeners could know nothing except numbers and 'hold please' with and without inane music, and nurses helping and overwhelmed and doctors on both sides hating the other, the doctor taking care of the patient annoyed his or her judgment is questioned, and the doctor on the other side disdaining of self and reduced to okaying others' service. It was lucky if doctors were talking on both sides of the line, many times it was a clerk, questioning a physician.

Julie and a hundred like her did come in and were taken care of. It was scary though, when you still believed that suicide was not the answer but you were categorized as the vilified greedy doctor among all the managed care CEOs making an average of a whopping seven million a year in California.

Julie was called a "borderline personality disorder" and gave everyone a headache because she had a history of sexual and physical abuse, spousal abuse, losses from gunshots and auto accidents, and then suicide attempts and stomach bleeds and shooter's abscesses and prostitution for drugs that no soap opera writer would find credible. No one cared to begin with, nor would they pay for it. Maybe permission might be given to hospitalize her till the crisis was over and send her out into her hell until the next time.

The new mantra was keep her out of the hospital to bother only a few people in a "managed care program" with capitation and to conserve many thousand dollars a year per potentially and usually already sick heads. If they need more, you eat it or let them suffer, she guessed. The compromise was to take the patient to a hotel room with an attendant, watch them there, and avoid hospitalization because it costs more for the extensive care. Strange how the United States was going to have the two-tiered system that was so criticized in England, cash or third world treatment with HMOs. Yet it was here too, and she was susceptible to it, so much easier to select certain patients and not bother with the rest.

Trying to fight for patients now took so much time to arrange approval on the telephone, and sometimes you never even got a response. Yet she had already felt obligated to take care of them. Phone time was donated time and lost time. She wanted to call her brother back and banter about retirement. She hadn't heard from her kids now for weeks, blending days into routine without talking to anyone outside of work, patients, and staff. She'd had no time for friends as they moved away from the neighborhood. No time out for twenty years. Inertia is a continued state of motion. Her ear and arm ached from having to wait for the "Press this number for that service" messages and then, if your lucky and don't get voice mail, talk to someone who never was a health professional of any type to get permission to practice what she knew very well. It would be tempting to be a salaried employee or get out all together.

She put her paper on projection away. What else could she do today? Her life was a void without taking care of someone. No husband, no kids, no patients, no friends. She went to her bed strewn with pillows to prop her up and read *Time* magazine and the Robert Hughes article on some painter he revered or reviled, which she had folded the magazine pages to reveal. Wandering from magazines to novels to putting dishes away was easier than thinking about what to do with the practice of medicine on her supposed days off.

CHAPTER 36

In academia, the researchers think most clinicians are unfocused, unimaginative drones and dispensable worker bees, and the clinicians think most researchers are out of touch with reality and saving their own tenure-seeking tails with worthless publishing in the majority of cases, queen bees.

"WHY DO YOU think millions are so fascinated with drugs? I mean, the media, the police, the government? For maybe a couple hundred thousand to a few million hardcore drug addicts?" Frank's son, George, asked him during one of his monthly calls.

"Well, I guess there are many reasons," he returned, beginning to list some in his mind.

"Of course, of course, but what do you think, as a researcher, I mean?" his son answered impatiently.

Frank could feel that gentle push into becoming only a source of passé wisdom, relegated to a slow thinker and an old thinker by his own assured offspring. He knew now what to say, "Why? What do you think?"

"We were looking into the number of alcoholics in this country. Close to fifteen mill but zilch attention compared to drugs. You can bet the alcohol industry has made a strange but beloved bedfellow out of the righteous Christian right. Don't you see how it fits? All the pressure is off of alcohol," he concluded.

"Ja, I see that, although there are other factors like lack of natural brain opiates in some patients and the forbidden aspect that intrigues

when Amy was sleeping with the guy that she later married after their divorce. The idea bored him now.

He looked in the refrigerator and saw brown Budweiser bottles, which he preferred to cans, and something in a white doggy bag from a restaurant he'd been to at least a week ago. He peered in and took out a half-eaten chicken breast. It was covered with a fine coat of ice; the fridge hadn't been opened in a long time again and even fruit would ice up. He touched the chicken again and stepped back in shock. Stung by the memory of his first dog. The dog he remembered felt like that the morning he found the her lying on the porch frozen to death. His mother had let her out late at night and had forgotten to bring her in. The dog had waited patiently by the back door and curled up and died. He remembered asking why. He was angry at the dog for dying. The dog had been outside many times in winter. He tried to make her move and pushed her, but she stayed curled in her repose, calm and stiff in death. His mother said they'd get another one if he wanted. He never asked what became of the body.

Strange to think of this old childhood memory he mused, and he pushed the bag and its contents back into the refrigerator. He took a bottle of beer and went back to his desk.

He sat down on his swivel chair, pushing on the back and using it like a rocking chair. He sipped his beer and surveyed the books, papers, journals, and the jugs of pens and pencils like thin breadsticks. On the shelves above the desk, there were collected rocks, a sign saying "Keep calm," and some old toy cars, all from the kids. There was a clear glass bottle found somewhere he couldn't remember, a couple of rundown clocks, cartoons for speeches, and books lying on other upright books and slanting books trying to find comfortable positions. He liked to use *Calvin and Hobbes* and the *New Yorker* cartoons in his presentations. He always smiled at "What do cows make when they sing? Moosic." The boys loved that one, and he'd kept that book of riddles, but now it was too childish for them.

He finished his beer in a large gulp, holding it in his mouth for the memory of it. It sprung his taste buds alive. He liked the bubbles on his tongue. He swallowed it as he went up the carpeted stairs to his unmade bed. Tomorrow, he would be at work again and wouldn't have to think.

He didn't need an alarm. When seven o'clock came, he opened his eyes and knew what time it was. He completed his usual routine and trimmed his mustache before putting on his shirt. He didn't always wear a tee shirt under the button-down cotton shirt anymore, and so with the moist shower towel, he had to dust away some of the little hairs that got caught on his chest. They coasted to the floor, and he reached down to wipe them up. The maid wasn't coming for another week.

The drive on the freeway was uneventful if you left early enough. He could see the cars lining up on the ramps to enter the moving mass he was part of, but they had to wait for the green light that paced their entrance since they were entering late. He would have a nice day today as the saying goes. Scheduling was no big deal anymore. Now the fellow and a graduate student were doing all his data collection for his analysis. They were motivated to ride on his name into the journals and squeeze some CV glory from the research. The staff said hello respectfully and turned to their individual pursuits.

His ideas weren't the hot ones now, but he was still a respected researcher, and this next study would be an important one, not a flashy one. He wondered if this would be his last good work. He didn't try for the big money, but then he could hang on like other "tenured profs" stealing into their offices about ten in the morning and leaving at three after two-hour lunches and meager attempts at writing old ideas in new ways, "status of the field" editorials, or "review of the literature" papers and summary books for pharmacy students.

He opened his mail and found an early retirement offer by the university. He'd heard from Fred in Chemistry that the letters were coming, but it was hard to believe. The University Medical Center had timed everything wrong. It had built state-of-the-art programs with PET scanners, MRIs, and operating arenas to transplant everything from livers to lungs and probably brains too. *Oh, all right,* he thought, *implants not transplants.* The plan had been to also genetically engineer everything from bacteria to bodies at the multi-million-dollar labs, but society mutated into HMOs saying save us money, not people.

Now the dean was broke, and the president of the university wouldn't bail him out, and so he was trying to get hold of any contacts for primary care in the medical world to prescribe cough medicine. Frank felt he was expendable because he had ideas and that really didn't matter anymore unless they were related to making money or saving it. The emphasis was in money, not furthering the cause of healthy life. His grants were good ones, even the smallest was respectable, but he didn't like the assessment of his ideas only in terms of what they paid the university. Idealist and naïve, he would have told anyone else admitting to this. He rubbed his mustache and shrugged his shoulders a couple times to loosen them up.

He threw the offer in the waste basket, pulled it out, held it in his hand, waving it back and forth, and finally put it on top of his third-priority pile of manila envelopes and articles on the upper left side of his desk, near the telephone. He wouldn't surrender. He was too young to retire, and he liked what he did. He'd know what the others were doing in the next faculty meeting. Consider. What would he do? Travel. Write. Garden. Golf. Shit.

Finishing his paper mail, he checked his e-mail and looked at his calendar and set to work analyzing some new data.

By ten to one, he knew Jean Volk was not showing. She was to be there at noon. He had been understanding, he thought, and made the appointment near lunch so she wouldn't have to change her clinical schedule. With an impatient sigh, abruptly rubbing his mustache, he asked his secretary to page her.

No one was reliable anymore, except maybe his secretary, he concluded as his hand rubbed his whole face. Maybe. Even she was more involved with going to see her grandkids in Santa Rosa and taking Fridays and sometimes Thursdays off. She was a person with a life, he mused, and he didn't like it. At least she put in vacation requests. Those clinicians, they were forever having emergencies and were resistant to crunching numbers for the statisticians. He wondered what kind of life Dr. Volk led. It was an easy name to pronounce, not like Schlager, which people were always massacred. Wanting to put a *t* or a *d* at the end of it. Gert, gerd, laggard, braggart. Both of them had German names but were so different.

She never answered her page. He had his secretary call her department. She was out on "medical leave" as of yesterday. He knew it. Never rely on anyone, he swore to himself, when he heard she was not coming for sure.

CHAPTER 37

On Call

"TOM, TOM, TOM," she beat his name into the air. He had come out of the shower and heard her call like she always did when he was running a little late. "I'm not waiting any longer because I have an appointment with the college counselor. Your eggs are on the stove," she yelled and left with a door that closed sounding as annoyed as he knew she was. He wondered if she understood he masturbated in the shower on Friday mornings.

He combed his hair straight over his forehead and parted it near the left ear and then combed all the hair over across his head to the right side.

This technique was better than a toupee and more natural-looking. He liked to be neat and perfectly groomed without any bald spot showing at all. He knew that his hair had become thinner and thinner, and it was increasingly difficult to hide the bald area, but combing helped. He finished dressing, selecting a paisley blue tie, nodded approval to himself in the mirror, and went downstairs.

He never liked scrambled eggs. He made himself some sunny-side up eggs and lifted the yolk unbroken into his mouth. He pushed it against his palate, feeling the warm liquid run over his tongue, then he smiled. Three eggs, three perfect yolks to burst.

It was seven o'clock and time to go to the office. He would have coffee there before his eight o'clock patient came in.

The drive to the office was about twenty minutes long, and his parking place was well marked. He looked through his mail, had his coffee, and then got ready for his first patient. He combed his hair very neatly before the meeting. First, he pushed the hair forward and pulled the comb through it, and then he parted it by his left temple again, as close to his left ear as he could get away with, and then he combed all the hair across his balding head to blend in with the fringes on the right side. He straightened his tie by running his hand down to its tip and retucking it. He brushed his herringbone jacket, which he had worn predicting it wouldn't be that warm today. He sprayed the vinyl patient's chairs with Lysol and cleaned them carefully. His papers were all off the desk and in his file room. He was ready; he got the nurse on the com line, and after he let Mrs. Harris in and faced her attentively, she still yelled.

"I've come here for six months and I'm nowhere. I'm sick of getting nowhere and still fighting the damn HMO to get any treatment."

"Where is it you want to go?"

"I should tell you where I'd like you to go with your insipid questions. Oh God, how'd I get into this mess? It's like going to a doctor who needs more help than I do. Sitting in your little citadel, pontificating about the fact that I have a history of melanoma and I better come here rather than get a divorce. All you do is check to see if I've got any metastases. I refuse any more x-rays, scans, and blood works. Fuck you. You're a fraud and a shitty doctor and you're worse than my husband. To hell with courts asking couples to get counseling, and to hell with you telling me I'm the sick one and letting my husband free. What about his cancer of the soul? Why did you take his side? You're an agent of the stupid HMO. You've got no guts"

"What? What is bothering you this morning?" he said patiently. He knew how both of them had begged the insurance company and they had only given her a few follow-up visits and she was supposed to stay with her primary physician.

There was silence as she dropped her arms over the sides of the chair and leaned back, tilting her head and sighing with exasperation. He blinked his eyes very deliberately because he didn't want to disturb the contact lens, which had lately bothered him, and because he didn't want her to think he wasn't watching her. Last time, she said he was so unable to understand her that she wanted to bury him like a stinking, putrefying anachronism. That he was worse than the Nazis. "Shit, you should commit suicide. You're so out of it. You stink. Dr. Thomas Zeitman, you stink, MD and all."

Patient after patient had been upset this week. Summer coming and kids getting out of school and parents getting out of nothing. He took a deep breath while she blew her nose, and he wondered why he was so tired. Initially, he thought he hated her for her bitching and blaming him. Then he thought it best for her to get her hidden anger out and knew she wasn't really mad at him but at the thought of dying. Insults didn't bother him now. He'd had his share as a kid and at least his patients didn't shun him, they just praised him.

"If I wish you dead, are you going to die?"

"What do you mean?"

"Jesus, are you evasive. Are you going to die if I hate you?" she asked with disdain.

He imagined himself holding her. She wasn't bad-looking, trim body and long fingers. He didn't like her toenails as they peeked through her sandals. He hadn't found anyone with really pretty feet. His were less calloused than most women's. His were almost as soft as his penis, asleep, warm, and safe in his pants. A suffering woman didn't wake it anymore. Maybe he could hold her, comfort her, and she would slide down and take him in her mouth. Maybe they could lie together and spoon.

"Answer me. You're my doctor!" she demanded.

He stirred out of his little diversionary fantasy immediately and recalled her as a case. The first time she had come to his office, she was post-op from the complete excising of a lesion on her left scapular area. She had still been in shock over the whole idea of dying so young but was determined to "fight this thing" in whatever way he advised. She was only thirty-five. She was a lifetime sun worshipper now having to wait for metastasis and avoid the sun.

At first, she reminded him of his wife when she was that young and how sweet and wise and eager she was. He still looked for those things in his wife, but she spit back poison, saying he had neglected her for years. Had he really shoved her away when she'd wanted to be hugged or have sex?

"Who's going to be with me? You promised you'd help and what happened? My husband ran away on another business trip instead of being here trying to fix our marriage. He's a coward and won't face the possibility of me dying," she cried.

"Look, there is no evidence of metastasis now. It's been three years. You've got to think positively. Have you been going out with friends like I suggested?"

"That's another thing, you university doctors think it's great to advise all the little lady patients. Beverly Hills docs don't tell you anything, including whether or not they're even thinking. What's the deal? My friend June says her doctor's better and you're wrong."

"Have you gone out with friends?" he repeated. "Is your sister going to stay in the area?" The last time she came in, he felt a need to help her get some support. He'd referred her to Jean Volk, one of the psychiatrists who consulted on medical patients. Mrs. Harris never made an appointment. He tried to speak to the husband, but he never got his calls returned. Friends seemed the best alternative.

"Yes, yes, I, the self-sufficient Mrs. Harris, have returned to life after my extensive excision of my primary cancer. Mrs. Harris is also looking for men. Hump them and dump them, fuck 'em and chuck 'em as my brother used to say. That'll show my brave husband how much support he's been."

He didn't know what to say to that tirade except "I have given you the name of a psychiatrist. Please call."

"Are you going to die for me, Dr. Zeitman?" she asked simply. "No one will help me. My kids need me. Who will care for them? They're only eleven and nine. You die for me, so I can take care of them. Or tell the insurance company you have to come home with me and take care of me."

Mrs. Harris was obsessed, in limbo, afraid to live and afraid to die. She looked to him to change her problems, to cut them away like the tumor. Tom stood up to counter these strange ideas and proceeded to check for nodes, take her blood pressure, listen to her chest, and palpate her abdomen. He also did a quick neurological, but she began to cry when he tried to examine her eyes. She pushed him away and said that was all she could tolerate. He acquiesced and made notes in her chart. "Patient irritable, much more angry than usual. Refused fundiscopic, PERRLA. Exam negative for nodes, lungs clear, abdomen soft, pulses and reflexes normal. Schedule repeat studies in six months." He finished listing the negative findings and recommendations including a psych consult while she quietly continued to cry. He put the chart in his pile to be filed.

He told her he'd call her with the results of the routine bloods later in the week and scheduled another appointment in two months. She used to be attentive and motivated to get things settled when she discussed her family situation, what would happen to her kids, and chemotherapy side effects. Now she was irritable and unreasonable. She'd come in the couple times only to bitch. Her husband wasn't available to yell at. She feared he would leave her for good. Instead, she yelled at her oncologist. Afterwards, she left messages saying she was feeling better and wasn't going to use up her authorized visits. He couldn't remember this wife being that angry and then apologizing when she felt better.

He was strangely pleased when two patients cancelled their morning appointments, and he tried to keep things quiet for the rest of the day. He played his messages from the machine. The drug salesman with the deep voice had called him again. He was always touting some new anxiolytic for patients who got anxious about having cancer. That sales rep irritated him, his voice so smooth and confident, and yet he couldn't tell him to stop calling. It was important to know these new drugs.

A couple afternoon patients and then a dinner break for his salad and diet Pepsi and then rounds with his hospitalized patients. Maybe after this year, he'd cut down, but he'd made an additional $35,000 last year. He needed the extra money to get enough for the kids' college education. No surgeon's income, but inevitably, oncology would always get patients. The cell was always losing its ability to ward of aberrance. Cancer was always there, and enough times, it broke through to become a full-blown disease. Oncogenes and viruses at work.

He did the absolutely most complete and thoroughly comprehensive workup and presented all the options in perfect clarity to the patients. It was a chess game against the king, death. HMOs inhibited some of his ideas and wouldn't always agree to pay for the CAT scans, MRI medications, and chemotherapies. Still, he argued well. Medicare was less obstinate, and most of his patients were able to use it.

He knew all the statistics on the survival rate of each cancer and what was the newest treatment of choice. Before having them come back to his office, he always ran a journal search for all updates on the cancer protocols. He couldn't understand why more of the patients, especially women, got so mad at him, but later when they were dying they looked at him, with their pleading, worshipping eyes, and he would give them Dilaudid, Fentanyl patches, or the morphine pump and they would finally be grateful. The men didn't seem to care so much and went along with it all until they weren't thinking anymore. His parents had never complained to him and died quietly. He wished they had been angry at something.

He walked across the street, went through the quad to get a candy bar at the bookstore, and then up a block to get to the hospital, which was devoted to oncology. It was a big moneymaker to advertise a center devoted only to cancer, and of course, a hospital affiliated with a major university created even more drawing power in a day and age when hospitals have to advertise.

Medicine was changing from the little self-run business thirty years ago when he started to doctors as employees of business majors as it was today. He took out his date book as he walked and noted he should go to the next hospital staff meeting and not forget. He took the elevator to the fifth floor ward and combed his hair slowly in the bathroom and washed his hands carefully. He closed the door behind him quietly and greeted a few nurses with nods and then sat down to review his first chart.

He began by checking the lab values and saw the hematocrit was down today to 29 from 38 Tuesday, and he started to cry. Tears came banging on his cheeks and then his hands like giant raindrops as though he'd been caught in a Michigan summer shower. He could not get his thoughts together to analyze what was happening. He got up, got a paper towel from the sink to smear the tears off, and looked around trying to find some noxious agent that must have irritated him. He mustn't let the nurses see him; they relied on him. Again, he approached the chart and saw the stains from the tears on the computer print out of the lab values. He flipped to the progress notes and looked at the physical therapy entry and then shut the chart and walked out into the hall toward the patient's room. Which patient was it? He realized he didn't know which chart he'd been reviewing.

He returned to the nursing station and washed his hands and began again. He picked up the same chart. It was Mr. Mooney, white, male, 68, mets to liver, probably GI bleeding again. Yes, Mr. Mooney, bowel resection three years ago and now lesions all over the liver. He was ochre-looking, maybe darker, but like an enormous yellow summer squash. Marcie Walker, his favorite internist, had referred the patient.

He went in and said, "How are we doing this evening? Able to eat anything?" He realized he tried to use the word *we* to join in the suffering.

"Not much, Doctor. Still nauseated," Mr. Mooney said slowly between breaths. "I'm hanging on for some reason. I can't let go. Isn't that a hoot?"

The rooms were all the same cubes. A TV hung in space across from the bed, and the blue drapes hung on a window that faced other windows in a hollow courtyard. The bed was standard with the guardrails up and the head and foot control panel fastened close to Mr. Mooney's right hand.

He was dying, that's all, and he still cared to live.

"We'll make you more comfortable. How about your sleep? Is that okay?" Tom said as he opened the man's gown and pulled his stethoscope out of his pocket. He listened to the man's heart and his breathing and didn't quite catch what Mr. Mooney said about sleep. He felt the liver edge and then said, "Roll over now. I've got to do a rectal to check for blood, okay?"

Mr. Mooney turned his swollen yellow body over onto his side as far as he could before he hit the side rail, and he held himself with a puffy yellow hand like an oven mitt coiled around the smooth shiny bar.

Tom put his gloves on and scooped some lubricant on his right index finger, pulled the top buttocks upward with his left hand, and found the anus. It was like a hairy target but remarkably symmetrical with all its protruding hemorrhoids, a berry brooch. He inserted his finger and felt for stool. The prostate was relatively smooth for a man this age, 2 plus and it had only a few irregularities, but that didn't matter anymore. He could feel the tip of some soft stool, and he pushed in a little farther and then scooped. He brought back some yellow feces. "Bilirubin does that to stool. Doesn't look like old blood. This makes the stool light and then almost black," he told many an imaginary medical student and then wiped the sample for testing. Heme negative. "Shit, where was he losing blood?" he asked himself while pulling off the thin plastic gloves.

Mr. Mooney rolled back and closed his eyes. "Damn, you'd think I would be used to that by now."

"Well, it's a sensitive area but you cooperated nicely. Thanks. The stool looks okay," Tom said and took out his stethoscope and listened to the lungs carefully. Decreases along the right base.

"Well, you take it easy. We'll get another x-ray and I'll tell you about it tomorrow." He wanted to take good care of the man, really for Marcie's sake.

"Thanks, Doctor. I'll breathe on till tomorrow."

How many times had he heard "Thanks, Doctor" after he had poked and probed and prodded. Tom started to cry again and paused in the tiny foyer between the curtain near the bed and the door out of the room.

"Anything else, Doctor?" Mr. Mooney said with a sigh, realizing that Tom was still there.

"No, no," Tom assured him and took some Kleenex from a box on the bathroom sink to blow his nose. "No, no, I'm thinking," Tom repeated and left the room.

"What the hell is going on? Damn it," he said in a whisper to himself but definitely out loud, which was also upsetting to him. He was not one to talk out loud ever. His contacts had been fresh for the weekend. It was not irritation. He scribbled out the order for a repeat portable chest, pulled the flier, and went back to the nurses' station.

His next patient was Austin Bass, 33, AIDS, on DDI protocol and worried about a localized lymphoma at L 2. The room was brightly lit, the TV was off, and a tape of Hendrix was playing. Mr. Bass—"Call me Austin," he'd say—was round of cheeks and slightly potbellied. He had blue eyes and stocky fingers that constantly fussed with his face while he talked. The fingers would move hair by his forehead or stroke a little mustache or scratch a cheek and rub his eyes continually. He sat up immediately when he saw Dr. Zeitman.

"I've been shaking all over, but I did better last night with the Demerol and Vistaril. It will be a relief when I'm over this, Doctor, I tell you," Austin said, smiling.

"Well, you're doing remarkably well. The tumor has shrunk, and your T cells are up."

"I think I'd like to finish the work I'm doing for AIDS project LA, and I've got good communication with them now. I dictated some articles, and they want me to go to New York to look at the situation there. I'm real excited. Of course, I've got to wind up selling my shop.

You should take a look at some of the beautiful clocks I have still," Austin exalted and scratched his left ear.

"Are you going to stay with your parents for a while?" Tom asked as he planned a possible discharge day. Get them out for as long as possible.

"Mom and Dad have been wishing for that. I don't know though. I'd like to be with Bernie. Of course, he's not back from Chicago yet."

"I think it might be good for you to be with your parents to watch the medication. These new protease inhibitors need to be taken on time, and they could make sure you're eating. What do you think?" Tom said causally as he fussed with the chart, checking the temperature recording for the last twenty-four hours. He knew that Bernie had been very frightened by the seizure Austin had, and it would take him some time to come to see him dying. Other friends could call and stop by occasionally, but Bernie, even though they weren't lovers, would be the one who would be there in the end.

Chasing the virus and batting it down were what they all did once it got hold of the nervous system. New protocols were coming daily. There was no detectable lesion in his brain scan, but it was there. HIV sat smugly waiting while it multiplied, waiting until the drugs couldn't stop it anymore and everything went its way with no argument. What a strange victory to destroy your host. Clinicians demanded researchers move faster to provide better answers.

"Listen, I want you to go to my shop. I told Vicky to give you a particular piece. I want you to have it. Please," Mr. Bass said earnestly, stroking his chin.

"That's very good of you, but you don't have to do that." Tom looked down again to the chart as he spoke.

"I know that, but you'll like it. Here's my card."

"I doubt if I'll have time, but thank you any way. Try to let me know tomorrow what your plan is and we'll look for Saturday as discharge date, okay?"

"That will be spectacular. Thanks for everything." Austin Bass arranged his blankets, sank back on the two pillows he had propped up, and fussed with his headphones to put in the small red radio.

This week, Tom had only four patients in the hospital, and that made it easier. He combed his hair again and washed his hands as he was careful to do before and after each patient. Two more to go and he'd be home by eight o'clock easily. They were old patients of his. One was comatose so that was easy. The other was a woman he'd treated for an oats cell cancer of the lung and then she got ca of the larynx, totally unrelated. She had to use an electronic voice now so it was hard to understand her since she'd only used it post-op the revision of her tracheotomy Monday. He hoped he could understand her.

She'd put the plastic tube in her mouth and out would come this robotic voice. It droned, "I can't figure out why this should happen to me. Why is God doing this to me?" Then she'd take the tube out and wipe the saliva clinging to it.

She was crying, and it frustrated Tom since her surgery had gone so well and her electrolytes and hematocrit were stable. He checked her tracheotomy and then listened to her chest. As he moved the stethoscope to her left chest, he lifted the breast gently to get to the heart while he stared ahead in a professional manner. He was looking at her shoulder above the clavicle, and there was a discrete node. Was he going to have to work her up for metastasis? How would she take that bad news?

"Mrs. Finny, I'm going to have a psychiatrist see you so you can talk over some of these feelings," Tom said slowly and casually while he looked at his long white coat pocket and tucked in the stethoscope tubing neatly. Young doctors wore it around their necks, but he preferred the pocket. "And, Florence, such a fine name, we'll run a few more tests to check everything out, okay?"

She'd put her tube away and had to search for it, but he smiled and waved and left before she could say anything. He wrote the order for the psychiatrist and recalled the surgeon for the biopsy.

He got home by nine and went into the kitchen with the mail. He sat at the white Knoll table purchased years ago and took each envelope in his hands, scrutinized the address, laid it down again, and opened none of them. As the day had worn to a shabby twilight, he realized he was crying again. He took off his white coat, which he usually would have left in his office after changing to his suit coat, and was puzzled that he'd forgotten to go back to the office to do that nightly ritual. He hung it up with the jackets by the back door and got a paper towel to wipe his tears. He sat down again and looked puzzled.

"What is going on?" he asked as he looked around the kitchen for the cause of his tears. He got up again, removed his lenses, put on his glasses, and went from room to room. He knew no one would be home, but he turned on each lamp deftly placed on well-dusted tables and looked for someone. On the piano in the living room were silver-framed photos of his children and his wife and his parents and his aunt who had died when he was two, and some even of his wife's parents and his own grandparent or two. There were three paperweights his daughter had collected and some small enameled bowls from somewhere. He couldn't see clearly.

He could feel the tears, and he became frightened. He thought of the one trip to Mexico he and his wife had taken. When was it? Two years after they were married? They had laughed so much that he had gasped for breath as he did now.

He left the room and went upstairs to wipe his face with the big terrycloth towel his wife always put out on the sink counter for him. He took the towel to his bed and lay down on the multicolored pillows. He consoled himself with the idea that the contacts had irritated his cornea and glasses would be best for a while.

He'd better check his machine for messages. There had been no emergencies he knew because his beeper did not go off with the high-pitched whine like a newborn screaming. He promised himself he'd get a new cellphone soon. He dialed and waited as the machine began, but the first message was from the deep-voiced drug salesman wanting to come by and talk about the new serotonin reuptake blocker good for pain and depression. He felt this clunk of dread fall in his gut, and he hung up.

Once when he was young, he saw his cat run around the house trying to escape its tongue, which it had burnt licking a frying pan. His cat was named Mirabel, like his father's sister, and was so calm and loving. Then after the burn, she would stop and open her mouth trying to get rid of the pain, throw her tongue out onto her nose, and suddenly sprint away as if she could leave the sharp pain behind. She repeated this process until he begged his mother to take her to the vet. The vet said Mirabel—it was funny to hear him say her name—would have to wait it out. You couldn't give aspirin to a cat; they'd all hemorrhage and die from it. She hardly drank at all and never ate for days. He had cried then. His mother held him and said the cat wouldn't die, and she was right.

He always felt it had been easier to study and treat people than have to cut up cats. He went into medicine because of that, specifically oncology to chase the devil death. Yet he found out no one chased death, the grand master; it chased you. Humans and cats ran from it as best they could. You'd try to save the patient, transfuse and cut and give chemo and hope and good attitude and let everyone get relaxation tapes from ambitious social workers. There might be years, "five year survivals," and even cures of cancers of the cervix, colon, and skin, but he saw the deaths. He was there at the end. He thought of Cheryl. She had her fifteenth birthday in the hospital two days early. "I'm here to celebrate my life. I feel so sorry for my brother and sister because they won't have me anymore." Then she died of metastatic cancer to the lung. She did well to the last without anguishing gasps because of the low doses of anxiolytic with morphine the psychiatrist had recommended.

He remembered then that the low-voiced drug salesman had called him about more samples.

He went out into the hall and picked up the big tabby they had had for seven-plus years, took him back to the bed with him, and went to sleep in his shirt and pants. He did have the energy to kick off his shoes, and that was all.

In the morning, his wife called again, "Tom, Tom, your breakfast is ready. Tom, I'm leaving," and he heard the door slam again. They never slept in the same room anymore, and she was gone most of the time to the little antique shop she and Rene Rawly had opened in the corner pastel shopping mall near the Von's he liked. He had supported her venture into business almost more than she had.

It was Saturday, and he didn't open the office. He would still do rounds at the hospital. Weekends were the worst for patients because activities ceased in the hospital for routine procedures, and they all knew good things were going on at home. Saturday afternoons were for family. Single souls and the sick suffered when they couldn't have their share of the media-hyped happiness.

He was too tired to bother to go to the office for a new white coat, and deciding it was not too wrinkled, he put on the old one. He combed his hair and drove to the hospital. The nurses greeted him, and he bowed slightly as usual and took his four charts with him down the hall. The utilization review nurse was looking at someone else's charts right now, and the case managers were going to complain because Mr. Mooney was still in the hospital, wouldn't die, and make it cheaper for everyone. For him, it would be a loss anyway. He liked Mr. Mooney and wanted to help him. Mr. Mooney had a hemothorax, and he spent a good hour putting the chest tube in, sliding the huge trochanter at the edge of the rib, pushing into the plural cavity, and hooking up the suction to bring back all the sero-sanguineous liquid, all for nothing.

It did give him relief to know that Mr. Mooney could breathe easier as he went into his final coma in the next few days. No hospice would take him with tubes. He talked with Mrs. Mooney who was a bleached blond with big diamonds on her left and right hand and was always at her husband's bedside at night. She understood.

His already-comatose patient down the hall still hung on, but the breathing was much shallower and it would not be long before Mr. Gordon's son would have to bury him. The son and his wife would be in around noon for a few minutes and then leave again to wait at home.

Mrs. Finney's speech was much clearer, and he sat down and explained that she might as well get the biopsy while she was still in the hospital. She agreed and started crying and asking again, "Why me?" He couldn't tell her about another course of chemotherapy yet.

When he got to Mr. Bass's room, there was someone else with him.

"Dr. Zeitman, this is my brother, Ralph, in from up north to help me with the legal papers of the sale. Look what he brought from the shop for me to give to you," Mr. Bass said with excitement, "an original Seth Thomas clock! Isn't it wonderful? I insist you take it. Lordy Jesus, I am raring to get the hell out of here and go to dinner at Spagos." He began singing "Hallelujah! Hal-lelu-jah! I'm getting out." Periodically, Austin was a little hyper, a little manic but par for the course with these patients and their struggles. It seemed a good defense.

Tom had never been particularly resolved around the problem of patients' gift giving. He knew he was between psychiatrists who were very hesitant and general practitioners who took it in stride. He accepted the clock and said it was very nice, planned the discharge, wrote all his notes, and left the hospital to put the clock in his office with other gifts.

"Have a pleasant evening, Dr. Zeitman," the ward clerk had said.

"Thanks, I'm going to my office now. See you tomorrow," he replied.

He knew some of the other doctors in the building, accompanied by nurses and receptionists, were busy seeing patients. Still, it was hard to guess who was in and who was not. Big impressive veneer doors like tomb entrances commanded the way into all the medical suites, and silence, occasionally jarred by voices or scuffs from people getting in or off the elevators, settled in the halls.

He paused to savor a prolonged high-pitched laugh, which was then lost. It came again like a sparkle to his ear, uncensored in its spontaneity and inhibition.

In his office suite, everything was silent and still. The light from the windows was all that detailed the rooms. Brad Runfield, his associate, was on vacation, and Tom tried not to have Saturday office hours during the summer. He had started that policy a long time ago when the kids were young. It struck him that the office was like a giant old photograph, still and static.

He put the clock on his desk and sat down on his worn leather chair. It squeaked under his weight. He sighed and looked around the room. He had a plain large teak desk and bookshelves to match. Everything was covered with neatly stacked charts, articles, and books. There was a small narrow adjoining room where he kept personal papers in two black file cabinets, and on the wall, he had hung a mirror to comb his hair. He'd always wanted a big spacious back room where he could have put a couch and a little refrigerator, but he never made much of an effort to look for another office or even remodel his current one like Brad had done.

He got up and picked up the clock. It was like one his parents had had on their mantel at the Dexter house, he thought—*Yes, at the Dexter house*—and he wondered what had happened to it.

He walked into his little back room, and he put the clock up on one of his file cabinets. It looked very calm and appropriate, so Tom opened the small delicate window to access the pendulum. There was a note inside from Mr. Bass. "To be alive, to be alive, was good, celebrate" was all it said. That message stunned him. He paused, then wound the spring, paused again to deliberate whether he wanted the thing to begin or not, and finally pushed the pendulum. It began its tick-tock and Tom knew he had begun to cry. *How ridiculous*, he thought, *to cry over such an obvious symbol as a clock.*

CHAPTER 38

Physicians make the worst patients: they know too much and all the complications possible happen to them.

SHE DID A consult on the rehab unit. A woman with Guillain-Barré syndrome. The woman was depressed. She wasn't making the progress she wanted and didn't believe the doctors who kept telling her she was doing fine. She related to Jean that when she first had some numbness in her feet and legs, her husband and primary doctor told her she was overtired and implied she was "hysterical" and "fatigued" and needed to take a few days off from being the buyer for a department store chain. She said she resented their implications and was angry with her husband. It was second marriage for both, and tenuous besides, because of her travels and his involvement with his first wife who had a stroke at age forty-two. They even implied that she might be copying the ex-wife to get attention from her husband.

"I certainly hope you're not here to give them ammunition that I'm crazy. This Guillain-Barré illness is so bizarre. I can feel my legs, and the strength in my hands is returning, but yesterday I felt weak again."

It was a strange disease and one that usually had complete recovery after total paralysis. Jean listened to the frustration the patient felt and the suspicion that her perceptions were again doubted. She hadn't been put on a respirator although the chart showed the neurologist's note who considered it. She'd lost her ability to move and feel, and she'd lost trust in her main support. She had no children, and her mother was dead. Her father was on the East Coast and was eighty-four. Jean searched through the history for more understanding. As with many rehabilitation patients who have a hard time, her past resonated with the illness.

The patient had been in a brace from the age of eleven through fourteen for scoliosis. It had been an extremely painful time because of the teasing, the orthopedic surgeons insistence that she wear it even to school, and her mother's own illness at the time, some sort of arthritis. The patient felt alone. Jean helped her compare the past with the present, and they looked at ways to deal with her feeling of alienation. It went relatively well because at the end of the session, the patient thanked her and asked for her card. "I'd like you to come back."

Jean left and walked over to her office. She could feel her need to stretch and moved her shoulders up and down, flexed her fingers repeatedly, and, in the elevator, went up and down on her toes. It took extreme patience to endure the brace in scoliosis. She had seen those children in the textbooks, in torture devices, and now the woman had to deal with being restrained by a neurological prison. The patient's story hung in her mind like some plaintive Mobius strip, always cyclic captivity.

She had worked hard, running a seminar, supervising, and then having her own patients that day. The day dimmed into evening as the patients came and went, talking of more than Michelangelo and of suffering. The last patient was a huge man, six foot four and overweight, who presented with depression. He had his own lighting business and was married and had three teenagers. After stabilization, they'd been really working together for months, while he reflected on himself, past and present, and then he turned his thoughts into the room for developing his transference to her. The session included the moments of insight in therapy and occasionally illuminated the glory of the mind. Uncovering layer upon layer of meaning, she wished she could explain it like the archaeologists divining history in the strata of cliffs or astrophysicists deciphering Hubble telescope images burning incomprehensible gossamer beauty beyond our world and words.

He had explained he was always anxious every time he came to see her. She made some nonjudgmental remark and let her mind open as she listened. While she listened, images would form and dissolve, as though his thoughts without words could transmit to her impressions sculptured from what he was struggling with. Holograms of feelings. She waited, never imposing, hearing patterns and themes. Timing was everything.

He presented a dream in which there were soldiers and he saw a woman throwing bombs at them, which turned into bright yellow color over everything. Jean gently encouraged him to relate what came into his mind when he told each part of the dream. At first, he associated the soldiers with being in the army and walking together with his buddies. He's been in Vietnam. They had grenades. They feared the Vietnamese would throw grenades at them. "I wasn't afraid in the dream, not at all."

In reality, he and his buddies had been lucky, he said. It was at the very end of the war, and they'd run to the helicopters.

"Do you know anyone of the soldiers, or is there anything distinguishing about them?" she asked, thinking of his father who apparently had been authoritarian. He smiled and acknowledged the soldiers had been goose-stepping like Nazis.

"When we were young, my father would be gone on business trips, and mother would have to report my and my brother's bad behaviors. He would beat us for any stupid thing she reported. When he was gone, we would play soldiers goose-stepping. Commodore Klink was the name we called him like in the TV program, you know."

Suddenly, the patient questioned, "But why the bombs to destroy us?" Jean pursued the idea. Who was the woman throwing? Why the color yellow and the destroyed bodies? She was imagining these images, searching, looking for connections.

"Yellow, I don't know," the patient hesitated, "but there didn't seem to be any blown up bodies. It was more like we were all yellow, marked like."

"Was there yellow on your faces and hands too?"

"I don't know. Our clothes, I think. She wanted to make us Jewish, the yellow patches, stars of David, like we were scum. I just saw *Schindler's List*." He paused and started the soft cry of grief. "My wife hates me because I get so angry, and I'm afraid I'll kill my kids too."

"What do you mean 'too'?"

"I get angry at them sometimes. I wasn't hiding any kid killing in Vietnam. I was in intelligence. I love my family."

"No, I mean why the 'too' like also?"

He stopped and looked up, reached for a Kleenex on the table next to him, and blew his nose. His face was flushed, and he let the Kleenex fall on his rumpled shirt as he reached for another one. He blew his nose again, and it sounded like a small explosion. He picked up the fallen

Kleenex and crumpled it with the one he already had in his hand and threw them both in the wastebasket. He was thinking of the question, stunned by it.

"That's it, the 'too.' I'm afraid I'll kill my kids too. It was my father. He told me that in Ireland, my grandfather had killed my father's brother, beaten him silly because he painted a fence yellow, not white. I'd been playing war with my brother and threw a rock, which busted one of his front teeth. My father beat the hell out of me then. He told me I should never feel I had it bad compared to how his father was."

"Do you say that to your kids?"

"I guess I have, but I don't hit them. I would never hurt my kids."

The room was quiet, and Jean heard a door shut as one of the other psychiatrists finished for the day. It was important to remain silent, let the patient really understand what he believed, who he was.

Still unresolved was the woman in the dream. She couldn't leave that lie even though the session was almost over. She waited until he looked up again, as if for guidance.

"What was the woman like in the dream?"

"I don't know, maybe tall. She wore a long green dress. She seemed to smile when she threw the bombs." He bowed his head. "You know, I got this flash in my brain. Like she was really, you know, those Mother Nature pictures and it was sunshine. You know how they paint it in cartoons. The news always has those big bright jagged suns reporting the temperatures, last night said it was the first day of spring today. It showed some painting of a woman in garlands. All over the world, the day is twelve hours and eight minutes long. I heard that last night before I went to bed.

"In the dream, it's strange. When I think of it, we're not afraid. We all seem to go toward her. I never much trusted my mother. She didn't seem to manage me and my brother easily, and my wife is always telling me to watch myself with the kids as though I were dangerous. You've got a German name, but you don't hate. You never seem to get mad at me. I guess I'm afraid you'll change. I'm not a bad person really, no matter what anybody else says." He cried softly.

Within a few minutes without her signal, he got up, knowing the time was over and probably because he was anxious about his confession. Jean left it at that, choosing not to overwhelm. He said, "Goodbye until next week," and she said, "Take it easy."

FRITZ WOLF

She closed the door and went back into the office, sat down at the desk, and finished her notes summarizing the session. Her back needed stretching, and her seat was burning from sitting so still. She celebrated the end of the day with her routine of turning off the lights, looking out the window at the city, and leaving for the car.

It was always best to drive the freeways at night after the traffic. The air was fragrant, and her mind played over the sessions that worried her, like the Filipino widow who saw her husband's ghost but was afraid he'd come to take her with him. She was so guilty that she was enjoying her life. She might begin to believe she had killed him with her anger at being harassed. There was also a young woman who'd been molested by her uncle and who loved her boyfriend but couldn't stand his sarcasm when she went to do massages instead of waiting tables. This licensed pursuit had become the supplementary income aspiring actresses in LA pursued instead of waitressing. It was much more interesting and lucrative. She supported him with it, and he raged but didn't get work of his own. There was the middle-aged man who was afraid to ask the woman he loved to marry him but was afraid she was going to leave him if he didn't. There was the film school twenty-three-year-old who lost his leg in a motorcycle accident and felt he was not a "whole man."

So poignant and trite.

Session after session, making sure there would be no destruction, no uncovering of memories and fears without protection and refuge, no despair without hope, splashes of sun in shadows of sadness when possible. Not false hope and placating of a mother's love but true new chances.

She pulled off the freeway at her usual exit and stopped at a light. Then there was nothing. A blank space. A blank time. She focused. She looked up through the windshield and realized she was in the car moving toward a street light. There had been no sound, no screech, no bang, no yelling, but she knew then she'd been hit. She knew too she was alive because she could think watching the streetlight, *I am thinking*. And she could see that streetlight hanging its head of light above her like some ministering angel. Her car coasted to a stop as she lost sight of the light and seemed to rest under it and close to the pole itself. She waited, trying to grasp what had happened.

The unexpected.

She'd been hit on the driver's side and thrown against the console and the gearshift. The window was smashed into a mosaic of safely glass and hung valiantly to the frame. She began to realize her left leg was caught and she couldn't sit up. The bag had not inflated. A few people peered in the passenger window and asked if she was okay, but no one opened the door. She answered obediently, "Yes, I'm okay, I think," but she couldn't understand why she was left in the car. The pain did not come until a man in a yellow fireman's slicker ripped open the driver's door and her foot seemed to fall away with the door. It was limp and seem to be separated from her. She watched over herself, and the swelling leg was somehow still attached to her while she was carried to the ambulance. Her mind periodically opened to painful consciousness only when her eyes did, responding to the goings-on of the paramedics' radio talk, questions about her name and the date, and the trip to the hospital.

She was without any will to determine what would happen and was lifted and positioned and arranged as the compliant patient on hard surfaces for x-ray and on soft surfaces for treatment. She became a body with her mind only observing, not commanding the body.

That day, she tolerated the pain and decisions about x-rays of her leg, CAT scan of her twilighted brain, MRI of her neck. She waited to hear about what was found and what was to be done. Pain and medication filled the waiting. She was asked if she wanted someone called. She asked for her children. No one else. Her doctor? She had no one special. Her brothers were out of town.

At last, she was placed in a bed and told she would spend the night there in starched sheets and plastic-sealed pillows. She had to ask what was wrong. "Take a look, honey," the nurse said and left. She was a patient, prone, looking up to others, not down on them like a doctor would.

She was a fucking patient. How foreign. How discombobulating. How dependent and how helpless she was. She tried to process this, and it seemed impossible. She was a patient at the mercy of orthopedic surgeons. Damn, damn, damn. Who was the asshole who hit her? May he rot in hell. She shrugged her shoulders and asked herself, what did it matter. She was a goddamn patient. Caught.

Jean surveyed the room. There was a clock and a calendar directly facing her and a TV hung from the ceiling. The date, her nurses' and doctors' names, and "regular diet" were on an eraser board. A sheet covered her body, and she pulled at it with both her hands until it came off. There was her left leg with external fixtures sticking out and screwed together in a scaffold around her leg. She sent messages to her toes, and they curled in recognition and pain. Her right foot moved easily, and she gingerly brought her right leg to a flexed position rubbing her knee in appreciation of its being.

Six weeks of crutches and a wheelchair and physical therapy. At first, she had no opinion of it all. She was an observer who wanted to erase it all like a word processing sentence that wasn't right. Put her finger on the delete key and watch all the words popped into oblivion one letter at a time or better yet block the whole event and click "cut" from her history. Yes, yes, she could have died, but this was limbo.

Her children came in shifts to watch her doze or stare at the TV with her or tell her what was happening to them, but she felt removed and studied them like friendly aliens. They had been busy with life, and in recent years, she knew them mainly by telephone. Her life had been her work. Her brothers called, and she told them she was okay. They were busy with plans for their spouses or spouses to be. She tried to leave a coherent message on her voice mail and to call as many patients as she could. She had the division secretary let the other doctors know, and she left a message with the chairman. The rest was put on hold; she couldn't think about how she was going to carry on with her leg stuck out on the wheelchair support like a battering ram against the world.

The rehab social worker came to see her and asked her if she was depressed. They talked about being women in the field and what it meant, and both decided she was doing all right considering her restrictions. She avoided sharing her fear and was the best of patients when the focus was on her. She was confined to that role until she could get home away from scrutiny. Then she could cry.

Dr. Schlager called her while she was propped up in bed at lunch the second week she was in rehab.

"Hello."

"Hello, this is Frank, Frank Schlager. How are you doing?"

She tried to place him, thinking of the surgeons and the physical therapists and the x-ray technicians.

"I'm sorry, you must have the wrong room. Who are you looking for?"

"Isn't this Jean Volk? This is Frank Schlager, Dr. Franz Schlager, the researcher, don't you remember?"

"Yes, this is Jean. Dr. Schlager, Schlager. Oh my God, of course."

"Well, I guess I'm not too memorable, but anyway I heard you'd been in an accident and I wanted to call to see if you were doing all right."

They exchanged pleasantries about accidents; she apologizing for not showing up for the meeting and he about not calling earlier.

"You know, I had the wrong idea about you. I thought you didn't care about the project," he said.

"You mean you thought I would stand you up?" she replied.

"Well, we researchers have had our bad experiences with clinicians."

"You mean the clinicians might put their patients first?"

"Well, you sound feisty even from the hospital bed. Is that right?" he laughed, diffusing the exchange.

Jean paused for a moment. She had been ready to defend herself.

He added, "I really did assume the worst, and I feel guilty." He laughed again. He was trying to be kind, he wanted to be nice, but she didn't seem to appreciate it. "Probably doesn't need me bothering her now," he mused.

She listened and felt relieved. "Ja, I guess I did too. Thank you for calling. I'm doing okay although the whole experience has an unreal quality about it. I guess I felt I was still an invincible twenty-year-old."

"Yes, broken bones cause broken illusions all right. I had ribs cracked and a spleen ruptured once, but I was twenty then."

"That must have hurt," she said and immediately regretted it.

"Ja."

There was the silence that happens in phone calls that should end but somehow both parties don't want to hang up, communicating through silence. She thought of other questions for him, and he thought of himself at twenty.

A nurse came in with her tray, and Jean felt interrupted but said, "Thanks for calling."

"You're welcome. Hope you keep on the mend."

"And I do hope you find someone to help you," she said quickly.

Jean had always found herself the giver in her relationships. She was pursued, and the attention somehow converted her to serving the man's needs. She was going to avoid putting the focus on him, and he'd have to lap it up somewhere else. Her ex-husband had easily developed his entitlement stance, which stood even before the children's. There had been the pain of refusing his needs for the babies, and he had never been gracious when she was torn between choosing who came first. When the children were under ten, he left for a job in Chicago to make money on some Saudi Arabian deal. He wouldn't give up the salary, and she wouldn't give up LA to stay in the Midwest. A few years later, they were divorced.

She could feel her children wanting her to find another man and almost waiting for her to do this so they could commit to someone too. Yet they always found something wrong with anyone she had sauntered about with. To choose her kids over others became automatic. Yet somehow she and they allowed her to have a career; it brought security when their father didn't send his support money.

Now she had nothing for at least the next month or two. Because of the accident, she had to refer all her private patients to someone else or they could wait for her or stop. She had to let other staff take over supervision of residents and medical students, membership in committees, and her specialty lectures. All of her work was on hold.

She tried to recall the accident, the day and the hours and minutes before it, but the accident's moment was lost in the limbo of the crash, wandering, unclaimed.

The orthopods talked about the callous formation cuffing her broken bones, and she waited for that comforting support that time was to give her. It didn't come.

When consulting, she had seen all the devices that the orthopedic surgeons, medicine's carpenters, had devised to keep bones aligned: steel halos sitting on the shoulders, making frozen gyroscopes of heads; corset braces for the scoliosis of the lumbar spine of young girls that resisted their bones wish to tilt; Striker frames that suspended the paralyzed skeleton softening pressure for its skin and muscle coat, and, of course, the casting in plaster and in plastic that held everything hot and still.

Restless, her leg was contained by the external fixations for weeks. There were the rods, coming from her skin like bullet trajectories, tightened with the wing nuts, caging her bruised left leg. While her right one waited patiently, able to flex and stretch, hoping for its companion to agree and comply with their purpose. She had to walk again and recreate all that she had woven together as a life. Life without friends for every day, life without someone to stay with her at night when she went home, life feeling like a burden to her children. Where was the steadying cane to care for all that?

Finally, time did its good as well as unrelenting bad and she was unpinned. Her leg was stiff, but it was metal free. The first day at home, her oldest daughter spent with her. Her children were going to alternate looking in on her due to self-mandated obligations. Jean could tell Estelle was irritated. "Bills" and 'this is not a bill' statements came in deluges. She piled pink, blue, green, and white papers together on the desk in the hallway. Orthopedists, hospital, anesthesiologist, physical therapist, social worker, radiologist, insurance company. Jean's car was still in the shop where the debate about the front axle continued.

Estelle was a very successful broker and had organized someone to come in and help with the meals and laundry, but Jean had refused. She wanted to be by herself, not with some woman who reminded her of all the babysitters, maids, and housekeepers she had had to rely on when the kids were young. Some well meaning Spanish or Pilipino woman, probably as old as she was, still having to serve, moving things to let her know that they had cleaned here and there, breaking things that disappeared and were never spoken of again, asking about pain for their stomachs and taking old clothes and old refrigerators gratefully. No, she didn't want that now.

"Why can't you accept a little help? It would make it so much easier," her oldest daughter offered.

"What's there to do? I have food and the bathroom. Please understand the hospital left me with no privacy. I need that now."

"But you need some help too. Honestly, Mom, it would be easier. Peter and I have to go to this damn open house. I want to learn remodeling with the money I made on the IPO. We have to go. Can't you think of us a little and make it easier?"

Jean thought about why it would be easier and for whom. Her daughters were busy, and now Jean was the one who was left at home. Had she so infantilized her own mother those last years when she had moved to California and her mother was in a retirement home? Her stepfather had died of a heart attack while he had been at a bar smoking a cigar and drinking his un-Italian Manhattans. The sweet sticky drink brought up the image of emptying all the booze bottles from the cupboards while her mother said, "He really liked his after-dinner drink. That's all, Jean."

"I think I hated him, Mom. He was so controlling."

"I did too, honey," her mother said in a matter-of-fact manner and dropped a full bottle in the trash. It cracked and splashed and splayed the tangy liquid out into the air.

They laughed at the mess on their clothes and kept dumping. "Why did you marry him, for God's sake?"

"I had to, really. No choice," she stated in her persistent matter-of-fact manner.

"What do you mean 'had to,' you weren't pregnant, right?" Jean asked impatiently. "No."

"But why then? Why if you hated him?"

"Well, what was I to do. I married your father in Munich and left business school in 1924. He came here and then sent for me, and I quit the bookstore. He provided for us with his tool and dye shop, one of the best in Detroit, even the River Rouge plant used his gears. Your stepfather hadn't been drafted, couldn't hear in his right ear. He said it was because of a ruptured eardrum. I had three children. In those days, you didn't have day care centers, and my parents were both dead when I came from Germany in 1926."

"Didn't my real father leave any insurance?"

"Why? We never thought he would die. I had Ralph and Eric years before you, then your father was gone. Your father, a full American citizen, he was drafted before you were born. It was with the army engineers. He was blown up in some accident in France, that's all. I was alone with three children. I got some death benefit social security, and Joe came along then."

"He was so cruel and he hated all of us and he hated Germans and women and anybody who disagreed with him. He called you Katy Kraut. I couldn't stand to have him pat me on the rear and say, 'Hi, little Heine, give me a kiss.' What the hell did you two have in common?"

"Well, Joe, his wife, she died of TB. Right in Herman Keifer near where you went to grade school. He didn't have any children, and he . . . I don't know . . . he kinda took over, moved in, and I, I was in shock I guess. In those days, women couldn't own their own property. I couldn't carry on the business, and I didn't have a job yet. I don't know, I cooked for him and he brought home money. It happened, and then I couldn't get away."

"Oh, Mom, he was so mean to you."

"Well, it's over now. I would like to move and you know what? I can do what I want within my means. Isn't that wonderful?" her mother said as she dropped all the glasses in on top of the bottles. They made mad clanging bright sounds as they broke into shards.

They both had decided she would be better off in a retirement home, freed of cooking and laundry. It amazed her how quickly her mother gave up the house she had lived in for over forty years. All the ugly craft show dog paintings and statues her stepfather had collected, all the dishes and odds and ends of cracked crystal he bought to polish the flaws. All of it. She didn't even ask if Jean or her brothers wanted any of it. She gave up Detroit and the few friends she had talked to a couple times a year. She picked a home overlooking the ocean in Santa Monica five miles from Jean.

Her mother bought all new furniture except she did take her two matching cupboards that had shelves and a base that opened into storage area, two lamps made out of huge brass cannon shells she said she bought after World War I, and a small mahogany inlaid music box with her few pieces of jewelry and photographs of her first wedding with Jean's father. In one photo, he was holding her mother's hand and looking intently into the camera. His eyes were dark, burrowed under thick eyebrows, and forever lost to the daughter he never saw.

The old furniture were made by Jean's father in Europe, and they had brought it with them for the dining room's dishes. Large table cloths of embroidered linen were destroyed by her stepfather's cigarettes. Jean's mother ordered new tablecloths and beddings from a Neiman Marcus catalogue, again without telling Jean or her brothers.

The retirement hotel included her own suite of a living room and bedroom with bath. She could have a little hot plate and a refrigerator in which she stored small cans of beer and jars of herring in sour cream. She drank instant coffee made from tap water for years thereafter.

Jean was haunted by the last months visiting with her mother as they sat in the retirement lounge. She watched her go through that dark blue purse with the gold clasp sticking out like a polyp, opening and closing it ten times or more, making sure she had the key to her room. Then she would agree to go out for lunch. Jean had been irritated like her daughters were now. Impatient and frustrated with her mother because she had different ideas about what to do with her life and its ending. Jean wanted her to go out and socialize, but her mother was content to sit on the porch and read murder mysteries and talk to the other ladies when necessary.

Yet her mother had been there for her, sent her the hidden saved money for medical school tuition, supported her decision not to stay married, and helped with the babysitting when it was still called babysitting, not child care. It was sad to hear her say, as though she got permission, that it was "all right with your stepfather" if she came over for a couple hours but she had to be back to make dinner. Jean had been so grateful but guilty that her mother had to bear the anger he had at Jean for not agreeing to treat his high-blood pressure and making him go to his own doctor. Then when he had died, she had wondered if her mother might live with one of her brothers or with her. Her mother said no and would visit only for an overnight stay at any of their houses. She liked her retirement home apartment, and later, she used the microwave Jean had given her. She thought it foolish to spend money on elaborate dinners, which were only "dollops of food" and she would only agree to lunch reluctantly. She loved to go to a movie or the museum. Suddenly, she became such a strong-minded, opinionated person while on her own.

Toward the last years, she talked about her family when she was young and seemed to consider Jean her confidant more than her daughter. She talked about how her own father, an officer, had been shot in some trench in Belgium early in the Great War and had died of an infection, and she talked of her mother and how she had died very late in the years of the influenza epidemic. She said she had no one and that Jean's father was a kind man whom she met while working in a bookstore and taking classes at the business school. They read Rilke together and planned to come to the United States of America. At night, she always came back to her coughing mother and watched her toss with fever, forbidding her child from entering the room so she wouldn't catch the illness. "I could do nothing for my mother. But you, you're a doctor, and that wouldn't have happened now." Her mother insisted. Jean wondered.

Her mother had died in her bed one night. Jean hadn't been there. In the morning, Jean had called, and there had been no answer, no answer at the usual time they talked. She knew there was something wrong. She left work, drove quickly to the apartment, parked on the street just as another car left the spot, and hurried in. When she got to the apartment, no one seemed to care. Activities were going on, and they blithely said Katherine hadn't been down yet.

Her gray hair was pushed out from the back of her head as she lay on the pillow, her body turned on her right side; the hair framed her calm face with her slack jaw and mouth wide open. She was relaxed. Jean saw none of the agony that she felt in her own heart at this quiet death.

Pushing her own head against the down pillow, Jean came back to the present and thought to herself that she could be more flexible. She could please her oldest daughter without feeling controlled.

She thought she could offer "I tell you what, why don't we let this woman come in for a couple days," but the idea of not being alone depleted her patience even before the woman could get there. She couldn't agree, she couldn't. "I'm sorry, Estelle, but I can't do it now. Maybe later I'll have someone clean the place. Please understand," she cajoled.

Her daughter left her propped in bed with sparkling mineral water, the newspaper, all the mail that hadn't been brought to the hospital, and a portable TV in a pink plastic case. She promised to be back in a couple days after her series of client meetings and her boyfriend's big annual firm dinner and said that Selena, Jean's youngest, would be by tomorrow. They were two years and three months apart and very close to each other.

The minute the gunning of the car engine faded, Jean got up and stepped her way slowly down the stairs to the kitchen and made toast with honey. She felt like Long John Silver with his wooden leg, one side of her body stiff but weak, maneuvering the steps like a swaying ship. Yet she was free.

After walking around the downstairs and checking her plants, she returned upstairs to the bathroom and ran the hot water in the bath without pulling the drain shut. She had gained at least ten or fifteen pounds sitting in that wheelchair even though she'd done PT. She patted her belly and lifted her breasts. It amused her to be so full. All her life she had been relatively thin, and now she didn't recognize her body and her weak leg. She sat on the edge of the tub one white leg in and one white leg out and then timidly put the injured leg in the water. She felt the hot water and sank into it, covering her head and rubbing her scalp.

Washing carefully, feeling the rough clean washcloth, luxuriating in her choices, she thought of her husband's hands touching her with those firm big finger, blunt and straight. She could feel his penis, the uncaped crusader they had called it, pushing pass the sway of perineal muscles into her. Sex had been easy and separate, but it got lost in life's other climaxes. She left the bath, dried herself, and lay on the bed to reach orgasm, and then she cried.

Hours later, she awoke to a phone call from a neighbor asking her how she was doing, and then her younger daughter, calling from her art gallery, complained that Jean didn't have call waiting and asked her "How's it going?"

"Doing better every day," she lied.

CHAPTER 39

Physician, Heal Thyself

"I'M SICK OF the damn pain and the doctors can't get rid of it," Frank's mother yelled over the phone.

"Does the nitro help?"

"Oh please, of course it does, but I hate to take it. It makes me feel weird. I don't want the open-heart surgery. It will leave a scar, and my ribs will hurt. I know it. The man down the hall had it done and his wife says he's a bear."

"Have them send me your cath results and I'll have someone look at it here, then we can decide," Frank offered.

"Your sisters don't give a damn, busy with their precious husbands and their trips."

"Now, Mother, they have to go where the businesses send them. Corporate life is like that."

"If only Franz had lived."

He heard his mother refer to his lost brother. It angered him. Hadn't he, the live Frank, done enough? Ever since she moved into the condo, he had sent her checks and birthday gifts and Mother's Day flowers and damn well paid for all the collect calls she made to him at least every other day since she retired and today again at the office. He was a dutiful son, and yet it was the same old story. He was never good enough.

Frank had an office view of the freeway and the hill going to the hospital. He looked out and watched the nurses and clerks walking diligently to work and the patients with multiple family members trailing or holding them to keep them steady. The Hispanics always came as families: a man or two holding a child and many women and many little kids dressed in smart matching outfits while the old people, mainly women, wore their gray hair in buns and dressed in their frayed sweaters over flowery dresses. He mused about all their closeness and their disregard for the convenience of leaving everyone home.

He had finished interviewing a student to work in the lab and felt her eagerness still hanging in the air like kite strings flying hope. She was an Asian woman, both parents born in Vietnam and now running a grocery store in Orange County. She was in her late twenties, came from Vietnam as a child, studied hard at Berkeley, and now was on break from the first to second year of medical school. She could remember the fires and the helicopters and the stink. She liked her car and genetics.

She listened quietly and smiled broadly, proud at the idea that she might contribute to research. She didn't or maybe didn't care to know it was merely one project and then another and another. Should he tell her science and research were never-ending? After he walked her over to the head technician so she could see the lab, he wandered around it himself, holding her already impressive CV with credits and second author papers on molecular biology.

Machines with intricate filaments and wires connecting the racks for test tubes and pipettes dominated his sight. He remembered the time when he was in graduate school and the mapping of the chromosomes was completed, gentle fat crossed larva of life's destiny lined up in a row of forty-five Xs and one Y, with the lost arm to make up the set. The double helix of DNA with its almost infinite combination of those four simple amino acids was described then. He owned the *Nature* issue where the article suggesting the helix was published; the journal copy itself was battered, but it was thrilling every time he turned the page gently to the small printed column.

He was in on the first use of the tricyclics to keep norepi in the brain. Now all the molecular biology and PCR to detect strands of viral forbearers of DNA were commonplace. There were the markers and assays for cancer and predispositions. Personalities were shy and sensitive or thrill-seeking and risk-taking.

Still, he carried on research on norepinephrine and serotonin and the multiple receptors for dopamine as well as his clinical studies correlates. The grant applications were due again, funding was tight, but at least his fellow relished the writing, which consisted really of begging for money again.

Yet he knew he was in a better position than one of his friends in the basic science department. Mike had been hit hard by the downsizing and the overspending on exotic transplant surgeons who had gotten the university into big debt on the medical campus. The attempt had been to cut salaries of the faculty to make up the deficit, and yet they were all asked to keep teaching and keep lab schedules. Mike taught anatomy. Strange and paradoxical how that became less and less important the more medical knowledge there was and gross anatomy in particular became squashed into sections of time only in the first year. Mechanics, form, and function were far less important than physiology and molecular biology now.

"You wait, in a couple years there won't even be a mandatory gross lab, and students will look at some videos or Netter-like models," Mike postulated repeatedly at their pathetic tennis games.

Frank smiled to himself at the way they would run around the courts and always avoid doubles with some of the available women at the club who hoped to play other games as well. Amy had been interested in joining the club years ago to learn tennis and "belong" to the right groups. Mike's wife still went to dinner there but was more active in the volunteer groups at the church they attended.

Frank picked up the phone and called Mike's office. Dr. Broadhurst was in, and the secretary connected them.

"Got time for lunch, Mike?"

"That would be great, Frank. No committee meeting on year 1 until two o'clock. How you been, Pancho Gonzales?"

"I'm trying to be Sampras, but age is weakening my knee joints," Frank joked. They usually would go to the faculty dining room with its ersatz British gentlemen's look, but Mike said he'd like to go to a little Mexican restaurant on Broadway and would pick Frank up at the parking lot entrance.

The old light blue Honda slid out into the driveway and Frank pulled the door handle, popped it open, and plopped into the seat. The car was still hot from being parked in the sun, and Mike had the air-conditioning running and the windows down.

"Still defying your wife about windows and air conditioning, huh?" Frank quipped.

"Yup and in winter, it's heater and open windows, but hey, it's not like I'm killing trees," Mike retorted.

They settled in a booth and each ordered a small beer and enchiladas as well as soft tacos with carnitas. Every time they went there, that was their order.

"Well, what's new with you?"

Frank unloaded his frustration with the administration and the loss of tenure connected to assured money, how the dean screwed everything up and still was the buddy of the university president while the provost hated him.

Mike talked about the class action suit the basic science faculty was filing and that their salaries had been only restored temporarily. He winced suddenly when biting into his taco and stopped. "I've been getting this damn pain in my front teeth. The dentist says there is nothing wrong, but damn it hurts."

"X-rays negative?"

"Absolutely, not even tender to the touch. I don't even have caps on these lower front teeth. Ah well, they'll probably take dental and health insurance away soon anyway. You know, the university's early retirement offer was only health insurance for ten years. Clever, that way you're on the verge of getting some catastrophic illness at seventy or seventy-five when the insurance stops. We're going to be in the same boat as the poor patient suckers that the county is going to make managed care casualties."

"I don't know, hard to think of retirement yet. Tennis and golf every day is not for me. Would like to travel and maybe finish that book on neurotransmitters. I don't know. Are you going to retire? You're my age."

"Sixty-six this coming July. Couple years older than you. The university can't force me out yet, and I can't think of anything else I like better. The students are really sharp. Might as well spend my time doing this, it goes faster."

"Ja, that's what we're doing, spending time. Do you think it goes faster because actual time increments are smaller compared to the total time we've lived, or do you think it's because enlightenment is far and few between routines?"

"I think it's a little of both. Still, you can't let boredom take over, then time is endless, right?"

Frank looked at Mike while his friend picked up his taco and caught some of the overflowing salsa on his sweater. Then he did a Mike thing, bringing the cloth and the salsa to his face and with his hidden fingers pushing the bits of onion and tomato into his mouth. This was a good guy, a fine man, and his buddy over twenty years. He looked a little grayer but still tan and didn't dye his hair like many of the other men on the faculty were doing. Mike had those big eyes behind the old horn-rimmed glasses and the dark blue sweater he always wore at the office even in hot as hell weather. He'd been there for Frank when the divorce had been final, had him to dinner a couple times every week for the first year, and saw him for tennis much more often than when he and Amy were married. He'd even brought him one of the puppies Mike's dog had birthed. The dog had been dead now five years, maybe even ten, but it had helped with the boys and had slept with Frank many a night when no one else was there.

Their lunch lasted through another beer, and then they returned to their offices, sleepy and bored.

The smog was particularly bad that day, and it was hot even for LA, 95° by noon and not done rising until about two or three in the afternoon. Frank had wondered if he should have gone to the university on the other side of town, near his home and the cooler weather. He could have gone east too, to upper New York or to the southern coast, Duke or Virginia. There had been offers in the Midwest as well, but he couldn't conceive of leaving the boys and seeing them only occasionally. Now they were gone north, and he was stuck in the smog.

He crossed the campus and arrived at the meeting ahead of two or three others and waited patiently until the committee chair began. He was a tall thin man who had been placed in charge of getting senior medical students interested in research. He was notoriously gay, not quiet and discrete like the university preferred, and about five years before had even run a medicine introduction course giving and getting rectals for the sake of "demystifying and desensitizing" the exam. He was proud of offering himself up for the exam and invited medical students to his and his lover's cabin on spring breaks. The medical students weren't as enthusiastic about having rectals, or pelvics for that matter, performed on themselves by their classmates. They tolerated his ideas but avoided participating until one year, a male Christian student complained. Then the university made participating "completely optional," compromising for political and financial reasons like wanting the teacher's money since he wasn't going to marry but owned a lot of real estate. Now the chair was very involved with curriculum revision and no longer teaching clinical medicine.

The meeting lasted through five o'clock and was supposed to resolve how seniors were to spend at least a month with one researcher or another. One hundred and fifty students and maybe twenty medical faculty with ongoing projects at the campus. Some students wouldn't work with animals, some wouldn't condone double-blind studies with placebos, and some still had to be told to treat AIDS patients like all other patients especially in research protocols. It was a nightmare, and Frank thought it should all be voluntary. He'd never had a problem with students volunteering and the chair pointed out sarcastically, "Not everyone is as popular as Frank."

"Look, Ralph, the emphasis of managed care is all on primary care physicians. Specialists are shunned and researchers are not necessary in the business world. In this climate of fast deals, fast deaths mean money saved. I don't think you should force students to pursue something like this. Instead, let's give them a series of lectures on what we're doing that should capture their interest, then they'll be our best emissaries out in the world or come to us for more," he fired back.

No such luck, the committee moved on to scheduling details and disbanded that session about six.

Afterwards, he stopped off at the mall on the way home and picked up a new book on HMO trends and lawsuits. He mulled around the bookstore, looking at big clean matching shelves with precisely stacked books, and then went over to the dirtier eclectic arrangements and mixed crowds of the Midnight Bookstore.

At home he corrected some proofs of a book chapter, ate a TV dinner of pasta and vegetables that tasted like the carton that it came in, and finished another beer.

He awoke to a colorless sky and an erection. A long shower facilitated relief and then woke him up. Saturday was the day he usually washed his car and did some yard work. His assistants covered the lab weekends. He wasn't sure why he kept the house. It did give him lots of minor repairs to do and reasons for going to B&B hardware. He was between taking up golf and giving up tennis, so clipping and pruning suited him. In the old house, he had puttered around until one of his neighbors came out and talked about cars or games or politics, but no one talked to anyone in this neighborhood where all the kids were grownup and the younger families were off in car pool pools.

He picked through cans and bottles he's filled with nails, screws, nuts, and bolts, found a washer, and carefully took it to fix a leaky hose faucet. He tightened the upper hinge on the side gate, broke up a small mud wasp nest under the front eves with the jet spray of the hose, and then washed down his car. The front tires produced black oily streams that followed the driveway into the street. He sprayed the lawn, washed some corners by the garage, and then he was done. He ate a big slice of salami and had the last beer. Then he napped until about four.

When he got up, he went to his desk. He moved some papers around and stacked some chapter proofs, sharpened two pencils, and smiled when he saw the little green address book his youngest son had given him after he complained about women hitting on him. He flipped the pages and didn't find a name he wanted to call. He wanted a woman but not the ones in the "green for growth" book, as his son called it, not a black book.

There had been the types who were still figuring out what career they wanted and were fifty and above, there were the forties types who wanted to do all the organizing and dinner partying for him as a doctor's wife, there were the thirties types who wanted children and a man who did house work while they went to school, there were those with failed marriages like his but with younger kids, there were the bleached blonds in real estate, the black bob-haired smart-dressing lawyers, the corporate-suited leggy administrators getting a little heavy incorporating vice president success, the social workers who connected best to helpless patients, the nurses who were like his children's wives, and the woman doctors struggling with their own careers. Amy remarried right away, but he couldn't. He could look anywhere and nowhere but still hadn't found what he wanted.

Getting up, he walked over to a stacks of books and standardized testing tools. Jean Volk's phone number was on one of the piles. He was going to call her no matter what anyone might say. Why not? She interested him.

The connection was made while both parties were still in their separate homes: Jean lying on her bed, brushing her hand over the duvet cover, which matched a group of pillows in shams, and listening; Frank shuffling through papers on his worn desk, and talking.

"I wanted to say hello. How are you doing?" he asked after mentioning his name.

"Well, thanks, I'm doing fine for a peg leg attached to a restless body. Orthopedists have no idea of what it means to be immobilized." She wondered why he would call and what he wanted from her.

"Why is it that we doctors can be so insensitive to anything but our specialty?" he commented cautiously, hoping to convey sympathy.

"Tunnel vision and an avoidance of the anguish of sympathy in an ugly world, of course," Jean replied, laughing. What did he want? Was he after getting her to do his research dirty work?

"Well, we solved that, now how about dinner? Unless you're busy reading Aristotle on medicine," he added to cover himself. He felt she didn't seem eager to talk.

"God, I've turned into an alpha wave TV freak. I didn't realize how awful daytime TV is. An understatement. It's worse than staring at the walls. At least then I don't have to hear these pitiful stories." Why would he be asking her to dinner? It put her on guard. What could he ask of her while she was laid up?

"But the old *General Hospital* soap opera must be your favorite," he followed through.

She hadn't accepted his invitation and was making small talk. He felt disappointed.

"I haven't found a thing in common with any show except the photograph they used and the actual outside of the hospital." She felt pressured to keep talking and yet suddenly had to go to the bathroom.

"Oh, so you did watch it," he joked. This was hard. She didn't give him any clue of what she felt. Another self-contained woman. Why did he always find them attractive?

"Well, I have to do my clinical . . . surveys"—she hesitated to use the word *research* and instead chose *surveys*—"so I know what patients are talking about." She liked the sound of his voice. Playing pillow talk pleased her. He was being gentle, but her gut sent this vague anxiety back to her mind, and she bolted with "Well, thank you for calling. I hope to be back at work soon."

Her voice sounded tentative. He tried again, one more time. "Don't you think a little survey of the LA restaurants might be in order? Your patients eat, don't they?"

"I'll think about it. May I call you later this week?" She couldn't understand what was going on. She obviously had other interests and was being polite.

He sighed and was about to hang up.

Jean interjected impulsively, "May I, could I have your number?"

"I thought . . . not a brush off, eh?" He laughed again and gave her his number. *We'll see*, he thought.

They said goodbyes, pressed the off buttons on the cordless phones, and settled them into the rechargers, each letting a hand hold the receiver a moment longer as it rested in its cradle.

The silence left in the room settled into their moods, and they returned to their separate tasks.

CHAPTER 40

Peri-Millennium

WHAT WAS HE thinking? She was dislodged from her inertia not having a telephone call that was a wrong number or a computer voice. He wouldn't let her disconnect quickly. And dinner? Was she going to have to hobble through a huge dining room? Would he laugh at her?

She rubbed her face and went to the bathroom. She didn't practice exercising her urethral sphincter control like all the women she knew did to avoid cystoceles but sat happily with relief coming quickly.

The telephone rang again. It was her youngest daughter, and she was coming over with some dinner.

Her daughters were lovely although they insisted that had they been beautiful, life would have been easier. Illogical as it was, to this day, they would tell her that she should have married a better-looking man than their father so they could have been better-looking themselves.

Selena came in the door and up the stairs, announcing herself, laden with all sorts of bags from Pavilions.

"Mother, I've decided to get two Siamese this spring."

"But what about Steve?"

"I don't know. He's a workaholic lesbian. No balls, as far as I can see."

Jean laughed and commented that they must have been fighting about something. Her daughter always cut herself off from whomever she was with if they gave her any trouble. Very efficient and confident. She thought of the patients who were women from the Philippines,

India, and Mexico who came to Los Angeles and worked in labs, in ORs, in homes. They each told her many times how much better off they were without men. They didn't have to resent their roles as housekeepers if they only kept house for themselves and maybe an occasional child coming and going, but to tell her daughter this? No. Jean had done it, and she knew how hard it was to raise children alone and cats to her daughter were no easier.

"Couldn't you work it out? Maybe see someone?" she asked in her softest voice.

"You remember that asshole we saw? He had to be a misogynist, although he hated Steve too, told him he was too rigid. Imagine an opinionated therapist," Selena complained. "Here, have some of this. It's pâté all made up."

Estelle and Selena had been named for the stars and the moon, when the world was doing its first moon travel in the 1960s, a romantic time in Jean's hopes. Her children seemed to have a clarity in perspective and didn't want to fall into any "traps" of their "physiology" as they described it.

Jean was still confused and worried what would happen to them if they waited too long and became the women she saw trying IVF, getting shots from their husbands, running in to see if they were ovulating, getting ready for "harvesting" and the like, and waiting in limbo over and over again for a pregnancy. Somehow she'd lost the ability to advise her daughters and use her knowledge for their protection. They were in their own process of learning and could only blame her in years past for not pushing them to get music and tennis lessons.

She had been successful in raising competent, kind adults. Yet it was strange to be nowhere with your children, they wanting to show you how much they knew, how little you could tell them, and what they could do for their mother. It made her feel helpless and displaced, with no role to play and yet on the stage, awkward and tentative in their presence. It was almost like being a kid again, teased for being smart or German or a girl getting breasts and ashamed that badgering hurt, but now ashamed of wanting to be a protective mother. It wasn't her need to be a grandmother that was thwarted, that would have been enormous work and a diversion from finding her own needs, but it was a little earned precious wisdom that could go nowhere and sat in her mind like Cassandra's unheeded cries.

The pâté was in a little plastic container covered with clear wrap, and she watched her daughter cut a piece and place it carefully on top of a fresh cracker. They talked about its taste and whether Jean had much pain, and then her daughter looked at her watch of gold and said she had to go. There was a show at the gallery tonight. She'd call later to see how things were going, her favorite phrase.

When the door shut, Jean took another cracker without anything on it. She wondered how her mother had been able to do without someone and her children also fine at a much younger age without anyone. Jean was the one in limbo, the "transitional woman" lost.

What should she do? Was it time in her life to think of her mother mothering her and her regrets and then die in bed. At her death, her mother had been twenty-five years older than Jean was now. She knew she was scheduled to return to work in a few days, to the hospital and her office. The secretaries, the residents, the staff, and the patients would make some comments and then she would be back at her routine.

There were the crisis of the budget, the endless "reengineering meetings" that was code for cuts, the new class of residents, bright foreign grads mainly, who did psychopharmacology where language didn't matter, and the calls to managed care to extend the time allotted for the authorized private sessions, pressures to earn private practice money for academic titles mandating tithes, to teach and do research and perform.

She thought of Frank Schlager. What a horrible name. She was glad she hadn't given up her professional name when she married, but she had been Mrs. Failure and her children had his name. At least Dr. Schlager had created a successful life for himself. She wondered if he were married and wanted to cheat on the side. Would it be good for her to work with him? If she wanted to stay at the university, publishing was the game? The caring and teaching and tithing were not enough, and she was never going to be given any more responsibility in the silver-haired solid white man's administration.

She let her mind wander around the idea of calling Dr. Schlager as she sat on the couch and looked at her bare feet. She marveled again at the idea that she could think *Move* and her toes, way down there, would move. Her left foot wiggled its toes as nicely as the right foot, and they held their little concert of movement at any tempo she commanded.

Amazing body, fine nervous system, amorphous mind in solid brain working together. She wiggled her toes again and smiled.

CHAPTER 41

A Summer Break

FOR THREE WEEKS, Tom awoke with an implanted alarm going off in his gut before his real clock could wake him. He was suddenly ripped out of unconsciousness, his gut swarming with fears and not understanding what thoughts caused this. The dread grew to become a living thing he carried in him like a parasite, some huge *Ascaris* worm of anxiety that coiled in his stomach. It could not be articulated nor excreted. He waited three more weeks before he mentioned the crying to anyone, and then it was to the psychiatrist who had seen Mrs. Finny when she came back to clinic.

He had a strange combination of respect and incredulousness for the mysterious workings of psychiatric diagnosis and treatment. Psychiatrists are generally strange anyway, Tom concluded in medical school, but he and other doctors still tended to call on psychiatrists for advice on medication for really sick patients. Psychologists, test givers, were seldom consultants on cancer patients. The mental status exam and neuropsychiatric assessments psychiatrists perform were strange and separate rituals.

As far as kindness and understanding, Tom felt he or the social worker or the family could do the same job as what he thought psychiatrists could or would do. He never really involved himself with issues about death because he felt the family dealt with those things on their own, that is, after he told them what was going to happen and answered their questions. He did have to answer the same questions many times, but he didn't mind that, and it gave people comfort to know that suffering wasn't necessary. Patients could be pain-free, physically pain-free.

Twenty or thirty years ago in the Age of Aquarius, many times he'd ask the patient's family whether he should tell the patient he or she was going to die. Half the time at least, the subject of patient's death was kept off limits. Family thought they were saving the patient grief and preserving hope. Tom always felt the patient and the family conspired in silence, both feeling it was too painful for the other. Now, since civil rights and all, the doctor usually tells the patient and the family. If the patient doesn't want to hear the prognosis he or she won't remember it, and of course, Tom would add very truthfully, statistics weren't everything. After a certain point, however, he could predict within days when most terminal patients would die. That wasn't statistics.

He liked Jean Volk as far as psychiatrists go, although she was over at the new hospital more and anyway he usually preferred to talk to a man. It was easier to explain things somehow or else he didn't feel so apologetic for his need of advice. However, this day Dr. Volk was on call. He noticed she was limping and wondered why she had to work so much. He didn't ask her what was wrong with her leg, and she spoke to him first and let him know Mrs. Finny was confused and markedly paranoid, which suggested an organic cause, and she recommended he should draw some electrolytes. He had called her back because Mrs. Finney's potassium was only 2.1 and he felt grateful that he could now take over. He went up on the ward after that.

"Did you keep Mrs. Finney, Dr. Zeitman?" Dr. Volk said as she sat at one of the nurses' counters and flipped through the notes of another chart. Her leg was in a soft blue brace.

"Sure did, thanks for the consultation. I'd never seen her like that. Electrolytes cause this kind of thing all by themselves?" he asked intently. He was trying to care and yet he was tired of Mrs. Finney; she always did something unpredictable and her being in and out of the hospital all the time. He would have to hear "Why me?" and he had only the scientific answers about oncogenes and such and she was tired of those and didn't understand them. Why did she have to have all these cancers anyway? Why her?

Dr. Volk was talking about paranoia and delirium and the brain being limited to thoughts and behavior in its responses. He looked at her and felt his eyes fight escaping tears like jailers trying to stop fugitives.

"Are you all right?" she asked while she handed him a Kleenex box nearby.

"Damn it. This had been going on for about a week. I can't figure out why me? I've never done this before." He watched her face as he said this. It was an oval face that has been etched with wrinkles in all the parts that get contracted by smiles and frowns. She was no longer smooth and pretty, and yet her eyes warmed in sympathy to his statement and he thought they were very kind. He got up immediately and wiped his face with a paper towel rather than the tissue and said offhandedly, "I'll have to get myself a CAT scan, see if I'm crazy."

"Maybe you need someone to talk to about it. Get a psychiatry scan. We doctors all feel immune to feelings, but they can really throw us for a loop too," she said and smiled.

He said nothing and looked at Mrs. Finney's chart, and she went on pursuing her patient's chart.

Hearing the nurses talk in the background about a patient's IV calmed him, and he then turned to her and said. "This is freakish and I have no idea why me. I probably need a break, that's all. Let's drop it for now. Thanks for the consultation on Mrs. Finney." He got up and walked out into the hall and went into the men's room to combed his hair. He arranged the long strands carefully and realized how long it took him to cover the ever-larger bald area. He patiently combed until he got it right and then washed his hands and went to seek the comfort of a sick patient and forget himself.

"I was going to my sister's in Texas for a couple months for a little vacation, but I can't think straight now. Why did the gasman poison the air?" Mrs. Finney said carefully with her little plastic tube placed on her tongue. "Why did he do this to me?"

"You're going to be able to go on vacation. Give me a few days and we'll get you better," Tom said, holding her hand and patting it and feeling guilty that he wasn't more understanding today. He poured out a little potassium supplement to have her sip besides the IV and held it up to her lips like a nurse would do.

"Oh, I don't understand, why me?" she said again and started crying.

"Now, now, I'll have the psychiatrist talk to you and you'll get better."

He left at four to go home. He felt excessively tired and had his blood drawn for routine chemistries and CBC at the lab on the way out. He began a differential diagnosis on himself by reviewing all his bodily functions. No headaches, change of vision, problems swallowing, coughing, coughing or spitting up blood? Well, occasional headaches, but relieved with ASA, began wearing reading glasses in his fifties, nothing else. Heart fine. Appetite and stomach okay except in the morning, bowels a little constipated lately, nothing he couldn't handle. Urination fine, good stream. No pain in chest or legs when walking, even up stairs. There was really nothing anyone would uncover.

He got out of his Jaguar in front of the open garage. He let his wife drive the Mercedes. It was not in there. He picked up a thrown newspaper and then got his key to go into the house. The door was a beautiful mahogany with an arch of beveled glass and a brass key plate. He stopped and looked at it and dread stung his gut again. He knew the house was empty, but he forced himself inside.

Again, he went from room to room, but it was not dark out yet and it was as if he could rediscover some of the corners of a house he'd lived in for nineteen years. The light made the furniture almost strange, as though it were still in some showroom. He remembered when he and his wife had first come upon that walnut chest. His wife had insisted he shop with her and the decorator. Beautiful wood was still his greatest pleasure, he thought. Greatest pleasure and yet it all gave him cramps now.

No one expected him home early. He'd read somewhere that cats become the soul of a house, and Bernard, who liked to sleep with him, was lying in the center of the hall by the top of the stairs. The seat of the soul was in the gall bladder in some societies and the heart in most or the pineal gland right at the center of the brain concluded others.

Bernard greeted him by getting up, stretching, putting his front legs out and pulling his rear up high, and yawning. He slowly came down the stairs and meowed for food. He got nothing but baby food since his urinary problems and his need for low-ash cat food. He was well taken care of and had the weight to illustrate that. Tom fed Bernard and then looked in the refrigerator and again walked aimlessly around the house. He returned to the kitchen as the cat finished eating and heard only the refrigerator humming and the cat lapping some water.

The dread was in him like the burnt tongue of his childhood cat, and he put on a sweater and decided he would go see his wife at the shop. He drove the few blocks and entered the small parking lot where the shop wedged itself between a cleaners and a florist. He pulled into an empty parking spot and looked in through the glass window. The shop was open, but only a sales clerk named Cindy was there. He felt some vague disappointment but realized he would have been more ill at ease if his wife would have been there and faced him with annoyance at his presence in her territory. He quickly left and went around the block to the big shopping mall and parked his car. It felt like he covered himself with a protective anonymity.

No one could see his dread although it felt like some pet cancer that trotted with him. The mall had become his sightseeing expeditions. He and his wife stopped traveling to Europe now that it was so expensive. Walking around Westwood was dangerous, and Santa Monica was sad to him because of all the couples, so he walked like the old people in the malls. Safe and busy. He liked to look in on the bookstores, stationary outlets, and nuts and candy places.

He methodically went up and down the corridors until he came to the end where a big department store swallowed and regurgitated other shoppers. There was never anything he could buy his wife; she would always return it. When he was at conventions, he used to walk through the men's department in different malls to see other styles as though he were out of town. Now he found himself in the shirts and tie area.

"May I help you, sir?" a blond stocky woman who smelled of loads of perfume asked him politely. She had some sort of European accent typical of all the middle-aged saleswomen in expensive department stores. He sneered to himself about the illusions of class superiority. If your accent were French, you were still something special, but Spanish meant commonplace.

"I'd like to see some ties. These over here," he spoke as he pointed to a case full of blue colors.

"That's real perfect with your hair, gray and distinguished," she said as pulled out a tray of paisley prints.

He looked at her to decide what her intention was with such remarks. He had never been sure whether it mattered who the woman he associated with was, only that she have that feminine presence that spoke to him. She had her hair pulled way back in a bun and had gold costume jewelry on her neck and ears and wrist. She dangled and swung one way with the jewelry and the other with her breasts when she walked over to get a mirror for him. "Let me put these next to you, so you'll get a better idea," she explained and then touched part of his sideburns as if to adjust some loose hair. He wondered if anything was out of place and quickly took his hand to smooth the hair down.

Tom fingered a couple ties and said, "Thank you, but they're not what I'm looking for."

"Well, what are you looking for? Do you want something a little more fun than stripes? We're showing all sorts of new prints this summer, and here's a lovely Armani made for the professional," she said with her eyes intent on his response.

"All right, let me see that," Tom said as he looked into the glass-enclosed shelves and tried to see his hair.

"So are you a businessman?" she asked.

"I'm a physician," he said. He never used the word *doctor* to laypeople because they mix up everything from a dentist to a PhD to a podiatrist with his hard-earned medical degree and everyone was a "doctor" nowadays.

"Oh, how wonderful! These are perfect ties for you," she seemed to gush with discovery, probably of his money potential, a myth today.

Tom knew he could take her out and buy her dinner and whatever. He wondered if it would make him feel good. But what would it do to his wife? He tried for a moment to remember his wife's name and couldn't. Who was she? She had the brown hair and the kind eyes. What was her name? Phyllis. Phyllis. Phyllis Zeitman. Phyllis Rosenberg. She had taken his name but began using her first name for her business cards when she opened the shop.

The saleswoman waited patiently and continued to put other ties in stylish arrangements on the counter in front of him. He looked at her again and picked up a blue tie and said, "This will do it."

"How would you like to pay for this, Doctor?" she questioned with a smile.

"Cash," he answered and placed the money in her hand.

"Are you sure I can't get you anything else tonight?"

"No," he said as he shook his head.

He recalled some of the opportunities life had easily given him in his career, in women, and in the stock market. He though about how he'd always been decisive and could appraise each situation to see what was best for him and for his patient. For him and for his patient. I've served them well, too, he thought.

"Here's your change, Doctor. Is there anything else?" she said again and smoothed her own hair.

He smiled and left. He was tired and hungry and didn't want to dance the ego dance for her or himself. As he walked out of the store, he thought it would be only somewhat pleasant if she sucked him off. He was tired, dead tired of it all, and he began to cry again. Like summer rain, he mused, big pellets of water. He immediately thought of Mrs. Finny and her supra-clavicular node and heard a strange series of words: "nugget of death and pellets of pain, nugget of death and pellets of pain." He sighed and stopped in front of another store window.

He could see both the mannequin men in their immaculate white linen suits for summer and the reflection of himself as a white face and gray shadow body superimposed. He reached up and smoothed his hair. Soon he would not be able to cover the growing area of skin under the long thinning stands. He remembered seeing a black man who had broaches on a satin shirt and who painted his head black with shoe polish and sang out to everyone in the hall by the hospital's medicine admitting. That was during his internship at the county hospital, too many years ago, he concluded. That man had been such a freak, but maybe he had also been right. Cover your head with paint rather than fake hair. The reality of coverage was there, not the illusion of real hair. Maybe he could carve coils and ringlets in his head like a Greek statue and never have to comb his hair again.

The tears stopped and he imagined himself chiseling his head. First, gently hammering the broad chisel over his scalp and watching the skin and meager hairs curl up and over each other like an orange he might peel in one long strip. Then he would dig out ruts and gullies and create his perfect curly-haired Adonis for his own head. It wasn't so insane. After all, he had done quite a bit of whittling while a teenager.

When he had been on his grandfather's farm every summer, he was given a new piece of wood to carve some interlocking puzzle or a fruit dish for his grandmother. He had cried the first year out there in this flat land without his parents. His father had been drafted, and his mother went to work, and he always felt they shipped him off to his unknown grandparents even though he had wanted to stay with the

FRITZ WOLF

grandparents who had lived above them in their brick duplex on Dexter Street. He never really forgave them for not fitting him in their lives during the summer when he could have been free of school and rising in the early hours. At the farm, he had to get up every morning even before the sun and always eat boiled chicken, which tasted like soaked string.

The mall fast-foods were all better than his grandmother's farm cooking. Everything was dry and cooked over and over. Her meals were all watery, and the bread became papier-mâché after soaking up the contents of the big bowls she always placed in front of them.

He remembered when he ate on a flat plate he was at home or above in his real grandparents' dining room. He always insisted that Phyllis feed the kids on flat plates. No food too runny for a flat plate was his motto. They seemed to like bowls as they got older and asked for stew and spaghetti and cereal and then everything wrapped to go in shiny paper and cardboard containers.

He came to the end of a corridor and had to either buy some food, a ticket to a movie, or go around and head back toward the other end of the mall. He bought a ticket to a movie. It struck him as strange, him going to a movie alone and in the early afternoon. He'd gone to a movie once in the afternoon while he was starting his practice, when he and Phyllis had found $20 worth of change in the jar she'd hidden in their dresser. It was such a celebration, full of joy and gratefulness. They had both been exhausted and felt deprived. Of course, they didn't know how to tell anyone that because they were such a success. A new practice and a new baby and all the potential for a dream life in most people's eyes. He was the scholar in his family and had one of the first combined MD and PhD opportunities in the country. She was the organizer and the prudent manager. They were the "best team ever," her younger sister used to say before she got married.

He bought popcorn and a soda and went to sit in the dark. The movie was some "cop kill, criminal kill, woman bashed, exploding car, and everyone get bloody" exercise. He watched it with the passivity that even his gut could not overcome in the chase parts. He was grateful that the dread had become distracted. He was alone without it, and he finished all his popcorn.

By six-thirty, the show let out, and he drifted slowly to his car and knew the only place he could go was to his house. To go to the office this late on Saturday would be strange; the hospital was all taken care of and shopping was hopeless. He had no friends that didn't have their own lives, and so it was to the house he went.

Lights were on in all the rooms, and Phyllis's car was parked in the middle of the driveway. Why was her presence in the house no help in warding off the smarting that had begun in his gut again?

She came to the head of the stairs and tilted her head down while she addressed him. "Thanks again, you son of a bitch. We were supposed to be at the Filberts at six."

"Oh God, I totally forgot. I really didn't even think of it."

"I left you two messages on your service today to avoid this. How often do I even ask you to do anything anymore?" she screamed and went back into the bedroom.

He took the steps quickly and repeated, "God, I'm sorry, Phyllis. I know this was important. I'll call them and say I had an emergency. We can make it by seven, seven-thirty."

"How can you be so utterly predictable? So consistently inconsiderate of everyone and be this god all your patient's worship? You've got to hate me to forget me so easily. You're so predictable," she said as she put a pearl necklace on and then turned to him and told him, "I've already called and made up some lie. Don't come if you don't want to. I don't care anymore. You can't hurt me anymore. You can't do it anymore."

"Phyllis, I forgot, that's all. I was even home early today. I went to see you at the shop. I forgot that's all."

"Why don't you forget your patients? Why do you only forget the kids and me? Our turn never came. Now the kids are off on their own, with Robert married and Rebecca engaged and graduating next year. Their father is someone they've heard about, that's all," she said, talking to herself as she faced the mirror again and smoothed a drop of liquid makeup over her cheek. "I'm old, for years and tears and wrinkles, I waited for you and I'm not waiting anymore. I never thought this would happen to me."

He dressed quickly and followed her down the stairs. Screaming had been their ritual before dinner parties, and they had always made their appearance relieved of anger. He got his coat out of the hall closet, remembering how long it had taken to find the right color paint for the door. He had the keys in his hand and opened the front door for her. She turned and looked at him and stared into his eyes trying to find some answer to a silent question. It startled him because he thought it might have been "Why me?"

She shook her head slightly and then said, "Don't come. I don't want you with me for this. I'll do this alone."

"Don't be ridiculous. Of course, I'll come," Tom said patiently.

"I'm tired of yelling and bitching. It's better if I don't expect you to be there. Don't come. I don't want to expect you for anything in my life anymore," she declared while she fumbled for her own keys out of her little sparkling purse and stepped through the doorway to her own car.

He followed her, but she would not let him get in the passenger's side of her car. He jiggled the door handle, waiting for her to release the lock.

"Tom, Tom," she yelled, "give me a break. I don't want to rely on you and be disappointed anymore. No more, Tom. Stay away!" She rolled up her window and drove off.

Tom stood in the driveway and then suddenly looked around to see if anyone would have witnesses the screaming. He looked again and slowly scanned his front yard. His eyes touched bushes and clusters of flowers and tall weed-like grasses and the spotty lawn he had always seen Phyllis try to weed. "Because the gardener never does it," she'd explain when he'd scold her.

There was a clump of some weed near his feet, and he bent down to pull it out of the ground. It resisted, and as he pulled, he stripped a few thin green blades but the plant stayed firm. He tried again but this time he surrounded the plant at the base with his hand and then yanked at it. He tore it loose and held its root ball in his other hand. Then he brought the plant in and put it in the garbage can under the sink and washed his hands.

He started up the stairs to lie down in bed, but he changed his mind and went back into the kitchen, pulled out the garbage can, and lifted the weed back into his hand.

He went out in the front of the house and tossed the already wilted plant into the bushes. *Let it try to survive,* he mused. *Why should it die merely because it's a weed?*

Then he climbed the stairs like an old man, sliding his hand up along the railing and pulling himself forward with each step.

The warm summer rain began to fall on his hands. *What had happened? Why me?* he thought. *I'd worked so hard.*

CHAPTER 42

Equilibrium

"WHAT IF WE'RE looking at a phenomenon of balance?"
"What do you mean, Dr. Schlager?"
"Suppose that the behavioral components of Alzheimer's like paranoid behavior, agitation, for example, are more similar than we had originally conceptualized with such conditions as schizophrenia and it is a matter of balancing the different neurotransmitters to obtain a harmony of brain as well of mind regardless of the actual amounts of the neurotransmitters?"

"You mean the lost acetylcholine in Alzheimer's disturbs the ratio between it and dopamine even though the dopamine levels are normal and yet shouldn't predict psychosis if you only think of the overload theory in schizophrenia?"

"Even further that might explain some of the serotonin-mediated mental conditions like depression and pain that are prevalent in Alzheimer's and schizophrenia."

"As far as pain goes though, aren't schizophrenics less likely to report pain symptoms?"

"I think the operative word is *report*. Schizophrenics have higher incidences of some ICD9 disease groups and lower incidence of others according to my studies, but depression is higher and pain has not been completely investigated, probably related to perception and interpretation of somatic stimuli."

"Should I do a Medline search, Dr. Schlager? I mean, it might help."

"Sure, do one for the last three years and see what the CDC data reports. I think though, it is important to reconceptualize and focus on the neurotransmitter ratio and balance issues and not think that patients with Alzheimer's, as well as the psychotics, are only reacting to their illness. It may be the brain at work, not only the mind."

This was his fun even though he knew most of the current researchers and their pursuits, get his fellows all worked up and think of new projects to give them the excitement of ideas. He smiled and mused that his own neurotransmitters were flooding his synaptic receptors; it felt good for once. He swiveled his chair over to his desk and looked at piles of papers, grant applications waiting to be finished, committee reports to be gone over, and teaching schedules to be honored. Increasingly, his salary had to be earned with grants, and yet there were also more demands for his time with restructuring. Too many responsibilities and too few faculty. He tossed another retirement notice and an offer from a drug company to do what he wanted, develop any projects, especially his cholinesterase inhibitor work.

He'd been at the university for twenty-seven years now, and he still was fighting for his job even though he was tenured. He knew that didn't mean much anymore other than in title. The medical school had spent money foolishly, like the sister university across town had also done, and now was going to conserve by means of pinching its supposedly treasured faculty. *Damn*, he thought, *Why couldn't I ride it out? The new golden boys can't get started without me or someone to ride coattails on.* Yet he felt this vague annoyance that no one really gave a damn about his past work, and the dean was looking for the school's young glory.

"Jean Volk on the line, Doctor," his secretary called through the open door, "and I'll be right back."

He picked up the phone. "Well, hello, are you back at work?" he said while rubbing his mustache with all the fingers of his left hand lined up together.

"I wonder if I might stop by your office this afternoon?" she said quietly.

"Of course, any time. I'll be here until about six or so." His thoughts continued with maybe she was ready. It would be valuable to get someone of her experience on the project so that the evaluations were accurate and reliable. Students were sloppier and less likely to pick up the nuances because of their language difficulties. There were more and more English as second language students, and their interests were not in understanding human thought as much as understanding its source. Dr. Volk was the ticket.

Jean held the phone to her ear for a moment before hanging up; she regretted the call and felt the desire to recall her words back through the receiver, back to her own ear, back to her own private struggles. She hated having to ask him for help, a justification in the delay of her participation in the project to counter the pressure she would get from the acting chair, who never did anything in research but was trying to please the dean.

Driving the Santa Monica freeway was slow going but steady. The din was newly noticeable after her reclusive quiet. She was aware of her foot doing its job on the pedal and how her leg shook from fatigue if the wait was too long at one of those unfathomable traffic holdups.

She drove her old repaired '86 Mustang, awakened from its slumber in the garage; her Honda was demolished in the accident. She would drive the Mustang until she had a new car and then trade in this old car. Estelle lauded her leased Mercedes but didn't convince her mother, and Selena liked her Jeep. The Mustang's clutch was hard, but the car was sensitive and loved first gear as much as fifth. Jean watched the traffic start to move again after passing the San Diego off-ramps and she could see up front the young girls cutting in and out of lanes without signaling, a few older drivers plodding in the right lane, the slow down again for everyone on areas where the damage had been done after the earthquake and the repair of white cement to bridge the gap.

She stuffed her hand into her purse while still at the last light on State Street to pull out her parking card. Always prepare ahead of time so she would keep no one behind her waiting. She had finally driven into the parking lot and been able to walk quite easily to her office at the hospital. Still, there was this vague sense of hesitation going back into the fray she had left, a deep muddy morass that she would have to put her feet in and pull out of again and again.

There were new messages for refills and patient appointments on her voice mail. Her desk was stacked with overflowing 11x8 manila envelopes and white letters with her name typed in official capitals, fliers and notifications of dues for this and that, letters to the faculty in general about how wonderful things were again and how they could make things even better by contributing to this fund and that effort. Money and time, money and time. Administration had copied the *LA Times*'s most recent articles on public health, managed care, the need for more hospital beds, and the poor treatment of the mentally ill. The scandal of the unauthorized cornea reaping reports had kept the university's name out of the newspaper and only the football losses were emphasized in the sports columns.

It was a gigantic mess. She wanted to go back home, prop her leg up, and read some Dickens about old lives.

Her secretary welcomed her back and told her there were going to be some more layoffs in the big county hospitals for the clerical staff and that the university didn't really care because they got their money for the doctors. Everyone knew the doctors were doing private practice at the outside hospitals and making the county-paid residents do the work at the new university hospital. It was a sham and a shame. The county didn't pay enough on its own, and the university didn't either.

She met with the rest of the faculty staff in her division and listened to their complaints about leadership and gossip, and she took two of the residents for some supervision by doing what was the good for her, seeing the patients on the wards. Time was strangely leaden with jetlag perspective, and soon it was five-thirty. She locked her door and then opened it again to call Dr. Schlager to make sure he was still there, locked the door again, and started for his office.

She walked down the stairs rather than wait for the always mysterious absent elevators with or without operators. The sun was waning in this season of long shadows, and there was the reliable late-afternoon breeze that helped LA breathe. She paused and let the warmth and coolness both touch her face. Since the accident, she had become aware of the sun and its position as the year moved through the earth's orbit. Strange, she never had really bothered with those angles and places of the earth in space for a long time, maybe since the first walk on the moon. Today was the fall equinox.

She looked up through the sunlight at the different colored and styled buildings, some with overhangs sheltering windows full of books and tangled plants or windowless walls with someone-with-money names on them. One window had a ceramic clown and a plastic gorilla holding a pennant taped up on the glass. Farther over was a surfboard dressed in a bikini and philodendron vines.

His office was on the third floor in one of the administration, faculty, and lab mixed buildings. The hall of scuffed and worn-out floor tile was bordered by gray, scratched file cabinets, assorted brown boxes, and old chairs spilling out from the open and closed doors of the offices.

His office was open at the exit door, but she went around to the front office, which had the neat desk of the secretary. It was empty. She knocked on his door.

He opened it and smiled, gestured with a sweep of his hand to come in, and plopped down again in his wooden chair with a green cushion molded to the wooded form.

She smiled and sat down in the same chair she'd been in before at the first meeting. She felt less angry for some reason. When she started to talk, her throat began to burn, and she was aware that she was going to cry if she said anything. It was the curse of her emotions that always haunted her in professional situations. *Women shouldn't cry,* she thought and yet her throat possessed these two columns of pain, caught her in their vice, and made her feel a helpless mute. No wonder she couldn't make it any farther in her aborted career.

He picked up her hesitation, felt she must be angry at having to meet again, and said softly, "What can I do for you, Dr. Volk?"

She raised her hand as if to stop him and swallowed hard. Please calm down, she begged herself. "I, well, I . . .," she sputtered and then stopped again.

He got up to get her a cup of water from the cooler. He would try to show her he was not unreasonable. She thought he was leaving and said, "Give me a minute."

"Of course, I'm getting us some water. Hold on." He left the room.

She swallowed again and swore at herself. She knew he would get mad soon and tell her to leave and forget it.

"Why don't I show you the lab, and then we can talk, okay?" he said as he brought a cup of water to her. She swallowed a large gulp and stood up in agreement. The lab was down the hall and had the black old resistant counters of chemistry but beakers and swan necked flasks were interrupted by stacks of machines with wires and plastic tubes and lights tangled together in mazes. He showed her the PCR procedure for detecting gene profiles and the viral loads, how they screen for everything from the different hepatitis viruses, multiple sclerosis, and AIDS and machines to assay bioamine loads; and by the time they had traversed the lab to the windows, she was remembering the comfort she had felt in chemistry classes when she was young and he the satisfaction he had in creating the lab years ago.

She wondered if she could talk to him now; this setup of his was so impressive even though it was messy as a kid's room. She was such a failure in her career trying to keep everything in order.

He wondered if she would think less harshly of him, be less angry in light of his beautiful lab.

They sat down again and she began. "I've come to ask you for a reprieve from the research I've been told to do for you. I need more time since I just got back and have to catch up," Jean said quietly.

"Well, I am surprised," he answered quickly.

"Surprised? What did you expect? You're putting pressure on me. I don't have the help you have," she said sharply and gestured by sweeping her hand around.

He sighed and thought of his mother yelling at him. "I am surprised," he repeated, "because you are still interested in the project."

They looked at each other's eyes for a quizzical moment and then each took a drink of water from the cups they had carefully taken from the desk. Then he stroked his mustache and studied her. She was a pleasant-looking woman, with mixed hair color, long eyelashes, and a full mouth. She didn't wear much makeup, but her cheeks colored as she talked.

"Look, I'm sorry. I can't do it now. Is that all right?" Jean asked plaintively. She was afraid he was still going to yell at her. He was stroking his mustache, which matched his gray hair with a touch of black left from years before. His eyes were brown and shielded by the careful frown of his brow.

Frank waited and thought. He wasn't sure what to say so she would stay in the office. It was turning dark, and she seemed to fade into the ending day.

"We can go ahead and line up some possible subjects this month, and the interviews can come later if that would help," he offered.

"That would really help. I could get caught up and then block out time for interviews," Jean responded.

A student in a full-length lab coat peeked in, looked at one and then the other, switched on the light to peer in more carefully, and said he was leaving to get something to eat and he'd see Frank in the morning. Jean and Frank looked at their watches; it was five to seven.

Jean still had her suit jacket on, and Frank put his on and said he'd walk out with her. They stood in the elevator side by side and said nothing. She stared straight ahead, aware of his height being a little bit above her, and he glanced at her hair clustered in a knot. Each was thinking about driving home, retreating to familiarity and a cold dinner of leftover soup for her and Hungry-Man TV dinner for him. It was black out.

"Look, I could explain to you what the project's timeline is all about over a bite to eat. Would you agree to that without feeling pressured?" he ventured. He thought to himself if he could reassure her that her part was vital maybe that would make her less angry.

"I tell you what, only if I can treat you, since you're being so flexible," she offered, grateful, surprised, and yet needing some control over this invitation.

"Anything around here you like?" he asked, making sure she didn't feel he was imposing.

"I don't know anything around here, only lunch joints. I'm on the Westside," she countered.

"Well, I could drive you and then bring you back. There's a little Mexican place nearby."

"Oh, that's all right. I'll follow in my car."

They met at the corner where the old pillars for the hospital entrance held ornate iron lanterns that were quiet and overshadowed by the modern streetlights. They passed through the dark streets with bright lights cutting out clean windows outlines in the calm colored buildings.

He drove slowly looking in the rearview mirror to make sure she was not gone, and she followed easily but somewhat impatiently as her precious car solitude was being invaded. The restaurant was closed. He waved her by him as he parked. She rolled her window down to hear him.

"That's life. I tried anyway," he yelled to her.

Her stomach gurgled; it would be a long ride home. "Well, thanks anyway. Maybe some other time." She thought of the McDonald's up ahead but figured that would not be good enough for him. She waved and drove on. Dinner interruptus, her stomach complained.

He sat in the car for a few minutes, looking at the sign with the restaurant hours clearly marked as open and then drove over to McDonald's to get a number three for eating at home.

The freeway was clear, and he moved through the city easily. He got out of his car in his driveway and looked up at the mottled moon casting cold clear light. He felt restless and unfulfilled. A beer was easier than running.

She drove through downtown and on to the fast-moving freeway, deciphering stars from airplanes and thinking about death and her theory of each person reaching his or her "singularity," imploding like the stars forming black holes at the end of a day or a life. She was lonely.

CHAPTER 43

Thanks for the Memories

"FOR CHRIST'S SAKE, stop being such a Nazi about it, Jeanie. I'm only a couple hours late, had to redo a brief."

"Damn it, I have to be at that stupid PTA meeting and you promised you'd be home to take care of the kids."

"All right already, I am. Give me a minute." He went into the bathroom and shut the door. She could hear the newspaper being opened and folded to an inner page.

"Sing me 'Silver Bells,' Mommy."

"Yeah, 'Silver Bells.' What are they again?"

"They're the little lilies of the valley flowers like we have by grandma's driveway." She ran her fingers through her girls' feather-like hair and kissed them while covering them up with their matching multi-pastel-colored comforters. She sang slowly and coming to the end with "Oh, how I wish that I could hear them ring, that will only happen when the fairies sing" and reached to turn off the light.

She went into the kitchen and put out his dinner and then into the bedroom to comb her hair and put on her jacket. She was thirty minutes late. She knocked on the door of their only bathroom.

"God damn it, can't I even take a crap in peace?" he bellowed back.

"I've got to go, Brad. The kids are in bed. Make sure they don't fuss around please. They have to get up early tomorrow."

As she put her coat on and opened the front door, he came out, zipping his pants and mumbling how hard it was to live with Hitler.

She felt hurt and closed the door quietly as though she could have been gone before he had said it.

They had been married ten years by then, and he'd had five jobs with different firms in Detroit; the first one a big beautiful office setup overlooking the river, which lasted only nine months and two big get-togethers with the partners. He told her he didn't like the cases, but she found out later he'd lost two clients with excessive billing and yelling. The others were with smaller firms that did family law, but he never had enough billing, and he would lament clients "never understood what I was doing for them." By then he worked for an insurance claims office finding evidence that people lied on their insurance applications about their health.

When she came home at ten-thirty, she found the kids on the couch watching TV and Brad on the big chair asleep. One of his World War II books showed a black-and-white photograph of guns lunged forward and retreated again lying on his disheveled shirt and his heaving and receding chest. He was constantly buying books about the battle of Berlin and about the Normandy invasion with money they didn't have to spare, and even though he had only been twelve then, he still had the newspaper clippings he'd saved in a thick black-paged album. Once when she had come home after doing insurance physicals for $12, she found, casually placed on the floor in their bedroom, a book about the holocaust. It was opened to a page with the photograph of a thing, gaunt, wasted, and dead. It stunned Jeanie when all she recognized was long and black hair on a shrunken skin-covered skull and the triangular patch at the junction of stick legs. There was no real face, no breasts, the oval hollow of a lost abdomen, bones of arms and legs with joint knobs stuck out like a stringless puppet. It was hung over a man's shoulder whose scapulas showed through the skin as huge as angel wings and who was dragging her along.

His grandfather was Jewish and never accepted Jean. Brad didn't observe any religion and wouldn't celebrate any holiday but took presents anytime.

They hated each other: he hated because she asked for things from him and she hated because she couldn't get them. He withdrew each year until there was no sex even when she saw him wake up with an erection. He would look defiantly at her, closing his robe and going into the shower. Through her last years in medical school, he would answer the telephone calls and abruptly hand her the receiver; she would talk with the calling medical students and study for her boards, hoping to finally apply for residencies and moonlighting in a medicine clinic for extra money.

If her brothers called, he would swear at her about liking them better than her own husband and call them losers. They stopped calling and writing, and she only saw them years later at their stepfather's and then mother's funerals. At neighborhood gatherings for kids birthdays, he would brag he was putting her through medical school even though it wasn't true and put on his exasperated eyes look toward the ceiling when talking about how long it was taking and why she couldn't be a "regular" wife. He never said anything about her mother helping with the tuition.

They had been such a potential team, a lawyer and a soon-to-be doctor. They had met at a mixer her junior undergraduate year. He had been the brother of one of the assistant administrators of the dorm. He knew what she had wanted to do, but every year, he hated her more as she became more determined. Finally, when the kids were seven and nine, he came home one night and, while watching the news after dinner, said he was moving out. "I'm going to Chicago to find myself," he said. He did consulting for anyone, including some of the Arab companies that he privately hated.

She applied for California residencies when she heard that he'd moved in with a checker at Kroger. Ola Harper had been her babysitter even during the one month she had to take off from medical school because of Estelle's birth. Her mother couldn't come much because her stepfather was angry Jean wouldn't get him his hypertension pills. By the time Selena came, she was in her last year and would be starting her internship. People said she was crazy, but she finished and worked in general medicine and in emergency rooms at regular hours until that night Brad said he was moving out.

Ola had come every day by bus to the apartment where Brad and Jean had student housing in one of Jeffery housing project's fourteen-story X-shaped buildings the university shared with welfare families. It was $33 a month. Two small bedrooms, a bathroom, and a kitchen–living room in gun battle gray. Ola followed them when they moved to a little house off Dexter. Brad had gotten that first job, and Jean took the bus to school when Brad had to use the old Ford they bought.

She'd had so may housekeepers and babysitters way before au pairs and care givers—Biolas, Violas, Harriets, Yolandas, Margaritas, Silvias, Mrs. Baker, Mrs. Johnson—but it was Ola Harper who she would always thank. She was the reliable chocolate presence the kids trusted and marveled at when she let them touch her hair and laughed with them over *Bullwinkle*. She came at seven-thirty in the morning in the same wool coat whether it was eighteen below or ninety above. Jean always gave her money and sweaters for Christmas. They hugged when she left for the last time, and Jean knew Ola was more to her than her family. Ola gave her children two books on the United States flag and the history of Detroit and said goodbye with tears in her eyes. They had their own sisterhood.

When she drove to California with the children and a U-Haul It trailer, she had only clothes, a few toys, two bikes, a typewriter, $843, and a handmade card with real rose petals glued on from Ola wishing her good luck. She wished she could have come with her, but Ola had a husband who was a welder at the River Rouge plant. Ringing in Jean's ear was her stepfather's remark,"What a stupid move," her mother's warning,"Be careful about the kids getting exposed to drugs" and her brothers' promises "I'll write," which they never did until she did.

There was still a Route 66, two lane roads, and motels with individual little cabins to hole up in and listen to the Beatles and her favorite, Santana. When Jean, Estelle, and Selena hit Palm Springs, it was eight at night. The car had no air-conditioning, and the air swallowed them in warmth. They stayed for two days and walked around the deserted town at night and swam in the hot pool water during the day. She smeared the kids with suntan lotion, and they turned brown while she hid her burnt shoulders and studied maps. The next night, she was going to the ocean, straight on through to Los Angeles. She had five weeks to get an apartment and find a babysitter before starting her residency at the LA County–USC Medical Center.

Ever since then, she loved driving the freeways at night, with the car windows open and the radio shouting glorious symphonies. White, red, green, and yellow lights dotting and blasting the dark, and cars moving fast into endless tributaries of city life and toward the ocean covered with the darkness.

The spring before Jean's trip, Frank had given his first poster exhibit in California at the American Psychiatric Association meeting. It was on suicide and the levels of serotonin metabolites in the cerebral spinal fluid.

Amy had come with him but stayed in the hotel room the whole time because she had a headache and didn't feel well. She never felt well on trips and sometimes even vomited if she didn't get enough sleep. She went out twice to shop at Fashion Island and then at Rodeo Drive. She bought a Hermes scarf with chains on it and wore it around the hotel suite with her robe. The boys were with his mother and grandmother who had come for a visit before the convention and stayed to babysit. His grandmother was seventy-seven, and it was the only time she left the farm and his grandfather. His mother was never home when he checked in, but his grandmother was thrilled at the privilege of taking care of them and said the boys were "wonderful little kinder."

"She better not give them cookies. I'm sick of having to deal with her spoiling them. Your mother is such a cold bitch. She's probably off again running around town looking at antiques," Amy yelled from the bathtub.

Amy had been trying to finish her thesis for twelve years and had decided she didn't like the subject anymore, "The Role of Women in Nineteen-Century Novels." He tried to make it easier for her, let her work at night in the study and not do the dishes after dinner. She usually wound up in the bath with *Vogue* or *Ms.* magazine. Occasionally, he would find a poem she had written, and it was usually about the lot of women "harnessed to nurturing," "sold souls penetrated by impenitent penises" while men "pounded out profundities, pillaging the helpless, committing pogroms for power, numb to needs."

He hated her alliterations and felt all the messages were directed at him; he was a failure at taking care of her and held her back from a career because of the children and his own selfishness.

"Your work always come first, fuck it! Why don't you have to go to the grocery store? I'm sick of picking out vegetables. You go. The boys don't like anything I get. They're always burping at the dinner table. They even have dirty socks that smell like yours."

He arranged for his mother and grandmother to come from the farm so she could go to MLA conferences in Boston and New York. He stayed in Chicago, wrote and lectured at the university hoping to secure tenure if he could, but still she would come back and complain about how lucky the people she met were because they could pursue their careers unhindered by "mundane responsibilities."

After their last boy was born, Frank couldn't touch Amy during the night, and in the daytime, she would stand still but turn her face away when he tried to kiss her. He felt allowed to give her a gentle peck on the cheek but never hold her too tightly with his hands on her arms, trying to steady her into staying still.

He placated her with trips and even agreed to the remodeling of the kitchen of their newly bought home in the North Shore Winnetka District she loved for its old homes and rich neighbors. He found her with the contractor in his oldest boy's bed one day and couldn't stand the house thereafter.

They came to California on his year sabbatical to do research, and he was offered a job at the end of that year. He loved Chicago and the seasons, but Amy seemed happier in the sunshine and they stayed. His grandparents were dead now, and nothing held them in the Midwest.

They bought a perfectly good air-conditioned house in Culver City, and he watched the smog of the city decrease as the fog of their relationship increased. It became unrecognizable in the early '80s. At the time of the Olympic games, he had ordered tickets for them all to see some track-and-field and swimming events. She refused to go, and he took the boys. They were all excited about Carl Lewis, and he quietly cheered for the USA and West German swimming team against the East Germans and the Chinese. It had been a party in LA without the cold war Russians as the political party poopers.

He and the boys walked along the old Adams Street with the huge houses and elegant porches, parked in bare dirt lots overseen by smiling young black teenagers, laughed and ate french fries in the car, which usually was forbidden by Amy. When they spilled into the living room, George held his flag and Matt yelled, "Mom, it was really cool!" She was sitting in the yellow-stripped chair having drinks with her advisor, B. L. Williams, who was sitting in the center of the couch with his arms extended over all the pillows and his hands hanging down, relaxed and in control.

She had been seeing this guy for about six months to finish her theses, and then she had suddenly stopped in 1982. Now two years later, they had revealed their affair to Frank with a simple statement by the balding thesis advisor with a state college degree in literature. "I think that your wife needs some space. I've offered her my apartment," he said right in front of the children, who were then twelve and nine.

Frank never forgot that moment—dead drama, mundane, trite, her hate hanging in the air as some sort of triumph over him. He would never succeed with her, which was her message to all his other successes. Unsure of what to say or do, he told the boys to give him some time alone with their mom, and they hurried out and slammed the doors to their rooms.

They divorced six months later, and she married the "asshole" as the boys called him. She never finished her degree, and they had a little boy who apparently had trisomy 21 or Down's syndrome. She took care of him all the time and never let anyone in the house. He heard she'd attempted suicide twice and worked at a shelter for battered women. She brought the little boy with her until he developed leukemia and died at eleven. Amy did volunteer work at a school for retarded children after that and then got a job as a marriage, family, and child counselor to support her husband who had developed renal failure and was on dialysis. Frank had wondered about the cocaine rumors but never asked if that was the cause of the renal failure. He wanted to keep away from the hate.

His boys stayed with him, and he got them through school with passing grades, and then they both went to college, but not at his school. That cost him a hell of a lot of money, but they did him proud and made decent careers for themselves. They always had very ambitious and fine girlfriends and never expected to get married. Each of them got job offers in Washington and Oregon, and each left for their new jobs in the early '90s. *Amazing,* he mused. *Now George is going to be a father and Matt is thinking about when he will marry Gina.* They talked to their mother on her birthday, and that was all he knew.

Amy did call Frank periodically to ask for more money even though initially she had refused the alimony and it was paid off into a trust. She always swore at him and told him he had ruined her life. He didn't understand the whole thing and only listened quietly until she worked herself up into a big enough frenzy to hang up on him.

CHAPTER 44

Tonight the waves march/In long ranks/Cutting the darkness/With their silver shanks . . .

— Langston Hughes

"THIS IS A lovely."

"Yes, we can go and do most everything is LA," he responded.

"You know, it's really great being a psychiatrist here, with all the cultures. I can go to different enclaves. I can hear all sorts of music, I can read anything I like, and it's all probably relevant for patient understanding."

"What do you read?"

"I've read Jane Austin, Thomas Hardy, Dickens, Conrad, Rilke, Goethe, the Russians, the French, and Pearl Buck and Walter Farley's *Black Stallion* too," Jean said, relaxing more. "The Japanese writers have many great themes."

"And philosophy and poetry too, I would suppose," Frank added.

"Absolutely. Dickinson, Yeats, Langston Hughes, Dylan Thomas, and Bob Dylan. Freud, Kant, and Nietzsche."

Frank and Jean had finally arranged to have dinner. He'd picked her up in front of Santa Monica Place. They sat at a window table overlooking the ocean. For the first fifteen minutes, they admired the water as the waves came close and then receded. Their voices relieved with the rush and hush of the waves they both knew well from many walks alone.

They each commended themselves for having accomplished sitting at a table near the big window and sponge-painted wall of the spacious PCH restaurant without any incident. She was not too clumsy before she sat down, and he avoided pulling the tablecloth enough to tumble a precarious water glass.

With the wine served, they returned to talking about people and events that had influenced them. She was wary not only of falling while traversing the tight paths between tables but in revealing her anger at feeling obligated to come.

He was frustrated about what would be okay to talk about and warned himself to be careful not to approach the research job yet.

Frank talked about the *Microbe Hunters* and Einstein, Fleming and penicillin and other drug discoveries, Freud, Watson and Crick, the uses of lithium, chromosomes and DNA, genetic profiling, Francis Collins's Human Genome Project.

He paused, thinking it was her turn again and hoping to encourage her. "I suppose you really liked Sylvia Plath?" Frank asked sincerely.

"Sylvia Plath?" she questioned incredulously.

"Well, you know because of the feminist movement and your career, when you were young," he back-pedaled, not wanting to offend.

Jean had agreed as they listed who had the greatest influences on the fading twentieth-century: Freud, Einstein, Karl Marx, the Steves, Wozniak and Jobs, Bill Gates, and, of course, the Roosevelts, Hitler, and Stalin.

They ordered sea bass. Everything seemed to get more pleasant. They had some wine and salad, and she said she also admired writers of poetry and fiction who had been medical doctors and secretly loved A. J. Cronin and William Carlos Williams.

"Sylvia Plath," she repeated. "You know I've liked some of her eye and sun imagery, but if you really want the truth unfettered and released through wine, I'll tell you."

He smiled at her sudden boldness. "Yes, tell me."

"Well,"—she paused and sipped more cabernet—"well, I am appalled at the worship by women of a woman who wrote about suicide, her own masturbatory obsession with suicide, couldn't live without her father, panicked when her husband couldn't keep up, abandoned her children, and stuck her head in an oven like a blond soufflé. This is no example of a feminist icon in my book. Poetry okay, behavior murky, helpless, depressed. Do you hear the irony of a feminist sticking her head in an oven? It makes me puke."

"That's quite an opinion."

"Well, there she was falling in love with Hughes, her teacher—whatever his pathology—and when he left her, it was like her father leaving her all over again, if you want a flippant interpretation. Some of us actually lived the life and made it through the hell of a woman having a career and children and don't want fathers to rescue us and don't want to be men either, just have them around."

"I'm glad to hear that. I thought you might be a little bitter about having to raise the children alone."

"You did it too. Are you bitter?" Jean asked and quickly looked down to her salad as the waiter's arm placed bread near the green mass with white crumbled goat cheese at her place. She was still affected by only small amounts of wine, but it felt good. Who was he that she should be demure and censor herself? He had pestered her to go out to get her to do his research like his laundry, and she wasn't susceptible to bribes of dinner or anything else.

"I did have my boys most of the time. My ex-wife remarried and had a little baby. She was busy. Really started completely anew. Can you believe that?" He thought about how easy it was for Amy to give him up and only see the boys when her new husband was on business trips. What did this woman know about men feeling abandoned?

"I can't really understand it, but my ex did it too. Left and seemed to forget. How can you leave your children?" Jean asked.

"Who knows? Better if we wait and they leave us as they grow up, I guess. Sometimes I think I'm still waiting as though keeping in touch meant that I couldn't go ahead with my own life."

She looked at him. "That was quite an insight," she mused while watching his broad hands encircle a roll and break it apart. "Yet you really are a success already. I mean a PhD in biochemistry and then a medical doctor, published all over. What more do you want?"

The roll was soft, and he ate each half without butter. He was disheartened, knew he wouldn't feel full with the skimpy decorated food, and felt she saw him as narrowly focused. She was bright and independent, probably been alone as long as he had. "Well, and you, aren't you feeling successful?"

"It's strange how hard I still have to try to earn respect."

He sighed and finished the last of his roll. He wondered about who he was trying to earn respect from.

She broke his reverie with "I didn't realize how lucky I'd been in not getting sick. I felt I lost all respect and was without authority. This accident was horrible. It made me so dependent."

"Did you need much medication? Was the pain overwhelming?"

"Not at first, and then not as bad as the feeling of helplessness. Being lifted and carried and told what to do." Jean winced and tried to hide her tears as they sprang up through her words by rubbing her eyes. "I've always been the mother or the doctor all these years and, you know, the strong one."

"Do you think we gave up on our needs?" he said and stabbed the last of a tomato. She looked at him and realized she had been more candid about her fears now than during the whole time of the recovery. She was shocked at herself and wondered why it took her so long to really understand what the accident had really done to her. "I couldn't walk at first. A left leg flapping in the wind, like a rag doll. Like it had left me but was still attached and then the external pins, coming out like arrows, medieval torture pins that didn't hurt but were as bad. Manacled to them." She let the tears drip onto her plate, and she ate them with the rest of the mixed leaves she studied carefully as she pierced them with her fork. "My children and hospital staff seemed patronizing and demeaning. I hated it."

"Sometimes when my boys call, I hear that patronizing tone as though I were on the verge of senility, and they were being patient with me. I hate it too. At the lab, the new fellows, computer programmers and facile with the data, they look at me as if I'm impaired because I have to learn the programs rather than intuit them. You know, I thought you were doing that to me too because you wouldn't work with me. I figured it was beneath you. Maybe you thought my work was passé."

She laughed. "I thought it was a stupid assignment by the chair who was desperate for some power. You're an expert. I'm a clinician, not a . . ." She was going to say *data collector*, but the waiter came by, poured some more wine, and wiped the spill from the table. She became silent. She remembered being forced to clean her stepfather's car, its red vinyl seats like the ones they sat on now. He would come out when she was leaning over the front seat to check the back of the two-door Chevy, and he would swat her on the butt.

Frank asked the waiter for more rolls and watched as the clean-shaven boy went to the back and returned quickly with another basket with rolls wrapped in a red cloth napkin. It reminded him of his grandmother picking up her rolls by fingertips from the oven tray and dropping them into a big cloth-covered basket to bring to the table. When they were opened, the steam rushed out like ghost of goodness, and the butter melted in yellow creamy mounds. His mother wouldn't let him eat them until the rest of the meal was finished.

"The plates are hot," the waiter cautioned and put them down loaded with grilled fish, shards of wild rice, and the usual vegetables of baby carrots with their trimmed tops lined up in rows next to tiny cauliflower tumors arranged with precious precision.

"More wine, even though we're drinking red with fish?"

He looked at her, and she took her wineglass in her hand and shook her head.

"No, but you go ahead if you like."

Jean had not been out to dinner in a long while. She was getting used to being alone and coming home to eat a bowl of cereal. The thought occurred to her that she was now over men and they belonged to the young women who could tolerate their ways. They didn't want her because she was too old for any love stories and she didn't want them because they were old news to her. Why was this man bugging her? He could get any woman he wanted, gracious as he was. What was the point? She carefully arranged her silverware again so that it was all the same distance from the table as her stepfather had always insisted or she wouldn't get dinner. Then she realized what she was doing and pushed it askew. *I can eat alone and like it,* she argued.

Frank immediately messed the food up and made sure that the rice and vegetables were in pleasant disarray. The silence was not the quiet relaxed time he had at home sitting at the table, eating some deli food and reading the newspaper. He felt pressured to say more. It was still hard to talk, and usually the other women he went out with chatted away about astrology or movies and he didn't have to say much of anything, merely absorb their company. Patient as she was, she didn't make it easy.

"So did you remarry, or are you dating someone?" Jean suddenly asked. "There must be plenty of graduate students to choose from," she added, aware of counting herself out even before she had really been invited in.

He looked at her, surprised at the forwardness of the question and its put-down. It was to be another fight, and he sighed, swallowed some wine, and focused on her eyes. "No, I didn't remarry, and no, I don't pick from a group of women twenty, thirty years younger than me. They aren't interesting companions, lovely and eager as they may be. Can you believe that, or are you one of those liberated women who are still defensive about your age?"

She studied his face and considered his question quietly. Then they both ate bites of their food by pushing pieces on the back of the fork with their knives while the waiter came and filled both their wineglasses. The restaurant's other guests filled the silence between them with laughs, dominant voices, fork against plate noises and some delicate happiness in activities that Jean and Frank missed.

The busboy came and gestured if it was okay to take the big plates away. They both sat back and let him and then looked at the other people at the nearby tables, busy and involved. The waiter came back and asked if they wanted dessert or coffee. How many times had dinners died for each of them with no sense of the satiety of well-being?

"No, thank you, I'll finish the wine," Jean said, looking at the young waiter with clean pinched face.

"Coffee for me," Frank said.

She wanted to say something but felt stupid when she commented, "The dinner was excellent. I guess I should apologize for my flippant question about dating. Sometimes cutting right to the chase eases my anxiety. I'm not a good social animal."

He nodded and said, "I really like this place, and I like your candidness. Hope you can take mine. I don't unleash it often."

"Truce then?"

"Truce."

When the check came Jean insisted she pay for her own dinner. Frank let her give him $20 as a compromise, even though she didn't know the bill's actual amount. He put the total on his credit card since he said he'd had the most wine.

They got up and decided to walk on the beach down from the parking lot. The tide was going out, and gulls were picking at the abandoned seaweed, sand flies were hovering low, the sky was streaked with pink clouds, and the sun was in bed by the mountains. Both of them took off their socks and shoes, held them, meandered on the cooling sand to the water, and stood looking out. Far away, a white egret floated on the kelp, keeping a lookout.

Laughing about the tar on their sandy feet, they put their socks on to protect their shoes and sought the car.

Later, when they were driving alone, she resolved not to be such a shithead to him, and he concluded if he couldn't get a right take on this woman, he'd never go out again.

CHAPTER 45

Free Will

AFTER HIS SHOWER, Tom lay naked on the bed. The house was empty, and the bright clear Sunday had soured into a translucent twilight. He called for his messages and heard the drone of the drug salesman trying to tantalize him endlessly with a new product, and Mr. Harris canceling Mrs. Harris's appointment because she had a headache and flu, Mrs. Finney rasping happily about her trip to Florida, and the Giannelis extending their gratitude for Mr. Gianneli's comfortable death. These were old messages from Saturday. He hadn't erased them he concluded and laid back on the bed rubbing his belly. It was September.

Even though he no longer measured his schedule in semesters, whenever the school year started, he reassessed his life. Time to begin learning and giving up on leisure were September messages. It never seemed right that there were August quarters and that hot month was not for relaxing. September, after Labor Day, was the mandate to begin trying again.

He hadn't turned the light on yet because he felt like fading with the day into a calm gray inertia and not having to think about making effort of any sort.

Since their last fight in the summer, his wife seldom saw him and went only to functions at the hospital fundraiser or staff dinners at his request. She never asked him to accompany her to any dinners for her friends, and they never had anyone over to the house. Their children called periodically, but after a polite chat, they usually asked for their mom.

There were no new courses in his life, he decided. He had only to go to the office again Monday and then the hospital. Endless effort, endless routine. He felt the tears again like separate beings emerge from him. They came at their own pleasure to humiliate him and take over. He could not resist anymore, and finally at that last seize of tears, he realized he had a brain tumor.

His stomach immediately calmed down, resolved of its turmoil by this straightforward answer. He was going to die. His brain was being eaten up by some damn astrocytoma. He reviewed the possible grades of tumor and their progressive virulence, the star cells branching out and infiltrating with long tendrils his thought. They were there in his brain. He tried to feel inside his skull to locate the exact area, the center of the black hole of his death. Trying to stretch his facial muscles, he squinted and grimaced. He wanted to feel the pain of the tumor, but nothing was elicited. He tried to visualize it growing in the parietal area, and he clutched his temples and rubbed them repeatedly. He wanted to touch some soft spongy mass, but all he felt was the bone as it tapered into his wet cheeks.

He imagined the malignant cells growing in back of his eyes, first on his right and then his left. He questioned how big the mass was and felt the back of his head to complete the examination as though his fingers could sense beyond the maze of hair that still hung on by his neck, beyond the rounded bumpy bone, and into the base of his brain. He held his whole head in both his hands and it was like a simple skull of some skeleton he might have examined in med school. He wanted to lift it off his shoulders and look at it, like an old school phrenologist predicting fates with bumps and grooves. He knew his fate.

This is facing death, he mused, *facing it and yet not being able to look at it in oneself.* He knew he would never deny the inevitable. He thought he had always been practical and straightforward in his dealings with himself. It was his time, and he was old enough to accept it. In fact, it was probably a glioblastoma multiforme or metastasis because it had come on so fast.

He jumped up to look in the mirror to see if his pupils were asymmetrical. It was an exercise he'd practiced when he was in medical school, trying to watch one pupil change size by comparing it with the other pupil. Look ahead in the mirror and then pass a flashlight in one eye and watch the pupil contract. He still didn't need reading glasses badly, so he could focus easily. He wondered if he could catch a discrepancy in the size of his pupils that could signify increased intracranial pressure.

An astrocytoma. A glioblastoma multiforme. The phrases astounded him. The glial cells, which supported the neurons, gone astray and eating up his brain. The brain was a sealed up organ, more than the heart or the lungs with their open cage. The brain had nowhere to escape if it became infected or something grew within. A space-occupying lesion would displace other tissue. Good healthy tissue would get squashed or pushed up against the boney encasement. All the thinking he might possess would not stop this.

He lay back down. There'd be the usual fear of vomiting from chemo, hair loss, and the purple crosses that would be made on his face and neck and head to mark the points for radiation. People always looked like heretics out of the Middle Ages ready for purging with their evil marks.

It occurred to him that he would probably choose to undergo some sort of treatment and get his legal affairs in order before he really felt the classical symptoms. He had to ask himself methodically if he had headache, vomiting, and blurred or double vision. Not yet, but it would come. What to do before he lost control? Before he couldn't think to make a plan. Before, all he wanted was something to stop the incessant headache. Finally then, who would take care of him?

It was September; the first-year medical students were starting clinical services. He remembered his pride at wearing his short white coat and talking to patients. He would be the best doctor ever and always be kind as well as knowledgeable. Marcie was there, his classmate. She took the beautiful notes that were always to the point. They had studied together before he knew they would be good together in other ways. It had been strange to realize that she and he were among the very few students that didn't have sick people in their families. That had been a primary motive for many of their classmates to go into medicine. When his parents died, he understood that. Marcie was lost to him when he left for LA after marrying Phyllis.

Phyllis, what would happen to her? He had provided her well with his good life insurance. His death could mean financial security for her and the children. Tears continued to pop out of his eyes and run down his cheeks to his ears and neck. He observed with a clinical remoteness that it was a strange sensation to have his tears create wet tracks into his ears. "Stop this," he said out loud. "Stop this. Start planning."

As though he had been called by the outburst, the cat jumped up on the bed and started purring. His big understanding face came up to Tom's, and he rubbed his cheek against Tom's. They stayed together until it was completely dark and Tom became too cold.

"Okay, buddy, I've got to get up and shut the windows." Tom continued gently, "And you know what, I'm going to go to the fundraiser and surprise Phyllis. Maybe she'll be pleased, and even if she isn't, I'll give some money to the cause and I'll feel better if I see her."

The cat rolled over and continued sleeping, and Tom got dressed in his gray suit, the one Phyllis always said made him look handsome. He looked around the bathroom that they had redone with a shower for him and a matching tiled bath for her with Jacuzzi outlets. She had asked him to take a bath with her that first night it had been all finished and he had said it was ridiculous and they were too old for that kind of thing. Now he would never get the chance again. *Why me?* he thought. *When I know I care? When I've been careful?*

When he arrived at the auditorium, he had an image of himself being a blob of cell among many. Each person parked his car and then was sucked into the wide glass doors of the lobby. The whole place reminded him of a slide with stained tissue of a glioblastoma, globular bodies of irregular shapes all dressed up and wandering in erratic paths over this purple rug. The cure took place quickly with the lights dimming on and off a few times and everyone taking their seats, which were aligned in proper rows and sequences. Each person with his or her fine outfit now nestled in his or her proper niche. *Ah,* he thought, *the cancer has been treated and order reigns again.*

To his surprise, he saw Phyllis at the head table on stage. She was talking intently to Rick Freeman, a cardiologist. Then they laughed, and he seemed to be admiring her dark blue silk dress. Tom was angry that someone might look at Phyllis as a woman. Before either of them spoke, he left the auditorium and went to the bar in the lobby. He thought he might order a beer, but the bartender took too much damn time to notice him and Tom got out of the place.

"Goddamn dirty old man. Freeman should have a heart attack. The lecher," Tom cursed out loud as he strolled to his car parked in the expansive lot full of pruned trees. He got in and placed the key in the ignition but didn't turn it. Where would he go?

There had been very few times in his life that he hadn't had a plan, a place, and things to do. He was always squeezing more in than he had time for his fellowships, medical practice, and teaching. They'd had one summer when they'd come back to Michigan for the reunion, then taken off to the West Coast meandering by car including Route 66. Phyllis, Marcie, the guy she finally married, Gary, no Larry, and himself. Free time and free will and free spaces.

He thought of Marcie. She had been both their friend for all those years. She'd had her kids before they had, and she gave them advice and baby clothes those first few years when no one had money. They had both marveled at her resolve to raise the kids without their father and to go back and get her residency in internal medicine to treat heart disease. When was the last time he'd seen her? Must have been over a year ago. They hadn't been there for her very much socially after she had moved out to California too. He'd seen her, he thought, when her mother had died. He wondered if he would ever see her again now that he was dying. They never spoke at work even though they knew each other. It had been a silent agreement, strange but less awkward than revealing that they had information on each other's lives outside the hospital. Who did he have to turn to outside the hospital?

He suddenly turned the ignition key, pulled the headlight switch, and drove out of the lot, trying to escape the thought. He wanted to talk to someone. Maybe he should call the kids and talk to them. His new cell phone was dead. Damn it, he'd left the charger in the other car. He drove into a 7-Eleven lot and looked for a phone booth. Two phones stood nakedly mounted by a well-lit side of the store. There was no secure enclosure even for his head and torso.

He had to call information for the numbers because he didn't have his address book on him. Neither of his children was at home, but their message machines willingly took his long apologetic and untruthful explanations of why he'd called. He felt an admixture of humiliation and guilt while he stood there and held the receiver like he was still listening to someone on the other end. The wind was blowing papers around the parking lot, and each forlorn sheet seemed eager to swirl and scrape along the asphalt in attempts to be his companion. A torn sports page wrapped itself around his leg, and he shook fiercely in an attempt to get the paper off and quickly ripped it from his leg as though it might take him with it down the street and into nothing.

He searched his pockets and came up with another quarter and got Marcie's number though hospital information. She was home. His gut secreted anxious appreciation, and he tumbled out grateful greetings before he let her give him directions. After he hung up, he went into the store to buy some token of thanks for his new gut feeling. He had to pause a minute to orient himself, the brightly lit place was a series of crammed shelves on which he quickly concluded he might find ties and tires as well as fast-food and laundry soap. He hadn't been in a grocery store of any size in years, and it pleased him to see all the absolute necessities of living so perfectly organized. He went and bought some raisin oatmeal cookies.

The courtyard was all green grass, lined with what looked like mums and some red berry bushes with extended branches that splayed out against the walls like scenes from Japanese screens. The one end apartment had a ramp near the stairs, and next to it was Marcie's.

He wondered why she'd chosen such a humble place when she could have afforded better. He squinted, hoping that it might help conjure up the name of the guy she was with. Why had she been so unlucky in her choices? Her husband hadn't been that great to her, leaving her and all.

He knocked on the door. It was painted a shiny dark green. He knocked again, and he could see from the change in the window one light go off and another go on nearer the door.

Marcie pulled it open. There were her huge eyes nestled in multiple darts of wrinkled skin pointing to them and the big grin on her full lips. He hugged her and then quickly put his hand on his hair to smooth it.

"Well, well, Doc Zeitman, to what do I owe the honor?" Marcie exclaimed.

Tom looked around the large room like he was searching for a corner to dump some huge burden he had to hide. He saw a big comfortable green patterned couch, wing-back chairs in the same material, hardwood floors and books on shelves, tables, and neatly stacked near a big walnut desk with a computer on it. The richness and color of the furnishings surprised him. He had expected threadbare sacrifice. He looked at Marcie questioningly.

Finally, Tom explained, "Marcie, I've got to talk to you. It's urgent." He ran his hand down his tie, lifting and straightening it in front of him and then tucked it neatly in place under his suit jacket. "I'm in great trouble, and I can't tell Phyllis," he lamented and ran his hand down the tie again, performing the same ritual and then smoothing his hair in some sort of preparation for what she would realize was a major revelation.

Immediately, Marcie's wrinkles swarmed into a face of concern, and she pulled him to sit down next to her.

"I've got a brain tumor, I know it now," he blurted out with what he thought was great poise. He stared ahead with a look of profound reflection.

"What do you mean? How do you know? What are your symptoms? Have you had a scan?" Marcie shot forth, putting her hands on his shoulders to make him look at her.

"I know," he said with a tranquil smooth face.

"For frigging sake, Tom, how do you know? This is awful. What does the workup show? Answer me," Marcie demanded.

He turned to her with a strange, quizzical look and said, "I don't need a workup. I know." Then he turned to stare straight ahead again.

"What are you telling me? Why do you think you have a tumor? What are your symptoms? Does the neuro exam show lateralizing signs?" Marcie said as she stood up to get his attention. Her size and full robe blocked the table lamp he had been staring at.

"You know, I've always been an unpretentious, straightforward person. No deception, to the point, so you don't have to use denial to help me," Tom said and smiled. "There is an astrocytoma or glioblastoma growing in my brain."

"Now, wait a minute, Tom. Give me a break. Start over," Marcie replied. She sat down in one of the chairs facing the corner of the couch he was in and scrutinized him.

He was quiet, and then the tears started.

He covered his eyes by extending his right hand and then began to gently rub the closed but constantly spilling eyes with his thumb and index finger. Periodically, he pinched the bridge of his nose, shaking his head.

Marcie handed him some Kleenex and then sat quietly watching. She could see the careful clumps of long hair covering the white skin at the top of his head. She figured out his technique of covering up and saw how far to the one side his part was. She could see his cheek moving as he clenched his jaw, and his fingers rubbing his eyes became almost rhythmic and soothing as the tears subsided. She looked at the rest of him. She could still see the traces of the young medical student she had known. He was settled and rusted. Years had displaced fat stores from cheeks to belly and sagging tone led her eye down his body. Little bit of a pouch in a beautiful gray suit, matching socks and loafers of gray leather, not mundane black. She'd always wondered why they had ever been friends. He was so invested in appearance and she was a gypsy type. Maybe it was because of Phyllis. She was the liaison.

Marcie decided not to speak and to wait for him to explain. For some reason, she felt very annoyed with him.

He took a deep breath in an effort to pick up his thoughts and finally said, "I'm dying, and I've come to you to help me calm Phyllis when she finds out."

"Why do you think you're dying, Tom?" Marcie asked.

"I've told you, I have a brain tumor. I thought first of an astrocytoma, but it's probably a glioblastoma. Why should I get away scot-free when both my parents died from cancer?"

"What the hell are your symptoms? How do you know? Think about it, Tom. Have you gone off the deep end because you haven't told me a thing that would suggest a tumor," Marcie said with a vehemence that bothered her and made her want to reflect on her own feelings, not his.

"I can't control myself. I'm constantly crying with no warning. I've lost control of myself," Tom said mechanically, like he was reading some list.

"Are those your only symptoms? Are you saying you're depressed?"

Her words seemed to puncture some enormous bubble occupying all his thoughts, and as it deflated, he looked at her with shock.

"Are you telling me those are your only symptoms? You really don't have a tumor, do you? Tom, answer me."

Tom continued to stare at Marcie.

She knew she was right. Another enormous joke on one's self, she thought. Her jokes had always been about men, how wonderful they were and how she could occupy her whole mind with a tumor of devotion, reaching for the astrocytomas of romance and love. It was never "I loved you and you are wonderful," but "I made so many mistakes. I did this and that. Help me." Never an acknowledgment of her needs. Now here was Tom Zeitman giving himself a real tumor so everyone would be devoted to him, she suspected. Phyllis was probably too busy with other devotions for Tom's likings. The idea prompted her to ask, "Are you and Phyllis fighting?"

Tom covered his face in both his hands, and they seemed to push his head into shaking no and then nodding yes. She said nothing but watched intently after sitting down and propping her head with her hands on her elbows. Like a restless cat, she grew impatient.

"You know, Tom, chaos is not always cancer. Remember the good old world beyond oncology?" Marcie offered. A spike of fear prompted her to say, "And it's not Phyllis. Phyllis is okay, right?" He nodded yes, and she felt relieved of the urgency to understand it all. She got up to get something to drink. While she stood with the refrigerator door open, she called into the living room, "What would you like to drink? I've got iced or hot tea, milk, hot chocolate, wine, beer, orange juice, diet Pepsi? Maybe you should see a psychiatrist. Did you think of that?"

Tom didn't answer.

She came back and sat down with wineglasses, a corkscrew, and some napkins. "I've got the wine in this apartment because Hank likes to keep it out of the other one. What would you like?" she said as she ran her hand down the built-in wine rack on the wall next to her chair. "I've got it. This is a very tasty Oyster Bay Sauvignon Blanc. We'll have that. You'll stay for dinner too, okay?"

Marcie set the glasses out and placed the wine bottle and corkscrew in front of Tom. Although they did not speak, there was a gentle communication of acceptance between them. Tom sighed loudly, and Marcie took that to be a sign of relaxation, resignation, and maybe relief. Tom took up the bottle and untwisted the cork. He said nothing until he had sipped away the whole glass of wine he had poured himself.

"I've been really stupid about this, haven't I? I guess it's all the stress. How could I have fooled myself so completely? I never do that. I am straightforward, honest to a fault," Tom pleaded.

"Hank will be here soon. We don't have to tell him about your playing out *Dark Victory* but at least tell me what the hell is going on. I mean you say you are straightforward and never in denial, but, Tom, what is the bit with you being Bette Davis? Who are you fooling?"

She paused for a moment and then risked saying, "Or how about your hairstyle? What's going on?"

Tom broke in. "What do you mean my hairstyle?" He smoothed his hand over his hair to make sure it was straight. He then ran his hand down his tie to straighten it again, like it was a tangled line he was hooked on.

"You don't have to answer, Tom. You know I'm trying to understand, not hurt you, right?" Marcie interjected.

He assented.

"Well, be honest for a moment. You're basically covering up some sort of depression with this damnable thought of a tumor like the fact that you're bald on the top and your covering the whole bean up with misplaced hair. Why?"

Tom sat with his head held gently in his hands and rocked it back and forth. He did not talk. Marcie sighed and took the open bottle and poured the clear wine slowly into all the glasses.

"We'll let it breathe in the glasses. You stay here and relax, and I'll get dinner started. Take it easy, Tom. You'll survive this one."

There are these reassuring sounds in life, Marcie thought to herself as she opened the refrigerator door to hunt for salad material. Pots and pans being used, refrigerators humming, and water running. She liked that thought, water running in the kitchen sink or for a bath. Maybe from a fountain. The old drought had made her less indulgent of these pleasures.

Of course, waves were the best. The ocean didn't stop, as of yet anyway.

Marcie called to Tom with the exercise of remembering old soothing sounds and assembled a dinner to cook at the same time. There were the city sounds: she liked the friendly squeaks and rubbings of old taxis, the old standard train rumblings, dogs barking in the distance, car horns and foghorns. She came to Frank Sinatra along the way as she put the salmon steaks in the oven and went back into the living room to put on a CD.

Tom hadn't answered. He was leaning back on the pillows now, and Marcie let him focus on his own thoughts. She took a sip of wine and then went back into the kitchen to finish the salad.

Slowly, reverie filled the little apartment with calm warmth. Marcie was in the kitchen entertaining herself as she usually did with thousands of thoughts darting like quarks in the ever-expanding universe of her reflective mind. Tom focused on one drop of memory swimming in a myriad of protozoal incidents, the time he had kissed her at a party twenty years ago.

About an hour later, Hank came in the apartment for dinner, and Tom was in the bathroom combing his hair back so he could expose the full extent of his bald head. He started at the idea that he looked like a cancer patient who'd had chemotherapy or a shaved concentration camp victim and he repositioned his hair to cover up his fear.

"I've got some wonderfully ripe mangos for you, Marcie," Hank called out and went into the kitchen to kiss her, then when Tom came back in the room, gave a greeting of "Hi, Tom, how are you? Glad you found your way here."

"Thanks, it's what we need with the cheese and crackers. Tom Zeitman's here for dinner, Hank."

"Are you okay? Something going on with Tom?"

"Tom," Marcie said and brought salad out to the coffee table.

As Tom came back into the living room, Hank extended his scared hand. Tom looked at it and then at him and then back at the smooth distorted greeting and finally grasped it in a handshake. "How are you?" they both asked.

"Fine," they both answered, and everyone laughed.

"Sit down, gentlemen, sit down," Marcie instructed.

"Hank doesn't know about what's been going on with you, Tom. I didn't tell him."

"Well, I came over because I had a hell of a scare," Tom said almost as an apology and relieved that he knew the name of Marcie's lover.

"Tom, it's good to see you. We don't get together very much, so it's a pleasure when we do. I hope the scare is gone and you can enjoy dinner now." Hank dished out the salad.

Marcie smiled at how unobtrusive Hank could be, and Tom took in a big mouthful of lettuce and tomato, relieved he wasn't asked to explain more.

"Hank, I got the estimate from Ray to paint the apartment," Marcie interjected into the wordless munching.

"That's great. When can he do it?" Hank replied.

"Probably next week, if that's okay with us," Marcie said.

"Fine, fine. I still want to do some searching for Cinderella this weekend," Hank reflected and then turned to Tom. "Would you be interested in a little treasure hunt to forget your troubles? Not to think about war, oil, water, cancer, the recession, and the lot?"

Tom pushed a piece of hanging lettuce all the way into his mouth with his fork and quickly said, "Damn, it would be wonderful to think I could forget all of the sickness unto death. What's the treasure hunt?"

"Finish your salad and I'll show you a picture of the treasure, if Marcie doesn't mind putting the dinner off a few minutes."

"No, no, you go ahead. It might be a great reprieve for Tom to go with us on the excursion. I'll give you fifteen minutes to show him. I'll turn the oven on now and then come back when I knock because the salmon will be a perfect pink inside."

There was a silence of words as the last of the munching subsided, and then Hank and Tom stood up. Hank handed Tom his wineglass and carried his to the door. "Follow me, Doctor," he said and raised his glass in salute to Marcie and walked outside.

"The picture is next door in the apartment for congregating supporters of our animal project."

"That's still going on?" Tom questioned.

"Many a year now. I guess you'd only heard about it and never been over here to visit us. We always went to dinner with you and Phyllis in town, didn't we? Come in."

The light suddenly showed the apartment was stuffed with books and real LPs. Hank was busy looking through the drawers of the dresser near the old record player, while Tom sorted through some of the albums.

"Ah, here we go. Take a look at this," Hank said.

The two men stood together, and each held a side of a big photograph. Hank pointed to the face of a brown dog of a shepherd collie mix.

"Another dog?" Tom asked in surprise.

"Well, can you think of anything more important? She got lost out in the desert, and no one can find any trace of her."

"Probably all decomposed by now," Tom concluded quietly. "No, dogs are ingenious, and we'll find her alive."

They continued to hold the photo while Hank related what had happened to the family who had camped with the dog. The camp got caught in a windstorm, sand everywhere, and they lost their teenage girl. She was found later at another campsite, but the dog wasn't. They contacted him when the police said they couldn't look anymore.

He explained the treasure hunts to keep members aware of the importance of loving friends above all the other pursuits in the city. He elaborated on who had gone when and to find whom. Tom would nod his head yes in pleasure and acceptance even as he wondered at the craziness of it all.

Hank explained that they don't give up until about six months or until they find the animal, dead or alive. They even had a farm where all the lost animals were kept and all their monies had gone to that, not to big people houses. Hank smiled and concluded his explanation while searching for another photo.

There were three bangs from the other side of the wall near Marcie's; and they downed what was left of their wine, put the photos on top of the dresser, left the light on, and headed back to Marcie's.

Dinner was salmon with beads of red caviar topping, broccoli with butter, and slivers of almonds and red potatoes cut into quarters and baked with garlic cloves. Tom noticed it all as Marcie brought out the plates and placed them on the table by the couch. Hank poured more wine, and they raised their glasses.

"To life," Marcie and Hank said to each other, and then Tom repeated, "To life."

"Why are you split up into these two little places anyway? You both used to have spectacular homes. Wasn't yours in the Palisades, Hank? Of course, yours in Malibu was spectacular. Why this?" Tom asked and turned to Marcie.

"No, Hank did not make me give up what I had. I sold it. We're like the Boffins. We 'Boffin' it, don't we, Hank?" Marcie said.

"Yes, it's true bliss."

"'Boffin' it?" Tom questioned.

"Obviously, you never read *My Mutual Friend*, my dear doctor. In it, the Boffins found the secret to domestic bliss. They literally drew a line down the center of the house, and she decorated her half of the house her way and he messed up his half his way. We have reality to boot, two really sweet friends in Seattle, Myrtle and Dean, who have lived the last twenty-five years in two separate apartments down the hall from each other. It works," Marcie concluded with a smile.

"Of course, Woody Allen made a mess of it, but hey, we're doing fine."

"Great idea," Tom said. "So that's the secret to happiness. Not separate beds, but separate apartments," Tom said and poured himself some more wine.

"Of course, our house is so big we might as well be in separate apartments. Our bedrooms are like suites."

The music evolved from old ballads to older English ballads, then to symphonies and finally to quartets. The conversation progressed from polite stories to Tom's confession of his tumor scare, then to professional demands and finally to lost loves.

"I think mine is the most obvious," Hank said. "It was a simple story for her. She couldn't stand to look at me, much less have me touch her. The scars from the burns were too much. We hadn't had children. We married so young, and I went to war. So I said goodbye. It didn't hurt that much because I was having too much physical pain then. I'd only seen her on weekends anyway. My life was in the VA hospital for two and a half years.

"Then there I was, neither a clean-cut good guy nor a millionaire, which was all you had to be in the late '50s to get women. Of course, you could read poetry and play beatnik and hippie, but it was obvious I'd been in war. You know people still thought the Asian wars meant something like beating the little island of Japan rather than understanding the unrelenting flow of humanity on the main continent. So they'd see me and think, 'What did you do wrong, buddy, to be such a mess and have no satisfaction in being the conquering hero?' Little did anyone know what Vietnam would turn out to be."

"Now, wait a minute here, Hank, old buddy, stay to the lost love turmoil so Tom can tell his story about Phyllis and him," Marcie cautioned.

"Absolutely. Sorry, you're right. *True Confessions* was still around while I was trying to get girls and then women. Most of the time, I lost my loves before it even got started. No nurses, although they laughed with me. No students when I taught even though there were a few women engineering students twenty, twenty-five years ago."

"So there was no one after your first wife?" Tom asked plaintively.

"Well, my dog and two cats still loved me and took care of me, didn't care about mirrors."

"Come on, Hank, cut to the chase," Marcie teased.

"Well, I think I could say I had two other women before Marcie and plenty of empty years in between. Of course, that's how I had time to write my book on tunnels, one on the development of roads and environmentally safe buildings. Stuff everyone really thinks about. Oh, right," Hank said, responding to a gentle push on the shoulder by Tom. "The first was Vera. She was a housewife whose husband had been an advisor in Vietnam and never came back for the election. Don't let anyone know but Vera voted for Nixon against Kennedy. She was twenty-four, and it was her first election. She followed her parents' advice. I met her at a party the university had as a fundraiser. She had two kids already. We talked and carried on for over seven years while she actual got her teaching certificate and then she met some sweet guy who said he'd take her traveling and she left. They never stayed together very long, but she was off and running with other guys thereafter. I guess I never thought I was good enough, as the cliché goes, and she never had the guts to push me."

"Classic cases of who had less self-esteem, right? Sounds like my life," Marcie said.

"The second was Joyce," Hank said and smiled at Marcie. "What's to tell? She and I were together from 1972 until 1982. She raised her kids, and I helped her while raising Vera's kids as well, and then she left too."

"You never had your own children?" Tom asked.

"Nope, there's insanity in the family," Hank sang out. "Another bottle of wine for us morbid three." He went over to the wine rack.

"But how did you mix Marcie up in this thing? I mean, aren't you two a little too educated for the likes of the bohemian life? And living here? I mean, you guys have found each other. Why this?" Tom said and scratched his head. His hair moved like a little pelt across his white scalp, and he patted it gently to put it in place again.

"You know, life is messy. Hank has made it through hell and still smiles. Life, it's not all neat like your hair disguise. I don't know why everyone whose educated and neat has to live in pretty huge houses," Marcie scolded.

"Damn, there you go again with my hair. If you had to see bald people dying of cancer everyday, you would cover your head too," Tom yelled.

"Hey, you two, take it easy," Hank interceded. "You see, that's the point, Tom. People become isolated and feared and disliked by so-called healthy people. It isn't that they mean to be mean. In fact, many families and friends are really great support, but the weird need to be with the weird and accept themselves and each other. I know. We communicate with the animals needs. Doctors, like you, you do care, but it's easier if you maintain some distance from sick people, even in the cases of great success in preserving life. How could you survive otherwise?"

"I couldn't, I couldn't," Tom cried. "You and your game of lost loves, Marcie. I lose loves day in and day out. I try. I fail. I try. I fail. It may take years sometimes, but I fail. I am sick of it. I don't want to fail with Phyllis."

"Shit, Tom. Then don't. You guys have been together for a hell of a long time. I remember when you met. She was your kindred spirit for sure."

"Phyllis. She's been there for me and the kids and all the time I had to work."

"That's right, remember. Here we are on the edge of old age, dealing with mortality. Did you think you could really overcome the whole death thing? Oncologist versus the black grim reaper. Me, I thought I could be the wonder woman of love and heal everything, especially broken hearts like Hank's. They'd love me, Sister Teresa of the heartsick, able to cure broken hearts." She paused, took a swallow, and jutted her chin towards Hank.

"His game, he rallies others for chases and hide-and-seek and treasure hunts to give them purpose. No matter how exasperated they get, they follow. They identify with the abandoned animals." Marcie wiped tears from Tom's and her eyes with a stained apron she was wearing. "My God, I haven't had this much to drink in years. Alcohol sure is a depressant even if it does taste good."

"Here's to depression and the messy world," Hank said, and they clinked their glasses and drank again.

"You know what, God, I'm sick of God. How come God has to solve everything? I'm sick of all the faces of pretty women all over TV and the magazines. I want some pictures of something besides humans. I want a horse head on *Vogue* or a killer whale on the bathing suit issue of *Sports Illustrated*. And I want to forgive myself."

"Marcie, my love, you're right. We won't be able to solve it all. We're still stinking narcissists, but we're better. It took us a hell of a long time to get to this point," Hank said as though it were a toast.

"I don't understand about the magazine faces bit, Marcie, but time is running out for us and it's true we aren't going to do it all," Tom said.

"Yup, it's 3 AM in more ways than not."

"Three in the morning! Damn, I've got to get home."

"Nope, you stay. I'll take you over to my apartment and you sleep there. Marcie, call Phyllis again, okay? I'll take him over to sleep."

The two men stumbled out of the apartment and commented on the stars, opened the unlocked door to the other apartment, and Hank gave Tom a gentle shove onto the couch and said, "Good night." Tom took a pillow off a chair and spread out on the floor instead. Hank covered him with a blanket, turned the light off, and shut the door.

Tom let his eyes become accustomed to the dark, then he got up, peed, and collapsed again. Marcie and Hank were damn decent, and he saw they were happy with their cause. They showed him different dreams. He was sleepy. He was not dying, and he took his hand to feel his face as he smiled. Faces and heads, smiling and bald. Now he understood. It was others, like his patients Mr. Watson and Mrs. Harris, who had the tumors. It was obvious now, and tomorrow he would help them. He felt his brain was like a whirlpool draining his consciousness. He let the tears of gratitude come and then fell asleep.

Mrs. Harris had already gone to sleep because of a headache. She had used up her authorized appointments with her primary doctor. Her husband was on a business trip. Her sister had come to visit and gone to Disneyland with the kids overnight to give her sister some rest. Mrs. Harris's brain herniated through the foramen magnum at the base of her skull about 4:35 AM; it was like putty pushed through a hole, and it stopped her breathing. She didn't know a thing about it. It was about the same time Tom saw her young face swirling in his thoughts. There was nothing he could have done.

In the morning, he got up early and left a note at Marcie's door thanking them both and saying he was going to the office of his own free will. He wished them luck in finding the little shepherd dog.

He breathed the cool air and knew it would heat up quickly to a hot smoggy day, but he would get home to shower first and, at the office, be protected by the air-conditioning.

Rosa and her husband Jessie were in the house cleaning. Rosa had all the cushions of the couch piled on the wing chair, had been vacuuming the lining, and began reassembling it all. Jessie was outside carefully soaping up the living room window.

"Miss Phyllis is gone early. Mr. Tom, how are you?" Rosa said after shutting off the vacuum and patting a cushion into place.

"Fine, Rosa, and you?"

"Oh, okay," Rosa said with her lilting voice. "But my granddaughter, Angelita, she is so heavy now. I lift her and get pain in my back."

"You shouldn't lift her anymore, I guess, Rosa," Tom commented while looking through the mail quickly.

"Ah, but I love her and it is worth it. Babies grow quick, and there will be time to heal later."

Tom looked at her as he was going up the stairs. "Shall I carry the vacuum up for you, Rosa?"

"Oh no, no, Mr. Tom. Jessie will do it."

"Hey, he's all wet with the windows. I'll do it." He went back and lifted the vacuum with its long neck up the stairs and set it in the hall.

"Muchas gracias, Señor Tom. Muchas gracias."

Tom sang in the shower and left for work. On his way, he resolved to work harder and not be so selfish. The hospital would have the whole new wing open as a result of the FEMA money from the earthquake in '94, and the leaks from the rain down the hallway from the garage would be all sealed this week. He knew he didn't need to see Jean Volk for himself, and Marcie would understand if he felt too embarrassed to call and thank her. He would be too busy to stop by again, but she would understand that too. Anyway, she had Hank and didn't need him. His patients, they needed him, and he would bring Phyllis flowers after work. What? Carnations? Roses? Violets? He'd think about it later.

CHAPTER 46

We are such stuff . . .

• - William Shakespeare, *The Tempest*

S HE HAD OPENED the door into her office and was startled
to see her desk totally cleaned off and the bookshelf empty.
Somehow, she knew the whole office had been appropriated. The office
next to hers was filled with multiple desks and strange women working
on them. The hall was clean with white shiny tile on the floor and
the area was well-lit, but there was no one to ask what had happened.
Again, somehow she knew that she was supposed to go to the end of
the widening hall and turn right. There, the hall was carpeted and the
ceiling was twelve foot with molding. Her new office was to be there,
she understood, and yet there was no number for her office and all the
blond wood doors were shut and the golden doorknobs wouldn't turn.
Then there were tall men walking through the carpeted quiet hall,
which seemed bigger than the hall where her original office had been.
The men were wearing suits with white doctor's coats. They didn't smile
or talk to her. She went back to the office with all the women at desks,
but they were on the phones and she didn't interrupt. She opened her
office door again, and this time, the desk and shelves were gone and
the room was bare as if it had never been used. She ran back down the
hall, and no one was there to ask where she was to be.

Waking up didn't help. All day, the dream came into her mind,
and the feeling of having lost, lost her office, lost her authority, lost her

ability to talk and communicate. She had to repeatedly tell herself it was a dream, but still, she felt this vague feeling she was lost.

Work was her anchor, her sail, her wings, her something to do now that her children were their own guides, now that there was no man. She was free to work. She finished her sessions with psychotherapy patients and did a hospital consultation about 7 PM. Gears had to switch between the regular careful progress of psychotherapy if it was really working and the immediate calculations of patient input to do a consultation and recommendations. The patient was a twenty-six-year-old man who had been in a skiing accident a year and a half ago and was a quad with some movement of his right shoulder. Cervical spine injury. She reviewed the chart and talked to the referring physician, Eric Schneider, about the mother being always around and then about the gossip due to the financial crunch and the taking of more of the staff's money from their private practice to run the administrative demands. The tithes were up to 60 percent of one's earnings. How could you work with the university taking that amount and the government taking 39 percent of that? Could you still eat? Physicians were screwed. Eric had three kids to put through graduate school, and he was always harried. Business was the way to go. Everything was a market. They laughed about selling pens and commiserated, and then he left to work up a new stroke patient, a gynecologist who fell during a C-section.

She walked in the room, and the patient was in the far corner by the window, which showed the parking lot lights. A young woman was sitting on one of the iron-armed chairs pushing and pulling an empty wheelchair with her foot caught in the space between the footpads.

"Hello, I'm Dr. Volk. Did Dr. Schneider tell you I was coming?"

Her standard phrase was sometimes answered with a yes, but usually with a no. The patient nodded awkwardly, and the young woman stood up.

She was his girlfriend from long ago, and now she spent hours in the room with him according to Eric and slept in the chair when it was piled with the thin felt like blankets used for pads in the beds to soak up any escaping dribbles. She would leave to go to the cafeteria only if he was in physical therapy, and she was weak with hunger. The nurses saw her crying all the time when she was out of his room. The mother started to visit more frequently and let the girl go home to her own apartment.

The patient was patient and stared at the TV most of the time, but in physical therapy, he worked and worked.

Get his story, assess his depression, see what was the dynamic between the patient and girlfriend and the patient and the mother were. That was what Eric wanted. All of it was distressing the nurses. Young patients always did. She finished her assessment after sending the girlfriend out to eat. The room was dark, and the patient asked for the TV to be on. Jean turned it on and asked about switching on more lights to which he refused, and so she left him there with the bright jumping light coming from the square box hanging on the wall. He would sleep soon. It was late, and the nurse had interrupted them once to give him his "nighttime medicine."

She came out to the hall and found a place to sit and write her consultation notes off in the corner of the long angular counter. She summarized the history: pneumonia, recurrent right lower and middle lobes, aspiration probably, C5–C6 cervical spine injury from trauma. She was writing about his family of three sisters and a brother, parents still married, when a woman came up to her. She was fifty or so and had pulled her hair into a tight bun. She had no makeup on and was dressed in a pink sweatshirt.

"I'm his mother. They told me you were the psychiatrist. May I talk to you?"

"Sure." This was the opportunity to gage the level of interference or infantilization that was going on. They found a little corner in the patients lounge, but they could still see some of the older patients struggling with their meals, hunched over the tables from their wheelchairs, arms leaning on the tables, trying to steady their spoons.

"My son will never be able to do that," the mother raised her head in a jerking gesture to look over at the tables.

Jean asked her about her son to get a take on how he has handled the accident because conditions like this don't get adjusted to from a vacuum but from personality substrates. How did he deal with the multiple hospitalizations. Three months in, two months out, four months in, and so on. She got the picture of a smart, book-reading, fun-loving boy who loved to ski and swim. His girlfriend had been with him that day and watched as he fell but didn't die. He encouraged her now.

"Let me put it simply, Dr. Volk. Sara has to get on with her life, and so I've become the interfering mother as a way to free them both.

I know it, and I do it whether the nurses or my husband scorn me or not. It is the best way I know. Later, I'll let him have his life with rehab and assisted living."

The mother began to cry, and Jean was quiet for a long time until the mother could look at her again. They talked for a good hour, and by then, the patient was asleep and the girlfriend went home for the first time in a week after the mother told her she would stay the night. Jean supported the decision and made another appointment to meet them both in a few days.

Jean left work at ten-thirty after all of administration had shut down for hours. She drove home carefully, tightening her grip on the wheel when near a stoplight. It was impossible to articulate the patient's situation and the anguish of it all. She wanted to comprehend and hoped she had done some good in helping the two women come to an understanding, picturing the endlessness and the resiliency. She was shaky from no dinner and wanted to go to sleep.

She needed someone and began thinking that somehow Richard would call even though it had been months since she had last seen him. She'd always driven to his house for dinner. Then she could decide whether to stay or not. He annoyed her with his handwritten menus and his meticulously followed recipes, the lock of hair falling on his forehead which he would comb back with his fingers and let drop again while stir-frying, his mocking of her abilities to follow street directions, his habit of cutting his fingernails while they walked from the movies to the car. He always talked about the young secretary he married and then divorced against his desires but with his supposed better judgment after she left him to live with a CPA. Once, he's even asked Jean to act like Simone de Beauvoir and fix him up as he read the author of *Feminine Mystique* had done for Jean-Paul Sartre. She didn't bother to tell him Betty Friedan would be offended.

Along with putting her in her place, Richard had regulated their time together. They had sex every other weekend, and she knew he must have been seeing other women on her weekend off. She cared and she didn't care. He would pull himself and the condom from her after it was full and he was small again, and she would roll over and turn her back to him. He would soon be asleep, and then she would decide whether she would stay to hear him breathe. Even though her neck got twisted, she missed putting her head on a man's warm shoulder and her hand on his rising and falling chest. That night didn't look too promising.

The siren woke her the last night she had seen Richard. There was a gray sky in the window, and for some reason, she thought of fires all over the city that summer before the earthquake and afterwards even more fires. She lay in bed aware she was still in Richard's bed with its strange quilt and thought of the calm, dissociated way she had driven to work all those days right through the turmoil as the freeway bisected the pockets of smoke. The rioting was only a scene on TV. Both her girls had yelled at her for driving, but she felt she had to get to work to reassure patients. Her daughters stayed home, and their bosses did too.

When the earthquake came, she knew immediately what it was, but it didn't stop like most of them. The rocking and jiggling and the predicament of nowhere to go lasted and lasted. It made relief impossible, and so she reached for the phone anyway and her call was fast enough to get through before the lines went dead or busy, and she was relieved that her daughters were safe. She always kept her plugged in phone by her bed and her cordless downstairs. She knew the cordless would not work without electricity. She had no electricity, and the water was shut off for three days. Everyone lined up at Von's and got Miller Lite bottles full of water. She kept one of them and still had it in her refrigerator these many years later. She went to work then and still to work from then on to comfort patients and kept her walking shoes and a jacket in her trunk and a wary eye on underpasses until she was past them.

The fires later burned right up to her house, and the heat on the windows radiated onto her face as she stared out at the raging light. The fireman in yellow slickers stood their ground and back burned the danger away.

All this time now, except for the rains of El Niño with its mud and leaks and soaked senses, things had been calm, and she had not disturbed that calm. Her accident had pushed her to face uncertainty and aloneness, and touching base with the memory of that sleeping man had been the only sense of security and escape she had found. She ate his meals and thanked him. She made him meals, and he ate them. They had sex and saw a movie or two, and that was her stability, her last link with some comfort of the "other."

Now he annoyed her, and she was not satisfied by his automatic sex. She was tired of the arrangement and was glad he didn't call. She didn't want to give any more effort at work or with him. She had wondered why older women stayed away from attachments and had seen her ex-mother-in-law avoid Jean's ex-husband after she was alone. She told Jean about bridge games and the gym and making money in the stock market and not wanting to cook. She laughed each time she explained to Jean about not wanting to cook for any old man and not wanting to take care of her ungrateful son. Her mother was the same. It was as though after doing everyone's bidding—children, husbands, aging parents—her mother-in-law and her mother finally stopped and said, "Now, for me."

What did that mean, no one else, and no job and no responsibilities? Serving, suckling, and dripping blood was over. She had her sexual drive for herself but didn't want the price a penis demanded for gratification. Who was she if she didn't give her body? Would the years of the twenty-first century leave behind death and destruction and give her a newborn life?

Now she was even debating the value of her ideas at work and wanted only to sequester herself in alpha waves, float in the brain's resting zone, not asleep, not awake and not thinking either. Was that why her dream left her without a desk? Should she relax and quit?

She remembered she had gotten up quietly, taken her clothes downstairs to dress while steadying herself and looking over the breakfast table, which was already set, near Richard's neat row of flour, cookie, sugar, tea, and coffee canisters all sitting obediently on the counter by the white microwave. He was all set and didn't really care who was in bed with him, merely wanted his weekends full. She was not set and wanted empty weekends, she mused.

That morning smelled of eucalyptus, and she ran her hand over the swirled trunk of a tree near where she had parked. She would have breakfast on the road.

When she got home after eating bacon and eggs and English muffins with butter soaked in them, making them soft and sweet, she was full. That was the last of him.

She pulled into her driveway, turned the ignition and her reverie off. She was resolute to make the best choices and dismissed her dream and Richard again. That was all past now she carefully concluded to help herself deal with the void.

She checked her mail and found letters from each of her brothers. They hadn't written in years, catching up with that occasional New Year's telephone call or at a hurried dinner on someone's milestone birthday. She sat down in her kitchen with the geraniums starting to play with the wind at the window even in the darkness and opened the letters eagerly. Letters were precious now that e-mail had taken over.

One wished her luck and said he was off to Detroit to play in a small jazz club near Greektown on Jefferson: "There we can see the boat races like when we were kids." His girlfriend of thirty years was still with him, and they found a beautiful old house in Indian Village.

The other said he was going to move to Las Vegas with his new wife since she had recently retired from teaching eighth grade. They found a place at the new condo development six miles from the strip toward the dam. They left addresses at the bottom of each "Love you" and "Tried to call but no answer for days."

Their letters seemed like the end of an era in their relationship. There were no descriptions of war like years ago, and no complaints about the cold war or the war on poverty or the war on drugs, the phenomenon of body counts, the stock market percentages of gains and losses, the TV ratings or political polls or IRS bitching, no Nixon, Iran contra scandal, nothing of Reagan or Gulf War games, Princess Di, Bosnia, China, not even a mention of the stink bomb of the Clinton machinations in the Senate or Michael Jordan's announcement, Hillary's hope and everybody's "mistakes." Kosovo dulled it all. Her brothers had been her reporters in life, and they were busy.

Now they offered legal pad papers, one white and one yellow, folded multiple times and one stuffed into a greeting card envelope and one cleanly arranged in a long white business envelope, each starting with "Dear Jeannie" and ending with "Love." She held the letters close to her. E-mail didn't have that immediacy, that tactile touch of actual letters.

So they were doing better than her in the relationship department even though they'd been tortured as kids too. Internalized objects and all. Ah well. The past doesn't have to determine all patterns. She'd learned that while practicing psychiatry and making decisions based on her wants.

She checked her answering machine, and it was blinking confusedly in red. All the tape had been used up. The last call was from Frank Schlager, and apparently he hadn't hung up right and the tape played out after his "Please call me." She wondered what he wanted, but she didn't feel angry.

CHAPTER 47

For every thing there is a season . . .

—Ecclesiastes 3:1

B ACK AND FORTH and back and forth, they rolled on the
freeway. Each morning and night, the great vessel carried the
metal cells as they moved and clumped and moved forward again. All
the tracks from the trolleys, which had covered the LA basin until the
1940s were run over and covered in asphalt and hidden. The car was
the conspicuous king, and its excreta, the smog, was being beaten down
in emission statistics but not in the lungs of needy patients wheeling
oxygen tanks in sturdy stands like stiff dogs trailing their owners.

First-generation Americans, three professional people, physicians,
a title once upon a time that meant education, service, respect, and
redemption. Doing better. Helping those needful patients. Going back
and forth past tar and concrete and the cemented river.

All the old defenses of sublimation melded into coping mechanisms
and then into routines, back and forth. They hardly had time to notice
the hardening crusts of their dreams. No Stop signs on the freeways. Yet
they had to know the value in what they'd been doing, regardless if they
were disparaged as greedy moneymakers. Only they could tell themselves
as they went back and forth. What do you get being an oncologist, a
psychiatrist, a researcher? What is a "successful person" nowadays?

They were doing penance for parents born in Germany maybe
without even knowing it. Listening to Beethoven, back and forth, they
travelled, carrying on.

CHAPTER 48

The spirit wants only that there be flying.

—Rainer Maria Rilke

S HE HAD THIRD-YEAR psychiatric residents to supervise today. The faculty was limited now after the cutbacks, and the residents got less and less supervision of the subtleties that a good physician needed to evolve further into a good psychiatrist. What distinguished psychiatry residents from all the other mental health specialties was the exquisite combination of their medical knowledge of the brain and body with that of the mind, she reminded them. Then she took them to see two patients.

After four years of college, the residents trained for four years in medical school and four years in a psychiatric residency. With one more to go, the residents are anxious about getting away. She was teaching them during their general hospital rotation. She always hoped that they had some eclectic background to give them seasoning in interviewing and conceptualizing. During the last twenty years, less and less medical students chose psychiatry for all the obvious reasons—little respect and money.

All of them looked older than the usual twenty-year-olds bordering on thirty. They were bordering on forty except maybe one. The group consisted of a biochemistry major who wanted to do clinical trials of medication, a former psychiatrist-pharmacologist in the Soviet Union before its breakdown, and an anesthesiologist who had a back injury. Pragmatic in their choice of psychiatry, hardworking, non-poets giving the psychologists and marriage, family, and child counselors all they needed to interceded with some form of talk therapy. She would help them develop their skills.

The first patient was a fifty-five-year-old Hispanic woman who spoke English. The consult had been a request to intervene on a possibly leaving AMA. Why she wanted to leave against medical advice was the question. The biochemistry major with the MD by his name volunteered to do the interview. He stood at the bed and looked down at the patient as she lay in bed, distressed when she moved her right leg, sometimes even lifting it with her hands.

Jean had to pull the curtain and signal to the others to bring chairs. She winced that they hadn't learned privacy in their years of residency although they probably didn't consider a general hospital ward could have some standards like the psych hospital.

The biochemistry major physician who was trying to become a psychiatrist, began the interview. "Maria, I'm Dr. O'Neil. Looks like you injured your knee real bad." Jean made a mental note about first name and the privilege of using it, about the use of *real* vs. *really* and about the close-ended question rather than a less-focused one to give the patient a chance to decide where the discussion would go.

"Yes, yes, that is true. Twisted it and have not been better for the whole year. I cry over it. I stay in bed. I cry over it."

"Well, are the doctors going to do something for it? Pain medication or operate or give you a brace?" Again, Dr. O'Neil was structuring and not pursuing affect, even though the crying was most prevalent.

"Si, they are trying, but I cannot walk without pain," she said slowly with tears beginning to form and spill over her already-swollen eyes.

"So tell me how it happened and what makes it better," the interview said, flipping through the chart. Jean sighed to herself. He cannot tolerate the crying.

"So do you have family that can help you?" Dr. O'Neil was pursing the family history. Jean was in and out of concentrating on the exchange while she watched the patient move her leg in between his questions as though trying to call his attention to her pain. There was no orchestration, no ease in opening up this person's life.

"My husband is sick with a stroke, and I have to help him. He cannot go out of the house, and I stay with him."

"Who's taking care of him while you're here?"

"His sister came from Mexico, but she has to go back"

"And your kids?"

"All working."

"Can't they come over?" The resident was trying for solutions without knowing the variables.

"One in Las Vegas, one in Chicago, one in Houston. They come at Christmas."

"Do you have any thoughts of suicide?"

Jean frowned at the lack of transition, and yet the connection to the patient's isolation could have been valuable.

"No, not even now. I was Catholic." The patient had shut down. The *was* interested Jean, but Dr. O'Neil went on past it.

"Any trouble sleeping, eating, or concentrating?"

"No."

"Do you know the date today?"

"Yes."

Jean rubbed her face as she heard the resident stumbling over his close-ended questions, asking "what is it?" to multiple inquiries and trying to get to the end of the interview, which took another ten minutes as he skipped around trying to fill in all the spaces for a history.

"Thank you very much. We'll be back to talk to you in a few minutes." Dr. O'Neil ended the interview and looked at Jean.

"I have a few questions, if you don't mind?" Jean said to the patient.

"No, it's okay."

"Mrs. Avila"—she began with an open-ended a question, feasible now that she had to acknowledge she's heard the resident's interview—"what is the most difficult problem for you at this time?"

The patient looked stunned and burst forth with "I'm caught."

"What do you mean?"

"I cannot leave my home, and I want to work at my job. I haven't been able to work."

"What do you do?"

"I make dresses and have my own shop, but his stroke has stopped me and now this," the patient pointed to her knee.

"How important is this to you?"

"It is my business, and I am very good at it. My father, he always made me stay at home and help my mother. My brothers, they got to be free and they left home, but I had to cook and clean and cook and clean. I never got to date till I was nineteen. Girls are good girls."

"Weren't you considered a good girl?"

"Oh no, I was too smart, and the aunts hated me too. I wouldn't go to church. I didn't want to cook. I was a bad girl. My mother was always disappointed in me and my father . . ."

"Your father?" Jean prompted.

"He beat me when I tried to leave home. I got away and came to the United States in 1962. I worked as a live-in, but the families, they wanted me there with them all the time. I went to sewing instead."

"It must have been very hard in the sewing factories too." She wanted to empathize and say, "Did you ever get depressed? Cry like now? Did you feel overwhelmed?" But instead, she asked, "How did you feel?"

"It was hard. I did cry at night. Caught all day in the sweat of the room, making pockets for the blouses. I can close my eyes and see the cloth turning and the patch I put on for the blouse, like the pocket for your white coat. I remember sitting at the machine for hour after hour. I almost went back to be a live-in, but I knew I could never go back to Mexico. Then I met my husband, and we moved in together. I didn't want to get married, but he promised me I would not have to cook. He was a cook in a restaurant, a real restaurant."

"How did you manage the children?"

"I had been making dresses at a little shop, and the owner sold out to me and then babies came. My father, he had died, and my mother came and helped me then."

Jean thought of the clothes and the frills of children's fancy dresses all over Olivera Street. She wondered why that popped into her mind, and she followed it. "What kind of dresses do you make?"

"Oh, Doctora, I make beautiful evening gowns of satin and beaded lace. Designer-like and sold at the merchandise mart. I did not think of health insurance. I didn't think of health."

"And now?"

"My mother, she is old and went back to Mexico, and I cannot leave my husband, and I am caught. This knee is buckled when I tried to lift him. Life is over for me, and he yells now that I am a bad wife."

"How does that affect your sleep with all this pain, worries, and physical limits?" Jean introduced the emotional aspects to help her acknowledge what she had denied.

"I worry and think I am being punished for the time of my happiness. I cannot eat my own cooking and am angry with my husband for his stroke. He and I have each lost over twenty pounds. I am bad and can't stand being in the house."

"Looks like you felt caught in your family as a child and then in your religion and in what you were supposed to be and now again with your husband at home."

"Si. I hadn't thought of that, but it's true. Back, I am back where I started from. I can't stand it," the patient cried.

"You're not standing it is the literal truth because of your knee right now, but is there another way out?" Knowing the patient was going AMA, Jean always felt the patient should have the first chance at an answer.

"I'm here. I wasn't going to stay, but maybe I could get the surgery."

"Why did you want to leave?"

"I couldn't stand being in bed. I needed to get out."

"Well, it might be worth the wait to get the knee repaired and we could give you some medication to help you. Dr. O'Neil will be back to talk with you some more and see what else can be done to help with home care for your husband. Does that sound reasonable?"

"Very much so. Muchas gracias, maybe I'll get better."

"I'm sure the nurse will let you sit in the hall for a while. Do you want the curtain open?"

"Oh yes. Thank you again."

The residents followed Jean out, and they huddled in the small room where blood and urine were spun. Dr. O'Neil was surprised that a Hispanic woman could have her own business and he knew how hard it was to lift at the gym when he had hurt his cruciate ligament. Other than that, the others comments consisted of what antidepressant medication to give the patient and how interested they were that the patient made evening gowns. They didn't seem to care that the women was caught in her history and how it was repeating itself in her mind, but they agreed the social worker could evaluate the situation to get some help for stroke victims and maybe meals on wheels.

Jean felt strangely alone in her wonderment over how this women's life fell into such a pattern and tried to explain it to the restless residents who longed for an early lunch.

The discussion had taken a long time with the first patient, but Jean had hoped to show the residents what could be done with a little appreciation of each individual patient. What could she tell them in the next half hour? How can she help them understand patients with conversion disorders like the woman who hadn't walked for ten years and was able to get up and walk with gentle suggestion and Ativan? Not a deception except to herself. How does one explain the dynamics of other somatoform disorders like pseudo-seizures? Or a patient who drank fifteen gallons of water to purge himself of evil and went into electrolyte imbalance every month or the depression of an old man because of trichinosis worms curled up in his arms or the double amputee from a fire who smoked a cigarette using her two stubs or the necrotizing fasciitis patient who must lose her arm and had carpal tunnel in the other hand or the swollen-faced Kaposi's sarcoma patient who handed his high school picture around to everyone to show them how handsome he had been before or the asthma patient who tormented his old girlfriend because he believed she was the only one who could relieve his dyspareunia? How to process the slight sliver screams from burn patients and not scream yourself?

CHAPTER 49

Last Rounds

THE NEXT PATIENT was a ninety-two-year-old man with squamous cell carcinoma of the face who refused treatment but wanted to stay in the hospital. He wasn't the first such patient with these overt lesions refusing treatment. He argued firmly with the resident from Russia, Dr. Lewski, who kept trying to tell him he had cancer. His face was half-eaten so that his teeth showed through on one side—all the skin, muscle, and buccal mucous membrane were gone—and when he talked, the loose tissue left by his eye puffed and fell with all his rancor as he told her, "This here was a sore, and it would get better." Every time he said *what or who says* the skin flapped, and his molars became completely exposed.

Jean finally interrupted the resident and again explored the history of this person and how he dealt with stress. He unfolded a full life. He had been a contractor, and he talked about Los Angeles in the '30s and '40s and how he had helped build Culver City when it was dirt roads, how he'd lived in tents and knew Topanga when you could find arrowheads along the fresh falling water from springs, how he'd broken his arm once and set it himself with eucalyptus bark bound up with the rest of a shirt, how he'd done his laundry in the LA River when he was a kid, and even road a mule on the beach near the Malibu railroad when it still ran. He'd need a little shelter lately and wanted to stay in the hospital until the weather warmed up a bit. He didn't need any cutting of his face, only some vittles and a bed.

Jean tested his cognition, and it was tight and clear. One finding didn't fit. He denied what was blatant. She thanked him for his time. The residents followed her out.

"So how did you feel about this man, Dr. Lewski?" Jean asked the resident.

She replied in a thick accent that it was "ridiculous" and he needed surgery. "How did you feel about him?"

"I think he is in denial."

"Those are important observations, but I wonder why you argued with him?"

"It's so obvious he's got the cancer. Why is he being so stubborn?"

"Is that frustrating? Patients don't always agree with our magic, and surgeons especially don't like that."

"But he's denying it."

"Yes, he is most likely delusional about his cancer. After you do your write-ups, we can talk about how to deal with the issue of mets to the brain, medication and legal aspects. But now, have you ever dealt with delusional or, as you call it, stubborn people like this before?"

The resident paused and looked out the small window in the lab that they stood in for privacy. "My grandmother had a sore on her breast, and it ate her away. She wouldn't go for help. I was little. My father was an engineer in Kiev and wouldn't come home. She lived with us, and my mother couldn't take time off." The resident rubbed her hands over her chest, smoothed her dress and tightened her belt.

They all went back to Jean's office, and she talked to them about countertransference in both the cases and how the Hispanic women had initially been denied her individuality because of assumptions and the old man had been approached with frustration because of previous frustrations.

She talked about understanding ourselves and analyzing the process between the patient and the doctor and how that could facilitate treatment for the caught woman by giving her some control in the hospital and for the independent man by giving him some time to adjust to getting help from others. The residents listened politely with notes in hand, and the former anesthesiologist closed his eyes, only occasionally catching his head from dropping to his chin in complete sleep. She stopped, they thanked her, and they went to lunch.

She stayed in her office and thought, *It's too hard. What do I offer that they can use? Medicating and cutting and putting legal holds to get people to do what you want, what you think is right? How much time is there for the understanding?* She knew in her private practice there was even less time allowed. Begging to treat because of patterns of destructive interpersonal relationships issues not overt cancers was even harder to tolerate than the impersonal approaches at the county hospital. She put her head down and thought of getting her purse and going home.

CHAPTER 50

Viral Loads

FRANK WAS IN his office too, and Rob, on a two-year fellowship, was talking to him, along with an elegant woman researcher in molecular biology and the perky medical student they had interview weeks ago. The rest of new group were Asian: one was a third-generation American-Chinese, from Berkeley, and the other was the young Vietnamese student from Irvine. They had discussed their backgrounds in front of him, which he had felt privileged to hear, and had then focused their eyes on him, intent on his direction. He smiled at them and their young eager faces, born during or after the Vietnam War and so versed in neuro, cell, and molecular biology.

They wanted to talk about viral load and gels and PCR research on frozen tissue as well as radioactive tracers, uterine fetal conditioning for schizophrenia and hypertension, and the role of serotonin vs. GABA, enzyme-blocking cancer agents.

He answered their questions patiently and then talked about where he thought the research was going and that eventually there would be interventions at conception beyond gene insertion. "In this close of this century, I think of all that I've been witness to like, that article, only a couple inches, in *Nature* suggesting the double helix, the map of the chromosomes when I was finishing college, the dopamine receptor delineation after Thorazine, measures of other bioamines, the detection of viral loads and IgG, PET scans, MRIs, and mapping the genome sequence of disease."

Rob said, "It must be fun to philoso-pause at your age."

"What do you mean?"

"You know, philoso-pause, that's the jargon, kinda of talk philosophically after all the actual research work you've done," he said and smiled.

Frank felt a distinct patronizing tone and was surprised because his fellow had been so respectful. He debated whether to attend to the remark. "And *pause* is the word, isn't that the issue? As though I was no longer able to generate new research, right? You're wrong, young man, you're wrong." Frank got up and walked away toward the lab. "Damn, I pay your salary with my grant money."

He looked around at the lab that did his bidding. The plastic tubes hung around the body of the machines like fine webbing, and the hum of the chemical sorting pleased him. These were clinical samples running from LPs to find the incidence of viral loads in random patients tapped for other reasons like CVA or space-occupying lesions of the brain. He rubbed his face with both his hands, and his fingers lingered on his mustache. It needed to be trimmed, he concluded, and he walked out the door with this lab coat left on a chair near the file cabinet. His tolerance was overloaded.

He took the stairs down in spurts, jumping past the last two or three steps before each landing, until he pushed the first floor's big yellow backdoor with its wide barred handle and was outside. He stood in the tarred alcove between the lecture halls and the research building and looked up at the gray sky, took a deep breath, let the cool air calm him, and decided to walk over to see Mike. "Screw it, philoso-pause was where innovative ideas came springing like Venus from the half-shell."

Mike was not in his office. His secretary had been let go, and the administrative assistant for the whole department told Frank that Dr. Broadhurst hadn't been in all week. Frank sat down at her desk and took the phone. Mike answered.

"Hey, buddy, what you doing at home at this hour? Thought we might go get some tacos and beer. I'm sick of my research fellow and the lab. Want to go?"

"Frank?" Mike's voice sounded soft and tentative.

"Of course, Frank, the old professor. How about it?"

"Frank. Frank, didn't they tell you? I'm on leave for the damn cancer. Zeitman is handling it."

"What do you mean?"

"Turned out to be some rare heart sarcoma, referred pain all right, right to the jaw. No one thought of it."

"Oh my God, when did this happen?" Frank felt his own heart get punched with shock. He tried to place their last lunch only a few weeks ago and looked out the window of the office at a peeling trunk from a eucalyptus shaking in a soft wind. He began counting the slender leaves; the secretary reached over him for some papers and faxed something as though she didn't know he was there. He could hear soft breathing from the receiver as Mike tried to compose himself.

"Can I come over, Mike? Is there something I can do? Is that angel wife of yours treating you well? Are they going to operate?"

Mike sighed deeply and then said, "Yes, she's been great. At the market now. Gone to get me some yogurt. I eat that like it was going out of style. No tacos and beer right now. Speaking of the angels, she's coming in the door. Here she is. I'll let her talk to you. Later, Frank. Goodbye. Talk to you later."

Kate explained it all rather quickly—inoperable, chemo, radiation maybe. No energy, much pain. No visitors, home from the hospital. Lots of rest. Kids coming in next week. "Thanks for calling. Nothing you can do. Maybe later, come by."

Frank hung up the phone and sunk his head into his hands, elbows held up on his knees. Then he got up and wiped his eyes, pinching them with his thumb and forefinger. He nodded at the secretary and left. He was going home. He was really sick of it all.

CHAPTER 51

Quad, an Abbreviation

H E WALKED OUT of his office and down the steps from the hospital toward the quad. He was thinking of the forth quadrant where the breast lump he had palpated lay and what the percentage of men getting cancer of the breast was. His patient was a man of only forty-two. So young.

Dr. Zeitman was seen on the quad every day, walking slowly with his white coat open below the carefully buttoned last button while his legs made their long strides usually towards his office. He constantly tucked his tie into his belt as he walked, this time over to the bookstore for a candy bar.

"What plans have you made for the millennium, Dr. Zeitman?" the cashier asked. She knew his routine and his preference for browsing among the pathology books and then buying either Baby Ruths or Tootsie Rolls if they had them.

"The millennium? Oh yes. I guess a regular New Year's . . . I think." He paid for his candy bar and listened as the clerk told him about her upcoming cruise with her church group and being out to sea under the stars when the new century came. The clerk was "fair, fat, and forty," which was a recipe for gall bladder disease taught when he was a student. She had been at the bookstore and processed his special order books for the last ten years. He nodded and wished her the best and left.

The millennium hype of 1999 was strangely irritating to him. Anyone with a touch of history knew the Greeks, the Egyptians, the Chinese, and the Hindu Indians were ignored in that hype. The Jews had five thousand years of written history. He sighed and peeled the candy bar to expose the dribbled chocolate cover like a keloid over the caramel sweetness. The millennium was such an arbitrary date, not even the right year to begin the new century really and not even the two thousand years since the Jewish boy Jesus was born. Really the end of the century, not the beginning, which would be 2001.

Looking down to study the chocolate pattern, he took a bite of the exposed candy and bumped into Dr. Volk, dislodging her papers onto the lightly tinted cement.

"Oh my God, I'm sorry," he exclaimed and tucked the half-eaten candy bar into his pocket so he could reach down and help pick up the scatter.

"Dr. Zeitman, you were intent on some profundity, I'll bet," Jean said, amused at his scurrying to gather the papers that had slipped out of one of the charts.

"How are you, Dr. Volk?" he asked sincerely.

"Jean, it's okay to call me Jean. I'm fine, I guess. What was occupying you so intently?" she wondered as they assembled her papers and put them back in her arms.

"Oh, the absurdity of the millennium when life, historical life, is so much older," he stated, tilting his head while looking at the tangled pages.

"Ja, we're going to become anachronisms of medicine whatever the actual dates are used. I feel it," she said, smiling, "and I've decided we have to call the 2000s the years of *oughts*, ought ta value brains, ought ta treat the environs better, ought ta treat children better, and ought ta treat animals better and ought, ought, ought . . ."

"I guess it is time to reflect on purpose," Tom agreed.

"Remember when the quad was a place to discuss ideas and raise consciousness, even ten years ago when the med students protested using bunnies for physiology experiments?"

"Well, we can't give up hope they'll be more like us in the future," he reassured. "Ah, here's the researcher coming to help us," Tom said as he raised his hand to greet Frank Schlager.

Jean stepped back and said, "I was going to turn in my dictation on the patient I saw. A left arm paralysis. Strange place for a brain aneurysm. How do you spend the next millennium of your life with only movement in one arm if you are a dancer?"

Frank walked over and shook hands with Tom and then bowed his head gently towards Jean. "Dr. Volk, hello." He turned to Tom and said, "You're taking care of Mike, right? How's it going?"

"Damn strange," Tom said and ran his hand over his scalp to the back of his neck. He had cut off the stretched spans of thin hair over his balding top and looked less artificial in his expressions including the frown of pain over Mike's condition. "What a shock to find that tumor, referred pain from the embryological brachial clefts. We'll do all that's possible."

"I can't believe it. Anything I can do?" Frank asked quietly.

"Maybe find a new potent inhibitor of adenocarcinoma receptors."

"We're trying. But about today and now?"

"No. He's at home," Tom said and looked at his watch. "Gotta get back for rounds. Sorry again for the mishap, Jean."

She smiled at him and said, "Any time, Tom. Take it easy. You look really handsome." Then she turned to Frank. "Dr. Zeitman walked right into me with his candy bar, and I dropped my papers."

The three of them laughed, and Tom started back to the hospital because he had another patient to see. He fixed his tie, not his hair.

Frank stood for a moment and then gesturing, said, "Going my way toward the bookstore?"

"Yes, I need a bookstore right now." She nodded.

"Shitty day like mine?"

"Yes," she said and smiled at his vulgarity, it was so homey and true.

"Shitty enough for a drink as well. You escort me to the bookstore and I'll buy you a drink at your Mexican place," she added impulsively.

They browsed among the shelves, touching the covers, flipping open books that weren't sealed in plastic wrap, dropping to the lowest shelves, and even sitting on the floor if the book was really heavy.

"Medical texts weigh a ton because of the glossy paper, but I wouldn't want it any other way. The reproductions are so beautiful," Frank mused when they wandered through the same aisle.

"The smell's so clean. I love old books, but new crisp texts are a close second," Jean said. "Of course I guess I'm a paperback addict too."

"No Amazon dot com fan yet?"

"For expediency, yes, but it's like a dating service. No good until you really meet the guy or the book. That's why I love bookstores that are old and musty, where you can hide in corners and greet and meet the book to decide if you want it."

"I can't imagine you needing a dating service," Frank teased.

"I can't imagine you needing one either. That wasn't the point, Doc Schlager. The point is I like old and musty," Jean retorted.

"I know, I know." He smiled as he responded to her banter. "Am I old and musty enough? My students seem to think so, but I'd like you to read me."

She felt herself being risky, daring to play with him. Part of her cautioned herself not to be presumptuous at her age; she wasn't some glamorous grandmother Marlene Dietrich or Sophia Loren, but an ordinary beyond-middle-age woman. When he turned and faced her and smiled while raising his eyebrows in mock anticipation, she laughed, and overcoming the attempt in her own mind to put her in "her place" as her stepfather would say or her ex's accusation of being "inappropriate," she said, "Let me see that smile again. Any snaggletoothed parts? Then you're perfect. We can hook up our teeth." With that, she blushed quickly, interpreting her remark and realizing that unconsciously she had imagined putting their lips and mouths together.

He smiled and rubbed his teeth with his index finger. "Damn, and I had thought brushing and going to the dentist was a more attractive old and musty." She seemed pleased with his gesture, and it occurred to him his mother had never liked his teeth because she thought they were too big like his paternal grandfather's and Amy had always wanted his mustache to cover what she thought was his too fat lips. Jean liked him at that moment, and he felt good. Something had happened.

Jean bought a book on consciousness, and Frank bought one on enzymes of the brain. They looked at each other's titles and opened their eyes wide with mocked surprise.

The clerk at the cash register asked each of them where and what they were doing for the millennium. Jean said she didn't know since it was still a year and two months off, and Frank said he'd read a book on history and go to bed. The clerk went on to extol the virtues of her starry night cruise called "Christ against sinners," and they listened patiently while getting their credit cards back at the clerk's leisure.

Outside, they smiled at each other, took deep breaths at the quiet, and looked around as the long shadows of October were melding into one whole nighttime of December. The quad lights facing in all directions were only able to puncture the dark occasionally.

"We can take my car and put the books in it," Frank offered.

Jean hesitated. "I can't go yet. I have to drop off the consultation, you know, on a lost kid who's maybe going to be a patient for life. Have to drop it off at the hospital now that I've proofread it for the medical records staff. Shall I meet you there?"

His smile deflated into a serious look, and she said, "Really, I will meet you."

He frowned and then said, "Tell you what, it's getting dark. I'll walk with you, and then we can go together. I'd like that, and then parking is no problem either. Okay?"

She knew that this was a last offering from someone worthwhile, and it was her choice to take the offered hand of exploration or walk alone. He knew too that this was the last time he would be vulnerable to someone who had earned the right to judge him and whom he admired. Those little defining moments of half conscious and half other, like the transitions of twilight itself, directed irrevocable choices for or against risk and change.

"Ja," she said in Midwestern casualness.

"Ja," he echoed and took her arm.

They walked in silence for half a block as the night took over and promised stars even in the city atmosphere.

"*Ja*, not *yeah*? Such a ubiquitous word. Do you speak German, Dr. Volk?" Frank inquired softly as though not sure it was all right to ask.

"No, we weren't allowed to because of my stepfather, and then I guess I was impaired linguistically anyway. Shy not bold in learning new languages. German is so, as they say, guttural, earthy."

"Well, you can imagine the kidding I've gotten with my name and the pronunciation massacres. My mother never even tried to teach us, and my grandparents were too intimidated by her to teach me or my sisters. I heard my grandmother sing sometimes in German and read poetry, and I took some German in college, scientific German for research. Had all the diligence without the fluency."

"And the guilt. Did you get the guilt and shame?"

"You mean about having a German background?" he asked as he looked at her more directly even as they walked.

She felt awkward and tried to keep her head down. She distracted him with a hand sweeping gesture and said, "Yes, there seems to be little chance to be proud like the Irish or the Italians are even with their drinking and the mafia. Even the Poles in Detroit celebrate their identity. Was it like that for you?"

"Strange that you should bring that up. The Swedes were big where we were, but of course, there was beer and some Oktoberfests. I'm not sure why I felt the outsider. Probably a combination of factors like my grandparents' foreignness, my father's death, my mother's disregard and who knows. You'll have to tell me." He looked down at his feet and kicked a small stone out in front of them.

It went to her side of the sidewalk, and she kicked it forward again. "Of course, you and I have worked hard to be good first-generation Americans, but I feel somehow this responsibility for having German parents. Some of that cultural heritage still feels secretly good to me— you know, music, poetry, philosophy, science but it's precarious in the light of the Nazis. I don't want *Time* magazine to make Hitler man of the century. Freud maybe. It should really be Einstein." Then she impulsively added, "Do you think the next hundred years will give a damn about the sins of our fathers' fathers?"

"Well, you are asking a lot of me even to speculate. What wars are remembered and what wars are forgotten are probably dependent on the needs of the country's mythology. I can say that I've worked hard and tried to contribute. Maybe trite as it sounds, the Germans embody all the extremes of humans. I mean, somebody said the greatest contribution of the last one thousand years was Gutenberg and his printing press. Not bad for being German."

"I know. I can list the greats too, but somehow, I still feel more ashamed for the horrors than openly proud of the glories."

"Ja, I know. It's World War II that stains everything."

"What's there to do but go on trying to do good."

"Ja."

They had reached the hospital, and the automatic doors responded quickly. The lobby was quiet, and the reception area staffed by only a few people. Dinnertime was a good time to get admitted. Jean led the way to the medical records department while Frank looked in the slit windows for administration and dietary offices. "It's peaceful at night, less administrators and only the essential people. Hospitals are better for us then."

"Kinda like the labs. All the real thinking goes on when it's quiet," Frank answered.

"Hi, Lena, this is the last of the reviewed consultations," Jean said as she pulled open the door and peered in.

"Thank you, Dr. Volk, great to have you so prompt," the imposing black woman said and hurried off to the files, carrying the consultation close to her full chest. Lena stayed in the partially lit room where she transcribed dictations all night.

Jean and Frank let the door close after them, walked back toward the entrance, and quietly left. Again, each of them looked at the sky for signs of stars.

"Look at the moon too. There is the Gutenberg quadrant, if you've read any astronomy. Can't forget the Germans and astronomy, Kepler and all," he said and laughed while periodically pointing the way to one of the parking structures that cluttered every other block of the campus.

Jean smiled and said, "Freud would have loved to analyze this conversation." They got into his small black Mercedes.

"Is the seat all right? I see you have long legs," Frank inquired with concern.

"I thought you had a Lexus?" Jean countered.

"No, gave it up months ago. Too big."

They watched the traffic, and Jean noticed she was not clutching the door handle or bracing her feet whenever a car came near them.

"I think I'm less vigilant about being hit again. I couldn't drive without jumping every time a car pulled up next to me. Talk about sensitization, but the Mercedes seems solid even if it is small."

"Yes, I like it, and I guess Chrysler and Daimler-Benz help to integrate this global world. I'll make sure we aren't hit even if we might be safer in this car, if you don't mind."

She laughed in agreement.

They found a small booth in the middle of the restaurant and had beer and tamales and enchiladas with rice while talking about the Michigan, Wisconsin, schools, siblings, teaching and teachings, loves, children, the goodness of being alone, and, as Jean said, "of sealing wax and cabbages and kings."

"Are you off tomorrow?" Frank asked.

"I am. Do you have something in mind?" Jean replied quickly, again surprised at her audacity. She didn't care anymore now that the beer had loosened her wrists and her tongue.

"How about lunch?" Frank said.

"Where were you thinking?"

"Well, that has to be decided. A restaurant. Still, that is prosaic. How about the Huntington or the Getty for a picnic or anywhere else you like?"

"A real picnic. Not even the Hollywood bowl? What about the La Brea Tar Pits for fossils like me?"

"Jean, are you baiting me with that comment? Come on, I can't imagine you needing reassurance. You've got to know I find you attractive." He smiled. "Moving on, what about the merry-go-round in Santa Monica or out in the marina."

"All right. I'm in. Long Beach and a harbor tour? Descanso Gardens and the Watts Towers?"

"Have they opened that up again? What's the guy's name that built it? Rodian or Rodia or something? Worked all his life with broken junk, bottle caps and dishes, milk of magnesia glass shards, imprints of tools and cement, and made his own spiral monuments like DNA helixes. I feel like that's what I've been doing. Building. Maybe later in the next century, people will appreciate it all."

"Yes, maybe. I'd like to think I helped people create better lives for themselves. Do you think the next twenty-five years will bring more than string theory, which you can't see, and more than things that you can sell? Maybe. I wonder if there'll be something we can still do after this century closes. Shall we have lunch in 2007 too?"

"Okay, lunch tomorrow and 2007. Any particular reason for that year?"

"Well, the seven-year itch in relationships, you know. Reevaluate. Revisit. Don't you think so?"

"Absolutely, although I hope to have you living with me by then. How about the beach for the picnic? Who knows with global warming where the shore might be by then?"

"A picnic on the beach. How original. Still, I agree, I'd love it."

Frank wanted to help Jean as they stood up to go from their table and she limped for her first two or three steps and leaned against him. They walked slowly to the car, arm in arm, like some couple on a promenade, and Jean knew it was not because of her leg, which didn't hurt at all. When they got to the car, they turned toward each other as he reached for the door. Then they hugged. Their heads were crossed over each other's shoulder. There was no kiss, but a still, complete moment of embrace. They did not move but held on until another car drove by and sprang its headlights on them. Then he held her arm as she got in the car. They drove in calm silence, looked at the quiet campus, and came to the parking structure.

"Till then," he said as he held her hand. "Auf Weidersehen."

She got into her own car and nodded. "Ja."

When does the age come to surrender fantasy? When can someone accept Kafka's coal bucket as really empty and that over the rainbow there is really nothing but air? Jean drove home feeling unfettered of constraint and humming loudly with a Schubert symphony.

She held the little moment of imagining a picnic and wondered how she would get all her chores done and pay her bills before their lunch. She'd have to poach the salmon first thing to let it cool. She hoped she still had a good tub of sour cream for the dill sauce. Maybe she should cook some roast beef tonight and slice it thinly tomorrow along with black bread and hot mustard. What did he like? What would be appropriate? Maybe cheese and La Brea bread and fresh fruit and vegetables. He might be a vegetarian.

She could bring the red blanket in her trunk and maybe even some beach chairs since the sand could be cold and hard now. It felt right to take this chance before it was all too late, and besides, she had worked enough; she had worked hard all her life, and it was time for a little play.

Frank drove home, opened three bottles of his best wines to taste which one would work for the picnic, decided on a Chianti Classico, and packaged a new bottle of it in an old gift wrap for bottles he had been given the year before. He looked at himself and shaved off his mustache and went to bed to sleep a deep, calm sleep. Tomorrow, he decided he'd buy cheese and bread at Trader Joe's on the way to her. He felt excited at the idea that he could take time off and have a little fun. It had been a long time coming.

CHAPTER 52

The Faux Millennium

SINCE IT WAS Saturday, she slept late and called her office voice mail from bed. She got a consultation request from Tom Zeitman on a patient who thought he had AIDS and kept wanting admission to the hospital but didn't have AIDS or a need to be in the hospital. He would send him to outpatient clinic for an appointment with her. She also got a call from Marcie Walker about a patient needing preparation for an amputation. She was told it could wait until Monday. When she went in the kitchen, her message machine was blinking. She hadn't heard the call. It was simple and sad.

"Frank Schlager calling. My mother has had a series of strokes. Have to go to Chicago. My sisters are both in Europe and are coming when they can. I'm very sorry about our picnic. See you soon."

She was aware that crystallization of hope into something substantial between them was dissolved in this reality. The might-have-beens were overwhelmed by now. There wouldn't even be a picnic in 2007, she thought and sighed. She read the newspaper, had her toast, and put the meat in the freezer again even though she knew that wasn't necessary since she'd cooked it the night before. It was better than eating it or throwing it out, she concluded.

The rest of the day, she thought of him up in a plane and all the terrain he would see if he sat by the window like she did. The corroded skin of the earth would be tattooed and scarred by the myriad of houses, circle crop plots and roads, or carving and raked by the winds and runoffs of rain and snow.

In the afternoon, she was folding laundry and she got another call. "Mom?" her older daughter asked as she always did.

"Ja."

"How are you?"

"Fine."

"Listen, I've got some news. We're going to have a baby."

"Oh my God. Oh sweetheart! Oh, Estelle. How wonderful!"

"You don't think the world is too ugly?"

"But your baby will add goodness. We need smart and loved babies. Does your sister know?"

"I'll tell Selena right now. You really think I should keep it. I'm not sure."

"Well, that's your decision, Estelle. Whatever you want. This is a choice, a sweet dilemma."

They talked for another half hour. She could hear her daughter's ambivalence and knew that was something she had to let be resolve on its own. After they said goodbye, Jean sat at her desk and thought of her own beginnings as a mother. She had been spinning beautiful babies both times, and all her husband could do was be Rumpelstiltskin and have his fits. She remembered his dismay, jumping up and down with bills in his hands at the idea of having a baby and how the timing was wrong and that they couldn't afford this. How he threw the bills and they scattered like body parts. Estelle had command of her life. She could choose openly and her man was grateful to be with her. Some things were different and better.

She would be a grandmother and go on working. She called her office voice mail, and there was a request for an outpatient referral. Her schedule was full, but she returned the call.

"My wife has found Christ, and she accuses me of not supporting her." She heard this earnest man struggling with what was developing in his wife and not accepting what was happening.

"She has talked to Christ, and he has told her that she was molested by her father and brothers so that she would come to him. I don't understand. She says his spirit is in her and she can do anything now. That John Kennedy Jr., Carolyn his wife, have talked to her and they are free of the plane and that their baby will come to her and she will give birth. She's not pregnant. But she says if she has this baby, her father will forgive her for running away.

"I met her when she was eighteen. She'd been on the streets and was working at Burger King. Then I took care of her. I was doing well as a stockbroker. We married three years later when she was twenty-one and I was thirty. We've been married for eight years. One little boy, four, who she can't touch now. Says he's impure and she must have only John Kennedy's baby in the first year of the millennium. I try to be understanding but I can't understand her. She thinks I'm cruel. Says I watch her like a neo-Nazi skinhead. Me. I belong to the ACLU."

"Mr. Bookman, has your wife seen a psychiatrist? Is she expressing any suicidal or homicidal thoughts toward your son?"

"No, she is a good sweet person. I have to understand her more. Believe in her. This isn't psychosis, is it? My internist says neurotics build castles in the sky but psychotics live in them."

"How long has she been talking like this, and has she ever been like this before?"

"'Bout two weeks now and no, never. She's always been quiet. Told me I was the only man she ever trusted. I love her and want to take care of her. Should we come in together?"

"Will she come to a psychiatrist? She needs help."

"She says she's fine and she does cook dinner and keep the house neat."

"And your son?"

"He's at my mother's now. She gets upset when she sees him."

"Is you wife better or worse in this last week?"

"She's quieter, but I hear her talk to herself. She says if I don't join her in Christ, we should part. I'm trying really hard."

"Mr. Bookman, I think you and your wife should get an evaluation for her immediately."

"Well, I've got to ask her? Can we come together? You know she goes wild when we try to have sex. She moans and cries and her legs tremble like a convulsion. Can we come together?"

"Yes, of course, but it may be necessary for you to think about going to the psychiatric hospital if this continues. I could arrange for you to come in with her now." Jean added carefully, choosing easy words that wouldn't offend, "Sounds like she is having a nervous breakdown and needs protection."

The conversation went back and forth, and the man seemed to think if he were only a better rescuer, things would settle down. Jean was calm but encouraging, and yet he wanted to call back and make the appointment after talking to his wife. He'd finish work early because it was Saturday. Jean knew it would be a night visit to an emergency room before he would listen. She had tried. This was the third woman with the Kennedy delusion she had come across.

"Your wife had not voiced any suicidal thoughts and the boy is safe, is that right? Would you let me talk to her? I'd be glad to call her."

"Oh, she's a good person. She'd never do that. I'll talk to her and I'll call you next week and we'll see."

So there it was—"we'll see"—and so she was not able to do any preventive medicine. The husband was making her feel as helpless as he seemed to feel. Jean sighed and hoped for the least pain. The woman was decompensating in the hopes of relief from emotional turmoil, and the disappointment of the millennium wasn't going to help her.

As Jean put together scenarios, the phone rang.

"Mom, I've been trying to call you. Your phone was busy forever."

"I'm sorry Selena. I was talking to a patient."

"How come the crazies bother you on Saturday? Anyway, Mom, I talked to Stellie. Mom, guess what?"

"I know, sweetie. Estelle is having a baby. Isn't that wonderful?"

"Mom, I didn't want to say anything, Estelle is due at the end of May. I didn't want to say yet till it was certain, but, Mom, I'm due to get my two Siamese from a litter at the end of April."

"You're due at the end of April this coming year? You're going ahead with this too. Oh my God," Jean said slowly and then added, "How wonderful!"

"Ja. Just did it with my man and that's that. Decided not to add humans, chromosomal abnormalities, biological clock, keep good sex. What the hell. Think, Mom, you're going to be a cat grandma twice and a human one too in the new millennium."

They talked for another two hours, and then Jean sat down quietly in the living room. She'd write her brothers about the babies, the two- and the four-legged, she decided, but she had no desire to call friends to tell them news or even cry. When Frank landed at O'Hara, Jean was having cereal for dinner and would go into her bed to watch Turner Classic Movies early that night.

Frank caught a cab, sat quietly in the back as it moved through the traffic and saw the slush and dirty snow shoved up on the street curbs.

The blackened mounds brought back memories of cold walks when he was an intern. Now, his hand crossed over his face, and feeling his naked skin above his lips, which he had shaven again in the morning, he concluded he would give up his mustache for good. He sat back and waited patiently to get to Rush's Medical Center.

His mother was in the ICU, and he was led to the bed by a gesture from a nurse at a desk. He wanted her to say "Please don't stay long, Dr. Schlager. Your mother is resting and we hope to get to rehab soon." However, she returned to her charting without any sign of concern.

He walked along the shined white hall bordering all the rooms and into one of the glass cubicles that looked like his lab, but in each of the them were bodies, not machines, who absorbed the tubes and wires as they lay in the elevated beds. Their heads lost in the rigmarole of huge monitors and dangling screens of dancing images, and their breathing drowned out by the beeps and inspirations of the respirators as well as the talk of the staff. His mother lay with her eyes open, nasal pronged oxygen tubing delicately strung over her face. *At least she wasn't intubated,* he thought to himself.

"Mother, it's Frank."

His mother looked at him fleetingly and then turned her eyes to the ceiling again. Her face was askew, with the left side of her mouth smeared down and slightly open.

"Mother, it's Frank. How are you doing?"

She looked again and then closed her eyes. It was the same dismissal he'd always felt, and it still got to him. He stayed and talked to her as she opened and closed her eyes periodically. He talked about his sisters coming soon and how she was going to be all right and that he'd stay with her and see that everything got settled. She breathed the steady regulated breathing of someone resting and said nothing, didn't try to say anything. He sat down in the small plastic chair by the bed and stroked his empty lip. It felt fresh and good, and he opened and closed both his hands multiple times.

Her neurologist came by and said that she was found very late and had initially refused any treatment. The chances were that most of the damage was permanent. It was hard to tell for sure and she'd be in the ICU a few more days. He could page him if he needed any more information. Her eyes followed the tall bald man as he walked to each side of the bed, shining light in her eyes and coming up to her face with the ophthalmoscope, and Frank knew she was alert.

The doctor asked her to squeeze his hand, and she did with her good hand but wouldn't do it for Frank when he held it afterwards. Frank sat down again and rubbed his face with his own cold hands.

He would have to stay for now. He waited until about twelve o'clock and thought of Jean tucked in bed, although it was only ten California time. He wanted her tucked in.

He left the hospital after giving the nurse his phone number and went to a hotel near his mother's condo. He didn't want to go into his mother's home yet, and he could have a fax at the hotel so his fellow could send him the draft of his latest book chapter. *Whatever*, he thought. *I don't have to justify my actions to anyone.*

At two in the morning, the copy of the chapter came in very clearly with a note from the fellow that there was a committee meeting Thursday. Mike's wife had called to say Mike had died quietly since Dr. Zeitman had kept him very comfortable. There were two acceptances of his papers with a few revisions only. Frank cried quietly, had a beer, and sat up all night.

The dark weeks of December passed, and Christmas for Jean was with her girls and the eager fathers of their babies at Selena's condo and for Frank in the rehab ward with his mother and the first of his sisters to get back.

Jean hid at home with sips of a Kenwood cabernet sauvignon and *It Happened One Night* on video for the New Year celebration. The aloneness was a reprieve and relief after the difficulties her patients had with the year's end. Frank stayed in his hotel room, had half a bottle of a California merlot, and watched an old Cary Grant and Irene Dunne movie he came across on TV.

January was anticlimactic, as everyone had been exhausted by the expectations. No end to the world and no beginning without the past. The rain in LA was good for everything, even if not good for everyone. Jean didn't know where Frank was and left him a written message at his office to be forwarded rather than using e-mail. She thought it less presumptuous and quickly crumbled up the wilted fantasies involving him.

Frank had felt embarrassed as the time went by and called her once—she'd been at the store that Saturday— the message said that all was stable and he'd accepted a visiting professorship there for three months and he'd call when he got back to LA. But he figured she might forget him. Jean didn't want to push returning the call since he hadn't left his telephone number.

The distraught woman who thought she was carrying Kennedy's baby came into the hospital. She believed her only salvation from the sin of being alive was to give birth to dead people's babies. Jean treated her for her depression with psychotic features and was seeing her as an outpatient for her abuse history. She sometimes brought her smiling son with her to the sessions.

Frank worked on his book chapters and began another one on the principles of neuropharmacological treatment of depression.

In February, Jean received a small package at her office. It was from Chicago. She waited to open it at home with a glass of wine.

The note said, "Dear Jean, The song 'The Glow-Worm' comes from a 1902 German operetta. Best to you and hoping to see you soon. Till then and before 2007, Frank Schlager."

Inside the package was a 20th century Master CD of the Mills Brothers Millennium Collection recordings. Jean smiled and listened to the harmony.

"Shine little glow-worm, glimmer, glimmer / Shine little glow-worm, glimmer, glimmer! / Lead us lest too far we wander . . ."

****

LYRICS

Robinson's English translation lyrics (circa 1905):

Verse 1:

When the night falls silently,
The night falls silently on forests dreaming,
Lovers wander forth to see,
They wander forth to see the bright stars gleaming.
And lest they should lose their way,
Lest they should lose their way, the glow-worms nightly
Light their tiny lanterns gay,
Their tiny lanterns gay and twinkle brightly.
Here and there and everywhere, from mossy dell and hollow,
Floating, gliding through the air, they call on us to follow.

Chorus:

Shine, little glow-worm, glimmer, glimmer
Shine, little glow-worm, glimmer, glimmer!
Lead us lest too far we wander.
Love's sweet voice is calling yonder!
Shine, little glow-worm, glimmer, glimmer
Shine, little glow-worm, glimmer, glimmer
Light the path below, above,
And lead us on to love.

Verse 2:

Little glow-worm, tell me pray,
Oh glow-worm, tell me, pray, how did you kindle
Lamps that by the break of day,
That by the break of day, must fade and dwindle?
Ah, this secret, by your leave,
This secret, by your leave, is worth the learning!
When true lovers come at eve,
True lovers come at eve, their hearts are burning!
Glowing cheeks and lips betray how sweet the kisses tasted
Till we steal the fire away, for fear lest it be wasted!

Made in the USA
San Bernardino, CA
23 October 2016